Praise for Th

"*The Stand-In* is a sparkly, cinematic adventure that combines emotional drama with hilarious and relatable moments. Lily Chu handles swoonworthy scenes and down-to-earth concerns with equal skill."
—**Talia Hibbert**, *USA Today* bestselling author of
Get a Life, Chloe Brown

"Lily Chu's debut is wry, moving, and utterly romantic. I was charmed by *The Stand-In's* vividly-drawn multicultural cast...wit and poignancy."
—**Ruby Lang**, author of *The Uptown Collection*

"*The Stand-In* is a charming, engaging rom-com that drips with glamour and sparkles with banter. Chu's exploration of multiracial identity was resonant and nuanced. *The Stand-In* is truly a stand out romance."
—**Andie J. Christopher**, *USA Today* bestselling author of
Not the Girl You Marry

"A sparkling debut rom-com from author Lily Chu. When Gracie is thrown into the world of movie stars, the result is a highly entertaining story full of heart—and a happily ever after."
—**Jackie Lau**, author of *Donut Fall in Love*

"Lily Chu's deft prose...had a way of taking unexpected turns, startling me into laughing out loud—or punching me right in the feelings."
—**Rose Lerner**, author of *The Wife in the Attic*

"With quick wit, beautifully developed characters, and a charming love story, this rom-com debut is a winner!"

—**Farah Heron**, author of *Accidentally Engaged*

The Comeback

LILY CHU

sourcebooks
casablanca

Published by Sourcebooks Casablanca, an imprint of Sourcebooks
P.O. Box 4410, Naperville, Illinois 60567-4410
(630) 961-3900
sourcebooks.com

Cataloging-in-Publication Data is on file with the Library of Congress.

Manufactured in the UK by Clays and distributed
by Dorling Kindersley Limited, London
002-337156-May/23
10 9 8 7 6 5 4 3 2

For Nyla

Always and forever

One

When my phone flashes a notification, I'm primed to be irritated before I even see what it is. It's been a busy morning, and my eyes are so dry my eyelids stick together when I drag my gaze away from the monitor.

Phoebe b-day, the message reads.

I automatically clear the screen and do some rapid blinking to rehydrate my eyeballs. My older sister has done a fine job of aging without a congratulatory note from me for the past few years, and there's no reason to break the tradition.

I'm not even sure what I'd write. *Wishing you a joyful day free of annoying reminders you have a sister* doesn't have much of a Hallmark ring to it. *Happy birthday! Hope you have a great time not telling me anything about your life as usual* might work.

I debate removing the event from my calendar altogether, but another notification pops up to tell me there's a new email from Dad. *Focus on your goals for success* declares the subject line, as if this is groundbreaking information. In the text, before the URL, he's written his usual inspirational message: Saw this and thought of you. Now is the time to work on making partner. Don't let life distract you.

I don't bother clicking the link because it's from the *Harvard Business Review* and I'm out of free articles for the month. Also, I've read enough of these to know it's probably some banal, common-sense dictum about prioritizing tasks or matching goals to outcomes written in that *I'm too busy to read full sentences* list format that businesspeople eat up.

In my case, success has only one metric—how fast I can make partner at Yesterly and Havings, the law firm where I'm currently an associate. That's not to say I'm not ambitious. The only person who wants me to make partner more than my dad is me.

I can't remember when he last emailed to see how I was doing apart from work. I suppose it doesn't matter. We don't have that kind of relationship anyway.

I put my phone back in my purse and am deep into the memo I'm writing for Meredith, the partner I've been trying to get as my mentor, when a knock comes at my door. Richard Havings, one of the managing partners and the great-grandson of the original Havings of Yesterly and Havings, ushers in a tall woman. "Ariadne, this is Brittany Cabot, who's joining us today."

Although a little resentful at being disturbed, I stand and put out my hand, wilting only slightly under the blazing onslaught of Brittany's smile. "Good to meet you," I say.

"Ariadne, I'd like you to show Brittany the ropes. I trust you to get her up and running." Richard bestows a warm glance on Brittany, who beams back at him. "We were lucky to steal her from her old firm."

"Of course." Showing Brittany around is worth the extra hour or so I'll have to put in tonight. Richard is very big on culture fit, so I do my best to be positive and courteous no matter what the ask.

Richard nods once he sees we're playing nice and leaves me alone with Brittany. She wears a camel sheath dress with a matching blazer, and I can't tell how much of her face is contour or her real features. "Happy to be here," she says. "Ni hao!"

No way this is happening. I struggle to keep up the smile. "I don't speak Chinese."

"Sorry. I mean konnichiwa!"

This conversation is not getting off to the best start. "I'm *Canadian*."

Her brow furrows, but it's not out of shame. I've known her for thirty seconds, and I can tell Brittany doesn't experience shame because the world's never found it necessary to make her feel bad about anything at any time. "But your name is on the door, and it says *Hooey*."

"It's Hui," I correct. "Rhymes with *sway*."

"Are you sure?"

"Pretty sure." I resist adding a passive-aggressive mispronunciation of *Brittany*. I also decide to mentally spell it as *Bryttanie* from that point on for my own personal satisfaction.

"Huh." She glances out the window over my shoulder. "Can you show me where to get a few things? I know where my office is."

Normally, one of the assistants would do this, but Richard has charged me with this task, so I lock my computer and lead her on the tour. We haven't made it two meters down the hall before Meredith comes around the corner. Her sandy-blond hair has been freshly blown out, and her makeup is perfectly applied. The nude pumps and navy skirt suit scream *Get out of my way or I'll cut you* in corporate. I've never seen her smile in a meeting.

I want to be like that. Invulnerable. Unchallengeable.

"Brittany, hello. Such a pleasure to have you with us. Let me show you around, and we'll go for coffee to talk about the client I mentioned."

Every invitation I've sent Meredith for coffee has been rejected or moved at the last minute.

Her eyes flick over to me. "Ariadne, I need that memo."

"Bye." Brittany/Bryttanie gives me a little finger wave. Dismissed, I watch them head down the hall laughing easily with each other.

I return to my office to do some triangle breathing—three counts to breathe in, hold for three, three counts to breathe out, repeated three times—and instantly trash any benefit this mindfulness exercise might have had by googling my new colleague-slash-competition. She graduated after me, and of course, her mother is friends with Meredith and some of the other partners.

I shouldn't be pissed about this since most of the office, including myself, got in through contacts and networking—in my case, Dad went to law school with Richard. However, I am a woman of contradiction, and this tidbit has me in a fury of injustice that I need to force down before I turn back to my files.

The Brittanys of the world might start one rung higher, but I'm with Dad in believing that performance is the ultimate differentiator. I only need to work harder.

———

It's almost eleven by the time I get home. Brittany came by several times to ask me time-wasting questions that a woman with a degree from one of the country's top law schools should have been able to figure out on her own, like the location of the well-marked washrooms. I'd have felt more generous had she not started every interruption by calling me *Adrienne*.

I toe off my high heels and set them by the door before laying my purse on the side table. More work waits in the black laptop bag I tug off my shoulder. If I'm lucky, I'll get to bed before two.

I close my eyes to enjoy the peace of the apartment and rub my face, sore from smiling politely all day. The place is empty since my roommate, Hana, who works as a diversity consultant, is away on a work trip. This one is at least a month, and right now the silence is exactly what I need to decompress. Yawning and rolling my aching shoulders as I unbutton my navy blazer, I pass a man sleeping on the couch and cross through the kitchen.

Two steps into my bedroom, I stop, listless synapses firing a belated alert. I passed a man sleeping on the couch.

A man. On my couch.

I creep back into the kitchen to check that I wasn't hallucinating. There is definitely a man there. My heart pole-vaults into my throat as I rock back and forth, unable to see anything but the stranger. I pride myself on always knowing what to do, but this has me floored. Do I call the police? Go on the attack? Hide in the refrigerator? Before I decide, he opens his eyes to peer at me through a mop of bleached platinum hair, and I stop breathing. My brain has focused on a single and totally useless thought, which is how angry Mom's going to be when the paramedics find me dead with raggedy underwear. I'm going to die in my period undies because I didn't have time for laundry.

Then he uncoils from the couch and stands.

My lizard brain: *Fight, not flight. You can take him.*

My neo-mammalian brain: *No, you can't.* Look *at him.*

That part isn't a problem; I can't stop looking at him because I'm too frozen to even blink. He's slender and taller than me with smooth lines of pure muscle on his neck and arms, dressed in a black sweater threaded with red.

Lizard brain: *Whoa.*

Neo-mammalian brain: *Whoa.*

All brain functions: *Whoa whoa* whoa.

Whoever this guy is, he's striking enough that my hormones register it despite my panic.

He clears his throat. "Hello." He takes two steps in my direction, lithe and confident as a dancer...or a serial killer homing in on his prey.

This breaks my paralysis, and I scramble for a knife. "Stay back." It takes me two tries to choke the words out of my dry throat. At least the counter forms a protective wall between us.

His eyes widen, and he raises his hands like he's under arrest. "I'm Jihoon. Jihoon?" He repeats his name urgently, as if it's a charm to protect against the sharp steel in my hand.

"I don't *care*." I grip the knife and lift it higher. The surging adrenaline makes my heart pound so hard that I wheeze, but I have a weapon, and I'll use it.

I also have a phone, and if I can calm down, I can use that, too. Without taking my eyes off the guy, who has not taken his eyes off me, I pull it out of my pocket to call for help. As my thumb goes for the nine in 911 because I can't remember how to get to the emergency SOS screen—I'm in a *crisis*, why did they make it so hard—the phone bleats out the tone I've assigned to Hana's texts, a discordantly cheerful *dah-DAH-DAH*.

Not now, Hana. Yet despite being in a very scary position, I check the screen immediately. If I die because I'm distracted, the fault lies with technology and its ridiculously addictive algorithms.

Hana: My cuz Jihoon coming over to stay for a bit. Left my key for him. Sorry, forgot to mention it.

Like a chameleon, I keep one eye down to scan the message again while the other swivels up to the guy. She forgot to mention it. Forgot to mention I'd be coming home to a strange man in my living room.

If I live through this, she's dead.

I drag both eyes up from the phone. The guy hasn't moved.

"What'd you say your name is?" I demand.

"Jihoon." It comes out as an almost imploring whisper. "Choi Jihoon."

"You're Hana's cousin."

"From Seoul." His shoulders sag. "I apologize. I didn't mean to frighten you or intrude. I'll go. I can stay in a hotel."

His expression is forlorn, but I'm immune, having experienced Hana's frequently deployed nuclear-grade puppy-dog eyes. Although I'm 99 percent sure he is who he says, it's not the 100 percent I require in this high-stress situation. Or any situation, frankly, because I only ever proceed after achieving total certainty.

"Put your passport on the coffee table, then go into the bathroom and close the door." I need to talk to Hana, and I want him at a safe distance while I'm occupied.

"Is this really necessary?" he asks, eyeing the knife. When I wiggle it, he sighs and bends down to a black leather bag sitting on the floor. After he tosses a booklet on the table, he inches toward the bathroom without turning his back. We maintain steady eye contact, and the click of the door when he throws the lock sounds like a gunshot.

If this guy really is Hana's cousin, he must be sincerely regretting her offer of a place to crash.

I put the knife on the counter within close reach and call Hana.

"Hey, Ari." Hana's breezy voice sings out of the phone. "Good timing! I'm picking up my bag. Is Jihoon there yet?"

"There is a strange man here, absolutely yes." I keep watch on the bathroom door in case the presumed Jihoon Hulk-smashes out of it and edge over to grab the passport.

"I know, I'm sorry. I meant to tell you earlier, but work was a mess, and I was late to the airport." Hana does not sound at all contrite. "Then I forgot until I arrived in Vancouver."

Forgot. It's the new f-word.

"You never mentioned him."

"I'm sure I did. I don't know. How many times do you talk about your cousins?"

"I would if one of them were going to be staying here," I say.

There's an increase in background sound as if she's left the terminal to get a cab. "I know you don't like surprises, but it came up kind of quick."

I open the passport and thank God the name is romanized so I can read it. Choi Jihoon. Picture checks out, though he must be the only person on earth to look good in a government ID photo. I almost swear it's Photoshopped.

"Say his last name." It didn't sound like *Choi*.

"He'd say it *Chwey*. Looks the same as mine, but we say it like white people. *Chooy*." She draws it out with exaggeration.

Another mystery solved. I'm now 99.9 percent sure but require one more check. "Describe him."

"Umm." I can hear her thinking. "He's my cousin, so Korean, obviously. Taller than me, about five ten. Unbelievably super stylish. A couple years younger than us."

His passport confirms that makes him twenty-eight. It's inappropriate to ask for a judgment on the quality of his looks, but Hana supplies it unsolicited. "Everyone says he's good-looking."

I snap the passport shut and drop it on the table. "Why do you know that?"

"Eomma never fails to point out how handsome he is when his name comes up. Then she tells me I need to groom my eyebrows better. Also, you saw him."

I did, and that's definitely the guy I banished to the bathroom. I sag against the counter. "I thought he was a murderer and pulled a knife on him."

"Did you hurt him?" she asks with alarm.

"No."

"Good. I'm sure he has health insurance, but stabbing is a really unfriendly welcome, cross-culturally. Ari, I'm sorry to spring this on you, but he's family and in a bind."

I can't throw Hana's cousin out, so I'm resigned to Jihoon's visit. "How long is he here for?"

"Not sure. He's quiet," she adds.

This will be a change, since Hana has what I think of as a big personality. "What's so urgent that he needed to jump on a flight to Toronto?"

She heaves a weighty sigh. "It's a breakup. A rough one."

This is bad news. I don't want to be mean, but I have a heavy workload. Having a stranger mope around drinking merlot from the bottle and stalking his ex's social media while listening to maudlin ballads is not going to be great for my productivity.

A new dread rises. "Will your mom come by to visit him?" Hana's eternal struggle to build boundaries with her mother has yet to result in any tangible success. If she knows there's a wounded Choi bird in her vicinity, I can kiss a peaceful home life goodbye.

She snorts. "God, no. Jihoon's keeping it a secret. No one knows he's here but me, so don't post any photos of him on your social media. You know she checks it to see what I'm doing."

"As if I would." She did say he'd be quiet. "He can stay."

Hana squeals. "I'll make it up to you, I promise."

Before I can answer, she blows a kiss into the phone with an obnoxious *mwah* sound and disconnects.

I put the phone on the counter and the knife back in the wooden block. After quickly rebuttoning my blazer, I go down the hall and knock on the bathroom door. "Ah. Jihoon?"

"Are you armed?" Now that my fear has abated, I notice he has a deep, raspy voice without much of a Korean accent.

"I put the knife down after Hana vouched for you."

The door swings inward, and Jihoon, who has skipped back to the far wall to maximize the distance between us, inspects me cautiously. I can spot the family similarity to Hana. Both have the same sharp curve under the eye that dips down to a strong jawline and pointed chin. Under that flawless bone structure, he looks absolutely beat. Dark circles ring his eyes, and the corners of his mouth are tight.

"I'm Ariadne," I say with the professional smile I activate for work and most social interactions. It's enough to say, *I am friendly and mean you no harm*, but not so welcoming as to invite anything further.

"Ariadne." He comes forward and says my name carefully, pronouncing all the syllables so it sounds like music. "Choi Jihoon." He bows slightly. There's an uncomfortable silence until he says, "Am I allowed out?"

"Right." I step away. "I'll show you Hana's room."

He drags over two of the world's largest suitcases and closes the bedroom door after giving me a polite smile. Excellent, I don't have to navigate any awkward conversation and can focus on the memo due tomorrow. The headache that's been lurking all day starts to take over. I pull out my laptop case, but I'm too distracted to work. Instead I pour a glass of water and bid a silent and mournful fare-well to the serene solitude I had planned. A stranger in my space means being social and friendly instead of relaxing with unbrushed teeth and ripped leggings. I'll have to be "on" all the time, instead of only at work. It's exhausting to think about, but I agreed and that's it. I'm stuck.

I finish the water and send Hana a quick text outlining all the ways she owes me. Then, unable to delay it any longer, I put Jihoon out of my mind and open my laptop.

Two

I have an unvarying morning routine that involves a single hit to the snooze button, a mental review of what's coming in my day, some deep breathing to cope with it, and a struggle to roll myself out of bed. Today, my ritual is interrupted by a text.

Alex: Favor time.

Alex Williams is the public relations vice president for Hyphen Records, and this message bodes ill for me. I stare at the screen with bleary eyes and try to force myself back into a work headspace despite only getting four hours of sleep. I fail.

Me: No

The phone rings, and I pick it up while kicking off my duvet. "*No* is a complete sentence, Alex. Also it's six in the morning."

"No choice. You're Luxe's lawyer. Since Hyphen is Luxe's client, together we have a problem. I technically called this a favor to be nice, but it's not. Ines said to call you direct."

The most exhausting yet fascinating of my clients is Luxe, a luxury concierge firm catering to the rich, famous, and supremely dickish. Luxe can source any consumer good or experience for those who can pay, from exclusive dinners to carriage rides with white horses dyed mint green to seeing an acrobatic Argentinian clown troupe perform in a park. It's owned by Ines, an unflappable woman who goes by one name, like Madonna or Cher. Ines is the only woman I've met who can get away with that kind of personal statement, because she has a huge presence that fills every space she enters.

"Did one of your man-child rock stars screw up?" I leave out the *again*.

"Hey, it's like we've done this before."

"Give me the details." It's as I expected. A band with more fame than brain trashed a snooty restaurant after Luxe wrangled them a private chef's night. Since Luxe organized the event, it's their job to take the lead in working with Hyphen's PR and legal teams to soothe the restaurant and get it all swept under the rug. As Luxe's lawyer, this has now become my job.

This isn't as weird as Luxe's problems sometimes get—their clients can be a toxic combination of imperially demanding and oblivious to social norms—but it's aggravating to have to drag a bunch of entitled jackasses out of the hole they dug for themselves. One thing I've learned working with Luxe is that celebrities are the glitter of humanity: pretty to look at, useless except at parties, and an utter pain to clean up after.

Coffee. I need coffee to deal with Alex's problems this early. I put on a robe, collect the outfit I set out last night, and open my bedroom door, thinking through what I'll need from him.

"Alex, do we have the—what the hell?" The phone goes flying as my foot catches on something in the middle of the floor. I land ungracefully on my hands and knees, straddling a warm lump that manages to be simultaneously hard and soft.

It's Jihoon, and he moans in pain as he struggles beneath me.

"Holy shit!" I plant both hands on his chest but accidentally slam my elbow into the corner of a chair before I can lever myself off him. "Ow." I collapse, and Jihoon's warm arms wrap around me, no doubt to protect himself from further injury.

Alex's concerned squawks sound from under the couch. "Ari, are you okay? Do I need to call the cops?"

I roll off Jihoon to paw for my phone. "Alex, I tripped over my new roommate. Give me a second."

"Call me back." Few things faze Alex after a decade in the music industry.

After I hang up, I turn back to Jihoon. "I'm sorry for falling on you, but what were you doing?" My entire arm has a nasty shivery numbness. Jihoon sits up, rubbing his ribs with a grimace, and my brain shorts out because he's only wearing a pair of low-slung black pants. I don't even know where to focus my gaze as it moves from the indent between his impressive pectoral muscles to the curve of his shoulders before dipping down to the many, many rows of abs leading to a molded V. I didn't even think men had that outside of underwear ads, and I'm not ready to deal with this knowledge so early in the morning.

"I was meditating."

"On the floor?" *While shirtless*, but that seems like a detail pertinent only to me, so I don't say it out loud.

"I fell asleep." He twists to examine the red mark where I kicked him. I try not to gawk and almost succeed until the stylized black tiger tattoo that wraps around his body comes into view, stretching down from his side to cross his lower back. I have no choice but to give it the aesthetic appreciation it deserves because the tiger ripples on Jihoon's muscles as he moves. It's art, really.

Then it's back to business because I should be getting the details on Alex's dipshit rock stars instead of ogling Hana's cousin. I'm not even into tattoos.

I give my arm a test bend, and Jihoon turns to me in concern. "Are you hurt?" He reaches out to check my elbow as I suddenly realize my robe has fallen open to reveal my very skimpy tank top. I'm also sitting back on my heels, and my pajama shorts are...well, they're short.

He freezes, and we sit there eyeing each other for what seems like forever until we jointly come to our senses.

"I'm sorry!" His voice is almost a squeak as he crosses his arms over his chest.

"My fault!" I snatch my robe closed and scramble to my feet. I'm now maximally alert and can skip the coffee, so I try not to let my shorts ride up my ass as I bend to grope around for my dropped clothes. Behind me is a flurry of activity as Jihoon takes off to his room.

Wondering if daily shirtless floor meditation is one of Jihoon's breakup coping mechanisms—and how I feel about that—I head into the bathroom. I flip on the switch and survey the counter in disbelief. Overnight it's been turned into a Sephora.

I need to look groomed for work, so I have a standard collection of cosmetics that sit in a drawer, tidily out of sight. Jihoon clearly likes to see all his options, because his skin-care assemblage overflows the counter. I don't even recognize most of the products, which are presented in stark packaging that makes the serums and creams look like serious pharmaceuticals. Long cylinders of white and silver stand in a group next to sleek black tubs of various masks. Most have Korean labels, but the ones in English wouldn't be out of place in a chemistry class. Hyaluronic acid. Peptides. Niacinamide.

No wonder he looks so good. I peer into the mirror, noting the bags under my eyes and the freckles dotting my face from years of sun exposure thanks to my parents' 1990s disdain for any UV-blocking product. Am I growing a hair on my chin?

It's only a cat hair. That's one beauty crisis averted, although we don't have a cat, so where it came from is another question. A cold shower helps settle me, and after I answer a few emails from Alex between fitting my hair into its usual bun and spackling on my work face, I'm ready to go.

Jihoon is in the kitchen. We both pull up short. Now that my adrenal glands are not pumping my body with fear hormones, I can take better stock of him.

Even like this, puffy from sleep and travel, hair a tousled bird's nest, and wearing a huge green hoodie that reaches midthigh, he's almost surreally attractive. He has monolid eyes like mine but much bigger, and as Hana had indicated, his eyebrows are a testament to meticulous grooming. His lower lip is almost pouty, it's so full. I could only hope to achieve lips like that through cosmetic surgery or painstaking hours in front of a mirror with products designed to plump, sculpt, and highlight. His features look large on his smallish triangular face, which would look incredible in photographs, the same as Hana. Even in real life, I want to keep watching him.

He looks down at the sink, and I realize my open staring is rude as hell.

"Hi," I say, trying to act casual and as if we haven't already seen each other half naked. At least I'm in the armor of my work clothes. I can handle anything dressed like this, even though Hana sometimes calls it my corporate-android look.

"Good morning, Ariadne." His voice is so low, I almost can't hear him. Hana said he was quiet, and it hits me that he might be shy.

"You can call me Ari." I summon up the power of the structured blazer to cover the fact that I don't know what to say to him either. "Are you finding everything you need?" I sound like a flight attendant.

"Yes, thank you." He sounds like a man talking to a flight attendant.

"Good." I want to be polite, but he should know I won't be around a lot. "I'm going to be late at work, but help yourself to anything in the kitchen. If you don't feel like cooking, I can tell you a few good places to eat around here."

"I'd like that." He looks relieved to be left on his own, and I try not to take it personally, since it's what I want as well.

The lure of being able to give a visitor tips to enjoy the neighborhood outweighs the threat of running late. After all, I was up at six to deal with Alex's problem. I can get into the office at 7:45 instead of 7:39. I'll still be the first in.

I grab a pad and sketch out a quick walking map, noting restaurants in the area, where the subway stop is, and my favorite local hangouts. I love doing travel itineraries for people. I even have a special notebook where I log interesting places. It's silly because I've rarely left the province, but it's the perfect escape from...I'm not sure from what. It's a waste, since time is money when you work with billable hours, but sometimes dreaming about those urban spice markets or white-capped blue waters is what gets me through the day.

I snatch the thoughts of all those appealing places and roll them up into a tidy package before tucking them away. Those things exist for later, if later ever comes.

"Here's my number." I jot it down as an afterthought. "You should give me yours as well."

I give him my phone, and he pauses for an almost insultingly long time before putting in his number. Then he takes the map I hold out and aims a polite smile at my feet. "Thank you," he says.

I nod at him before going out the door. My attention has already narrowed in on the day's concerns, none of which have to do with tiger-tattooed men or scenic vistas. So it's annoying that I keep thinking of both those things instead of preparing for my client meeting. I shake my head and return my attention to my screen. No use—I'm distracted by my screen saver, a cityscape of Buenos Aires.

I should have read Dad's article about keeping focus after all.

Three

Wednesday, 7:13 a.m.

Living with my new roommate is like living with a ghost. I assume his jet lag causes him to wake at odd hours, because I rarely see him, although I sense traces of his existence. Whenever we see each other, caution emanates off him like he's wearing an electric fence jacket. He's watchful, taking my measure, and I would be lying if I didn't find this irritating in my own house, where he's a visitor.

———

Thursday, 7:58 a.m.

Three cups of ramen fell on my head when I opened the cupboard foraging for coffee this morning. I text Jihoon when I get to work.

Me: You like ramen.

Jihoon: Yes. Ramyeon is a Korean food group.

Me: I'm not a fan, particuflarly when it falls on me. Can you put them away properly?

Jihoon: I'm sorry.

He adds a GIF of a sad cat for emphasis. It makes me smile, but only a bit because how hard is it to put ramen away so it doesn't fall out? It's shelf-*stable* in multiple ways. I ponder possible responses and send back a cat with a noodle cup on its head. Amusing, but also—don't let noodles drop on me.

Friday, 10:10 a.m.

I rub my neck as I turn away from my computer, wondering what to tackle next. Work is a hydra of tasks to be completed. The moment a project closes or the email is sent, another seven pop up the queue, ready to take its place. Even if I did miraculously finish everything, there would be that nagging sensation I should be doing more.

Before I can decide, the phone rings. It's Alex with good news: Hyphen Records is expanding and wants to bring me on retainer.

I cheer up because bringing in new work looks very good indeed, even if a record label isn't as high-profile as some of Yesterly and Havings's more blue-chip accounts. Then he asks what I know about K-pop.

"K-pop?" I draw a blank but think fast. "It's pop music. From Korea."

The silence on the other end is enough for me to know my answer was sorely lacking. Finally Alex says, "Hyphen works with one of the big Korean entertainment companies to distribute their artists in North America."

"I'll study up," I promise. I've learned about glass installation and cat food (not together) for other clients. I can watch some music videos for Hyphen.

"Newlight Entertainment's biggest band is StarLune," he says. "Might want to start with them. I'll send you a playlist and some fact sheets about the industry."

We chat for a bit longer before I say goodbye. Reflected in my monitor is the big smile I'd never wear outside my closed door. Hyphen wants me. Not one of the partners. Me. Richard assures me I'll get put on the bigger clients if I keep proving myself.

"What's got you so happy?" Brittany didn't bother to knock before opening my door.

My smile falls off as if it's been power washed. "Nothing," I say.

"Sure. Well, Meredith told me to tell you not to bother with the thing she assigned you."

"What thing exactly?"

Brittany shrugs, already shutting the door. "She said you'd know."

I don't, and now I'll look ignorant for asking.

That's not me proving myself.

———

Saturday, 2:30 p.m.

Hana: Jihoon says you're not at home. It's Saturday.

Me: He snitched on me?

Hana: I asked him.

Me: I'm at the office finishing up some stuff.

Hana: You've got to be kidding.

Me: Did you text me to nag about work?

Hana: That's my secondary purpose. I wanted to see if you were being nice to Jihoon.

Me: You know when a man goes on a rampage and all the neighbors say how shocked they are because he was a quiet guy who kept to himself?

Hana: Hoonie is not a serial killer.

Me: That could be why he had to leave home so fast. Police were closing in.

Hana: Like I TOLD YOU he takes a while to feel safe with people and is going through a rough time. Doesn't like to talk about himself.

Me: You sure he's related to you?

Hana: Funny. He's had some bad experiences meeting people, so he's a bit cautious. He likes privacy. It's not you.

Ah, the classic *it's not you*. It seems a little bit me when the guy shies away when we pass in the hall. I don't want to take on the emotional labor of having to coax Jihoon out of his shell. Why is it my job to get him talking?

Because you're the host. In fact, I'm the Triple Crown winner of making it my responsibility: I'm the host, I'm older, and it's my apartment. I make a face at the wall before submitting to the inevitable.

Me: I'll try to try.

Hana: That's my girl. Got to go.

———

Sunday, 1:36 p.m.

Me: Hey Jihoon, checking to see how you're settling in. Finding everything? Jet lag better?

I add in a happy face emoji for good measure.

———

Sunday, 5:09 p.m.

No answer from Jihoon. Fine, not everyone checks their texts frequently.

———

Sunday, 6:32 p.m.

No answer from Jihoon. I frown at the blank phone screen. It's not like he has a lot to do. It's simple courtesy to text back, especially when your host contacts you. What's with this guy?

———

Sunday, 7:56 p.m.

I can't tell if he's in his room. He could be dead for all I know. Ten minutes and I'll go knock.

———

Sunday, 8:05 p.m.

Jihoon: I'm fine, thank you.

It came exactly nine minutes into my waiting period, as if he'd timed it. I got all uptight for nothing. Why was I even worried? He's an adult and can take care of himself. I send back another happy face because, unlike Jihoon, I know it's polite to reply promptly.

He doesn't want to talk to me any more than I want to talk to him. The problem is I kind of do want to talk to him because it's weird to have to sidestep him all the time. Or I want him to want to talk to me so I don't have to go out there and make the first move and risk rejection. Is it too much to ask the guy freeloading at my place to be friendly as well as hot so I can live in peace?

I look at the phone. I guess it is.

———

Monday, 9:10 a.m.

I reread Richard's reply to my Hyphen news.

Good work, the email says. I know I can trust you with our most unconventional clients.

I've got two wins here: *good work* and *trust.* Then we have *unconventional.* That's a problem, since Richard is not a man who appreciates any deviation from the norm. He won't even wear a tan suit. Only black, gray, or navy, and the fanciest his tie gets is diagonal stripes. For him, a good client is an established one, like an oil company, where everyone around the table looks like him. It occurs to me that getting Hyphen might have potentially damaged my reputation. What if I pigeonhole myself as someone who can only handle quirky clients?

No, I'm reading too much into an email that probably took Richard twenty seconds to write. I'll stick with the plan to show what I can do with clients like Luxe and Hyphen. I'll do so well, Richard will fast-track me to partner. Beaconsmith is my brass ring, a high-status client like the ones that fill the dockets of others in the firm, and Hyphen will help get me there.

———

Monday, 10:38 a.m.

Another email from Dad about bringing an entrepreneurial spirit to the corporate office. He's added: Start joining meetings even if you aren't invited. Shows resourcefulness.

Or a stunning lack of judgment, but there's no point in telling him that. He'll say I need more confidence. I email back: Thanks, Dad! Great tip.

In the hall, Brittany calls out to someone that she's on her way but to go ahead and start the meeting while she gets a coffee super quick.

I don't bother to read the attached article.

———

Tuesday, 12:48 p.m.

Jihoon: Where is the bleach?

Me: Under the bathroom sink.

It takes three minutes until curiosity gets the better of me.

Me: Why?

Jihoon: I need to clean the hair dye.

Me: The what?

Jihoon: You know that tile in your shower?

Me: Yes, it's white.

Jihoon: It was white and I promise it will be white again soon.

Me: Send me a photo.

Jihoon: ...

Jihoon: Best not.

Me: Jihoon.

Twenty minutes later:

Jihoon: Where do I buy more bleach?

This time I send that cat GIF. It's crying.

———

Tuesday, 5:31 p.m.

Brittany pokes her head in my door without knocking. "You coming for drinks?"

It takes me a minute to get my head out of my work. "What?"

"Drinks. Are you coming?"

No one mentioned drinks to me. I'm tempted, but Meredith has assigned me two more tasks, and I'm getting stressed thinking about it. "Maybe next time."

Brittany pouts. "Oh, boo. Everyone will be there."

That tempts me even more because drinks are always a good way to connect. Then she adds, "It's to celebrate me joining the firm! It's so sweet of Meredith to have planned it."

Screw that, then. I mask my annoyance with my usual smile. "So sweet," I say.

She waves at me with the tips of her manicured fingers in a toodles gesture and leaves.

Later, I don't bother to look up from my files when I hear the rest of the group head for the bar.

———

Tuesday, 10:26 p.m.

When I get home, Jihoon is lying on the floor, which seems to be his happy place. He unwinds to stand, and I see he's about 80 percent very muscled leg, emphasized by his tight jeans. His oversize gray shirt reveals part of his shoulder. Hana is right, he's got style and not only in how he dresses. It's the way he holds himself. His hair is a stark blue black, and I resist running to the bathroom to check his cleaning job.

"Your hair looks nice," I say politely.

He runs his hand through and tilts his head to the side. "Does it?"

Well, when he looks at me like *that*, it does. Before I can answer, he gives a brief nod and disappears back into his room. I watch him go, a strange ache in my chest that I can't quite identify.

I'm probably hungry.

———

Thursday, 9:15 a.m.

Me: I tripped over your shoes this morning. There are a lot of them.

Jihoon: [photo of a suitcase filled with small cloth bags] I like to be ready for any occasion.

Me: Those are SHOES? Why are they in single-serving bags?

Jihoon: You don't shove Pradas into a suitcase without protection.

Me: Prada.

Jihoon: You've heard of Prada? You have.

Me: OMG, I've heard of Prada. It's that I don't care about Prada.

Jihoon: You are a monster. Look. [photo of brown shoe].

He must have sent the wrong image.

Me: It's a shoe. It's brown. Is that Prada?

Jihoon: [GIF of horrified cat] Levlin. Hand-stitched with copper awls. It takes a cobbler weeks to make. Years of expertise. It's not only a shoe, it's imagination made real.

Me: I can get a pair of shoes for $20 that will keep my feet off the gross sidewalk the same way.

Jihoon: I repeat, a monster.

Me: A monster who doesn't want to trip over shoes in the hallway.

Jihoon: Fair. Admit that shoe is a work of art though.

Me: No.

Jihoon: It's ok. I forgive you.

The next image is of that goofy cat, one paw raised in benevolent benediction. I laugh. At least he's less awkward on text.

———

Thursday, 2:01 p.m.

I look through the streaked window at the traffic sitting idly on Bay Street and visualize the corner office where I'll be working in a few years. I know the exact one on the fifty-fourth floor, complete with leather furniture and dark wood. At night I'll stand in front of the floor-to-ceiling windows as the lights of cars make the roads look like streams of liquid gold. I'll have exactly what I want and what my parents want for me. After all, I'm Ari, the younger but dependable and ambitious sister, not Phoebe, the flighty dropout.

Will you be happy? That snippy little voice sounds like Phoebe, who was so good at getting under my skin that I can hear her even after she's been AWOL from my life for years.

Shut up, disembodied Phoebe voice.

I squeeze my eyes harder and try to ignore it, but at times like this, weighed down with a weariness that's not from physical exertion,

I wonder if that voice is onto something, if there's more out there than what I've set my sights on.

These aren't productive thoughts. These won't help me reach my goals. I push them away and get back to work.

———

Thursday, 8:29 p.m.

When I get home, Jihoon is in the living room sitting on the couch surrounded by half-empty chip bags. In his hand is a tall boy. His laptop is open on the coffee table, and he pauses his show to smile at me. It's small, but this is the first truly positive expression I've seen since he arrived. It looks good on him.

"Hi, Ari."

I debate saying hi and then going straight into the kitchen to avoid conversation, but that's rude. Also, I want some of the chips. "Hey." I poke through the bags. "You didn't get hickory sticks. Those are a classic."

He groans and puts a hand over his stomach, his black shirt covered with crumbs. "I wanted to explore new flavors we don't have at home. It might have been a mistake. Help yourself."

I grab the bag of cheesy garlic bread chips and try one. Then I make a face and go for the sriracha ruffled. Those are better. Meanwhile, Jihoon goes to the kitchen and comes back with more beer and two glasses. He pours me a glass as I glance at his screen, which shows a handsome man in a wide-brimmed hat and a black jacket.

"What are you watching?" I ask.

"My favorite K-drama." He hesitates. "Do you want to watch?"

Not really, but I'm too lazy to go to my room. I nod with my mouth full of jalapeño chips.

He adjusts the settings to include English subtitles. I'm lost within minutes but don't bother pestering Jihoon with questions. It's pleasant enough to nibble on the gross chips and watch stunning men in turtleneck sweaters bicker with each other.

We finish the episode, and Jihoon glances over at me. "Another?"

I nod. "And a pizza?" Chips aren't a proper meal.

He lights up. "Can we get one with Gorgonzola ?"

"I know the perfect place."

We watch another episode until the pizza comes, and we drink more beer and don't talk about much at all except for confusing plot points. It's kind of a perfect night, cozy and unexpectedly comfortable.

I make a mental note to apologize to Hana for calling her cousin a serial killer.

_____

Friday, 3:13 p.m.

Yuko waves me into Luxe's open space office, which is shared by her and Ines. Ines is on the phone dealing with the personal assistant of an actor insisting on a dress a design house has promised to someone apparently lower in the fame hierarchy. Her voice is soothing and calm, but she shoots a glare at Yuko, who is pretending to gag behind her desk. Yuko stops and waves me over to whisper in my ear.

"Remember that travel itinerary you did for me when I went to Sicily?"

"Sure. It was fun." I included a catered picnic at the Zingaro Nature Reserve, which they loved.

"My friend's going to Singapore, and I was wondering if you can do one for her."

I get a rush of pleasure. Planning trips is my joy, soothing my detail-oriented and results-driven soul and providing some of the adventure I don't have. "Absolutely."

Yuko gives me a few more details about what her friend likes, and I take notes in my travel notebook. I glance up to see Yuko's screen saver is an Asian guy posing in front of a blue star with a full moon peeking behind it. "StarLune," I say, recognizing the logo. I'd checked the material Alex had sent me before deciding to go more in depth later. I don't start with Hyphen for another month, so I have time.

"That's X," she says. "Don't tell me Ariadne Hui, straitlaced lawyer, is a Starry?"

"A what?"

She makes a face. "I knew it was too good to be true. Starry is StarLune's fandom name. How do you know them?"

"A client."

Yuko pretends to swoon. "If you get to meet StarLune and you don't bring me, I'll kill you. I watch a lot of crime shows. They'll never find your body."

I roll my eyes. "You're vegan."

"Vegans can inflict violence on the deserving."

"Why do you like them so much?" I ask curiously. Yuko's in her thirties. Even when I was younger, I never had posters of the latest heartthrobs on my wall.

She raises her hand and begins ticking off her fingers. "Talented. Hot. Good-hearted. Funny. Performance gods. Lyrics that make me cry and dance at the same time." She pauses and strokes the man on the screen with fond fingers. "Did I say gorgeous?"

"You said hot."

She sighs. "So hot."

I look back at the screen saver. X is indeed attractive, but pop stars aren't my thing.

Ines calls me away from Yuko. "I have a project I'd like you to consider," she says by way of hello. "It involves travel."

"How much?" I'm intrigued. I don't go anywhere because I don't like taking vacation time at Yesterly and Havings. I don't want anyone questioning my commitment.

I think about it, though. A lot.

"I'm planning to branch out to more group luxury travel."

I'm instantly transported from Ines's office to a candlelit dinner on a black-sand Aegean beach. I had a photo of it on the vision board I kept for a few months until I put it away because it bummed me out. "That sounds fascinating."

"I need someone on the ground in places that do better with face-to-face negotiations."

My heart inflates for a moment. "I can do that."

"I know you can." Ines's smile is like sunshine. "This is critical work that requires relationship building. I want you to join Luxe permanently."

Instant deflation.

Swallowing my disappointment, I shake my head. "I can't." Dad was bragging about how soon I'd make partner right after Richard hired me, and I only need a few more years. I'm so close.

Ines is silent for a moment. "Think about it? You're my first choice."

I don't hesitate. "Sure."

I won't, though, and it hurts a bit to say. I've committed to Yesterly and Havings for the long haul. I can't miss my chance here, not after all I've put in.

It would have been fun, though.

Four

My Saturdays follow a standard routine: call my parents, work, and clean. I do best when my life is predictable. Hana scoffs at it for being boring, but she's the one who's always complaining about how much money she spends buying lunch because she forgot to make it.

Routine is good, especially now, when I'm doing my best to not think about Ines's job offer. It's tantalizing. Travel. Working with Yuko and Ines would mean an office where people talk to me or at least smile. They'd laugh at my jokes.

I might even make jokes.

Don't let those thoughts take root. Like ivy in a wall, if those doubts grow, they'll bore into my plans, flaking off little bits here and there until there's nothing left.

I check Jihoon's room to make sure he's out before hunting through my playlist for the perfect song to motivate me for the day. "Paradise City" blares into the quiet apartment seconds later.

That's the stuff. I start slow but am soon scream singing my frustrations into a wooden spoon snatched off the counter as I fill the kettle and pop it on the stove to boil, full-on Axl Rose-ing it with high kicks around the kitchen before standing with my legs apart and leaning back to squawk my way into the chorus, one hand jabbing upward. My baggy pajamas flap around me, and for the first time all week, the tension leaves my muscles. I'm in the middle of channeling Slash with my spoon-cum-air-guitar as I beg the cup on the counter to take me home, *yeah-yeah*, when I attempt a complicated jump turn and nearly knock over Jihoon, who is standing behind me.

A week and a half ago, he scared the shit of me when I discovered him sleeping on the couch. That was nothing compared to my reaction now. The spoon goes flying as I trip and fall on my ass in the middle of the kitchen, my braid whipping up so the elastic at the bottom hits me in the face.

"Oww." I cover my eye. "What the hell are you doing, sneaking up on me like that?"

"I called your name, but you couldn't hear me." Jihoon's eyes are wide under the ball cap he's wearing so low, you can barely make out his features. He's been running, and where I would be a red and sweaty mess, he merely glistens charmingly. "Were you, ah, singing?" He stumbles over the last word, as if he knows technically that's what I was attempting but feels it's not an appropriate fit.

"No." I silence Axl and Co.

"It was…" It would be amusing to watch him struggle for an inoffensive way to describe my yowling if I weren't about to melt from embarrassment. "Interesting," he offers finally.

I'm looking at the floor in sheer humiliation but catch his expression out of the corner of my eye. His shoulders are shaking with the effort of not laughing.

"Oh my God." I groan. "Go ahead. I'm terrible. I know it. Hana's mom made her get off the phone when I was singing in the shower because it hurt her ears."

He explodes with laughter. I didn't realize how tense he was until his shoulders drop and his face opens. He was keeping iron control around me all this time, but now he's laughing so hard, he ends up leaning over with his forehead on the counter. "No, no," he gasps into the granite. "Music is about passion. You're passionate."

I can't keep a straight face. And it *is* hilarious. Eventually we both stop laughing and wipe our eyes.

"I really am kind of mortified you saw that," I admit.

"I'm sorry I laughed. I shouldn't have. That was mean. You aren't that bad."

"Don't lie."

"You're untrained, that's all. Music is an art and a craft." He grins. "And Axl Rose is hard to imitate."

He heads off to the shower, and I continue making coffee, feeling lighter now that Jihoon is acting more like a regular person. I linger over the dregs in my cup and stare out the window as the water runs in the bathroom, thoughts flittering like moths through my mind. One by one they get zapped until only the biggest and strongest one remains, its pale wings made of emails and memos. I don't want to work. I don't want to do my usual Saturday things. Instead, I'm filled with the unusual desire to do...nothing. No, not nothing. Anything but opening my laptop.

I get up quickly. That's not the attitude I need right now, so I settle down at the table with my work. Jihoon comes out looking at his phone. He's dressed in black jeans and a loose black T-shirt with bare feet and shower-damp hair.

"What is this?" He shows me the screen, which has a text I sent him last night. I hadn't been able to get to sleep and was doing some travel research to relax when I thought about what Jihoon could do to check out the city.

"Hana mentioned you don't like crowds," I say. "I sent you a few places around Toronto that should be quiet if you wanted to explore."

"Because you're working and want me out of the apartment?" he says, his mouth quirking up at the side.

"No! Of course not." Well, yes, but I'm horrified to be so

transparent. I don't want him gone, but it's fair to say I was also not looking forward to Jihoon being home when I was trying to work. Quiet though he is, Jihoon has a distracting presence.

"It's not a problem, Ari. I should get some air."

He doesn't say anything as he scrolls through the message, and I nearly whack myself for intruding. "They're only suggestions," I tell him, trying not to feel defensive. "I didn't mean to interfere."

Jihoon shakes his head, the small smile growing. "This was kind. Thank you."

The way he looks at me is strange, and I can't read his expression. It's almost wistful, but why would he get emotional over spots I like to visit? It's the least I can do. Hana's voice whispers that the least I could do would be to keep the guy company for an hour, but I can't. I already feel so behind at work that my heart races when I look at my laptop.

Jihoon leaves, and the hush of the apartment descends around me. When my timer goes off to indicate it's time to take a break, I pull out my phone to call my parents.

"Hi, Dad," I say when he picks up.

"Ariadne, good to hear from you. How's work?"

I glance at the files spread across the table, due diligence for a client who never remembers my name. "Good, I guess."

"Work hard. Here's your mother." He hands over the phone, and I check the time. Eight seconds worth of conversation—that's about the usual.

Mom scolds him in the background. "You can at least speak to your own daughter."

"I need to finish the garage." His voice fades as he walks away.

"Hi, Mom," I say when she comes on.

"Hi, sweetie."

We talk about how the squirrels are digging up her tomato plants. Then she says, "Your sister called me the other day."

"Phoebe?" As if I have another sister.

"She's back in Canada, living in Montreal."

I laugh. "Like that'll last."

"Ari." Mom's voice holds a warning that I ignore.

"She'll get bored and leave after a month. We all know it."

She tsks at me. "I wish you two got along better. You could call her."

"We get along fine as we are. Plus, Phoebe didn't bother to give me her new number. I hope you told her the same thing as you're telling me."

Mom's silent, and I know she didn't. It rubs me the wrong way when she acts as if I'm the one who should be doing all the work to be a good sister.

"You two are so alike," Mom says.

As always, speaking of Phoebe sours the conversation, and I want to get off the phone as soon as possible without Mom getting upset. "What else are you doing today?" I ask in my best neutral voice.

Three minutes later, I disconnect and jump up from my chair. Phoebe's back in the country, but it's got nothing to do with me. Montreal is the same as her living in San Diego, or Chiang Mai, or Mexico City. She didn't think about me from those places or from all the other places she's been since she left. I was thirteen when she dropped out of school and took off. One day she was in my life, and the next, she was doing more interesting things than whatever her boring little sister could offer.

Expelling my breath too hard for it to be a sigh, I set my timer for my next working session. I have things to do, important tasks, and thinking about Phoebe isn't one of them.

Five

Work is more annoying than usual on Monday. When I leave, I gulp in the air until I feel dizzy. It's not fresh since this is Bay Street, but it's better than the office. In the middle of my breathing, Hana texts me one word: People.

That's all she needs to say. Hana's job as a corporate diversity consultant means talking to people about why it's not cool to be racist, sexist, ableist homophobes and asking if they could please not be like that. Her work trips are a poisonous combination of physically and psychologically exhausting.

Me: You ok?

Hana: Work sucks. The hotel air con is arctic. Eomma says I'm eating too much fast food because I posted a picture of a matcha latte.

I'm not surprised, because Hana's mom is a piece of work. Trying to get Hana to see how she looks unfiltered by her mother's constant negative comments—all provided under the guise of being helpful or being for Hana's own good—is an ongoing, eternally heartbreaking battle.

I grit my teeth and text back: Your food is your business.

Hana: I know.

We message about things we hate for a bit longer, and then I head home. Jihoon's already in his room. I don't want to knock on his door, but I wish he'd been in the living room so I could feel less alone. I sit on my bed, mind both empty and buzzing. I want to do something, anything, but I also want to do nothing. Inertia wins out.

My phone rings, and I glance at it. It's Mom, and I decline the call. I don't want to talk about Phoebe, and that's the only reason she'd be calling at this time.

The phone rings a minute later. Mom again.

My palms tingle. She never calls twice like that. I pick up. "Mom?"

There's a quick gasping noise. "Ari? Sweetie?"

It must be bad. "Mom, is everything okay?"

"He's safe, that's what you need to know. I don't want you to worry. Do you hear me?"

I hear the words, but it's hard to understand, as if my brain is sifting out every second syllable, leaving me with a broken message. Everything goes very slow.

"Mom? What's going on? Is it Dad?" I stumble over the words.

"He's at the hospital. We're at the hospital."

"Mom!"

"He's okay. It's fine." Is she reassuring herself or me? The first is scarier. "He had a heart attack, sweetie. The ambulance came, and he's going to be fine, I promise."

"What hospital?"

"You don't need to come. They said he'll be out in a couple days. He doesn't need surgery."

"I said *what hospital*."

She sighs and tells me, then she says, "I called your sister."

I take a moment to absorb my rage that she called Phoebe before she called me. Now's not the time. "Okay."

We hang up, and I watch my hands shake. Dad had a heart attack. He could have died. What if Mom hadn't been there to call an ambulance? What if he'd been alone?

I don't even notice I've moved to the living room and am standing in the middle of the floor until Jihoon cracks open his door.

He's in front of me immediately, hands warm on my shoulders. "Ari, what's wrong?"

I open my mouth to tell him that nothing happened and I'm fine, but instead I tell the truth. "My dad's sick. He had a heart attack. He's in the hospital."

He steps in and tucks my head under his chin as I sniffle. I'm not *crying* crying, but I can't seem to control the speed of my breath or the tears leaking from my eyes. Jihoon whispers softly in Korean as his hands stroke down my arms. He walks us to the couch and urges me to sit beside him without letting my wrist go.

The comfort of his touch wars with my shame at crying in front of a relative stranger. I choke out a laugh to try to save some dignity. "Sorry I got your shirt all gross."

I expect Jihoon to take the out I'm offering and make a joke that will be the first step in extricating himself, but he only looks at me. "Is your father safe?"

"Yes." My breath is light and uneven.

"Your mother. She's safe?"

"Yes, with Dad at the hospital." I feel a little stronger. In this moment, they're both safe, and I cling to that.

He hums an acknowledgment and sits with me silently, not loosening his hold, as I alternate between staring mindlessly at the red lines threading through the floor rug and thinking through what I need to do.

Finally I pull back and wipe my face. "I need to go to the hospital."

He nods and releases me.

Although my thoughts are darting around, my body sits unmoving on the couch. Keys. I need my keys and my wallet. Should I change? Call a cab. No, drive. A cab is better. What do I need to bring? ID? It's all so draining. I feel I need to move slowly, almost gingerly, like something in me will break if I rush, but I'm filled with a contrary need to hurry.

Jihoon's dark eyes are trained on me. "Ari? What do you need?"

"Nothing, thanks." My reply is automatic.

He doesn't take this escape either. "Tell me so I can help."

What I want, what I need. I want this not to be happening, but that's not on the table. I want Jihoon to pinch me and tell me it's a dream.

I want to not be alone, but I can't ask him for more than he's doing. That's not fair to a guy who's spent most of his time being very clear he wants nothing to do with me.

"I'm here, Ari." This time he runs his hand up to my elbow. I crush a cushion under my other hand and avoid his eyes. My need for company is bigger than my discomfort at asking for help.

"Uh. Will you come with me? To the hospital?"

There's a moment of silence, and I start apologizing, embarrassed for showing weakness. What was I thinking? I can do this by myself. I'm used to handling things on my own. "Sorry, I shouldn't have asked. It's a pain. I'll be fine." I get up, and he stands with me.

"Of course, I'll come with you," he says, his voice soft. "I wanted to offer but didn't want to make you feel pressure. Where's your bag? I'll get it."

In the cab, Jihoon keeps hold of me with a light touch on my hand that grounds me. A text comes from Hana, filled with hugs and hearts. I glance over at Jihoon. "Did you text Hana?"

"Yes. She wanted to call, but I asked her not to because you might be busy."

"Oh." I look at him out of the corner of my eye. It's nice to have someone watching out for me. "Thanks."

We travel the rest of the way in silence and then navigate to the emergency room. It's crowded, and the people on their phones or talking in low voices create an atmosphere heavy with tension and resignation. I wouldn't be surprised if Hospital Waiting Room is one of the featured tortures of Hell, and they wouldn't even have to change the seating. I find Mom staring at a wall near the vending machines. Under the strong light, her face is drawn and haggard, the bags under her eyes more prominent. The gray streaks in her short black hair look thicker than before, and for the first time in my life, I understand she's getting older and that one day her heart will also...

No. *No.* I'm not thinking that.

Her gaze shifts over when we approach. "Hi, sweetie." She looks past me, and I step aside so she can see Jihoon.

"This is Jihoon, Hana's cousin. He's visiting and came with me."

Jihoon bows as I lean over and give her an awkward hug with my right arm. "How's Dad?"

"Resting. He's in a shared room, so I left to give his roommate some privacy with the doctor. Did your sister call you?"

I take a deep breath. Phoebe again. "No."

"I told her to."

"We can talk about Phoebe later. When can I see Dad?"

"It's his own fault," she snaps, eyes fixed on the vending machine. "He was working too hard. I told him, let's take a break. We haven't gone on holiday together in years. Why work to only work more?" Mom's voice is rising, and the older woman beside her nods in sympathy.

"Mom, I don't think..."

"For what?" She shakes her head. "So when you die you can get *he answered email at midnight* on your tombstone?"

"How did it happen?" I don't want to talk about Dad's work ethic. Jihoon touches my arm, murmurs about coffee, and disappears.

"He mentioned heaviness in his chest in the afternoon but said it was fine. He waited five hours! Then he collapsed after dinner. All sweaty."

"How long is he here for?" I ask, trying to keep her focused. I read somewhere that getting people to think about numbers or facts can calm them down. "A couple days?"

"They think so." Her phone alarm sounds, and Mom stands so quickly, she almost stumbles. "We can see him now."

I feel bad I've already asked so much of Jihoon by bringing him here, so I text him that he can go home if he wants. He replies with a heart emoji, which is a sweet if inconclusive answer.

The hospital corridor is bright with that light that comes down through the tops of your eyes in a jagged and headache-inducing line. In Dad's room huddles a crowd of people chatting around the man in the first bed, who has the privacy curtains thrown open wide. They greet us with disconcertingly cheerful smiles, and I manage a terse nod in reply.

Mom slides open the curtains around Dad's bed, the slithery rattle of the metal rings making my shoulders inch up. She only widens them enough for us to squeeze in before closing them firmly behind us. Her arm rests against mine for a moment before she steps away.

Dad's asleep. It's been a long time since I've seen him with his eyes closed. He's in one of those blue cotton hospital gowns with an IV buried in his arm and wires coming out from his chest.

"Did they give him pain medication?" I whisper to Mom. I want to cling to her hand, but she has her arms crossed in front of her. It takes all my energy to keep the tears out of my eyes and collected in a tight ball in my throat where they can't escape.

"He's on a lot of meds. They're monitoring him."

It's creepy to stand and watch while Dad's asleep. His black hair, streaked with gray in the same places as Mom's, looks dull against the harsh bleached white of the pillowcase. I could sit down and hold his hand, but that feels unnatural. We don't touch very often. I can't remember the last time he hugged me.

I look at the lines on the heart monitor and desperately wish I could pull out my phone to have something to do that isn't this. Beside us, the roommate's family bids him a boisterous goodbye as they file out. "You'll need to leave soon," Mom tells me, eyes not moving from Dad's hands. "I told you there was no reason to come."

"I wanted to."

She reaches out to give me a little side hug, and I burrow into it. I'm thirty years old and need my mommy. "I'm going home soon, too. Phoebe will be here tomorrow."

"What?"

"She's taking the morning train from Montreal and staying with a friend."

I don't answer. The last time my older sister was in Toronto, we had a fight that ended in her telling me I was a repressed child who needed to grow up. Then she stormed out of the café where we'd met for coffee.

What infuriated me was that she'd left before I said what I thought of her. No, that I didn't get a chance to tell her I never think about her. That's what I would have said. That's what I was going to text her before I decided it wasn't worth the effort.

"She misses you," Mom says.

I glare at her. "I don't need you to try to fix things like a 1950s mom, thanks. We're adults."

She doesn't answer, and we watch Dad sleep until the nurse comes to say visiting hours are ending soon. I slowly go to his side of the bed and give him a squeeze on the arm. He doesn't move, and Mom ushers me out.

We stand in the corridor for a moment. "I'll keep you updated," Mom says.

"I'll come tomorrow."

"We'll see what happens after the test results, okay, sweetie?"

"Mom."

"I promise I'll keep you updated." She gives me a hug. This one has the reassurance I crave, but she's also captured my arms close to my sides so I can't return it. It's over as quick as it happens, and she steps away from me. "Go home and get some sleep."

She waves me down the hall as she retreats into Dad's room. I don't look back as I make my way to the waiting room.

My heart thumps with relief to see Jihoon sitting there with his cap pulled down and a face mask on. I didn't know how much I wanted him to wait. He jumps up when he sees me.

"Home?" he asks.

I nod.

"Want to talk?"

I shake my head.

"Then let's go." He wraps an arm around my shoulders, only for a moment, but I feel the absence when he moves away.

Six

When we get home, Jihoon waves me away when I reach for my wallet and pays the cab driver. I idly watch a group of dude-bros barrel down the sidewalk, slapping each other on the back for no apparent reason. Dad is safe, so I shouldn't be worried, but it's not like I can schedule my anxiety.

Jihoon walks around the back of the cab to join me, but I don't want to go in. The thought of being cooped up in the apartment is unbearable. "I'll be up soon," I say. "I'm going for a walk."

He glances up the now-empty street. "May I come?" he asks, pulling his mask down slightly.

"It's getting late." It's almost ten.

"I don't mind, and I've spent a week lazing around." He touches my arm so lightly, I barely feel it. "I'd like to join if you want company."

I'm ready to say no out of habit, but he rocks back on his heels as if nervous about getting rejected. It would be good to have company, and Jihoon has a comforting quality, present but not intrusive. "Sure."

We head down a small side street. Each step lessens my fear about Dad a bit more. Mom said he's fine, and she wouldn't lie. Beside me, Jihoon respects my silence and strolls along looking curiously at the houses we pass. He pauses at one decorated with disco balls along the front porch and turns when I point at the car parked out front in the street, an old Chevy that's been bedazzled to within an inch of its life. The steering wheel is lined with fake fur, and a small hula girl bobble figure sits on the dash. "I don't know if these would be fun or nightmare neighbors," he says thoughtfully.

We decide against peeking into the front window and move on, slowly creating a story about the house and its occupants. By the time we've walked two more blocks, it's stretched to incorporate a hidden entrance to an underground cavern, spaceships, and a taco truck, and as we try to one-up each other, Jihoon relaxes further. When I stop to create an elaborate sketch, using a stick and some dirt, of the aliens who live in the space taco truck, he laughs loud enough to startle a nearby cat.

"Your aliens are hideous," he says with a smile that crinkles the corners of his eyes and illuminates his whole face. "Here, give me the stick."

"Yours are worse," I inform him when he's done.

He frowns. "They really are. I blame the stick. It wasn't sharp enough."

I haven't laughed like this in a while, and it's tinged with guilt that I'm enjoying myself while Dad's in the hospital. Shouldn't I be lurking in a dark bedroom, feeling morose?

Jihoon glances down at me. We're under a streetlight, and the shadows play on his face, highlighting the geometric planes and corners of his features. "Ari?" Even his tone seems different, almost softer.

I take a step but stop at the slight pull on my sleeve. All his movements are gentle and precise. "What?" I ask.

"Something is bothering you."

"Well, my Dad's in the hospital," I snap. I can't help it. The best defense is a good offense when it comes to feelings.

"I know. I'm sorry." He doesn't lift his gaze, and I twist around uncomfortably until it's clear we aren't moving until I spill something.

"Being out here is nice," I say finally, staring at the sky to avoid looking at him. The streetlights block any stars that might be out.

"That's good. You need to distract yourself."

I snort. "No, that's the point. Isn't it wrong to be having fun when he's sick?"

"You feel guilty."

"I guess."

"What do you think you should be doing instead of this?"

Three dark pines partially obscure the gate in front of the house across the street. "I don't know," I say. "Sitting around being sad in solidarity?"

"Would that please your father?"

This makes me laugh. "Only if I'm also working. Otherwise he'd consider it a wicked waste of time when I should be trying to get promoted."

I start walking again, not wanting to elaborate. Normal people would let it go at this, understanding that it's a sensitive topic.

Jihoon doesn't. "He wants you to succeed."

"That's one way of looking at it." I get the feeling that I could drape myself in a gigantic red flag to warn Jihoon off but he'd ignore it to get the bottom of something he found important.

We turn left and into a small park. I'd never go there alone at night, but with Jihoon, I feel safe enough to cross through. We walk along the well-lit path to where it branches into a small stand of birch trees. I pause at the fork for a moment before deciding to go straight.

"My parents want the same thing," he says finally. "For me to be a success. You know my mother and Hana's are sisters?"

"I did. Are they similar?"

He makes a noncommittal noise, which I take as a tacit agreement. "I grew up in Busan but wanted to do an arts training program in Seoul when I was a teenager. My parents were against it. They wanted me to stay in school so I could get a stable government job that would last my whole life."

"You live in Seoul, so I assume you ignored them?"

Jihoon kicks a small pebble out of the way. "When I left, there was much drama. My mother refused to speak to me for a year. My father told me how disappointed he was in my choice every time I called home."

"You stuck with it, though."

"I did." Jihoon takes off his hat and runs his hand through his hair. "It was hard, but I knew what I wanted. I made some friends and began to learn what I needed to know."

"How do your parents feel now?"

He laughs. "I made a career for myself, but my field has high turnover. They still think I should have taken a government job."

This makes me laugh, too. "Parents."

"You can't do anything for your father now. You have nothing to feel guilty for."

"Yet I do." It's about eleven now, and the warm night combined with our solitude makes me more open than I would normally be.

Jihoon touches our shoulders together. "Hearts are strange things. They never do what you wish. Never take the easy path."

"No. Let's cut them out as sacrifices to the god of doing the right thing."

He wrinkles his nose. "I'd take the heart and its twists and turns over feeling nothing, though. Wouldn't you?"

I think of my role model, Meredith, who would rather die than express an emotion. Before I need to answer, we emerge onto a busy street and get crowded to the side as we pass groups of laughing people barhopping.

We head east, but I'm distracted by my companion, who has started walking with his face pointed at the ground. All I can see is the brim of his hat. His hands are stuffed into his pockets, an impressive feat given how tight his pants are, and his shoulders are pulled inward as if he's trying to look smaller. It's how I'd expect someone in a witness protection program to navigate the world.

"Everything okay?" I ask.

"What?" He swivels his head up and promptly walks into a fence that partly blocks the sidewalk. I do my best not to laugh, but his expression as he warily eyes the area for more obstacles is priceless.

"You look a little anxious."

This makes him look more anxious. "I'm fine."

"Sure." We keep walking—me normally, him not. I wonder if Hana's been completely honest about his sudden departure from Seoul. Maybe it wasn't a breakup but something more exciting like running from the mob with rows of diamonds and cocaine sewn into his very fitted jeans.

Clearly preposterous, Ari.

But...he did arrive suddenly. Very suddenly.

"The other day I learned the strangest thing. There's a mobster museum in Las Vegas." I watch him carefully, but he doesn't react to the word *mobster*.

"There is?"

"I bet there might be one for jopok somewhere. Or the triads or yakuza. The Mafia." I dangle every organized crime name I know like candy.

No change of expression except slight interest as he stops at a window display of artisanal cheeses. Then he gives me a conspiratorial look. "Did you know that one man rules Seoul's underworld? They say he's too young to manage it, but he has the city under his thumb. He disappeared recently. The city is in turmoil because all the gangs are turning on each other."

"What?" I stare at him.

"He's said to be as witty as he is brilliant. Well-dressed. Charmingly handsome, especially with black hair."

"Very funny."

I feel myself go red, but then he gives me an exaggeratedly wicked wink, exactly as a sleazy rich son would give before climbing into a

Lambo, and it makes me laugh. He looks pleased with himself. "I'm only a man who needed a change."

He sniffs the air as we pass a burrito food truck. "Hungry?" I ask, to change the topic. "I like this place."

He's reading the menu. "Chana masala burritos? Chicken wing burritos."

"I promise they're good."

"Ice cream burritos." Jihoon looks suspicious. "Really?"

"They're better when you're drunk," I admit. "Even sober, you won't regret it, cross my heart and hope to die."

His eyebrows rise. "Dramatic for a burrito. You order for us. I like surprises."

I shudder. I hate surprises.

I order two burritos to share: the tofu and the pasta. We take the silver-wrapped rolls to a bench on the corner. The streetlight is broken, making it feel dim and intimate, with the people walking by on the sidewalk becoming performers in a show we're watching.

My conversation defaults to Canadian Standard Basics: Occupation Query. "Hana didn't mention what you do for a living."

He hesitates. "I'm in the entertainment industry."

"Ah, that's what you meant about your parents wanting a more stable field."

He nods as he inspects the pasta burrito. It's packed with cheese ravioli and mini vegetarian meatballs in sugo that's been covered with parmesan before being rolled in a spinach tortilla. "It's competitive."

"Entertainment. Do you work in K-dramas?"

He takes a bite, then another. "It's good," he says in shock. "Dramas aren't your thing? You liked the one we watched."

"Hana loves them, but generally I find them too melodramatic."

Jihoon raises his eyebrows. "This from the woman who thought I was a mobster."

"I never said that, but in my defense, you wear a mask and hat everywhere. What should I think?"

"That I value good sun protection," he says with a serious expression.

"It's night."

"They also keep me warm."

"In the summer?"

He clears his throat. "Back to your dislike of K-dramas."

"I don't have a lot of time, and the episodes are movie length. Is that what you work on?"

He shakes his head. "I'm a music producer and a songwriter."

Interesting. "Any songs I'd know?"

Jihoon glances away. "How well do you know K-pop?"

I frown. "Not at all, but I need to learn more for a client. Have you heard of a band called—" I falter for a moment, trying to remember. "Starry?"

The tofu burrito has a wasabi mayo that I forgot to warn him about until he bites in, sniffs, and gets glassy-eyed. He said he liked surprises, but I assume that doesn't include a horseradish-based chemical burn in his nasal passages. I pass him a napkin. "Sorry, I should have told you about the wasabi."

After recovering, Jihoon says, "The band you're thinking about is StarLune."

"That's the one. I hear they're popular. Do you like them?"

He pauses. "You never heard of StarLune?"

"They came up for work, but I don't listen to much music in general."

His eyebrows shoot up. "You don't listen to music or watch shows?"

"I do, but not a lot. I do better when it's quiet." One of the assistants at the office always has a murder podcast playing, and I have no idea how she concentrates.

He shakes his head. "What about graphic novels? Webtoons?"

"No."

"Video games?"

"Please."

"Podcasts?"

"BBC World Service."

"Movies?"

"Only if it's action for the special effects. I don't pay twenty bucks for dialogue."

"Books?" He sounds frantic.

I glare at him. "Yes, I read."

Jihoon closes his eyes with relief. "I thought we would have to stop being friends."

It's churlish to point out that we've known each other about ten days and are hardly deep into friend territory, so I don't.

"I work a lot," I excuse myself. "All that media takes time. An hour of TV a night and games on your phone and a movie on the weekend? Let's say that comes to sixteen hours a week." I work the numbers. "Thirty-four solid days a year of casual content consumption. That's time an entertainment company controls instead of me."

We're done eating, so we gather up our trash. "You don't get joy from stories?" Jihoon says as we start walking again.

"All I'm saying is there's a lot of mindless stuff designed to get you hooked so they can sell more."

"Music and art also bring meaning and help people define their humanity."

A thin line now divides Jihoon's dark eyes. I belatedly remember he makes his living in entertainment. "I don't mean the work you do is useless," I hasten to assure him.

"Thank you!" He gives me a slight bow. "Very generous."

I sigh. "I deserved that."

To my relief, he laughs. "You haven't found the right thing to touch your heart yet, Ari."

Again with my name. I didn't think I needed validation this much, but every time he's said it tonight, I had a warm sense of being seen. It's after midnight now, but neither of us suggests going home. It's like he's finally decided I'm safe enough to at least have a civil conversation with. More than civil, even. Friendly.

Being with Jihoon is easy, and we start chatting about nothing and everything as the topics come up. We pass a boba store and talk about our favorite bubble tea flavors (rose milk for me, lychee green tea for him). A vet clinic brings up the question of the best animals for pets (cats, unanimous). A convenience store starts us on the best snacks, which quickly turns into a debate over which country has the best selection, Korea or Canada. I have a sure advantage with Coffee Crisp chocolate bars, but Jihoon makes a strong argument for Kkokkalcorn corn snacks.

Jihoon is really listening, even though there's nothing special about what we're saying. Hana is amazing, but she has a habit of lapsing into her own head sometimes and not paying attention. I also wouldn't rank open and easy communication among my own family's virtues. Jihoon looks at me as I speak and then asks follow-up questions instead of using whatever I say to launch into his own story.

When we hit the subject of roommates (one for both of us), I say, "I met Hana in university. How'd you meet yours?"

"Through work," Jihoon says. "It's strange to be without him. We're at the same company."

"You don't find it nice to be alone?" I love Hana but relish having the place to myself. Or did, until she sprung a guest on me.

He kicks at a small rock. "It's boring. We've been together for years, so I feel better when he's around. My other friends as well."

Wow, we are very different people. "Why did you come to Toronto, then?" I ask.

His face clouds. "They understood I needed some space away."

I want to ask more because I can tell there's a hell of a story behind this epic breakup. I also know I won't be able to respond with the sensitivity the circumstances, and Hana, would demand, so I back off with a wimpy, "Makes sense."

Jihoon casts me a doubtful glance, as if waiting for prying questions, but he catches me mid-yawn. "It's late," he says. "You have work tomorrow."

I do, and a fierce irritation overtakes me. I have work tomorrow and the next day and the next and every day until I die.

He sees my expression. "You don't want to go to work?"

"Doesn't matter if I do or not," I say, turning the corner that will take us home.

"It does."

I pull my hair over my shoulder. "I'm a lawyer. I have to work in an office. That's how it is, so it doesn't matter how I feel about it."

"Law is what you do, Ari. It's not who you are."

He draws close to me while we walk, and our hands brush as I consider his words. It's a nice sentiment out here, wrapped up in the dark with no one around, but Jihoon is wrong. In the morning, I will be the same old me, doing the same old thing because I work so much at my job that it's become both what I do and who I am.

I guess that's kind of sad.

But that's how it is.

Seven

It's clear Jihoon has successfully hurdled over both his lingering jet lag and any reservations about me.

I know he's fully adjusted to eastern daylight time when I hear him singing as he gets up at six in the morning. It's not "Paradise City," and I'm certain he's on key. Or on pitch. Whatever you call it.

I know he's adjusted to me when he pops his head in my room and asks if I want breakfast at shortly after six in the morning.

I'm buried under my duvet, enjoying my usual seven minutes of snooze, but I jerk upright when I hear his voice at my door. Shoving my sleep mask on top of my head and knowing my hair must be wild despite its night braid, I stare at him in shock. Not even Hana, our friendship resting on a sound foundation of years of goodwill, would dare come into my room this early.

Jihoon stands there in a loose black shirt and fitted gray sweatpants—and those things are the devil's garment leading people to sin—looking at me as if this is normal.

The alarm goes off, and I silence it with a vicious motion. "What?" I snap.

Though I sound crabby, he takes it in stride. "Breakfast. What would you like? I'm a good cook."

"No. Nothing." I rub my face. "I don't eat breakfast."

He frowns. "It's the most important meal of the day."

What, is he on hire from Canada's Food Guide? "I'm fine."

"Not even cereal?" He pauses. "We have lots."

"God, no." I'm not awake enough to be polite or to deal with the thought of eating whatever repulsive sugar bomb he's into this morning. He must have bought out the cereal aisle judging from the number of brightly colored boxes in the kitchen.

"I'll get you coffee, then." He ducks out before I can reply.

It's clear Hana fibbed. Despite his initial reticence, Choi Jihoon in his natural state is a Choi and, as such, not the type to keep quietly to himself once he's comfortable.

He's in the kitchen assessing his collection of cereals when I'm ready to leave for work. His smile gives him a funny, impish look, but his eyes are shadowed, and it fades almost as soon as it appears. He might be acting more natural, but it's clear whatever he's been through has taken a toll.

"We can watch a movie tonight," he says. "If you have time."

I think it over. It sounds relaxing. Dare I say...fun? Too bad I have a heavy day today.

"I'll be home late." I know the regret makes my voice harsher than usual but don't know how to stop it.

"I understand." His eyes drop to the floor. "Bye, Ari."

I open my mouth to say something that will soften the rejection and let him know that I appreciated his company last night, but I'm not sure how to phrase it without sounding graceless or putting my foot in deeper. A reprieve comes with the ding of my phone, so I nod at him and escape, the emails coming through making it easier to feign distraction.

When I get to work, I text Jihoon the address of a café I like, hoping to make partial amends. We got to bed late, I tell myself. He'll need the caffeine.

My concentration at work, already being tested thanks to fatigue, is not helped by constantly checking my phone for updates from Mom, which come through as if being squeezed through a dropper. Dad is awake and feeling better. They're running tests. He's being moved to a new room. Phoebe missed her train and will catch a later one.

Exactly what I'd expect from her.

I'm about to do my next email triage when a text comes from Jihoon, a photo of a cinnamon-flecked cappuccino from the café I'd mentioned.

Jihoon: I was going to bring a croissant home for you but it looked so good I ate it.

A wave of pleasure tingles my skin.

Me: Probably for the best. Squishing croissants that perfect is a crime.

Jihoon: Do you come here often?

Me: That's the worst pick-up line ever. Tell me you never use it.

That could be on the edge of too flirty. My pulse quickens as I wait for his reply even as I tell myself it's only a joke, so a rebuff wouldn't be a real rejection.

Jihoon: I never use pick-up lines.

Me: Confident.

This is definitely flirty.

Jihoon: Except this one. Ready?

Me: Probably not.

Jihoon: If I could rearrange the alphabet I'd put U and I together.

I run through six different responses that could either nip this in the bud or see where it goes. I settle on my default, which is a little bitchy but teasing. Flirtsults, Hana calls them.

Me: That's horrible. Did you google worst pick-up line ever?

Jihoon: No. I searched bad pick-up lines not worst.

I'm laughing at my phone when it dings again.

Jihoon: Have a good day, Ari. It was nice to be with you last night. I hope your father is well.

When I get to the hospital later that evening, I pause in front of the gift store. It's filled with little volunteer-knit booties and saccharine get-well-soon cards (no sympathy ones, I notice with morbid interest), and I hold an internal debate over whether to get a gift. Flowers are a no-go, since both my parents think they're a waste of money. Chocolate might not be the best for a man recovering from a heart attack. Books are safe, but as I linger in front of the display of books on how to lead a better life, inspirational autobiographies, and a selection of romance and thrillers, I'm struck by the realization I don't know what my own father would like.

Forget it. I head up to Dad's room empty-handed and find him asleep when I arrive. Mom is by the bed filling a cup of water. Phoebe lounges in a padded plastic chair.

She reacts first. "Hey, sis. Long time."

I bite back my gut response, which is a cheap variation on *whose fault is that?* "Hi, Phoebe. How was the trip?"

I congratulate myself on my neutral tone. I didn't even point out how she missed the train to visit her own father, who barely cheated death twenty-four hours ago.

"Not bad. I met a woman who plays cello in a rock band. She invited me to her next show."

"Only you," says Mom fondly.

Only Phoebe, that's for sure. "How's Dad?" I ask, getting the conversation back to the priority topic.

"Good," Mom says. "He'll be back home tomorrow if all goes well."

"He'll need to take it easy," says Phoebe. "Maybe start taking those Zumba classes with you, Mom."

I want to argue with her, but I can't. She's right, he will have to change his lifestyle, but I don't want to admit it.

Phoebe stands up and stretches, causing her lace kimono-style robe—which I'm fairly sure is a negligee—to fall off her tattooed shoulder. Her style has always been eclectic, and next to her, my tidy, work-appropriate suit feels beige even though it's navy. Her bleached brassy hair with inch-long black roots is cut in a choppy shag that reaches her shoulders and highlights her eyes. They're the same long and narrow shape as mine and have been accentuated with liner that extends them to her temples.

According to science, it takes four seconds for silence to become awkward, and I count to eleven before Mom, used to being the peace-maker, intervenes with a detailed rundown of what's going on with Dad. I try to listen, but I'm distracted by looking at him on the bed. At least if he were awake, he'd be more alert, but now his face is sallow and sagging, and his hair is a greasy mess. Dad is always very put together. He tucks in his shirts on weekends and throws out any sock without a match. It's almost transgressive to see him so weak, and a faint sense of shame rises in me, like I'm seeing something I shouldn't or that he wouldn't want me to witness. Phoebe moves close to touch my arm. I shake it off, and she backs away with her hand up and rolling her eyes.

When Mom's done, I ask a couple of questions, and Phoebe heaves a dramatic sigh. "Lay off Mom. She's doing what she can."

I don't even look at her. "I was only asking."

"Girls." In the past, Mom's voice held a slight pleading tone when-ever she wanted us to get along. Not today. She's firm as she points a finger in turn at both of us. "Enough."

We sit—or, in my case, stand—in an obstinate silence, nei-ther of us willing to lose by being the first to talk. This lasts until a nurse comes in.

"How are we doing?" she greets us.

Mom glances at the door, and we obey her wordless order to vacate the room. I lead the way, Phoebe's bootheels clicking behind me.

"Why do they always have this spotted floor in hospitals?" Phoebe says, tapping her foot as we stand in the hall. "What even is this? Linoleum? Tile?"

Since she was the first one to speak, I take that as the win it is and answer her in kind. It's easier to talk about inane things like hospital flooring than why she's here. "It's probably vinyl. Easy to clean and slip resistant."

Phoebe grimaces. "Of course you'd know that."

"There was a case study in law school that involved flooring."

"Right." Phoebe style, she gives the single word, that one syllable, a mocking intonation that says so much more. There's no point confronting her about it because she'll hide behind her usual defense.

That's not what I said, Ari.

You didn't have to. I know what you meant.

I didn't mean anything. You're being paranoid.

The silence gets to be too much, and I crack first. "When did you move to Montreal?"

"A few months ago. I wanted to improve my French, capisce?"

"That's Italian."

She gives me a long-suffering look. "Damn. Guess I've got work to do."

Against my will, I snort. Phoebe's superpower is that she can make me laugh with the silliest comments based on years of in-jokes. It drives me wild that she continues to know me so well this still works.

She looks satisfied, as if she's scored a point by making me react, but I let it go. "How long are you staying in Toronto?" I ask.

Phoebe points her thumb back over her shoulder toward Dad's bed. "Guess we'll see."

We stand and watch a harried nurse bustle down the hall before Phoebe says, "You never called me."

"What?" I shouldn't be surprised that she jumped right into it. Phoebe goes after what she wants with the tenacity of a bulldog and the impulsivity of a child.

"After I saw you last and we had that fight. You didn't call."

"You want to do this here? Now?"

Her eyebrows lift. "When else?"

"It was obviously your responsibility to call since you were the one who walked out," I point out. "Not me."

She bites her lip. "You could have emailed."

"Wow, so could you, if you weren't such an immature asshole."

A man passing by with his toddler glares at me. We wait until they pass, as frozen as the statue game we used to play as kids except for the deep flush I feel traveling up my neck from embarrassing myself in public.

"Me?" she finally says. "Me, immature. That's rich."

"Right. Like you're not the one always running away and expecting me to chase after you."

Phoebe huffs and stares at the ceiling. "Yeah, because that's totally what you do."

"It's what you want me to do."

Her eyes snap down to me. "You don't know jack about what I want."

The nurse comes out and smiles, oblivious or uncaring of the tension woven between us. "You can go in now," she says. "He's awake."

Phoebe thanks her in a sugary voice. I do my best not to shoulder Phoebe out of the way as I go in, even though I want to slap her. I'm not violent as a rule, but Phoebe brings out my worst self. Her boots thump behind me, and when I look through the curtain, Dad is propped up and frowning at his hands as Mom sits beside him tapping on her phone.

"Ariadne." His voice sounds a little rough. He looks past me to where my sister has pulled the curtain open to reveal herself. "Phoebe. What are you both doing here?"

When I turn, I see the gobsmacked expression on my sister's face. Despite our fight in the hall, we share a glance of understanding. Dad being Dad.

"You had a heart attack," Phoebe says slowly. "Of course we'd come."

"I'm fine," he says with a dismissive wave. "I'll be good as new in a couple days."

"That's not really how a recovery works," Phoebe says. Both Mom and I shoot her a look, and for once she pays attention to the social cue and lightens her whole attitude. "I mean, sure, Dad! That's great news."

"Can you pour it on any thicker?" I mutter.

"Shut up," she mutters.

Dad pulls lightly at one of the wires. "All unnecessary. Doctors always play it too safe."

"Martin, I can't believe you." If possible, Mom's arms fold tighter over her chest. "This is a wake-up call."

"I'm fine."

"This is not fine."

"Soolin." We all know that voice, which is the one that always ends the conversation. There's no point in arguing with Dad when he's in this mood. Mom's lips pleat, but she keeps quiet and busies herself moving around the items on the side table.

Dad turns his head to look at me. "Ariadne, how's work?"

"Great, but Mom said you need to..."

He holds up a hand, then stares at it as if surprised it's pincushioned with IV needles. "I can take care of myself," he says. "You need to worry about you."

"Right." I feel flattened. "I brought in a new client." That will make him happy.

"Good." His eyes flutter a bit before opening. "I've told you your hair is too long. Shorter is more professional."

"Okay, Dad." The hair comment is a biannual ritual.

The room eventually settles into silence, the opposite of the family last night, who huddled close and talked over one other, connecting with soft touches. It's been years since we were all together, and even when we were a real family, we respected each other's physical space. I always thought that was the best way to exist. Then I remember how Jihoon touched me on the arm or the shoulder as if to reassure me that he was there and I wasn't alone. In this room, my family is close enough to touch, but somehow they're too distant for me to even try to reach out.

"Time to let your father get some rest," Mom says, rubbing her hands on her pants. "We'll be home tomorrow or the next day, so I'll tell you when we get settled."

Phoebe gives Dad a hug, and I watch as his arms come up but then drop back down to the bed before he raises them again to gingerly tap her shoulders. I wave from the end of the bed and make my escape.

"Want to share a cab?" Phoebe trundles her suitcase beside me. "My friend's place is in your direction."

"Sure."

I don't want to talk, and luckily, I don't have to because we'd have to shout to be heard over the phone call the driver is taking on speaker. I take the respite gratefully as we head back into the city. When we turn south onto Jane Street, Phoebe waves her phone at me. "I should give you my number, in case something happens."

I'm leaning against the back of the seat, letting the streetlights shine through my closed eyelids. "Fine." Even before I finish the word, my phone buzzes with a text from Phoebe.

Hi, it says.

I experience total disbelief. She hadn't lost my number. She just... didn't want to contact me. The knowledge that she couldn't even be bothered to type A in her contacts list to bring up my name sits like a rock in my stomach, but it's not unexpected. Even if she had lost it, she could have asked Mom or emailed, but that would take effort, and that's not her style. There's no point in bringing it up. I'm too tired to have another fight, which is what will happen if I do.

We turn onto Bloor Street. "This is me," she says. "Tell me the final fare, and I'll transfer you the money."

"Never mind." I don't turn from the window.

"Thanks." The cab pulls over, and she hesitates. "Look. Ah, we should get together. For a drink or coffee."

When I look at her, she seems uncharacteristically unsure of herself. She must want something from me, but I don't want to think about what it could be because I've had enough Phoebe for today. I take the easy way out. "Yeah, okay. Text me."

There, the ball is in her court, and I have a feeling it'll bounce there for a while. She nods, and I hear the *thud* of the trunk as she collects her bag and leaves.

"Where to, lady?" The cab driver leans back to look at me.

"Wait a sec." I watch Phoebe, shadowed by the light coming through the bay window, as she yanks her suitcase up the crooked front steps. The door opens to show a woman with a high ponytail. She laughs as she brings my sister into a close hug and then pulls her into the house. Neither of them looks over to where I wait in the dark cab.

I tell the driver my address and head home.

Eight

On my way up to the apartment, I push away thoughts of Phoebe and think about what to eat. According to my weekly meal plan, tonight is chickpea bowls. Healthy and nutritious. I prepped the quinoa on Sunday the way I always do. Suddenly my chest feels hollow, but I don't know why. Chickpeas are good, and as a treat, I got organic for an extra two dollars a can. I like having the same thing every week. Streamlining my life means I can focus on what's important.

Jihoon is lying on the couch staring at a pen he's holding but sits up when I come in. I hadn't known how badly I'd wanted him to be home until I saw him. I throw myself in the chair opposite him, then get back up to put my purse where it belongs. He watches me before rising with a graceful motion and fetching two glasses and a bottle of wine.

"How did you know I wanted this?" I ask as I take my glass.

He puts down the bottle. "I did, too. How's your father?"

I fill him in and feel a surge of relief when I finish the story of Phoebe and the visit. I survived but don't want to linger on it. "What did you do today after the café?"

Jihoon updates me on his day as though it didn't happen until he tells someone about it. There's no detail too random for him to leave out, and even though I should find it aggravating, I don't. I close my eyes as he describes the two dogs he saw playing in the park near a high stone wall. He has an eye for small details that make a scene come to life: the red collar and dusty paws on the black dog, and the dry, crumpled leaf stuck in the fur of the gray one.

Then I open my eyes to a delicious aroma wafting over from the kitchen and a blanket over me.

Oh my God, I fell asleep when Jihoon was talking. That's the rudest thing I could have done, even if the low rasp of his voice could be sold as stress relief therapy. He should run an ASMR channel.

I tumble off the couch, yelping as my knees thump on the floor, and Jihoon calls from where he's standing at the kitchen counter, "Ari, are you awake?"

"Sorry, sorry." I get to my feet, rubbing the pins and needles out of my arm. "I have no excuse for that."

"You've had an exhausting time." He doesn't seem to take my nap as a commentary on how interesting I found his conversation. "It happens to my friends and I often. Are you hungry?"

"Very." This is a welcome escape from my chickpeas. When I stumble into the kitchen, pots are bubbling, and his hands move confidently to give one a stir and another a shake. I check the time. I've slept for an hour.

"Good, because I made too much." He brushes his hair back, and it immediately falls into his eyes again. "I'm used to cooking for five."

"I thought you only had one roommate."

He pauses. "Our friends are over a lot."

He spins around and grabs a bottle of red wine, giving a pan a liberal splash before pouring more into a glass and handing it to me. I take it and go into my room to change so my work clothes won't smell of cooking. I unravel my hair from its bun before giving my scalp a quick massage with my fingertips. I have a headache from lying on it as I slept, and having it loose sometimes helps.

Back in the kitchen, I perch on a chair to watch Jihoon work because it's soothing to have him cook for me. Neither Hana nor I are creative gourmets, since I strive for efficiency and she for convenience, but Jihoon seems to take real pleasure as he slices and stirs.

Jihoon's hand halts over the saltshaker. "Your hair."

I glance down and run my hand through to check it over. It feels fine, no knots or kinks. "What about it?"

His eyes follow to where the ends fall at my waist. "I've never seen it loose before."

I pull it behind my shoulders. "I need to wear it up for work, so it's become a habit." My hair contravenes one of the office's many unspoken rules: Thou Shall Not Stand Out in Thine Appearance. It's one I'm already pushing by being visibly Asian, and I don't like to add to it by having my hair on display. One of the partners referred to it as my geisha look when I wore it down at a holiday party.

"It has waves as dark as the memory of a night river."

Jihoon throws off the compliment casually, like it's no big deal, and grabs the shaker. At least I think it's a compliment. I've never had a man say something like that to me before. "Thank you?"

He smiles and checks the rice cooker. It's a boring Canadian one since I refused to get the expensive imported version that chirped, "Your rice is done!" in Korean. Hana had pouted for three days. I sip the wine to cover my confusion as he spoons rice into a sizzling pan.

My phone rings, and I glance at it. "Work."

I deal with a last-minute update on one of my due-diligence projects. It's late for a call, and although I do my best to be professional, when I end it, my jaw aches from trying to keep my voice calm. One of my law profs told us to keep the expression we wanted in our voice on calls, and it's harder than it sounds.

Jihoon glances at me when I'm done. "You sound different at work."

"Yeah?" I nibble on a chive. "That doesn't sound good."

"Harder, almost. Severe."

I roll my head over to look at him. "Makes sense. I need to be those things so people don't take advantage of me. Can you imagine a soft lawyer? People would think I'm a pushover."

"All the time?"

I rub my temples. "It depends on what people expect from me. With others, I need to be peppier. More keen and positive."

He tilts his head. "You're not like either of those at home."

"I mean, I can be, if you prefer," I say stiffly. I feel like I've been caught out in something.

"I like that you're like this with me. It seems more like the real you."

I want to scoff at him because he's known me, what, days? But he's a little right. I always feel like I'm playing a role in my job. "I guess it is," I say.

He smiles at the rice. "Good. I like this Ari."

I don't know what to say—cultural differences mean I can't tell if he's only being polite—so I watch Jihoon arrange the food with delicate fingers and an expression of intense concentration. He even snipped chives for a garnish. I would never bother doing that, but it looks as pretty as it smells delicious. Japchae shares space on the table with braised tofu, fried rice, and salad.

"No meat," he says. "Hana says you're vegetarian."

"You checked with her?" I grab chopsticks and dig into the glass noodles.

Jihoon tilts his head to the side, then fetches kimchi from Hana's inexhaustible store, which he cuts with scissors before plating it. "Of course. I wanted to know what you'd like but didn't want to wake you up."

I can't believe he's real. Who does that?

"You're a fantastic cook." I've been too busy eating to have properly congratulated the chef. "Why do you eat so much instant ramen when you can cook like this?"

"I don't like to cook only for myself." Again he bites his lip. "Eating together is good. I missed this from home."

Since I'm now on my second glass of wine, I decide this is as good an opening as I'm going to get. "Hana said you left Seoul because of a breakup. Do you want to talk about it?"

Jihoon snaps his chopsticks on some kimchi and examines it before lowering it slowly to his plate. "The breakup."

"They're hard," I say. I'm trying, but I'm not the best at talking about relationships and wish Hana were here to pilot the conversation. She's a solid INFP on the Myers-Briggs, an Enneagram Type-2 Pisces. Or so she tells me, because those things are bull. She says that's exactly what an INTJ, Type-8 Aquarius would think. "Breakups."

"Yes." He sips his own wine, frowning as if deciding what to say. "We'd been together a long time, and I wasn't sure who I was outside of it. I came here to think about what I wanted and whether people would accept me for what I have to offer on my own."

Despite his words, the longing in his voice is so clear that I wonder if he's not completely done with his partner. I wouldn't judge, even though part of me is almost jealous of this person who has so much of his attention. Even after the brief time we've known each other, I feel the power of his focus. When Jihoon's listening, it's like he's entirely in the moment and that moment is all about you.

I've only known him for two weeks, but that much attentiveness is addictive.

"You couldn't sort it out back home?" I ask.

His nod is so decisive that his hair flops over his forehead like a living thing. "I needed to get away and clear my head. If I were there, I would get drawn back in. How can you explore yourself surrounded by all the same things that have determined who you've been for so long?"

I don't bother with a lot of self-reflection, but I see where he's coming from. "I've never left the country, so I wouldn't know."

He tilts his head to the side. "You don't like to travel?"

"Never had the chance, but I'd love to." I poke at some bean sprouts on my plate. "I plan trips a lot, for fun."

"Ah." Jihoon doesn't say anything else, but I'm left with an uncomfortable feeling that I said more than the words. "That sounds relaxing."

It is, but I look away, self-conscious about my private obsession. "Oh, you know."

"I don't," he says. "Tell me."

I deflect. "It's nothing, only something to look forward to. Like looking at the menu before you go to the restaurant."

"Anticipation."

More vicarious living, since none of these trips are for me. "How about you?"

"My trips are usually for work, so I don't see much besides the hotel room and where I'm working. Someone does all the scheduling."

That's almost worse than not going at all. We both eat silently until Jihoon pauses, holding his glass midair.

"Let's plan a trip," he says. "Our ideal trip."

It could be the wine and the intimate, warm feeling of eating with Jihoon that causes my first question to be "Where to?" instead of *why would we do that?*

He grins and pushes himself back from the table. "Anywhere. Everywhere. We could take an around-the-world cruise. Or find a small village in the Alps and feed goats for a month."

"Did you know goats can climb trees?" I think about it. "I'm in."

We clear off the table as we narrow down our location. "Relaxing or active?" I ask.

"Moving relaxes me. I like to walk." He brings the wine and glasses to the living room and comes back to clear the water jug. "Busy or quiet?"

I consider this as I wipe the table down. "Both? I'd like to experience a big city, but I also want solitude. I don't want people around me all the time."

"I want that, too," he says. "I like being with people I know, but I get nervous when strangers get close to me."

We go into the living room, and he hands over my glass. Our fingers brush slightly, and I almost jerk back with the electrical shock that flashes through me. He must have been shuffling on the carpet.

"Do you need to speak the language wherever we go?" I ask.

He shakes his head. "I'm fine looking confused until someone helps."

"Your English is great," I say. "Did you learn from Hana?"

"I went to an international school and then practiced on her and a friend from Vancouver. Do you speak..." He hesitates, looking at my hair and face. "Any other languages?" To his credit, he doesn't start naming Asian languages at random.

"No. My mom speaks enough Cantonese to order dim sum, and Dad only speaks English, no Chinese at all."

He leans back on the cushions, jawline on display. In a way, I wish he were the same distant Jihoon of the last few days because I can tell this warmer version is going to be difficult to live with.

Live with without drooling over, I should clarify.

We hammer out a few more details. Neither of us needs luxury but do require regular showers. Shopping is important for Jihoon and not for me. I want to hit some major landmarks, and he's happy looking at them online. Neither of us likes standing in lines.

"I'm not used to them," he says.

"What, there aren't lines in Seoul?"

He glances at his glass. "Not at the places I go."

"Okay, Mr. Fancy Music Producer. We'll avoid places where you need to queue like the common folk."

Jihoon goes red. "Do you have any ideas on where we can go?"

"I do." My travel notebook is in my bag by the door, and I go over to check it without bringing it back to the living room. No one has ever read it. Even Hana thinks it's only a journal.

As I flip the pages, he calls, "What are you doing?"

"Nothing." I stuff the notebook back into my bag and go back. "I have a place."

He looks at me suspiciously. "What aren't you telling me?"

"How do you know I'm hiding anything?" I put on an injured tone.

Jihoon gestures toward my bag near the door. "Ari. You're not subtle."

I know when I'm defeated, but when I look at his face, I decide to trust him. "I keep a travel notebook. It's where I jot down notes of interesting places."

He doesn't laugh like I fear, only nods. "It makes sense to have a place for your ideas. I have notebooks for my music, but I keep losing them."

"You can set up a special email account to send yourself notes. My friend did it for her kid and sends photos and messages so they can read them when they're older, like a digital journal of their childhood."

He brightens. "I love that idea. Where are you thinking would be good for our trip?"

I hesitate. I can find what I need online, but my notebook has the perfect route already mapped out. Jihoon catches my eye and smiles at me. He hasn't let me down yet. I make up my mind and fetch my notebook.

Sitting back beside him, I flip through the pages. The book itself is nothing special, a plain grid-patterned A5 Leuchtturm1917 with a canary yellow cover. I like all my travel notebooks to have the same look, and I have filled ones with blue, green, and purple covers on my shelf. There isn't much of a rhyme or reason to the notes either, like being organized by continent or country, or hotels and attractions. It's a hodgepodge of ideas and information that strike my fancy gleaned from conversations, social media, and news stories.

Jihoon looks over with interest but stays silent until I find the page I want. I take a deep breath and pass over the book. "Here. The Camino de Santiago."

He takes it carefully. It's a two-page spread featuring a rough map of southern France, Spain, and eastern Portugal. I've marked my preferred pilgrimage path across northern Spain and down south.

I figure he'll glance at it and give it back, but instead he examines the path before reading the notes about hostels, sights, and packing tips that crowd the corners of the pages. "May I look through the rest of the notebook?" he asks.

"Why?"

He looks at me. "This is fascinating. I want to know what other places have caught your attention."

In for a penny, right? I've already come this far, so I nod. Part of me is happy to be able to share it. There are so many enthralling places in the world and to talk to someone about the ones that interest me is...well, it's fun.

Jihoon takes his time working through the pages. There aren't many, since I only started this one a couple months ago. He points to one of the entries. "We can see the world's oldest ham?"

"At the Isle of Wight Museum. They also have the oldest peanut."

"Let's log that for a later trip." He turns the page. "Ah, I've been here!"

"Atlantis Books in Santorini?"

He nods. "It's very twisty and crowded inside, but you can buy a book to read on the outdoor patio. The town has one of the best sunsets in the world."

I sigh, and Jihoon leans in so our shoulders touch. "You'll go one day," he assures me. "Perhaps we should go to Greece for our getaway instead?"

I'm torn before I remember this is all make-believe. We're not going anywhere. "Let's stick to the Camino."

"It's perfect," he says. "Walking and quiet."

"You can shop in Seville. Or we can fly into Paris."

"Then we can go up the Eiffel Tower," he says. "I've never been to the top, only saw it from the hotel."

I look at my notes. "The best times to go are spring and fall."

"Fall," he says with certainty. "It's my favorite season."

"Mine, too." I check my phone. "I say we do three days in Paris and then get a train south. We can have a bus take our bags ahead each night so we don't have to carry all our clothes as we walk."

He frowns. "Doesn't that negate the point of a pilgrimage walk?"

"Do you want to carry a huge bag for twenty kilometers each day?"

Jihoon weighs the actuality against the purity of the experience. "No."

I shut my notebook and lean back against the couch. "I wish we could do this now."

"We can," he says. "I jumped on a plane to Toronto. I can get on another to Paris."

"I can't go to Paris. I have work."

"Then let's do this next year. For now, we can go somewhere that doesn't involve crossing an ocean," he says.

"We should," I say. I'm not sure what he means, but I'm tentatively open to the idea.

"I'm not even sure what I like to do anymore. I've been too busy with work." He tosses the pillow aside. "Books. Do I like stories or facts? Am I a man who enjoys puzzles? Graphic design? Horse racing?"

"Can't help you there." I grab the glasses and refill them. Then I pause. "Wait, I can."

He swirls his glass. "Do you have a flowchart?"

I ignore that. "Are you free this weekend?"

"I'll have to check my calendar since the zero people I know in the city are all begging for some time."

"Decline all zero. We'll have a Who Is Jihoon Day while you're in Toronto."

He lifts his perfect eyebrows. "That sounds like the worst name for a national holiday."

"Well, we have Canada Day. Not very creative."

"We have Hangul Day, when we celebrate the creation of our alphabet."

I pause. "That's pretty cool, to be honest. Are you in?"

"I'm not sure how I can resist."

It's not until I'm almost asleep that a text comes in. It's an itinerary for next year's Camino walk from Jihoon, with all the details we discussed, complete with flight availabilities to Paris from Toronto and Seoul. It's in my calendar, his message ends, with a link to a meeting request for today next year.

He's called it Jihoon and Ari's Super Awesome Getaway. I accept the request. Mine too, I type.

Then I lie in bed and look at the screen. We can have a fun day exploring while he's here, but obviously this big trip will never happen. Jihoon's only here for a few weeks, which is no doubt why I feel so free with him. He's safe because nothing can happen. Our Super Awesome Getaway is safe as well, a dream I can plan for and anticipate without worrying about taking time off work or getting sunburn or blisters. It will be always unrealized and perfect.

I click the map link he's included and trace my finger from Salamanca to Merida. Perhaps one day I'll do that walk, and if I do, I wonder if I'll remember Jihoon. Or if he'll remember me.

It would have been fun to do together, though.

Nine

*I*nstead of preparing for Who Is Jihoon Day, I sit on the balcony staring at the tops of trees, selfishly wondering what I would plan for a Who Is Ari Day. Hiking? Scavenger hunt? The beach? I pause. Have I ever liked swimming or only thought I should? In fact, most of my thoughts end up boomeranging back to one question: whether I like the things I thought I did.

Such as my job.

I grab my travel notebook and flip through the pages. In Istanbul, I could haggle for saffron in the spice bazaar. In Belize, go cave tubing through a Mayan archaeological site. Visit Tanzania and climb Kilimanjaro. The world offers so many options, and yet I only write them down as I sit here in Toronto with stress and a job I worked years to get in an office that makes me feel like half the person I could be.

Who the rest of that person I'm missing is, I don't know.

Movement from inside the apartment catches my eye. Jihoon sees me, waves, and comes out to say hello.

"You'll be late for work," he says as he leans over the balcony, nose buried in his arms and unrivaled ass curved out as he stretches his hamstrings. He's in shorts and smells like the synthetic coconut of his sunscreen, which means he's about to go for his usual eighty-kilometer or whatever run as the healthy person he is.

I check the time. Jihoon's right; I will be late for work. I haul myself out of my seat. "Duty calls," I say. "What are you doing today?"

He doesn't answer, so I don't press him. I've seen the open notebooks around the house, filled with crossed-out lines and doodles and suspect he's suffering from writer's block, if that's something music producers get.

Hmm, artistic block. An idea sparks for what we can do.

————

When Saturday morning finally comes around, I first call my parents. Dad's home, and both Phoebe and I have made separate trips to the house. Mom made it clear I wouldn't be welcome this weekend because she had enough on her plate trying to get him to relax instead of doing his usual weekend tasks.

No surprise, Phoebe hasn't bothered calling me.

"Are you ready to go?" I call to Jihoon. I've sublimated my discomfort at skipping my normal Saturday things into organizing an outing with the precision of a military campaign. "Today we help you find yourself."

"As long as I can spend the day with you, Ari. That's all I need." He glances up as I fix my hair. "Will you leave it down?"

I peer at him, both my arms back and behind my head. "Why?"

"It swings when you move. It's pretty."

I hide my flushing face behind my elbow because I like the idea of looking pretty, and that makes me feel like some sort of anti-feminist throwback. "I usually have it tied back for work."

He gives me a sweet smile. "Whatever you're most comfortable with."

I tuck a tie in my pocket just in case but shake my hair so it tumbles to my waist. I instantly feel more like myself with the comforting weight of it distributed rather than always tugging at one spot on the back of my neck.

Jihoon reaches out as if to touch it but then blinks and ducks away. "What's first?" he asks.

I'm staring at those long fingers, wondering what they'd feel like tangled in my hair. "What?"

"Our day. What's first?"

I snap out of it. Now is not the time to be fantasizing about Jihoon, although given his breakup, living in Korea, and being my current roommate, I'm not sure when the right time is.

Back to business.

I check over our itinerary for today. I had Yuko help me with some of the details, and she was effusive in her praise of my plan. "Damn, you're good at this. Can I use these?" she asked, flipping through some of my discarded ideas. "It would totally suit some of our clients when they need to keep people entertained."

"Go ahead," I told her. It was only a silly thing for fun anyway.

Five minutes later, we're ready to go. Jihoon watches me pull on my shoes with an air of polite disapproval, and I check his feet. He's wearing a pair of spotless sneakers.

"Another pair of Pradas?"

He looks appalled. "These are Balenciaga. Balenciaga!"

Teasing him is too easy, so I lay off and turn away so he can't hear me laugh.

"Ah, Ari." He rolls his eyes. "One day I'll buy you a pair of shoes so cute, you can't help but adore them."

I never felt any particular way about my name, but when Jihoon says it, it's like a caress. I stuff my wallet in my bag. "I don't need shoes."

"You can have wants as well as needs." As I'm about to dissolve into a puddle at the low purr of his voice, he straightens. "Let's go."

We get on the subway, and Jihoon watches people from under the low brim of his hat as if he's been stranded in space and starved for human interaction. Meanwhile I watch him. Jihoon's face—well, his eyes, which are all I can see over his mask—is so expressive, I can read almost every thought that passes through.

I'm 100 percent confident if there were ever a man unable to out-right lie, it's Jihoon. It's nice to be with someone like that.

I sit back, the rattle of the subway around me, and relax.

The first stop is a bookstore, and Jihoon peers curiously through the window. "Used books?" he asks.

"Not just any used books," I correct. "This place has the most random selection I've seen." In front of us is an assortment of books that are visually unified and topically chaotic. A hand-drawn guide to mushrooms of North America is beside an explanation of fencing strategies. A treatise on how to be a competent secretary sits above them.

I usher Jihoon in and let him look around for a few minutes, picking books up curiously, before walking over. "We're going to play a game today. At each place, the winner gets a point."

He perks up. "I'm competitive," he warns me.

"I once refused to talk to Hana for hours because she got a package in the mail before I did."

Jihoon nods, understanding how serious this is. "I'm ready."

I take out my notepad from my bag with a flourish. It's more for the drama, because the game's pretty simple. "Round one. The perfect book." I look up. The cashier is staring at her phone, totally uninterested in us, so I continue, "We have two minutes to find the most inspirational book."

He looks around, hands on his hips. "In cover design or topic?"

"Entire package, and inspirational is broadly defined. Winner decided by mutual consent."

"The most inspirational book." He looks down at me. "Why that?"

"You seem frustrated with whatever you're working on." I flip through the pages of my notebook, not wanting to meet his eyes because, as usual, what seemed like a good idea at first now seems laced with potential drama. "I didn't read any of your notes," I add.

"You can't," he points out. "They're in Korean. You don't know Korean."

"There was that, too." I put the notebook in my bag. "I thought it would be good to find a book to motivate you."

I avoid looking at him as the silence grows. I completely misjudged him, and my soul collapses down into a black hole of shame. Passions can be difficult creatures, I suppose. I never had one. Making itineraries for fantasy trips I'll never go on doesn't count because it's not serious. I'm about to ask if we should leave in the least defensive way I can muster when he speaks.

"You are observant, Ari. And right. I have been having trouble. Music used to flow, and now there's nothing but a watery flatness. Nothing to grip." He tilts his head to the side and rubs the back of his neck, contemplating the shelves before he smiles at me. "It feels better since I've been here but not as it should be. I like this idea."

Emboldened, I raise my eyebrows. "Do you accept the challenge?"

"Do I have a choice?"

"Sure, if you want to be a quitter."

His eyes narrow. "Set the timer, Ari."

We separate as the numbers count down, each of us retreating to a different part of the store. I look at a 1970s tome on pickling before turning to a book on road maintenance. Neither seems particularly inspiring to a songwriter, so I pull out another. *Bread Sculptures for Fun and Profit.* There's a photo of a toasty golden brown mermaid on a shell, raisins decorating her throat in an edible necklace and almonds covering her like a bra.

I put that in the maybe pile.

Across the store, Jihoon reads through the titles on the shelves. I feel a pang of guilt. I assumed his English was as good when reading as it is speaking, and I hope I didn't embarrass him. I should have asked; Hana is always telling me to use my words.

He catches my eye, and my knees get sweaty. As we've gotten to know each other, Jihoon has become even more attractive. I think he's starting to stand closer to me when we talk or touch me more, but I'm not sure if it's wishful thinking. Occasionally, when he laughs or looks at me a certain way, I wonder what he'd do if I caged him against a wall and kissed him. I have that feeling right now, and as if I'm somehow broadcasting my thoughts across the store, Jihoon's eyes get bigger.

They drift down to my mouth. Or so I think.

Definitely I wish.

My phone softly beeps out the *James Bond theme song*, which Hana set as a joke, and we both step away from the shelves. Since I've been busy mentally undressing Jihoon instead of paying attention, I grab a book without looking and hope for the best.

Jihoon comes over, waving his book triumphantly. "I win," he declares.

"Not so fast." I look down at the book in my hand, *Theater Interiors for You!* "Proscenium arches are very stimulating."

"Really, Ari?"

I'm ready to defend my terrible choice. "Theaters mean plays and plays are art." No lie there. Before she left, Hana and I saw *Operation Oblivion* with Sam Yao and Wei Fangli. It had been stellar, even for a Philistine like me. The chemistry between the two had been off the charts.

"It doesn't matter. I'm confident." He shows me his book, which, incredibly, is called *Inspirational Exercises for Mental and Physical Strength*.

I can't even be mad at how bad he's trounced me. "Unbelievable."

"I know." He pages through. "It says I should dictate my ideas to a willing helper as I do a handstand to take advantage of the blood flowing to my head."

"A willing helper?"

"Are you volunteering?" Jihoon touches a finger to my bare arm, and to my horror, I come out in goose bumps.

I do my best to edge away without looking obvious so he doesn't notice. "I'll consider it." Pleased with how steady my voice is, I take him to the back of the store, where a cheery turquoise vending machine sits, and hand him a toonie. "Put it in."

"A book vending machine?"

"Think of it as an idea generator."

Bemused, he slots in the coin, then reaches down after the soft thump indicates his prize has been dispensed.

We unwrap the brown paper and look at the book, which is called *Hannah, the Story of a Girl*.

I gawk at it. "You've rigged this store."

"You could be onto something with this game, Ari." His eyes crinkle as he smiles. "I'm keeping it for Hana."

He pays for the first book, and I take both purchases and pack them into my tote. "I'm winning," he says complacently and, frankly, unnecessarily.

I try not to be sore. Today is about Jihoon. "For now."

He grins. "We'll see."

Ten

I organized a car and driver today through Luxe, and Gregor, who had now finished with an earlier job, is waiting to take us to the next destination. We greet each other as I introduce Jihoon and put my tote on the seat between us. I've known Gregor since a small incident involving another one of Luxe's clients last year, and we get along well.

Jihoon pulls off the mask and rubs behind his ears. "You've put so much work into this."

"I liked doing it for you." I glance out the window at the people passing by on Bloor Street. It's always busy in this stretch, with people grabbing coffee or buying mangoes and flowers at the corner stores.

Gregor drives us to the weekend farmers market that is our next destination. The summer harvest is on display under the high warehouse ceiling, and Jihoon walks between tables of corn on the cob and rustic baskets of beautiful frosted plums. I buy him a goat cheese and roasted butternut squash panini and take him to a picnic bench by the ponds.

I drink my cider as he looks around. "What is this place?" he asks.

"Reclaimed industrial space. They used to make bricks here, so we're sitting in the old quarry."

We check out the pond when we're done, a picturesque view of overlapping water lilies. A ripple catches my eye, and I point at it. "A snapping turtle!"

Two things happen at the same time. Jihoon turns, and my outstretched hand hits him square in the chest. He falls back, arms shooting out as he tries to regain his balance.

He's going to fall into the water. I am such a bad host. This is why I never have guests.

Then he does this wild superhero twist and sort of leaps back onto the boardwalk. I can't even describe it. It's like a gymnastics move. He's a little wobbly, and I grab his shirt and haul him away from the edge.

Bad move, Ari, because now his hands come around my waist, and he steps into me. I can feel the warmth of his body against mine. I haven't been this close to a man for a year, let alone a man like Jihoon. He's so different from the ones I usually meet, who might as well be spit out from the same factory. They all like craft beer and Jet Skiing at the cottage with guys they met in university, who are all like them.

My face tilts up and his down, and his hand slips lower to tighten on my hip.

"Daddy, look, a turtle!" The squeal of a small child, in combination with the appearance of many other small children flanked by frazzled, coffee-clutching adults, breaks my reverie. I step back, carefully, but Jihoon follows me.

"Ari," he says, watching me intently.

I shiver when he says my name like that. Before he can continue, a kid Naruto-runs down the boardwalk with her arms extended behind her, chanting, "Birthday, it's my birthday." It's anarchy, and I take the opportunity to disengage.

I'm fairly sure, like in the high-90s percent sure, that Jihoon was going to kiss me, or he would have, had it not been for the mask he wears everywhere. I need to think it through because, wow, I want that, too. I also have to be certain. Flirting is fun and fantasizing is fantastic, but kissing is a whole different level. It changes things. Exactly how done is he with his ex?

"The game," I say with the least amount of desperation I can manage. There was no game for this stop, but I need a moment to corral my thoughts into their usual tight order.

"Right." Now he moves away, and I have to restrain myself from closing the distance between us. *Be smart, Ari. Consider the consequences.*

I think fast. "The point goes to the first one to see a water animal. Frog, fish, heron, duck, or turtle. Start on the count of three. Eyes closed until we count down." I wait until he obediently squeezes his eyes shut. He's so cute. I want to kiss him tenderly and romantically and then wrestle him to the ground.

"One," I say.

"Dul," says Jihoon.

"Three." We both open our eyes and start scanning. Jihoon bends to gaze deep into the murky depths, and I do my best to not check him out and risk my inappropriate rubbernecking being reflected in the water. It's a losing battle because he's right in front of me, black jeans clinging to every curve.

I yank my eyes back to the water as my heart rate slows from the dual shock of nearly sending Jihoon into the pond and then having him pressed against me. Jihoon, apparently engrossed by the search for fauna, seems unperturbed by the incident, so I follow suit, pushing the mess of thoughts to the side. Nothing can happen, nothing should happen, so I need to concentrate on being a good host.

Too bad the way he felt against me, and the way he looked at me, is something I can't easily forget.

I see movement on the shore. It's a duck. Could be a mallard, might be a canvasback, but I'm no biologist, and those are also the only duck species I know. "Duck," I say with great pleasure.

He swivels to look. "You win."

Jihoon's such a graceful loser, I feel bad about my triumph over gaining a worthless point in a meaningless game I created. "We're tied."

I make a tally mark next to my name in my notebook and try not to look at him. He's standing close, closer than he needs to be, and watching me with those big brown eyes. An orchestral song should be playing in the background as a montage of us laughing slides in over our faces.

Think first.

I step back. "Ready for the next place?"

"Lead the way."

———

Gregor drives us to Graffiti Alley, a dingy, stinky back laneway that runs parallel to Queen Street West. Puddles of rainbow-flecked water fill in the cracks of the broken asphalt and reflect the magical murals that cover walls, doors, and garages. I hand Jihoon a special mobile phone and the new earbuds that Yuko left in the car for me. I owe her big. "Audio tour."

He takes my hand and presses one of the buds into my palm. "We'll experience it together."

We linger in that dirty, fantastical lane listening to a woman narrate the stories behind the graffiti: the tags, the motifs, the artists. Some have already disappeared, painted over by new ideas. Beside me, pressed close because of the earbuds, Jihoon has a blissful expression, and he occasionally hums to himself and types notes into his phone. He's utterly lost in the experience, and I have that sweet feeling of getting it perfectly right. My work at Yesterly and Havings is intellectually satisfying, but that's about as good as it gets. None of my colleagues ever seem contented by what they do because it's more about winning for the win's sake. This is about—and I mentally squint at this—being happy. I get a little of what Jihoon was trying to say the other day about art and meaning.

"Ready for the final point in the game?" I ask when the tour ends. "It's an easy one."

"I am." He takes out his earbud and waits.

"Find the painting that best represents your life. Two minutes on the timer."

He looks around. "There are so many."

"If you'd like to forfeit, I'll take the final point for the win." I pull my hair around to the front of my shoulder.

He stiffens. "Hana, dul, set, let's go."

After thirty seconds, I'm cursing myself. This is too revealing, too vulnerable. I see a school of fish with one going the opposite direction, but that's Phoebe, not me. I move on to a cubist landscape of a tree on a hill and consider it before deciding that, although I don't know what it means, it's not me. When the timer goes off, I'm standing in front of a purple silhouette of two little girls in short dresses holding hands and looking at a high wall. If Phoebe and I had been closer in age, would our relationship be different? Would we have been able to confide in each other to build something that could have evolved past our shared DNA?

"Ready?" Jihoon calls.

I turn quickly away from the image. There's no point wondering about what-ifs when we have the relationship we have.

"Yes." I look around and point at the tree I saw earlier. "That's mine. I'm the tree, and I like overseeing everything." That's a safe response.

He looks at me as if he knows I'm hiding something, then steps aside. Behind him is a door, a real one, and it's been painted with two doors, each of which open to two more, and so on until the doors are the size of dimes. It's hypnotic.

"Why?" I ask.

Jihoon stands in front of the image, tracing the thin red outline of one door with his fingers. "Every time we go through one door in life, there's two more closed ones to choose from."

"What if you choose the wrong door? Do you go back?"

He doesn't look away. "No. You keep going and hope the next one is the right one."

The air is raw in a way that makes me jumpy. When my last boyfriend broke up with me, he said I had the emotional intelligence of an eggplant—I paraphrase but also couldn't argue with the sentiment. I'm out of my depth here, like there's something I don't understand and saying the wrong thing will tarnish whatever it is.

I clear my throat and decide to leave it rather than risk going deeper. "You win," I say. It's not even a question.

He gives me a deep bow. "You were a worthy adversary, but I humbly accept my triumph."

At least he's an amusing winner. "Dessert?" I ask.

He gives the alley a final look and nods. We get back in the car, and I keep up a running commentary as we drive. We pass a restaurant with an old-school diner sign. "Hana had a crush on one of the servers at that place."

"Did anything happen?"

"Hana spilled a drink on him and then knocked a plate of fries on the floor because she was nervous. She never even got his name, and we didn't go back."

He looks out the rear window at the restaurant. "Why did she like him?"

"Why does anyone like anyone? Pheromones. Good hair. How their mouth tilts when they smile." Like his does, but I steadfastly avoid looking at him.

"You believe in love at first sight?"

I laugh. "Hana wasn't in love with that guy. If she were, she would have stayed and made the best of it."

"I believe in it." Jihoon sounds intense.

I brush off a red thread stuck to my shirt. "Then I hope you find them." I keep my voice light, but I'm uncomfortable with the conversation. Jihoon's a good person. I want him to be happy, but the thought of him falling in love with someone makes me unjustifiably upset. It's like we've built a strange little world, the two of us. I've even started coming home earlier from work to see him, and every time I open the door and he's there, my heart gives a happy hop that's not in the slightest diminished by knowing he's only here for a limited time. In fact, that might make this easier. It's like our summer fling. I'm Sandy and he's Danny. Sort of. I could never pull off those skintight satin pants.

Soon we arrive at Uni-Land, a hole-in-the-wall store in a quiet side street.

I lean over the front seat. "Gregor? You in?"

He stares out the windshield. "Ms. Hui, you shouldn't tempt me while I'm working."

"You know it's Ari, because Ms. Hui is my mother. You love ice cream. Green tea or birthday cake?"

He laughs and bows to the inevitable. "Birthday cake. Extra sprinkles."

"Be right back."

Jihoon follows me out, eyebrows lowered as he considers the narrow street. "We eat here?" I understand his concern because it's not the most prepossessing of vistas.

"There." To the left is a small, curtained door and behind that, fantasy. We walk into a gumball of an ice cream store, swirls of pink and mint green punctuated with dark blue unicorn heads displayed on the walls. I found this taiyaki place on a city stroll and had been instantly enchanted. I hope Jihoon likes it.

He does, and I smile as he sleepwalks toward the display of cones, which are filled pastries shaped like fish instead of the usual regular or waffle. "You go first," he says, eyes flickering from one option to the next.

I order for Gregor and get a custard-filled green tea ice cream for myself. Jihoon ponders before ordering the unicorn special, a multi-colored extravaganza complete with little pastel-pink mochi ears and a golden horn.

Once we get our orders, I point my chin to the far wall, where two women pose with pursed lips and thrust-back hips to take shots of their ice cream. "Photo wall," I say. "Want to take one for your social media?"

"No." The brisk response is so unlike the usual calm Jihoon that it takes me aback. Noting my reaction, he looks at me from under the lowered brim of his hat. "I'm taking a break because of my aunt."

"Of course." Hana would kill me if I let her mom find out Jihoon's here. At least one of us remembered.

Back in the car, he pulls off his mask. All three of us eat in bliss and then try to mop up the stickiness with napkins that shred on contact. Gregor starts the car, muttering under his breath when his palms stick to the steering wheel.

I give up and run my hands down my pants, leaving paper fluff along my thighs. "Did you have fun today?"

"You must be excellent at your job," he says seriously. "You know how to pleasure me."

I know that English is his fourth language—he mentioned he also speaks Japanese and Mandarin—but his phrasing makes the blood rush to my face. "Some lucky guesses."

"No." He shakes his head. "You took a conversation we had and matched it with your knowledge of the city to make something perfect. You pay attention to details."

"I feel bad for not spending more time with you," I admit. Take that, Hana. I can be a good host.

He smiles. "Thank you for a beautiful day. I could forget my worries."

I look at him curiously. "Did it help you, though?"

Jihoon turns to me, and I lose my breath when he looks into my eyes. "It did. It was inspiring." Then he looks out the window, leaving me to concentrate on his jawline, which, no joke, is casting a shadow. I want to run my hand along it.

Oh no. No. It's been a long time, but I know this feeling. It's a crush. I have a crush on Jihoon.

Damn.

Eleven

Top five reasons I might possibly have a potential thing for Jihoon.

1. That face.
2. That body.
3. Don't be shallow. He's sweet.
4. Authentic.
5. Sensitive, good listener, great cook. Technically this brings the list to seven.

Top five reasons I should not have a crush on Jihoon.

1. Are you twelve? Adults have relationships, not crushes.
2. Work. #makingpartner
3. He lives in Korea.
4. Hana's cousin. (Better star this one. Might be reason number one.)
5. Don't be the rebound from his breakup. (Could be number one. Or living in Korea is number one. It's a three-way tie because those are all solid reasons.)

Jihoon is out when I wake up on Monday, and I experience a dip of dissatisfaction. I'm used to his morning routine—coffee, chatter, and filling me in on what's going on in the Korean news cycle—and it's irritating to shift back to my usual habit of moving straight to work emails.

I flip on the news to fill the space up with some sound. Wars, trade deals. Sadness, negativity. Some Asian singer is supposedly missing, but it's not thought to be foul play. Sam Yao's new action movie trailer is out. I turn it back off because it's time to get going.

At work, I take two Tylenols and drink some water to get rid of my eternal headache, then stay until the lights start to power down all over the office. When I finally leave, it's to a dark rainy chill that slides through my wool blazer.

The phone rings on the streetcar, and I answer without looking. "Hello."

"Hi, Ari."

It's Phoebe, and I seriously consider lying and saying I'm about to go into the subway to buy some time. The only reason I don't is that it means I'll have to deal with it later when I have even less energy. "What's wrong?" I ask.

"Who said anything had to be wrong?" Her voice is tight.

"Phoebe, I haven't had the best day." The unspoken order is there: tell me what you want because I am far from being in the mood to deal with you.

She sniffs. "Mom wants you to come for dinner tomorrow."

"Why are you calling me and not her?" I glare at the phone, wondering if this is Mom's way of trying to get us to reconcile.

"Mom is busy trying to get Dad to eat a carrot to kick-start his heart health and hiding his laptop so he can't work."

Phoebe's delivery is so dry and her words ring so true, I can't help it. I laugh. "I'm busy with work."

"So?"

"So..." I stop. Too busy to see the Dad I might have lost? "Nothing. I'll be there." I'll have to work even longer tonight if I have to waste three hours at my parents' house, but there's nothing to be done about it.

Waste. I roll that around. I don't like that it was the first word that came to mind when I thought of spending time with my family.

I grab some flowers at the corner store to cheer myself up and head upstairs, where Jihoon is on the phone. His back is to me, so he doesn't hear the door open or me putting away my things.

He also doesn't hear me because lovely, kind Jihoon is in a rage. I stop with one shoe off. I've never heard his voice so loud or harsh. His shoulders are hunched forward as he paces and speaks faster. Then he stops and listens, one hand against the wall and his head bowed, the phone pressed to his ear.

Shit, this has big ex energy all over it, and I'm torn between tiptoeing to my room or standing there like a creepy eavesdropper because he's talking to someone who can clearly generate a lot of passion, and I want to know more.

When he hangs up, he slaps his hand against the wall.

"Everything okay?" I ask from the door.

He spins around. "You're home. Did you hear that?" His eyes are huge.

"Yes, but my Korean is less than stellar." I decide to ask. "Were you talking to your ex?"

He shoves his phone in his pocket. "That's private."

Of course it is, but I'm already keyed up from work and Phoebe, and now he's made me feel like I overstepped, so I'm ready to fight. "Hey, sorry I asked."

"It was a difficult conversation with someone back home." He sounds conciliatory, but my passive-aggressive mode has been activated.

"Like I said, sorry I asked."

"Ari. It's nothing to do with you. You have no right to be angry with me." His mouth is a thin line. I should de-escalate this. I should be a good host. I should give him the space to have his feelings.

However, I can't even do that when I'm having a good day, let alone when my sensitivity reservoir has been drained to an arid pit. "Whatever."

He rubs his eyes. "Please don't be like this."

"I'm the problem?"

"Can I not get some privacy?" he snaps. "A moment to myself?"

In a fight, I've always been fairly good at knowing when to stop before I've crossed the line. Phoebe is the only one with whom I never paid attention to that border. With her, I didn't tiptoe over it, I strut through like I was coming down a runway. It never mattered because Phoebe would already have leapfrogged over and be waiting for me to turn around.

I don't say anything to Jihoon.

I don't have to, because my eyes drift around the apartment—my apartment—and he gets the hint that he's the one intruding.

"Forget it." He snatches up his hat, jams on his slides, and is out the door.

I call Hana about three seconds later.

"Hey, hey." She's on video in her hotel room and wrapped in a robe. "What's wrong?"

"I want to see how you are."

"No, that's a text. This is a phone call."

True. The hierarchy of communication does put phone call above text, which ranks higher than social media post. God forbid you show up at someone's door unannounced. That's for deaths only or Mrs. Choi doing a drive-by room check disguised as a food drop.

"I have a problem, and I need advice."

"Is it Jihoon related?"

"You know, not all my issues are about your cousin," I say, insulted.

"Sorry. What's it about, then?"

I hesitate. "Okay, it's about Jihoon."

"Mm-hmm."

I check the time. "It's only six in Vancouver. Why are you in a robe?"

"Because I hate humanity, so I put on my failure robe to call it a day."

"I hate humanity, too."

"Good." She moves over to a chair near the window. "What about Jihoon?"

"You go first."

"Mom."

"What happened now?" I ask.

"The usual. What am I eating. Why so much of it. Why am I traveling for work instead of settling down. When am I visiting next. Why did I leave home in the first place."

It's no surprise that Mama Choi has conducted boundary oversteps number 1,043,431 through 1,043,435 because the woman can be difficult. She believes the Korean—at least Busan—way of doing things is superior to all cultures at all times in all areas of competition, particularly when measured against the Chinese and absolutely against the Japanese. When she brought over gimbap and I called it Korean sushi, Mrs. Choi called me an ignorant child before deconstructing a roll to explain in detail how it differed (and was better) with regard to flavor, texture, and composition. When I told her I couldn't eat the ham, she refused to believe it and held it to my mouth until Hana grabbed it away.

"I don't want to talk about it now," Hana says. "Tell me of your hatreds."

It comes out in a rush. All the minor work irritations I can't seem to shake off. The fight with Jihoon. Phoebe. Seeing Brittany meeting with both Meredith and Richard in the big conference room.

"That's a lot," Hana says finally.

"Thanks. Your turn again."

"Don't you want to talk about what happened? How you feel?"

I make a warding gesture at the phone. "You know how I feel about feelings."

"You know how I feel about talking about feelings."

She loves talking about feelings. "Guess we're at an impasse."

"Hold on." She leaves the phone on the table, so I now have a great view of the ceiling, and I hear the muffled sound of her thanking the pizza delivery person.

When she comes back, Hana already has a slice hanging from her mouth like a backward tongue. Time to divert her. "What about your day?" I ask.

"Good try." The words are muffled, and she takes the slice out of her mouth.

"You were planning to go for a walk around Stanley Park," I say. "There's a reason you're holed up in your hotel besides your mom." The pizza makes me hungry, so I go over to the kitchen. Looks like Jihoon was in the middle of cooking because there's a sliced onion and the rice is out. I don't have the energy to cook, so I grab some bread and stuff it in my mouth.

Hana cracks open a Diet Coke. "A guy argued with me that sexism didn't exist. In fact, men are the ones who are discriminated against these days."

"Did he cite his source?"

She gets another slice of pizza. "Yeah. It was the internet and his personal experience as the father of a daughter."

"Can't argue those."

"Then he told me that being told to smile was helpful because women look prettier when they're happy."

Now we're both laughing, even though it's not at all funny despite being painfully hilarious. Then Hana sighs. "The worst of it is that, honest to God, one hundred percent, he didn't get it. He insisted he didn't need to be there because, and I quote, he 'was a nice guy.'"

Nothing to say there. She eats more pizza, and I eat more stale bread. "Don't worry about Jihoon," she adds. "He can take care of himself."

"I feel bad."

"Did you share a feeling?" She makes exaggerated prayer hands over the pizza box.

"Shut up."

Hana looks down. "He's got some stuff going on, but he told me he's going to talk to you about it. He needs time."

I laugh uncomfortably. "I mean, he doesn't owe me anything. We're not in a relationship."

She looks horrified. "Eww. With my cousin?" Her eyes narrow. "Ari."

"What?" I busy myself in the fridge.

"Why would you even say that? Is it something on the table? Is it even in the room where the table is located?"

"Of course not. Don't worry."

She gives me a long look. "Okay."

"I need to get back to work," I say, deploying my go-to excuse to get out of anything.

"I don't know why you want to make partner at Yuckerly and Jerklings so bad," Hana grumbles, brushing crumbs off her robe. "You don't like anyone there. You don't have a single work friend. They don't treat you well."

"Work is for working," I say. "It's the best firm in the city, which means the best lawyers in the country work there."

"You're spending your life on something you don't like. It's a waste."

"It suits me," I say.

"You haven't given yourself a chance to suit anything else."

I make a face at her, and she gets the hint that I don't want to talk about my career choices right now—or ever. I've made up my mind on the correct path for me, and you don't get to the finish line by taking detours.

She manages to get off the phone before I can press her about her mother, and I pass the table where Jihoon's notepad sits open and filled with scribbles. I change out of my work clothes and come back out dressed for coziness in sweatpants, my hair in a loose knot. It's late but I haven't had dinner and I should cook. Instead, I take a bottle of wine and go out on the balcony.

The sounds of the city rise as I prop my feet on the rail and lean back in my chair. I have a memo due tomorrow, but instead I pull out my travel notebook and flip through the pages. All these places I've never seen. I told myself I'd go later, but later never seems to arrive. I toss the notebook away, frustrated with myself in a way I've never felt before.

Behind me, the door to the apartment clicks shut, announcing Jihoon's return.

Twelve

The appropriate thing would be to get up and apologize.

Instead I sit and drink my wine and pretend I don't know he's home despite being very aware of each movement he makes. There's the slight tap of his phone as he places it on the counter. The sticking noise of the fridge door and the creak of a cabinet.

Then a long silence where I imagine him standing in the middle of the living room. I try to act normal, but my hand feels almost numb, and my arm jerks unsteadily when I lift my glass.

Apologize.

It doesn't make you weak to say you were overreacting when you were in fact overreacting.

His steps come toward the door.

I put the glass down with more force than necessary and twist around.

"I'm sorry."

We both blink at each other because Jihoon hasn't even echoed my apology—he said it at the same time. He's at the balcony door, arms crossed over his chest so he can grip his elbows.

"I was in a bad mood, and I took it out on you," I say, speaking to his left armpit because I don't want to look in his eyes. "It wasn't cool for me to make you feel unwelcome." I take a breath. "I'm glad you're here. I like being with you."

That was honesty in action. Hana would be proud, but I feel a bit nauseous. This communication thing sucks.

"I shouldn't have snapped at you," he says. "I was upset by that call from home."

"I get it." I point at the bottle. "Drink?"

"*Please*." He fetches a glass and sits next to me. Some tension remains but it's bearable.

"It was my work," he says. "On the phone."

I nod, trying to hide my relief. Work problems are better than hearing about his busted relationship.

"I've always known what I wanted," he says. "From my life, I mean. I had a goal, and I worked hard."

"I get that," I say.

"I love most of my life. I'm lucky, so *lucky* to be able to do what I do."

"Okay."

"I want more, though. I feel trapped by my luck. It's like being successful has put me in a cage." He buries his head in his hands, and when he speaks again, his voice is muffled. "I'm ungrateful."

"Hey." I reach out and grab his hands to pull them away from his face. "What you feel, that's valid."

"What?" He looks at me, eyes reddened.

"They want you to keep making the same magic happen in the same way so you don't mess with a good thing, but it feels like you're repeating yourself."

"That's it," he says, eyes on the ground. "I worry about going against them, but I want to grow."

"Change is scary," I say. "Can you leave for a new job?"

Jihoon is shaking his head even before I finish. "I love my team and leaving would put them at a disadvantage."

"That's tough," I say. "How about making small changes you can build on? It might be easier for you, too."

"I tried." He rubs his face. "The bosses told me to stop, more or less."

"Messing with the formula."

He smiles at his glass. "Yeah."

"The opposite thing is happening with me," I say. "You know the change you want. I always thought I knew what I wanted at work. Now I don't."

"You want to make partner," he says. "That's your goal."

"I guess."

"It's not anymore?"

"I don't know how I feel. I never used to have doubts about what I did." I look at him. "Did you?"

"Not until I got what I wanted. Then I didn't know if I had been wanting the right things."

"Me neither," I say.

"I've never said that to anyone," he muses. "Not even my friends. I don't know if I've ever said it out loud even to myself. It felt good."

I frown. "Really? Because I hate it."

"Why?"

"I like to have a plan," I say. "To know what I'm doing. Now I'm not sure. I don't do well with ambiguity."

"No," he says. "I've seen your to-do lists."

He waits until I'm done laughing, then he says, "You bought flowers."

It takes me a moment to remember the bouquet I left on the table. "Got them at the store to cheer up the place."

"One looks like a tiger flower," he says. "My birth flower."

"Your what?"

"At home, each day is associated with a flower. That's mine. When were you born?" He checks online when I tell him. "Primrose," he reads from his phone after a moment. "It means loveliness. How accurate."

Normally I'd shrug a comment like that off or laugh, but his compliment feels so genuine that it makes me warm.

"We should eat," I say.

We both stand and reach for the wine at the same time, banging our heads together like a Three Stooges sketch. Instead of grabbing his own head, Jihoon reaches for me, his face creased with concern.

"I'm fine," I say as his fingers touch my head. "You?"

He doesn't answer. Instead, his hand moves over my hair, which has fallen out of its knot. "Your hair is down." He runs his fingers through it, his eyes on mine. "You only wear it down at home, or with me."

"I like it better this way," I say, hoping he doesn't notice my shaky voice. I step back into the shadows. "Do you want some ramen?" It isn't my favorite, but it's fast and easy. Plus, thanks to Jihoon stockpiling it, we have a lot.

"What?" His eyes go huge as his mouth drops open.

"Ramen. For dinner?"

"To eat. Ramen to eat, you mean." Jihoon starts laughing, but I don't know what's funny, and he won't tell me. He shakes his head and blinks before he smiles at me. "Another time. Today we can cook together."

He leads the way to the kitchen, and although the moment is lost, all I can think about is his hand on my hair and his eyes on mine.

I want more.

———

After dinner, Jihoon lies on the couch with his notebook propped on his knees. It's warm in the room, and he's shed his sweater to lounge in a V-necked shirt with short sleeves wide enough to show half his chest if he raises his arm. He seems completely unaware of how hot this is, and I beat back the urge to have him reach up and pass me things from high places.

I curl on the chair with a book I've been meaning to read for ages, but as usual I have trouble concentrating. My eyes are on the page, but my mind drifts away from the gritty but delicate coming-of-age story. Instead I think about Phoebe, of all people. We used to read in the library during summer afternoons, when the heat made time feel slow and endless. I thought those days would last forever, and now look at us. Barely talking. Estranged and uncaring. Or too scared to care, which might be even sadder.

Uncomfortable with these thoughts, I toss the book away and lie on the chair with my head on one arm and my legs on the other. Jihoon has unbuckled his watch and is staring at it with intent focus as he twirls it in a circle.

"That's a nice watch," I say. It's got a modern 1960s look, with little lines instead of numbers on the white face and a brown leather band.

"It's my favorite," he says idly. "A masterpiece of craftwork. This is the watch that made the Swiss watch industry cry for mercy after they tried to change the rules on the Japanese."

"What, that?"

"Yes, this." He rolls it between his fingers. "I bought it to remind myself that improvement is iterative and constant and the work is up to you."

I take the watch, still warm from his wrist, when he holds it out to me. It's a classic watch design and doesn't look special to me.

"The magic is underneath, because work happens under the surface," he says. "The Japanese kept improving the mechanics until it looked like it might win a very prestigious Swiss competition. You can imagine how they would have taken a Japanese firm winning."

"What happened?"

He buckles the watch back on. "They closed the competition and, when they reopened it, changed the rules so only Europeans could enter."

"That's so unfair!"

"Very." Jihoon gives the watch a loving pat. "But who were the real winners in the end?"

I look at his notebook. "Is that what you're working on? A song about watches?" This might be nosy, but I told him about my notebook. I'm owed a secret.

"A song that might be about watches. Or something else." His frown deepens to cover his forehead in lines. "It's not going well."

I shimmy around to see him better. "How do you even write a song?"

He rubs the back of his neck. "I've been asking myself the exact same question."

I toss a pillow at him. "Seriously. Do you start with the words?"

"Sometimes. Usually a melody. Occasionally an idea or a feeling."

"What do you have so far?"

He sits up and smiles at me. "Would you like to write a song, Ari?"

That makes me laugh as I stretch my legs. "I'm not creative."

"We're all creative," he says. "Every single person is, but some have been discouraged. Give it a try. Help a poor, lost songwriter."

Why not? "What are you stuck on?"

Jihoon tosses the notebook aside to pace the room. "There was another mural in that alley, beside one of a flower. It was a clock painted in a cage. And I think of this."

He hums a part of a song to me, and even without words, I have a sense of longing and desire. "That sounds like the singer wants something."

"They do." Jihoon looks pleased before he taps the side of his nose with his pen. "The question is what they want."

I point at the watch. "They want time."

He gazes at his watch. "Time," he muses.

"Watches break time up," I say, thinking of my billable hours. "The act of measuring makes us think differently about it."

Jihoon's head is bent over his notebook as he writes. "Keep talking. Please."

So I do, about not much and everything. And Jihoon listens and writes, and again I have that sense of being not only listened to but heard.

"Do I get a songwriting credit?" I ask when I take a sip of water.

Jihoon looks at me with wide and shining eyes, his smile huge. "I'll give you anything you want, Ari."

Anything could be interesting. I restrain myself from looking down to where his shirt has ridden up to show the edges of that tiger tattoo and instead wish him a good night and leave him on the couch writing away.

As I go to bed, I wonder what the song will sound like and if I'll ever hear it.

Thirteen

Jihoon texts me short thoughts and photos of what he's doing. He's a stream-of-consciousness kind of guy, so I get random snippets of what he overhears on the street and his observations watching people try to fix a broken gate in the park. They're the bright spots of my day, and slowly I start doing the same. We end up in long, free-flowing asynchronous conversations that serve as a satisfying digital reminder that other people exist and there's life outside the hallowed, dark wood-paneled halls of Yesterly and Havings.

Because work seems a bit off.

A lot off.

At first, I thought it was me. My head used to be about 90 percent dedicated to work and 8 percent thinking about Hana and my family. The remaining 2 percent went to grooming and other human tasks. Jihoon and my dad and Phoebe have barged in to claim more than their allotted share. Work has lost out.

I glance at the time. I'm due for a meeting with Richard. Formal meetings with Richard are usually good news, and this must finally be about Beaconsmith. I *know* it. It has to be. I've worked hard, harder than anyone else at my level. Definitely harder than Brittany. Being added to a big name like Beaconsmith is a declaration of how much the firm values you. I'm ready.

I arrive at Richard's office at the exact meeting time, and his assistant nods me in without looking up from her screen. Richard is finishing a phone call, and he points me to one of the leather seats in front of his desk. I smooth my skirt over my knees, notebook balanced on my lap as I cross my ankles. I never go into a meeting without something to write on.

Richard hangs up and smiles at me. "How are you, Ariadne?"

"Good, thanks."

"How's Marty?"

Richard is the only one I've heard call my dad *Marty*. I'm not sure Dad would like me to spread the story of his heart attack, so I say, "Doing well."

"Good man." He rests his hands on his desk. "I have some news for you today."

This is it. My heart rate picks up, but I make sure to stay calm, at least outwardly. "Yes?"

"You'll be pleased, especially in light of your work with Hyphen Records. A most unusual client for us. Ah, Brittany. Here you are."

What's she doing here? Brittany slides into the seat beside me. "Sorry I'm late. Meredith was telling me about the changes the marina is doing near the cottage."

He waves this away as if he hadn't told me multiple times about the importance of punctuality. "I know how busy you are. I called you both in because we're making a few changes." He doesn't wait for a reply. "Ariadne, you've demonstrated a real skill with our smaller clients. I've heard good things from Luxe about your dedication and professionalism."

I'm holding my breath as I wait for him to continue. This is good, really good.

"We're going to capitalize on that. Effective today, you'll now also be responsible for the Queen's Bride, which was one of Brittany's clients."

"The what?" I say.

Brittany gives a fake frowny face. "Lucky. They're a spa, so fun."

A spa? He's giving me a spa?

"This frees up Brittany to take on work with Beaconsmith." He smiles at her. "An excellent learning opportunity for you."

"I look forward to it," she says.

"I've told Meredith and the rest of the team to bring you into meetings starting today," he says. "I know you'll do well. Have the Queen's Bride sent over to Ariadne."

I know the smile has remained on my face because it hurts my cheeks. I need to keep up a positive attitude in front of Richard, but I'm overcome by the unfairness. Instead of me impressing the bigwigs, Brittany's going to be the one in the room with the decision-makers. I've been here longer. I put in more hours. I did the work. I *deserved* Beaconsmith.

He looks at both of us. "That's it for now."

I drop my notebook on the floor accidentally on purpose to give me an excuse to stay behind as Brittany breezes out the door to a friendly farewell from Richard's assistant.

When I look up, Richard is already typing away. He stops when he realizes I haven't left. "Something you need, Ariadne?"

"I'm glad to have the new account," I say, deciding to lead with a positive. Men like Richard don't like to be challenged. Since I spend most of my workday around men like Richard, even when they're women, I've learned how to speak with the most marshmallow of words when necessary.

"Good," he says, eyes going back to the screen. "I know you'll bring your usual hard work to it."

"I'd like to talk about when I can join the Beaconsmith team or one like it," I say. "The chance to learn would be very useful for me."

His watery blue eyes rest on me. "It's natural you'd think that," he says. "If you prove yourself with these clients, you'll be in a good place."

I want to point out that I already have been proving myself, but I say, "Is there an area in particular you want to see some growth from me?"

Richard holds up his hand. "You're a good lawyer, otherwise you wouldn't have the work you do. These placements are sometimes about fit. We look for the lawyers who are suitable for the team."

I take a deep breath as shallow as I can so Richard can't see the rise of my chest. Yesterly and Havings is a cold place, not only so men can wear their blazers every day of the goddamn year but emotionally frigid. I normally don't mind because that suits me. Today it's landing harder, and I'm not sure what's changed.

"Thanks," I say.

"Thank *you*, Ariadne."

I have back-to-back meetings the rest of the day, which means by the time I leave, I'm numb to what happened but also angry. Suitable for the team, he said. Nothing about my work or dedication but that ephemeral and inarguable quality of fit. I know what that means and also that I have no defense. Brittany and I have similar qualifications, so what is it that makes her fit and not me? Could it be that she resembles all the partners and most of the lawyers, although the support staff is as diverse as the brochures at a university job fair? I'm trapped into silence, though. Richard would be angrier about any insinuation of being thought racist than he would about the actual racist shit he's pulling. To complain would be to paint a target on my back and go against the cheerful and obliging reputation I've been trying to build.

A text comes from Phoebe, reminding me about dinner, as if I'm the irresponsible one. I don't even bother to reply, and I feel my mood drop another eight percentage points. I look at my phone and text a message to Jihoon.

Me: I'm going to my parents' for dinner. Want to come?

Jihoon: They won't mind?

Me: Of course not.

Even if they did, right now his companionship is more for me than them. I deserve it after today. Plus, Jihoon's presence will force Phoebe to be on her best—or at least better—behavior.

Jihoon: Thank you. I would love to meet your family.

Me: I'll be home soon.

Knowing Jihoon is coming makes me look forward to this dinner. I like having him near, with his crooked smile and the way he throws his head back when he laughs. I like how he looks at the world, so different than I do. He gives me a break from myself.

The professional smile I put on as I leave the office is a little warmer because I'm thinking about Jihoon. It doesn't matter. I don't see anyone as I make my escape.

Fourteen

hat's with the presents?" I point to the box of chocolates and flowers he's carrying as we walk to the car.

"I'm going to the home of your parents," he says. "It's polite."

"They won't care."

He raises his eyebrows. "I do."

We're quiet for a bit as we get in and I start the car. Finally Jihoon leans over. "You're thinking so hard, I can hear you," he says. "What going on?"

"Nothing. Work stuff, but it's not a big deal."

"Ari. You helped me with my work issues. Tell me. I'm here if you want to talk."

To my shame, tears prick at the back of my eyes. I don't want to talk, but if I don't, I'll explode. That's not a good mindset before going into a family dinner. I give in. "They're giving me less important clients. I know they are."

"What happened?"

I keep to the facts as I tell him about Beaconsmith and the Queen's Bride, and he hums along to show he's listening. "I'm not sure what to do," I say at the end.

"Do you want me to listen or give advice?"

"How are you so good at this?" He makes me feel like I live in a cave and throw sticks as my primary communication method.

"My company has therapists come in and train us in conflict resolution," he says. "You can't create together without being able to talk."

I think about it. "Advice, then."

"You need to decide what you want out of this," he says. "Do you want to take Beaconsmith from Brittany? Do you truly care about the Queen's Bride?"

"The Queen's Bride might be more interesting, but there's more to it."

"Richard is not valuing your contributions."

"That, too." I stop at a red and glance over. He motions for me to keep talking. "I expected it, you know? I'm embarrassed that I misjudged it. Like I was a finalist for an award and waiting to hear my name but hers was called."

"I understand."

Only two words and he doesn't add on any useless reassurance. Just sympathy. I feel he really does get it, and that's enough to make me take a deep breath. "I feel better," I admit. "Thanks."

He smiles. "I'm glad you trusted me."

We're in our own thoughts for the rest of the ride, but it's a comfortable silence. The rush hour traffic eases, and we make good time to my parents' house, a standard suburban bungalow with a yard edged by a high wooden fence and two cars in the driveway. We get out, and Jihoon stops to fluff up the flower blossoms. He's frowning, and I touch his arm.

He takes my hand and laces our fingers together as he leans against me. I'm taken aback by this show of vulnerability and the intimacy of his hand in mine.

"They won't bite," I assure him. I give his hand a squeeze for good measure.

"I wanted to come with you, but I get nervous before I meet new people," he says. "That they're your parents makes it worse."

Emotional openness isn't really my wheelhouse, so there's no way I can meet him halfway on this, but I give it a shot.

"I feel the same way," I say. "Once, when I had to meet my ex-boyfriend's family, I chickened out and hid in their garden. They grew corn, so I thought they couldn't see me."

"Could they?"

I nod. "They were all watching me from the window and laughing. We didn't last long after that. What I'm trying to say is, no matter what, you can't do as bad as me."

"Are you trying to make me feel better?" He tilts his head to the side.

"If it's working."

He laughs and pulls my hand up to give it a kiss. "Oddly, it is."

"Good." I lead him toward the door and do my best to not think about the press of his lips on my skin.

We untangle ourselves to knock, but Jihoon retreats a half step behind me. Before I can say anything encouraging, the door opens.

"Ariadne, how was the traffic?" Dad looks better than he did, but there's a slackness around his face I don't remember from before. Or perhaps I'm only noticing it now. He glances past me to Jihoon.

"Traffic was fine. Dad, this is Choi Jihoon. He's Hana's cousin from Seoul."

"Jihoon, nice to meet you." Dad gives him a small smile before extending his hand.

Jihoon bows and shakes his hand, then passes over the chocolate and flowers. "Mr. Hui, I'm glad to see you're better," he says.

Dad looks confused, and I do my best not to nudge Jihoon into silence. "Jihoon came with me to the hospital," I explain.

"Ah." Dad steps aside to let us in. "They made it out worse than it was. Call me Martin."

Jihoon opens his mouth, and I interrupt before he can say something anyone normal would find caring and polite and Dad would find painfully personal. "Is Mom cooking?" I ask.

The house is quiet because my parents never have background noise like music or talk radio or the television. Mom comes out of the kitchen and waves hello to Jihoon. "Good to see you again," she says. "I'm finishing dinner, but go relax with Phoebe. Martin will help me."

"Coming, Soolin." Dad nods at me. "You heard your mother. Talk to your sister."

Phoebe's not in the living room, but she pops her bleached head around the corner a second later. "Hey." She waves at Jihoon. "I'm Phoebe. Thanks for bringing Ari to see Dad in the hospital. She probably wouldn't have left the office otherwise. Wine?"

"I was done with work for the day, and you couldn't even be bothered to get the right train," I say, my voice already tight. "No wine for me, I'm driving. Jihoon?"

"Thank you." He smiles as if unaware of the strain in the room, although I can feel him tense.

Phoebe manifests a bottle and two glasses like a magician, and I check the label. "Where did this come from?" My parents are not the kind to have a wine cabinet, especially since Mom goes maroon after half a glass of chardonnay. Thank God that genetic gift skipped me over.

"I brought it, of course. This house is drier than the Atacama." Phoebe gives Jihoon a glass and checks him over when he sits beside me on the couch. "Hana's cousin, huh? I see it. When's she back from Vancouver?"

She remembered. This is a pleasant conversation. It's going pleasantly. My shoulders drop down a centimeter. "Another week or so."

"I used to live there. It was gorgeous but had too much rain." She shudders.

I didn't know she'd lived there. They sip their wine, and Phoebe fidgets. "Can I put on the TV or some music?" she asks. "In the background."

"God, yes." I didn't realize how heavy silence could be until I moved away from home. Noise is a social lubricant, like alcohol, pets, or extroverts.

After a brief struggle, she connects her phone to the screen and starts running a playlist. "Hope you don't mind pop music," she says. "It's been a hell of a year, and the algorithm decided I needed to listen to the uppest of the upbeat."

The screen erupts into blue light before settling on five stunning Asian men staring seductively at the camera.

"K-pop, Pheebs? Really?" The old nickname comes out before I can think, but Phoebe doesn't seem to notice.

"The playlist picked it, but I bet it's catchy," Phoebe says.

"It's designed to be."

"Is there anything you can't be judgy about?" Phoebe looks honestly interested, like this is a question of great importance to her.

"I'm not judgy."

"Sure you're not."

The music is familiar. "Were you playing this the other day?" I turn to Jihoon. Instantly I feel terrible about subjecting him to my argument with Phoebe and what I said about the music, *which is his job, Ari, you bonehead.*

He's tucked himself into the corner of the couch and is staring at the screen with blank eyes as if disassociating. "It's StarLune," he says. "The song is called 'Candor.'"

"Hey, that's the band I asked you about." It's familiar because it's on Alex's playlist. I can consider this research for my new role with Hyphen.

Phoebe looks at the screen. "That blue-haired singer looks a bit like you, from what I can see." The men all have extremely artistic makeup that acts almost like a mask, complete with facial gems.

I give her a look, and she rolls her eyes. "Obviously I don't mean that in an *all Asians look the same* way," she says, waving her hand at her face.

"I get that sometimes," Jihoon says before he drinks down half his glass and hiccups.

"Great smoky eye," Phoebe and I say at the same time. We stick our fists out at each other without looking. "Jinx," we say in unison, and I get a flash of warm memory. That was one of the best feelings: a fleeting moment of someone getting you perfectly, like two waves coming in sync.

They start dancing again, and I whistle. "Did you see the one on the right?" I exclaim. "Black hair."

"Do you see how he moves those hips?" asks Phoebe.

It's hard to miss. There's a moment of silence when I wonder if it's appropriate host behavior to be gawking at a video of hot men in front of my guest—also an attractive man, don't get me wrong. As the performer completes an illegally hot body roll, Phoebe says, "God, did he vacuum seal those pants on his thighs?" She turns to Jihoon. "Do you know his name?"

His mouth is a thin line. "They call him Kay. He's known for his dancing."

Phoebe doesn't answer because we're busy admiring Kay flash his abs, which have stylistic flames painted across the lean muscle. Although Kay the Dancer is hot, my eyes are drawn to the blue-haired singer. It's something about how he moves, and yeah.

That guy is unreal.

"Not so bad, huh?" Phoebe elbows me.

I give in. "I stand corrected."

The song finishes and goes into "My Favorite Things" from *The Sound of Music* because, of course Phoebe's playlist would be as unpredictable as she is. My sister proceeds to bombard Jihoon with questions. What does he do all day? How long is he staying? He wilts a bit under the cross-examination but manages to answer to her satisfaction. Then comes the next volley. Does he live with roommates or on his own? Has he done his military service? What does he love?

This is the first question that Jihoon balks at. "Love?"

Phoebe is intent as she always is when digging past what she sees as the bourgeois bullshit of small talk to get to the real person. "You're on a deserted island. What's the thing you'd do even though no one is there?"

Jihoon's gaze goes hazy, as if he's looking at the white sand and palm trees. Imaginary deserted islands are always tropical because no one's going to pretend to be on some cold rock in Baffin Bay even as a mental exercise. "Music," he says finally. "I would write music."

"Do you do that now?" she asks.

He nods. "I work for an entertainment company."

"Do you like it?"

"I do," he says quietly. "Mostly."

Phoebe regards him with that look I always shied away from as a child, the one that went too deep. I was greedy about my secrets, and Phoebe was never one to leave well enough alone.

Mom pokes her head around the door. "Dinner, kids."

I jump up with alacrity, dragging Jihoon with me to wash our hands before we eat. "Sorry about that," I say. "It's how she is."

"Will there be more?" he asks weakly.

"Almost certainly."

"I should have prepared, like for school exams." Jihoon gamely straightens his shoulders to ready his answers for Phoebe's dinner round.

But Phoebe gives him time to dig into the plain grilled chicken (tofu for me) and steamed vegetables that Dad views with dejection. At least Mom has a chive cream sauce for the rest of us. The conversation in English might be a bit fast for Jihoon, because he's quiet and his eyes move quickly from person to person, checking their faces as they speak, but it could also be shell shock from Phoebe's barrage of questions.

"How's the office?" asks Dad as he passes me the rice.

"It's fine."

"This is the time in your life to be working for your goals."

"Yeah, God forbid you should enjoy yourself," says Phoebe dryly.

"You can enjoy yourself after you put in the work." Dad lays down his fork.

"Martin, there's a happy medium." Mom glares at him before putting on a smile for Jihoon. "More rice?"

Her attempts to shift the conversation go unheeded as Dad turns to Jihoon. "We always knew Ari would be a lawyer," he says. "Same as her father."

"I'm sure she's an excellent lawyer," Jihoon says diplomatically as he accepts a refill of wine from Phoebe.

"We were going to be Hui and Hui, until she decided against family law. Broke her dad's heart."

I try to smile. "Dad, you said you'd be happy as long as I went into law."

"Right, right." He points his fork at me. "I knew in my bones Ariadne would be the one to do it."

"Because I'm such a screwup, right, Dad?" Phoebe's voice is tight.

"I didn't say that, Phoebe." Dad stares at her across the table. "However, you can't deny it would have been hard for you to be a lawyer after you dropped out."

"I never wanted to be a lawyer, not like the golden child here. You wanted that for me."

My mother turns to our guest. "Jihoon, you didn't tell us what you do."

The poor guy. The conversation goes from there, Mom and I doing our best to avoid drawing attention to the fact that Phoebe and Dad refuse to talk to each other for the rest of the meal. It's not as bad as some of the Hui family dinners, but that's about the best I can say. I wish we'd stayed at home eating takeout. I wish I'd done this alone.

An hour later, we're back in the car with containers of leftovers. Phoebe had already left with a small wave and smaller smile that didn't reach past her lips. I lean back against the rope of my hair and quickly unbraid it for comfort. "Sorry about the drama. I should get you a T-shirt that says you survived the Huis."

To my astonishment, he wears a huge smile. "Thank you."

"For subjecting you to the verbal tennis game that was supposed to be dinner?" I cover my eyes with my hands. Why couldn't my usually repressed family have stiff-upper-lipped it for two hours?

"Ari." He leans over and tugs my hands down. I slump back on the seat, gusting my breath out. "Your family is coping with what happened. I'm grateful they opened their home to me."

I side-eye him. "No one says stuff like that."

"It's true." He runs his thumbs along my hands, which he hasn't released, causing my heart rate to hitch.

He's going to kiss me. I know he's going to kiss me. I can see his eyes flutter from my hands to my lips and then, oh my, his tongue touches his lower lip.

The stress of the evening evaporates. I want this, so bad. I lean in enough to encourage but not too far in case he pulls back and I need to pretend this didn't happen, like fake fixing my hair after I wave at someone waving at the person behind me.

He comes closer and my heart thumps.

I wait, but instead of a kiss, he drags his hand up my arm to my shoulder and trails his finger along the bare skin above my collar. His eyes drop to trace the path down my throat as his hand moves to my hair and drifts slowly across my back. He's acting like he has all the time in the world, and I wonder what he would do if I moved to claim him first. Instead I wait, enduring this sweetest of tortures to see what he does.

It seems like forever. Then his lips press against mine.

Fifteen

This must be my reward for getting through the evening. After that first soft brush of his lips, Jihoon pulls back and rubs his thumb over my cheek.

"Ari?"

"Get back here." Now that I know we're on the same page, I'm more confident about going for what I want, which is his hands on me and mine on him. I also know I've wanted it since I watched him cook me dinner that first time.

Jihoon laughs and meets me halfway. We make out like teenagers in my parents' driveway, Jihoon's hands running down my loose hair as he pulls me closer, both of us trying to avoid getting lethally gored by the gearshift.

Except this is nothing like being a teenager, because Jihoon knows exactly how to touch me until all I can think about is him. I dimly recall my decision to not get in too deep, but that was based on incomplete information—namely how good a kisser he is and how perfect his touch feels. My new knowledge has forced an extreme and satisfying course correction.

I lean back in and take my time as his mouth lingers on mine. His hand comes down to rest against my hip and he tries to pull me closer in a possessive move that's stymied by the console. He leaves a gentle kiss on my lower lip, another on the corner of my mouth, then sits back, smiles, and touches my face. "I didn't notice much about dinner because kissing you was all I could think about."

I start the car with shaking hands, eager to get going before I drag him into the back seat. "That would definitely have changed the direction of the conversation over dessert."

Because this is Jihoon, Lord of Feelings, he wants to talk as I drive, where I would like to silently relive the moment. However, I also want to know what this means and what it means to him. It has the bonus of keeping me from thinking about the ropes around my chest tightened by Phoebe and Dad.

"I've thought about kissing you since the day you pulled a knife on me," he says thoughtfully. "After I calmed down and realized I wasn't going to die."

For that long? I glance over to find him looking at me with that small smile that seems so private, a look for the two of us. He continues, "Perhaps I shouldn't have because I'm leaving soon."

I give the road ahead of me a neutral nod. This is true enough, although I'd do it again in a heartbeat.

"You've become all I can think about. Your lips. Your hair." Here, he reaches over and wraps a lock around his finger before releasing it. "How much I like to be with you and talk with you."

"Okay," I say. These are nice things to hear, but it's difficult for me to return them or even a close proxy. Instead of words, I reach over and touch his hand. He brings mine to his lips and kisses my palm, chin slightly stubbly and giving me shivers. I take my hand back so I can focus on the road.

"I don't know what can happen, Ari." He doesn't sound defeated or upset. Merely stating a fact.

I mull this over. "Are you usually impulsive?"

As I check my rearview mirror to change lanes, he curls back into the car seat. "I don't know."

"You are or you aren't," I say. "It's like being a talker or listener. You came to Canada on a whim, if that helps you decide."

"Perhaps it's the wrong question. I prefer this rather than impulsive or not." He speaks in Korean before translating. "It means to live with your heart."

Live with your heart. "Follow your passion, you mean?"

Jihoon twists in his seat to look at me. "Yes, but more." He thinks. "Everything involves your head and your heart. What you *should* do and what you *want* to do. Sometimes they are aligned. Often they are not."

"When there's no conflict, there's no decision to make."

"Yes. To live with your heart means that when there are choices to be made, you make the one that thrills your heart, not placates your mind. Impulsivity doesn't come into it because either it's the right decision or not. How quickly you make it is irrelevant."

I wait for the light to turn. "Is that aspirational or in practice for you?"

He hums a few beats to the song on the radio as he considers this. "Aspirational, usually." He shrugs so fatalistically I can feel it. "A guide rather than a command. Life is life and it's unpredictable. How about you?"

Living with your heart is exactly what I don't do. "Thinking with your head," I say.

"Does it make you happy?"

I feel my head and heart have been on divergent paths for a while and I've only just noticed. "Not sure."

We're quiet for a bit, listening to the radio. "Did your parents both come from China?" he asks as if he's been thinking about it.

"No, my mom's parents immigrated here from Malaysia before she was born, and my dad's family has been in Canada since the late 1800s."

It's a question I get a lot. People seem to forget Asian immigrants have been making homes here for generations. Some of my teachers had been openly astonished that neither of my parents had an accent, like somehow it was as much a part of the Asian phenotype as black hair.

"Your father's family came from China?"

"They came from southern China to work on the Canadian Pacific Railway. Dad says we're descended from one of three brothers. The other two died during the construction." Like hundreds of others. I remember in school the teacher barely pausing on that page in the history textbook. "My ancestor married a merchant's daughter, I was told."

"Your country has much immigration," he says. "So many different people."

"We look Chinese, but the closest Phoebe and I got to Chinese culture growing up was going to Chinatown for dim sum and getting red envelopes for Lunar New Year." Always with ten bucks, no matter how old we were.

"We got sebaedon," he says. "My favorite time of year when I was young."

I sigh. "It's weird. I look Chinese but I'm Canadian." It's frustrating to explain this because I am obviously Chinese, ethnically, and at the same time, I'm not. Or am I? What does that even mean? Why do I even assume that to be Canadian means you can't be Chinese at all, that only a Brittany or a Richard can wear that mantle? I can hear Hana's voice intoning, *Internalized racism, duh.*

Jihoon thinks about this for a bit. "You are expected to be someone you're not because of how you look."

"People sometimes have trouble when your face doesn't match your culture," I say. "They come to me with ideas of how I should be, what I should eat and like and think. If my grandparents were from France, no one would expect me to go around wearing a beret or come to me for baguette recommendations."

He nods as I keep going.

"I was raised here. Apart from my appearance, there's nothing that connects me to China."

He touches my arm. "You get to choose who you are, Ari. No one else."

I relent a bit. "It sounds like I hate being Chinese. I don't. I love being who I am. I only wish other people could accept me for me and not make up a person based on my appearance."

"That takes time, and many people would prefer the ease of superficial judgment," he says.

"I know." An ad about mufflers comes on the radio, and I turn the channel without thinking. "Hey, it's that song we heard before dinner."

There's no answer, so I glance over to see Jihoon staring at the dashboard as if it's going to sprout snakes. "'Candor,'" he says. He squints at the dial. "This is a Canadian radio station? Broadcast radio?"

I check the station. "Yeah, they play a lot of pop. First time I've heard K-pop, though."

"No," he says softly. He wears a big smile, I assume from hearing a song from home on the radio. "It's not usual."

"What's it about?" I ask when the song ends. I wasn't paying full attention to the English part of the lyrics. I hazard a guess. "Love?"

He laughs. "Most songs are, aren't they? This is about a love of honesty, to see what's in front of you with clear eyes unclouded by what you wish to see."

I frown. "Really? It sounds so peppy. Dancy."

I can feel him turn his face toward me. "There can be serious lyrics to upbeat music," he says. "You expected it to be 'baby, my life is nothing without your love *boom boom yah*' because it's a K-pop band?"

"No." I speak with some authority because, despite Jihoon's impromptu songwriting tutorial, I haven't thought deeply about what K-pop songs would be about in the first place. Although I've listened to Alex's playlist, most of the lyrics are in Korean, so I have no idea what the songs are about. My next step is doing some research into this StarLune, but I have time before I start with Hyphen. I'm about to ask Jihoon more about the industry, but he runs his hand down my thigh, giving me shivers. There's time enough for work questions later.

Traffic is light, and we arrive home quickly. I'm both pleased and anxious about this. A kiss in the car is one thing, but I don't know what's going to happen next. My doubts disappear when he gathers me close in the elevator and looks at me with his eyes half-closed and lips red and parted, a severely sultry expression that makes my thighs squeeze together.

Live with your heart, he said. Easier said than done, but for once I'm going to work with it and worry about the consequences in the morning. The elevator dings and we pull back.

I nearly drop the key trying to open the door. Jihoon pushes my hair aside to nuzzle at my neck, one hand on my waist and the other on the doorframe by my head, and we fall into the lamp-lit room. His touch makes it feel like he's everywhere, and it overwhelms me in the best way. We take a quick break to kick off our shoes, and then I lead him over to the couch. It's a good intermediary place because couches say *I'm into this* without the implicit expectations of the bedroom.

"This okay?" I ask him, sitting down and giving his hand a little pull.

"Very okay." He runs his fingers through my hair until I bring him close.

When I was kissing my last boyfriend, my mind was usually half on him and half on work. That doesn't happen with Jihoon. His touch fills my thoughts, but it doesn't feel strange or awkward. It comes in waves of sensation, his hand on my skin and mine running through his hair, soft despite the black dye.

I push him back until he's lying on the couch and bend over him, my hair falling around us like a tent, hiding us away from the world. He pulls me down so I can mouth kisses along that stunning jawline. The muscles in his neck tense as he turns his head to give me more access to his throat, and he makes a needy sound that makes me dizzy.

I'm so into him that I don't register the click in the lock until Hana's voice rings out a jaunty, "I'm home early!"

Sixteen

I've known Hana Choi for ten years.

She's my best friend and probably the most important person in my life. She knows me better than anyone. We've weathered a full spectrum of emotional crises including breakups and work setbacks and her mother and my sister.

I would trust her with my life.

Right now I could also happily shoot her out of a cannon. In my panic, I push away from Jihoon, who rolls off the couch with shocking speed and into the chair beside me in a single fluid motion. Before I can react to his cheetah-like reflexes, he's got his phone out, pretending to be scrolling. He ghosts me a wink as I rapidly smooth my hair down.

Luckily, Hana is too busy wrangling her bags to notice. Jihoon jumps up to help, and I head to the kitchen and casually shove my face into the fridge to cool my stubble-burned cheeks.

Once Hana's luggage is in, she beams at me. "I wanted to surprise you! My last training module was postponed, so I'm back a week early to spend some time with my favorite cousin." With a squeal, she grabs Jihoon in a hug. "Has Ari been treating you well? How's your dad, Ari?"

Jihoon casts me a doleful look over her shoulder. Now that Hana's here, whatever could have happened is temporarily consigned to the dumpster. They start talking as I heat some of Mom's leftovers for Hana.

She has the next few days off work to be Jihoon's tour guide. I try not to be jealous. After all, it's not like I could take off work to spend that time with him.

"I know me coming back messes up your plan to stay here," she says to Jihoon as she digs into the food. "Good news, though. There's a guy down the hall who does an Airbnb. It's convenient and way more private than a hotel."

This has potential. When I glance over, I see Jihoon wiggling his eyebrows at me and have to cover my laugh with a cough.

We agree Hana will sleep with me and Jihoon will keep her room for tonight. He follows me to the kitchen with the empty glasses and waits until Hana's back is turned to dip and give me a lightning-fast kiss on the cheek, near the corner of my mouth. "You don't want Hana nuna to know?" he whispers in my ear.

"Not yet." She'll give me the third degree about my intentions and what I'm thinking. I'm not ready for that.

"Whatever you want, Ari." He touches our foreheads together and squeezes my wrist before we go back to the living room to exchange polite good-nights. His touch was featherlight, but the imprint of his fingers stays on my skin as I go to my room.

Hana follows me to bed.

"What a trip." She yawns. "Thanks again for looking after Jihoon."

"It was no problem." I keep my tone neutral.

Hana collapses back on the bed. "How was dinner at your parents'? Was Phoebe there?"

I stretch the tightness from my neck. "It was a mess. Dad and Phoebe fought right in front of Jihoon."

Her eyebrows rise slightly. "You brought him to dinner?"

The look she's giving makes me a little squirrelly. "You told me to be a good host."

"It's that you never do that," Hana says. "It took six years before I had dinner with your folks."

"Well, be grateful you weren't there tonight because Phoebe quizzed the poor guy."

Hana bites the conversational shift bait. "Are you going to see her?"

"I saw her tonight."

"You know that's not what I mean," Hana says gently.

"What's the point?" I open a drawer with enough force that it nearly comes out into my hands. "She's the one who said she would call to meet up. News flash, she hasn't."

"Have you told her how that makes you feel?"

"I feel fine about it." I snatch out a pair of clean pajamas, neatly folded into flat squares.

Hana exhales. "I don't know what to say when you get like this, but I know you don't like how things are with her."

"I don't like lots of things," I say. "Like the water that comes out when you don't shake the mustard enough."

She frowns. "Yeah, but the liquid that pools on the top of the yogurt is worse."

"Debatable. My point is life's not about liking everything that happens. Sometimes you deal with it, and that's enough. You pour out the yogurt water. You wipe off the soggy bun."

"This is a different level than a wet hot dog." Hana tucks her arms under her head. "Phoebe's your only sister."

I don't answer because it's late, and I'm tired. As I stand in the shower, Hana's words come back, and I stick my face under the water so the rushing sound fills my ears. She doesn't understand how unreliable Phoebe is. How can you trust someone who leaves for something better, no matter how much you want them to stay? Love isn't enough sometimes.

I stick my tongue out at the wall and finish up. Nothing with Phoebe has changed since she left, and I don't anticipate that shifting now. I go back to my room and get into bed, Hana already curled up and asleep.

Sleep comes slowly as my thoughts oscillate between Jihoon and Phoebe.

———————

The early morning finds me on the balcony enjoying the last cool breaths until dusk falls. The day is already collecting a thick humidity that coats your skin and lungs until your body feels almost saturated. I haven't yet donned the prison of my nylons and am happy in loose shorts and no bra while I sketch out a day for Hana and Jihoon to enjoy.

It's self-indulgent to take the time to do this when I should be ruthlessly triaging my emails, but my pen doodles over a page in my travel notepad. I have a digital planner as well—I found one called Eppy that's great for day organizing and has the vacation planning module of my dreams—but I always start with pen and paper. I prop my feet up against the balcony wall and think. There are considerations when doing an itinerary: energy, goals, and external factors.

On the energy front: Jihoon will be fine, but Hana will be tired from her trip. A low-key day is best.

Goals: It's been a while since they saw each other, so they'll want to talk and reconnect. Don't plan activities that require a lot of focus or noise.

External factors: It's going to be a typical Toronto August day, with disgusting humidity, strong sun, and almost 40°C temperatures. They'll need coolness and shade. It's also high tourist season, and Jihoon dislikes crowds. No Toronto Islands or big museums, although the smaller ones might work.

I go in to grab a refill of coffee. One of Hana's hot-pink mules lies on its side by the door beside Jihoon's expensive Italian or possibly Japanese luxury brand leather sneakers.

Instantly, I know how their day looks.

I check a few things online and book a table for their lunch before I shoot a text to Yuko, who promises to work her contacts for me. I send Hana an email with instructions—since both she and Jihoon are lovers of surprise, I make them vague and provide scavenger hunt–style clues that are easy to puzzle out.

Hana comes out wearing a sheet mask. "You not going to work?" She sounds surprised.

"I wanted to do something first."

She nods and adjusts the mask around her eyes before staring vacantly at the railing in front of us.

"How was Vancouver, really?" I ask. Hana loves her work, but the long trips can drain her.

She rubs her hand on her knee. "Discouraging. It's like battling uphill, you know? I got an email telling me my anti-racist seminar was racist."

"How?"

She pulls out her phone and reads from it. "'I was disappointed to see the amount of time given to Asians over other disadvantaged groups, when it's obvious Asians benefit most from the system and suffer little from discrimination. I invite you to sit with the idea that having a Chinese woman in charge of the training inserted unnecessary bias into what might have been a thought-provoking seminar. After all, allies such as myself are working on listening and learning in order to hold space for those who truly require our help and understanding.'"

I want to punch the wall, and through the wall, this dipshit, on Hana's behalf. "I assume you're the Chinese woman?"

"All Asians are Chinese to Lady Wokeness." She shuts her eyes and drops the phone on her lap. "She kept interrupting me, too."

"You're doing good work," I encourage her. "Important. You might not see a difference right away, but over time you will."

"I guess," she says without enthusiasm. "It sucks to see all the excuses people will give to avoid thinking they should ever have to change. That woman can't even see how she's contributing to the problem."

I reach over and give her shoulder a squeeze. "Take some time to relax," I say. "You put a lot into your work, but you can't burn out."

She offers a tiny smile to the sky. "Too late."

I get the hint to leave when she closes her eyes. I'm definitely going to be late but can't bring myself to care as I check through their day once more to make sure it's perfect, especially now, knowing how beat Hana is. I want to give her at least a few hours to enjoy herself.

My effort is validated when both Hana and Jihoon send me messages that run from happy emojis to photos of where they are throughout the day. First is their private docent-guided tour of the Bata Shoe Museum, with Hana posing in front of a gigantic sneaker, then lunch at a little place with the best caprese salad in town. Each message gives me a satisfaction that I'm not finding in today's brisk emails and boring meetings. As I check my phone for the thirty-sixth time in the last hour, a notification drops down.

Phoebe: Hey

I slowly tip the phone back on the table and regard it like a tarantula. Phoebe is reaching out to me. Why?

You can figure it out by answering the text, genius.

I don't want to because I am a vengeful and small-minded human. I don't need to fully analyze the swirl of feelings in my gut right now because it's enough for me to know that if I pick up that phone, I lose the upper hand. My refrain for most of my life has been that if Phoebe wants to talk, it's up to her to make the move, family deserter that she is.

Now she's calling my bluff.

I look out the window, wishing life could be straightforward. I want my sister, but I want to keep this anger. It's familiar and protective.

She might not want anything from you. She might be telling you to pick up a pack of hot dogs for Dad. No, the heart attack. Tofu dogs.

Then it sinks in. I could have lost Dad. I didn't and I was lucky.

Now my only sister has sent me a single text that says *hey*, and all I can do is angst.

I pick up the phone. What's up? I text back.

Wanted to know if you were free tonight. Quick drink? I found a cool place near us.

I push away my instant no. It might be good for us to meet even though I'm suspicious about the timing. So little advance warning might mean she got stood up and she's bottom-feeding for someone to go out with.

I nearly smack myself. Phoebe might not be a great sister, but she's my sister. I need to have a better attitude.

Sure. I delete it. Too needy.

Fine. Nope, too passive-aggressive.

Sounds good. That's the Goldilocks of replies, positive but not desperate. I take off the period to avoid pesky punctuation issues and send it.

Phoebe: 9pm ok or do you need more time at work?

I eye the phone with suspicion, as this is not the Phoebe I know. That Phoebe would mock me for giving the man my youth and free time. I decide to take it at face value. That works, I reply.

See you then. She texts me the address.

Seventeen

The day drags on, and it's hard to focus when I'm thinking about my date with Phoebe. The only bright spot is an invitation to meet the team at Hyphen in two weeks. Alex has told me enough to know that they're a casual group, so that's something to look forward to. At least Hana and Jihoon are having fun as they have boba at the park under the perfect oak tree.

I'm not jealous. I'm *not*. Life's about trade-offs, and I didn't choose one where I have lazy weekdays because I want that corner office. The one with the leather and the view, the room filled with expensive furniture and awards.

The one filled with more loneliness and pressure.

My mind is a mess when I finally go to meet Phoebe. The door handle is odd in my hand, and I look twice before I realize it's a bronze cast of the arm from a record player.

Longplay. LPs. I open the door to a tiny room. Vinyl records cover the walls, and in the center is a rectangular bar that opens to a back room blocked off from patrons. The bar surface is covered with record players.

"Hi, sis." Phoebe waves from her seat. She's dressed simply but accessorized so well that I feel almost aggressively unexciting. My sister is comfortable in her skin and her clothes in a way that

I, camouflaged to blend in with the rest of the corporate drones at Yesterly and Havings, am not. "Isn't this place cute?"

There's a couple sharing headphones on the other side of the bar and a few loners lost in their private music. I smile at her, genuinely enchanted. This wacky hole-in-the-wall has a great feel. "I like it."

"I knew you would. Drink?"

I look at the menu, glad the drinks and the bar provide talking points until alcohol takes the edge off. "How do you get a drink called No Weddings and Four Funerals from three fruit liqueurs, soda, and grapefruit juice?"

"You going to try it?" She flips over the menu.

That thing is a hangover in a glass. I'm exhausted and should have a Perrier. Instead, I nod as my usual distaste of sweet drinks gets pushed aside by curiosity. "Yeah."

"I'll get the Cat on a Cold Brick Wall." She smiles and glances up to the bartender, who's lingering in the door to the back room. "It has Chartreuse. The queen of liqueurs."

We order and I look around. "It's cool you can listen to records."

She pulls over a couple of albums and a set of earphones that are split so each person gets a side. "It's not great for stereo sound, but here you go. They sanitize everything between customers."

The bartender comes back with our drinks in a few minutes. Mine is a pastel dream complete with swirls of smoke begging to be posted online with a pithy hashtag. Phoebe's is a poisonous green with a single ice cube shaped like a cat's head floating in it.

We tap glasses, sip, and silently swap. She tries mine and wrinkles her nose. "Fruity."

"Herbal," I manage to say about hers as I try to wipe the taste off my tongue by rubbing it against the roof of my mouth. It's like melted cough drops—the gross kind.

Drink ratings complete, Phoebe puts on PJ Harvey. I consider and discard several topics of conversation before I settle on, "Your place in Montreal sounds nice." That's neutral, since I didn't tack on a *thanks a lot for telling me you moved*. Phoebe left when I was thirteen and she was twenty, and it's possible our relationship was tainted because of all the ego and agony of my early teens.

"It's fun. I'm in a good neighborhood, and it's close to the ad agency where I work."

"You work in an office?" I'm surprised. This doesn't match my perception of Phoebe.

"When I need. I do freelance web design, so I can usually do that from anywhere."

I stare at her. "Since when?"

Phoebe pauses with her drink halfway to her mouth, and through the curve of the glass, the melting cat's face is malevolent. "A few years ago. I dabbled and found I liked it, so I did some online courses."

"I thought you worked as a barista," I say.

"I did. I pick up shifts at a friend's place for fun when I feel like it."

I hide my confusion in my drink. Phoebe seems content with her mix-and-match life, but I don't understand how. "Did you see Mom and Dad today?"

She rolls her eyes. "You'd think rapini had been put on this planet solely to torture Dad. He was mad because Mom won't let him back to work more than a regular workday."

That's like Dad. "Remember when he brought his files to my swimming lessons to pick us up and the wind blew them into the pool?"

"He jumped in after them fully dressed and held them over his head like trophies as everyone cheered."

We grin at each other. When we were growing up, we spent most of our free time together since she watched me after school when Mom and Dad were working. There's security in these memories, and Phoebe is the only person to share these experiences with me.

We order a second round of drinks. I blow caution to the wind and order a Little Trouble in Big China, a party of green tea and Sortilège, a liqueur made of whiskey and maple syrup. Phoebe decides on Kiss of the Titans, with ouzo, banana soda, and mint.

"How's Hana's cousin?" she asked. "He was a cutie."

"Out with Hana. She came back yesterday."

"Yeah? Having adventures?"

I nod and tell her about the day I planned for them. The bartender comes partway through my monologue to put down my drink, complete with a dragon paper cutout and unfurled green tea leaves at the bottom. Phoebe's has most of a mint plant sticking out the top. We sip and trade again.

"Banana soda's not as bad as I thought it would be," I say.

"This is amazing." She steals another sip of mine before I grab it back.

She exchanges the album for the Supremes, and we sit in a not-uncomfortable silence. I sneak looks at her between sips, but Phoebe is focused on the display of records.

I miss you.

I want to say it.

Instead I say, "How long are you staying?"

"Not sure." She glances over out of eyes so similar to mine that it's unnerving, like looking in a slightly distorted mirror or an alternate timeline. "As long as I need. I'm in no hurry."

"Don't you need to get back to work?"

"I can work from here as long as I want." She swills half her drink and grimaces. The Supremes inform us we can't hurry love. "It doesn't matter anyway, Ari. There's more to life than work."

"Yeah, but you'll leave anyway. You always do."

Her eyes widen as I tap on the counter, my ears pounding. What the hell did I say? I've avoided talking about our past for years. There's no need to bring it up. What's done is done.

"That's not fair."

"Forget it."

"No, Ari. I want to talk. I called you to talk. What happened with Dad made me realize I don't want to keep leaving things like this with you."

She doesn't hold my hand or do anything sappy because, as different as we are, we've both been raised by Martin Hui, emotional statue par excellence, and Susan (Soolin) Hui, an only slightly more emotional being.

"Okay," I say.

"That's it?"

"I don't want to talk about it. It's fine."

"It's not."

I feel trapped. "What do you even want from me? You took off when I was a kid. You never call. Never email. Now you want some special sister badge because you apologized for walking out on me again?"

"Of course not." She glares at me.

"Sorry. My mistake." I look at the time. "I should go. I've got a headache and work tomorrow."

"Come on, Ari. My life isn't only about you."

"You've made that abundantly clear." I dig around in my bag and slam some money on the table. "See you later."

"Don't be like that. Let's talk."

"About what?"

She looks down at her hands. That's all the answer I need. If I stay and we talk, then I have to dredge up years of pain that I've very successfully tucked deep down inside.

If part of me wants to stay, well, that's the part that always gets hurt. The part that needs to be protected.

So I leave.

————

Hana is in bed, in her own room, when I get home after a walk that left me both calmer and more confused. I don't know what I want from Phoebe, and I'm too tired to think about it.

I'm brushing my teeth when a text comes in.

Jihoon: I miss you.

I rinse before I reply: Did you have fun with Hana?

Jihoon: I love Hana. I wish you had come with us to enjoy the day you planned.

Me: Work.

Jihoon: Do you want to come over?

Me: To your place?

Jihoon: Yes.

Moment of truth. If I go over there, the implication of what will happen is clear. I will sleep with Jihoon or at a minimum get to the base that's after kissing but before sex.

Whatever unit of time is faster than a nanosecond is what it takes me to decide.

Me: Yes.

Worrying about explaining to Hana that I'm hooking up with her beloved cousin who is leaving the country soon is a job for later. I slip on some clothes and grab a condom so I'm prepared for any decision. I reconsider and grab one more condom before I collect my keys, feeling a bit like I'm sneaking out. Well, I guess I am. My heart races as I pull the door open slow enough to prevent any giveaway squeaks or creaks.

Then all my planning gets shot to hell as I slam the door shut with a scream. Because two men dressed in black and wearing baseball caps and face masks are standing inches in front of me, hands outstretched.

Eighteen

*H*ana stumbles out of her room clutching the protection bat she keeps by her bed. "What? What is it?" she yells. Then she blinks. "Why are you dressed and going out at this time of night?"

A polite knock comes at the door, and I back up as Hana moves forward, bat at the ready. "There are two men outside," I whisper.

"Who?"

"I don't know! I didn't ask. Why would any men be there? Jihoon is in the Mob, isn't he?"

Hana drops the bat and scrambles to grab it. "What the hell are you talking about? Of course Jihoon isn't in the Mob."

I barely listen. "I bet his goon name is Honey Thighs Choi."

"His name is not Honey Thighs."

"Hoonie Thighs, then."

Before she can answer, we hear another door open down the hall and a series of shocked exclamations. Hana drops the bat. "Jihoon's talking to them," she reports, hand cupped over her ear. "They're Korean."

"What, like that excludes them from being assassins?"

"As if assassins are going to come for you," she scoffs. "Why bother when they can wait for your job to kill you instead?"

"Not the time, Hana, seriously."

There's a mumble of voices from the hall, and she glues her ear to the door, eyes widening. "Jihoon's friends have come to visit."

"From the *Mob*. No wonder he wears a mask everywhere."

"I swear to God, I don't understand how you can function as a lawyer sometimes. They are friends, not goons or hoodlums or bosses. I know because I met them in Seoul." She marches to the door, bat in hand, and opens it. Now that my panic has receded, I see the two men have luggage that do not include gun cases. Hana greets them, and they all look over at me through the open door. The newcomers bow and I wave. At me, Jihoon mouths, *I'm sorry*.

It's clear my booty call has been indefinitely postponed.

A neighbor's door opens down the hall, and Jihoon snaps at his friends as he shoves them inside our apartment. Four seconds later, we're all standing in my living room surrounded by tumbled luggage and unease.

The two new guys are glaring at Jihoon. Jihoon is looking at the floor, face a dull red. Hana's eyes flicker between all three, her mouth a thin line.

Then there's me, feeling like a complete outsider.

Hana finally senses my silent entreaty to please do something. "How about some introductions?" she says pointedly to Jihoon.

"Yes, sorry. Ari, these are friends from home who are here for a very short and unexpected visit." He shoots them a look, but the taller guy simply folds his arms over his chest and shakes his head.

It turns out the tall guy is Kitae, or Kit, and must be older since Jihoon calls him hyeong. The other guy is Daehyun. They pull off their face masks, and we shake hands, and wow, what do they put in the water in Seoul? Even after a thirteen-hour flight, both of them are beautiful, with the kind of clear eyes and glowing skin I can only dream about.

At Jihoon's helpless expression, Hana obviously decides it's up to her to restore order. "I'm sure you three have a lot to catch up on, so why don't you come over for dinner tomorrow?" She ushers them out before any of the men can say a word then comes back in and shuts the door.

"You can meet them better later," Hana says as she balances the bat against the wall. "Care to tell me where you were going?"

"Out for a walk. Who are they exactly?"

"Friends of Jihoon's. You were going out for a walk at"—here she gives her wrist an exaggerated look, marred somewhat by the fact that she's not wearing a watch—"midnight?"

"Yes." I brazen it out.

"Right." She takes a deep breath. "Far be it from me to interfere with you getting some, because it's been a hell of a dry spell, but is Jihoon the best idea?"

I cross my arms. "Who says it's Jihoon?"

"Saw you guys making out when I came home from my work trip. I was going to be polite and not say anything."

"Oh." I bite my lip. "I didn't mean for it to happen. This is your fault. You didn't give me warning. You should have known having a man like that around me all the time would be dangerous."

She squeezes her eyes shut. "Please, he's my cousin."

"I'm only human."

"This isn't like you, Ari. If there were a poster for playing it safe, it would feature you wagging your finger back and forth."

It's true enough, and that bothers me in a way it hasn't before. "I thought about it, and look. Living together for three weeks is the equivalent of a hundred five-hour dates. At two dates a week, that's like knowing each other for almost a year."

"That isn't even close to being correct."

"All I'm saying is that living together sped up the comfort level in the getting-to-know-you process." I glance away. "I like him."

"Be careful, okay?" Her voice gentles. "He's going through a lot, and I'm not sure if you want to get involved with a man who's leaving the country."

"He's not leaving right away."

"I think you two should talk about that soon." She takes her hand off my shoulder. "Kit and Daehyun are here."

"Why would the mystery men matter? Why are they here anyway?"

"Work trip, they said."

"What kind of work trip? Don't they work for the same entertainment agency? Why aren't they in a hotel?"

The bat falls again, and Hana bends over to grab it. "Not sure," she says to the floor, her voice muffled. "They're on a budget?"

I'll find out more tomorrow. If tonight's interaction is any indication of what that will be like, it sounds like a dinner at my family's, filled with silent resentment and loud expectations. I'll feel right at home.

We go back to our rooms, and a text from Jihoon appears.

Jihoon: This isn't the night I wanted.

Me: It's ok and also Hana knows I was going to your place.

Jihoon: Sorry.

Me: I don't mind.

Jihoon: Me neither. Good night, Ari.

He sends me a selfie of him blowing a kiss, and it makes me smile before I turn off the light. Best not to dwell on what could have been and go to sleep. If I need to be home for dinner tomorrow, I'll need to get into the office extra early.

————

Hana greets me when I get in from a day of being busily bored and immediately grabs the bottles she asked me to pick up at the liquor store. "Soju as well as wine. That's sweet of you, even though I hate it. At least you got peach."

"I wasn't ready for the yogurt-flavored one."

I light one of Hana's many scented candles—Cabin Sweater Holiday, a mellow blend of smoky wood and pretension—before I get changed and fetch glasses for drinks. A knock comes at the door, and when Hana lets the men in, my eyes go straight to Jihoon. He hasn't texted me all day, and he looks exhausted. All of them do. They must have been up late talking, plus jet lag.

Jihoon hands me a box of strawberry mochi as he redoes the introductions. I shake hands and try not to stare. Daehyun is dressed in baggy cargo pants and a flannel shirt with a beanie low over his ears. Kit is in black jeans and a black cardigan over a white shirt. Both live up to my previous impression of being impossibly gorgeous.

Hana's usual social grace means we navigate the first minutes of conversation without too much trouble. It turns out they needed to come for urgent business with a collaborating artist and decided to stay with Jihoon, but he'd given them the old apartment number. They'd wanted to surprise him so hadn't texted and were very sorry for frightening me. Daehyun nurses his drink, and Kit, Jihoon, and Hana all take turns murmuring translations to him.

It's when the food arrives that I finally decide the strange atmosphere isn't me reading into things. I'm not an unintelligent woman. I graduated in the top 5 percent of my law class. I got my driver's license on my first try, even though the examiner tried to trick me at a right-turn-only intersection. I understood the plot to *Inception* without resorting to Wikipedia.

So I can see there are unresolved issues swirling around. Is Jihoon pissed they're here? That they're staying with him? My ego wants to think he's mad because their arrival interfered with what might have been a very entertaining night, but I reluctantly let that go. He can probably cope with not getting laid.

Whatever its root, the tension ebbs and flows throughout the evening. Jihoon sits beside me at dinner, and after we go back to the living room, I grab my glass and crack the soju open. "No, no," Kit admonishes me. "Never pour for yourself. You wait for someone to fill it for you."

My hand freezes on the bottle, and I glance at Hana and Jihoon for confirmation. She shrugs, while Jihoon nods enthusiastically as he takes the bottle from me. "What if no one notices?" I ask.

Kit looks slightly scandalized. "People should notice because it's polite and they are aware of what's happening around them, but if not, you pour someone else a drink, and they will pour you one."

"Even if they don't want a drink?" I ask. That seems rude and the whole ritual weirdly roundabout. But they all seem content, and I know that I'm the odd one here.

"Even then." Jihoon pours us all a drink.

I drink, then sniff the empty glass in nauseous recognition. "This tastes like every drink I made in university," I say. "Sweet mixer and vodka."

Jihoon is already pouring the second round. "Is that good or bad?"

"In my experience, it's usually bad, then better, then great. Then very bad." I can feel my bun falling apart, so I take it down and shake my hair out.

"You can also say geonbae when you drink. It's like cheers..." Kit's voice falters when Jihoon reaches out to play with a lock of my hair that's tumbled into his lap. Then Kit's eyes narrow. Jihoon stares serenely back.

There's a beat of dead silence before Hana checks the time. "Damn, it's getting late."

We stand in the hallway at our front door as we conduct the usual farewells and thank-yous. Jihoon ducks back in after the others head toward his door and pulls me close before pressing a hard kiss on my mouth. He's gone before I can react.

Hana rubs her face. "Dude. In front of me?"

"Sorry," I mumble.

We go in and start clearing dishes. "Your hair looked good tonight," Hana says. "Plus your ass is great in those jeans."

"Thanks." I grab a few glasses and put them in the dishwasher. "What's going on?"

"What do you mean?"

"I know you think I'm oblivious, but if even I could catch how they're acting, it must be a big deal. Are they mad at Jihoon? Is he mad at them?"

Hana finishes her wine. "All I know is when Hoonie came here, they were left hanging at work. They're peeved."

"He seems like a loyal guy, though. That breakup must have been impressive." He's never talked about it, and I pull back every time I want to ask. There's no point. He's only here for a while longer, after all, and then whatever we have will be nothing but a memory.

Hana rinses the glass under the tap. "People make strange decisions when they're at their end." She looks at me without her usual smile, and I'm the one to look away.

That night before bed, a text comes from Jihoon: Can I see you tomorrow?

Me: After work?

Jihoon: Please. I'd like to be alone with you.

How can I say no to that? I go to sleep with a big smile.

Nineteen

The phone rings as I'm sullenly lugging my heavy work bag off the subway. It's Jihoon. Odd, he's better on text.

"Where are you?" His voice is urgent.

"Hello, I did have a nice day. Thank you for asking."

"Ari, this is serious. Where are you?"

I swing my bag to my other shoulder. "I'm in the alley near the subway. What's up? Do you need something from the store?"

"What do you see?"

"Why?"

"Please."

I sigh. "The alley. There's a squirrel. What am I supposed to see? Two squirrels?"

My phone beeps a notification, followed by a few more. There's no cell reception on the subway, so these must be all the messages that came in while I was in transit. There's more than usual. No doubt another meaningless work crisis.

Jihoon doesn't laugh, and a wave of apprehension flows through me. His worry must be catching because I swear I hear shouting from the next street. There's a burst of Korean from Jihoon's side as he talks to someone. He comes back on the line. "I want you to do me a favor."

"What?" This sounds suspicious, but I bet it has something to do with his visitors.

Jihoon speaks as I come out of the alley, but I interrupt him and stop dead as I take in the scene. "What's going on here?"

"Ari…"

I talk right over him. "Oh my God, there must have been a murder or bomb threat or something."

In front of me is chaos. News trucks, reporters, and videographers line the sidewalk, crowding people with cell phones held at the ready. Whatever happened must have been terrible, but also, shouldn't they all be running the other way?

"Ari!" Jihoon's shout gets my attention. "You have to listen to me. Go back to the subway exit. There's a silver car there. Get in."

"You've got to be kidding." I stand on the sidewalk watching the scene. "What happened? How did you know this was going on?"

A group of young women jostle me as they pass. "I can't believe he was here the whole time," one says. "In my own damn city, and I had no idea. We might have passed him on the street."

"No way," says her friend. "I'd know Min in a second. I've got Min-dar."

"Jihoon?" My eyes follow them up the street, where they join the throng of people.

"Try not to say my name. Our fans found out I was staying in your building. My team is working on it."

"Don't say your name? Your team? What the hell do you have a team for?" My phone beeps, and this time I check. It's from Hana. IM SO SORRY. "Whose fans?"

I tap my reply as Jihoon mutters something in Korean.

Me: About what

Hana: That I didn't tell you about Jihoon. Listen to him.

I don't like this and go back to the call. "*What is going on?*"

Jihoon clears his throat. "There are a few things I meant to tell you."

"A few things?" I put him on speakerphone to scroll my social media. "Hold on." #JihoonFound, #StarLune, and #MinToronto are trending. Worldwide. I click on one and check the posts.

Min in Toronto?

Not helpful. I go to the next.

Jihoon in my own backyard @_starlune_ what you playing? #Mincognito

StarLune, that K-pop band? The one with the *video we watched together*? I promptly take him off speaker.

"Ari, you can't go home. I need you to go and get in the car." His raspy voice is low and coaxing, and I head back, too stunned to argue.

"You're in a boy band and didn't think this was something to mention?"

"I'm sorry."

"I'll take that as a yes. Wait." I lower my voice, suddenly conscious of why he told me not to say his name. "Kit? Daehyun?"

"They're members of StarLune."

"Okay." I watch another group of people—not only women and not only young—rush by me. "This is cool. I am good with this." I can't believe Hana. What the hell was she thinking, hiding this from me? Not only that, but keeping me in the dark when she knew I was into him? The anger is a white flash that bursts through to encompass not only Hana but Jihoon, the instigator of all this.

I speed walk through the alley, bag bouncing against my leg with the same rhythm as my heart banging in my chest. My hands are so weak, I keep losing my grip on the phone.

I turn the corner, and as promised, there's the silver car. The tinted window lowers to reveal Alex Williams waving at me. "Hello, Ms. I Hate Rock Stars. Look at us now."

"Are you fucking kidding me?" I get in.

He sobers up quickly when he sees my face. "Sorry, Ariadne."

I put Jihoon on speaker and turn back to Alex. "Why are you here?"

"As you know, I'm the head of PR for Hyphen."

I wait for more information as Jihoon conducts a mysterious whispered conversation on his end of the line.

Alex finally obliges. "As StarLune's North American distribution arm, this makes me the man on the scene and this beautiful mess my problem for the time being. We're controlling the situation."

The car slams to a stop as the driver tries to avoid a clutch of people running down the sidewalk. "Looks like you're doing a bang-up job," I say.

Alex looks up from his phone. "Be thankful your name didn't leak," he says. "This is nothing compared to what it could have been."

"Ari." Jihoon's voice comes through the phone, nearly making me drop it. "Alex is going to bring you to a safe place. I'm here waiting."

"I'll speak to you later," I snap into the phone. Then I put it on silent to do some online searching for my own answers. Beside me, Alex opens his mouth but shuts it when he sees my glare. I don't want to talk to him right now and hear whatever spin he's going to put on this. I want the unbiased and accurate information proffered by random strangers on the internet with zero insider knowledge.

"We can talk when you're done," he says easily.

I barely hear him as I gawk at my phone. Kit is StarLune's leader and main dancer, and Daehyun is the main rapper. They're known professionally as Kay and DeeDee. Jihoon? Stage name: Min. Roles: visual and main vocalist. I'm not even sure what *visual* means. I get off social media and do a search for Jihoon. The first hit, an English-language Korean gossip site, tells me what I need to know.

K-POP IDOL IN HIDING?

Rumors continue to surround the whereabouts of StarLune's vocalist Min, who hasn't been seen in more than two weeks.

Newlight, StarLune's entertainment company, has refused to comment on the hugely popular singer, saying only that members are busy preparing for their next comeback. A source close to the band says the quintet is exhausted after their last world tour, which sold out venues globally.

The story appears to have been an avenue to showcase a variety of Jihoon GIFs that I scroll through with increasing disbelief. The guy living in my apartment in sweatpants and drinking iced coffee is the same one with his tongue peeking out to touch his tinted lip? The one thrusting his leather-clad hips at the camera, hand gripping his inner thigh with his head thrown back? *This fucking guy*?

"Jihoon is in a K-pop boy band," I say, testing the words out loud. "He is basically part of a Korean NSYNC."

"Choi Jihoon is a performer and songwriter with one of the biggest bands on earth," corrects Alex. "He is known as Min."

"He's famous." There's a feed dedicated entirely to Jihoon walking stylishly through international airports. "A celebrity."

"Famous is not the word," my escort says with withering disbelief. "They outsell most artists globally. You know that, right?"

"I did not know that. Why would I know that?"

Alex shifts his whole body to eyeball me. "Because you don't live under a rock?" At my blank look, he sighs, apparently remembering that, for all intents and purposes, when it comes to anything outside work, I live under a boulder. "Didn't you read the background I gave you?"

"I skimmed it. I don't even officially start with Hyphen for another two weeks. It was on my list!"

"I can't believe you didn't recognize him even without that." Alex shakes his head.

"Why would I? Would you recognize the top singer from Norway? Egypt?"

"I would if they were as famous as StarLune, but we can discuss this later. Mr. Choi wasn't exaggerating when he said you couldn't go back to your apartment," he says.

"Why not?"

"They've had crowds at airports that were so big, some fans were nearly crushed against the barricades. Also, the potential death threats."

"I beg your pardon?" I put the phone down to listen more closely.

"Yeah, you don't get a fandom that huge without there being some people with issues, and those people would not be happy to know Min of StarLune has a girlfriend."

Death threats are too much for me to absorb, so I cling to what I can handle. "I'm not his girlfriend. He's my roommate's cousin. Hana's *cousin*."

Alex rolls his eyes. "Please, I saw his face when he was talking about you."

That gives me a bit of a rush, but now's not a good moment to savor it. I take in a breath so deep, I reach a count of eleven on the exhale. "Look, Alex, this is all very new to me, so I need you to go slow. Hana—my roommate—said her cousin was here because of a breakup. He certainly never introduced himself as a man who needs a security detail to go to the store."

Alex gets that PR face I've seen him pull on in meetings. "I'm taking you to Mr. Choi in a secure location. He can explain further."

"Oh my God. Work. What will happen?" My firm is so painfully traditional, I'll never get ahead if this gets out.

"Right now, it's all fine. No one knows about you." To my surprise, he turns to put his hand on my arm. "I promise I'll do my best to keep your name out of this."

"Can you?"

He pokes his tongue inside his cheek as he thinks about how to phrase his answer. "Currently it looks good."

"No guarantees, though."

Alex shrugs. "There are no guarantees in this life. StarLune fans are passionate, but the vast majority are reasonable people who understand Mr. Choi deserves a private life."

I consider this. "How did he even manage to get around the city before being recognized today?"

"Masks, hats, and being Asian in a pretty white area of town. No one expected him to be here, and I assume he had a huge chunk of luck."

"Then it ran out," I say.

We turn up Avenue Road. "Mr. Choi was spotted at a grocery store by a fan who took a photo and followed him back to the apartment. Normally the fan etiquette is to wait for a while to post a sighting to give an idol privacy, but Mr. Choi's alleged disappearance threw that out the window."

"That's how they know where I live."

"Where he was staying, since you haven't been mentioned yet," he corrects. "Luckily, she couldn't get in. Even luckier, you and he never left the building together after he was identified."

"Then there's no connection between us."

"Not at the moment, but fans and media will check your neighborhood to find out where Mr. Choi has been. Plus your roommate has his last name."

"At least they're related so I would only be the cousin's roommate."

He gives me a look.

"What?" I demand.

"Ari, I can't believe I'm saying this—and please take it in the most professional way possible—but people will never think you were only the roommate."

I frown. "Why not?"

He fidgets with his phone. "Jesus, look in a mirror. You are not... unattractive."

I feel the heat light up my face. "Alex!"

"It would explain his mysterious disappearance, especially if someone's seen you together. There's no way fans will believe it's coincidence that a pretty woman happens to live with his cousin and there was nothing between you. It won't happen. You know what people are like. An idol like Mr. Choi can't even be seen talking to a woman without dating rumors." He shakes his head. "Heteronormative as well as intrusive."

I cover my face. "This is not happening."

"Oh no, it very much is. I'm sorry to have to lay it out like that, but you know my job. I look at the perception. Optics can be more powerful than reality, and I'm doing what's best for all of you." He looks sad. "It's a mess, Ari. A real mess."

"Where's Hana? Those other two, Kit and Daehyun?"

"All secure and with Mr. Choi."

His phone rings as I watch a man pass us on his bike. Jihoon wasn't avoiding an ex but escaping his life as an international celebrity. Why? Being waited on hand and foot was too much? He was tired of getting fawned over for breathing? I put my head in my hands as a memory hits me. The work problems. I thought he'd been talking about everyday office drama, but he was talking about StarLune. He might have even written the song we heard in the car, and I had no idea.

My mind is a lazy Susan rotating through *Jihoon is a liar*, *Hana is a liar*, and that perennial favorite, *what the actual fuck*. I go back to my Google search and come across an image of Jihoon strutting down a stage runway, tiny against the tiers of fans in the background.

It's too much. I throw my phone on the car floor. Alex does me the favor of pretending not to notice when I bend to pick it up a minute later.

Then I start scrolling again.

Twenty

ou." I point at Hana. "We're going to have words later."

She grimaces and sinks into her chair.

Kit and Daehyun—sorry, Kay and DeeDee—sit on the couch looking between me and Jihoon and their phones in an eerily synchronized movement, like cats tracking a laser toy. I ignore them.

Jihoon opens his mouth. "You," I say. "Your turn is now." I glare around the room. "In private."

Alex wordlessly points to a closed door. His expression is easy to decipher: *You poor bastard*. Jihoon reads it as well as I do, and his face squinches up in a way I would have found charming an hour ago but am now too angry to acknowledge. I blow through the door without waiting. Jihoon follows and shuts the door carefully behind him, blocking it as if worried I'll try to escape. No fear of that because no one's leaving until I get the full story.

"You even lied about your name, *Min*."

He stares at the floor. "Technically not, as Min is my stage name."

"You know what? You can have your technicality because I have a fine collection of your other lies to choose from. You're a singer. A famous one, according to Alex."

He looks trapped but nods slowly. "Yes. An idol with StarLune."

Idol. It blows my mind that's even a real job title, but professional nomenclature is not the apex issue of my problem pyramid. "Kit and Daehyun aren't buddies here on a work trip. They're your world-famous celebrity bandmates."

He struggles with that for a moment before admitting defeat. "They are."

"What else didn't you tell me?" I sag against the desk. "You fed me such a monumental pile of bull. I guess you wanted to know what it was like to be a regular person for once. A good joke."

"No!" He reaches out but freezes when I lean back, shaking my head. "Never, Ari. I swear I wanted to tell you."

"How convenient now that you've been caught." I try to pull back the bitterness in my voice, but I can't.

Jihoon—Min...whoever the hell he is—passes a hand over his face. "It's like when you don't know someone's name and then too much time passes to ask."

"Those are not close to being comparable experiences. You could have told me at any time in the past month. You could have told me *yesterday*."

"What, while we were making coffee after dinner? Just, 'Yah, Ari, this slipped my memory, but I'm actually an idol. The men in the living room are members of my band. Pass the sugar.'"

I'm already on a new thought, because unlike my focused and linear work self, this self is leaping all over the place. "How about when we were watching the video you were in?" I groan. "How could I have not recognized you?"

"I have a very different presence when performing, and we had creative styling," he says primly. "Also you were mostly looking at Kit."

That's undeniable, but I can't even go there right now. "You *lied* to me."

"I know." He looks me in the eyes. "Every time I tried, the words choked me. I knew you would be angry. I wanted to keep you safe, too."

"Safe?"

Jihoon sits down on the chair, a calming gray tweed woven through with delicate red threads. "It's hard for idols to date. Some fans get upset, and it's a struggle to keep a partner's identity private. There's a lot of pressure and scrutiny that I wanted to avoid for you."

I gloss over the part where he considered us either dating or about to date because that's a whole other conversation. "It should be my choice to make."

"No."

My eyelashes tangle together with how hard I squint at him. "What did you say?"

"How can you make a choice not knowing the facts?" He rubs the back of his neck. "I can tell you what it's like, but that's nothing compared to the experience of always being watched."

"You're conflating telling me and telling the world," I snap. "It's not like I would say anything."

The silence lasts a beat too long.

"Whoa," I breathe. "You thought I was going to rat you out. That's why you were so standoffish when you arrived. I thought you were *shy*." How dense am I?

"No, no! Hana trusts you, and I only wanted to get to know you first. As Jihoon, not Min of StarLune." He looks at me piteously. "I was going to tell you tonight, I swear I was."

"Noble of you." I'm allowed to be snippy. It hurts that he played me for a fool, but Huis don't do feelings talk, and I'm not about to break the family tradition. Time to focus on cold, hard plans. "What's going to happen now?"

He seems relieved to get onto solid facts, which is probably an indication of how stressed he is. "Newlight has teams monitoring coverage," he says. "Alex is checking every place we've been together in Toronto and having them sign NDAs."

This will be part of my job when I start with Hyphen, but the irony doesn't make me smile. "You didn't get recognized for a month."

"I was very careful, and no one knew I was away from Seoul at first. It was bad luck I knocked my hat off in the store."

I tick through our time together. "You shopped with a credit card."

"It's issued in another name."

So cloak-and-dagger. A gleefully small-minded thought occurs to me. "Mrs. Choi will know you were here and didn't go to see her."

He winces. "I can't believe I'm not even concerned about that, although it will cause a family fuss worthy of a television drama." He pauses. "I can make this up to you, Ari."

"Yeah? How?" I wait while he works on a response, because of course he can't. I'm not even sure why I'm here talking to him. I should tell him where he can stuff his StarLune and cut off all contact.

I get up and look out the window. We're in a luxury penthouse condo on Avenue Road that Alex assured me was better for security than a hotel. To the south is the crystal architecture of the Royal Ontario Museum, and I get a wave of nostalgia so intense, it almost makes me gasp. Ten-year-old Ari only had to worry about spelling *pterodactyl* correctly on her worksheet. She couldn't even fathom the shit that would go down twenty years later.

Jihoon hasn't replied before I speak again. "Were you planning to ghost me? Go back to your rock star life without saying anything?"

"No, never."

Jihoon *sounds* sincere. "Why did you lie about an ex?"

"Hana said I was too unhappy to simply appear without a reason, and it seemed most plausible. The sentiment was close enough."

"I want the full story. All of it." I want to believe him, but honestly, he's not giving me a lot of runway.

He sits on the bed and crumples the duvet in his hand. "I don't know where to start."

"Try the beginning."

Jihoon releases the duvet and smooths the wrinkles out with a pensive expression. "Do you know how many hotels I've stayed in?"

"No."

"Hundreds. For almost a full year, we lived out of hotels. I'm in hotels more than my own room."

I'm not sure if this is leading somewhere or if I'm about to get a Tripadvisor summary. That's a lot of hotels, but hotels are relaxing except for those jacuzzi tubs I'm sure are never clean enough around the jets.

"I've been with StarLune for more than a decade," he says, frowning down at his hands. "The best years of my life. I'm alive when I write songs that fans treasure. The members are my family."

I wait.

Jihoon plants his elbows on his knees and bends so he's talking to the floor. "It's hard to be an idol. There's fame and money and performing. There's also no privacy. I can't breathe without a camera in my face. We do interviews and concerts and fan signings, and I don't even know what else. Every day I get a schedule, and I obey it like a robot."

"What happened?"

He looks up at me. "Our last show was Seoul Olympic Stadium. Do you know it?"

I shake my head.

He smiles at his hands. "It's a dream for idol bands. It means you're big enough to sell out a stadium instead of arenas. Almost fifty thousand people each show. It was a triumph."

"You don't sound like it was."

"I nearly couldn't go onstage for the last one." He wrinkles his nose and looks out the window, gaze dark. "It's always organized chaos before a performance. Everything gets checked three, four times. Backups on backups. Plans B and C and D because there's millions of dollars on the line for those three hours of expected perfection. Hundreds of staff members work hard so the five of us can shine for our fans the way we want to."

"What do you mean you couldn't go on?"

"I forgot the words to our first song. I forgot our choreo. My mind was a blank. My earpiece was feeding me gibberish because I couldn't make sense of the sounds. The show was starting, and I didn't know the words. I was going to forget everything. Every time I tried to remember, the knowledge seemed further away. I was going to fail everyone. The fans. My members." He's speaking faster now, and I'm a little scared.

I make myself blink because my eyes are so wide, they're drying out. "Then what?"

Jihoon jumps up and leans against the wall before starting to pace the room with jerky steps. "Kit saw my face, and he knew. He grabbed me, hard, and he hit me."

"He what?" This isn't what I expected.

He touches his right cheek as if reliving the blow. "He slapped me and told me to get it together. Then he made me breathe with him. Gave me oxygen. He tried every technique he could in twenty seconds as the crowd screamed from the other side."

I take a deep breath, tense even from hearing this. "Did it work?"

Jihoon looks distant, as if he were back on that stage. "I did the show, and no one complained. I went back to my apartment, and it was cold because I was meant to be in a hotel to celebrate the end of a successful tour. I couldn't remember a single minute. On the best night of my career, I sat on my floor and wondered if it was all worth it. All those cheers and I was alone, knowing none of that was for Jihoon. Only Min."

I stay quiet because although most of me—almost all of me—feels intense pity, the nasty and vindictive part thinks, *Isn't this what you signed up for? Boo-hoo, it's so hard at the top. People would kill for that.*

"Some other things happened then, and I had enough. We had two weeks off, and I told the others I needed more time. They covered for me as long as they could, until the company found out I was gone and they had to come get me. They're furious."

"Tell them you need a break. Why all the sneaking around?"

"We have a comeback soon."

"I don't know what that is." There's a coin in my pocket, and I absently take it out to spin on the table before I start to fidget with it.

"An album release. That means practices every day to learn the choreography. Rehearsals for music shows. Interview prep and photo shoots. People everywhere. Cameras." He gives a wry smile. "They once filmed me having a nap on a couch for five minutes. Half my face is covered with a hoodie. It has twenty million views."

"That's a lot." How invasive. Yet he allowed it, so part of him must enjoy it even though he's protesting now.

"It makes the fans happy, and that's the most important thing to us."

"You left, though."

"All I could think about was what if next time there's a stage and I can't get on it? What if I had forgotten the words or messed up the choreo during the show? What if my songs never get..." Here, he falters. "It was paralyzing."

I can sympathize with this performance anxiety, even if I experience it on a much less public level.

"Then a text came from Hana." He sees my face. "We text a lot."

"She never even told me you existed."

The coin gets away from me, and he rolls it back. "That's my fault. My company's fault, but they did it to keep Hana's family safe."

"That's for her and I to talk about."

He continues, "Hana said she was going out of town. I didn't even think. I asked if I could stay at her place and left Seoul."

"Without telling anyone."

"I told the members where I would be but not the company. I needed to think."

Living with his heart for sure. "About what, exactly?"

"My path." His pinched lips and curved neck make it clear he doesn't want to talk about it. That's fine, because in the end, the why of his arrival isn't the most important part.

I leave that alone. "Alex says you're one of the biggest bands in the world. You're living the dream."

"Fame wasn't the dream. Music was the dream. Connecting with people, making them feel and think and be comforted or happy. Not the rest of it. I never talk to *people* anymore. I talk to fans or crowds, and they talk to Min, not Jihoon." He stares out the window. "The fame is what you put up with for the good parts. I knew there would be sacrifices, but not like this."

I shy away and return to the matter at hand. "Sounds like you're not sure of what to do."

He bites the inside of his lip. "It's hard. When Kit hyeong and Daehyun came, I felt so selfish. The decision isn't only mine. It affects all of StarLune. I was a poor team member."

"Then you haven't come to a decision even after being here almost a month."

"I thought I had, and now I'm not sure."

"Not sure," I repeat. "Why?"

"If I don't go back, I'll let everyone down."

"If you're not ready, you're not ready."

He laughs, but it's a harsh sound that I'm not used to hearing from him. "I've been training for years. I will make myself ready and get over it because I owe it to the members and fans. My feelings are small when compared to everyone else."

"That's not how it has to be." This is much different from the *take care of yourself first* mentality I'm used to.

He gives a resigned shrug. "For me, it is. I suppose I knew how this would end, Ari. I knew I would go back, but I liked to pretend to myself that I could change things."

Where does that leave me? I'm not ready to ask it, not yet.

"What's next, then?" The coin slips out of my fingers and drops to the ground. We both leave it.

He looks sad. "I don't know. I want to be with you, to continue what we were starting."

"Right." I stand and clap my hands briskly. I had meant the general state of affairs, and I don't want to have this specific relationship talk, not while I'm working through this new information. "Get Hana in here."

"Ari, I—"

"Hana, I said."

His lips thin, but he leaves without another word. Most of my fury goes with him, and I huddle into the chair. I understand about not being able to find his way to telling me the truth, but there are too many layers of betrayal for me to consider forgiving him at the moment. He lied about who he was even as I thought we had a connection. I don't know if he was using me or for what. He's clearly an incredible liar—how can I trust a thing he says or ever said?

I don't know if I can. That hurts more than I anticipated.

Twenty-One

If Jihoon's treachery is hurtful but now slightly understandable, Hana's is unfathomable.

She sidles in, eyes downcast. "Hey." It's the same tone you'd use to placate a bear as you step between her and her cub. Her mobile face is pale and guilty—as it should be, because that was a hell of a truth she hid from me.

I say nothing and she crumbles. "I'm sorry," she moans, covering her face. "I should have told you."

"That you were cousins with a man I'm told is one of the most famous singers in the world? Why would I need to know that, even though we tell each other everything?"

"I know, it looks really bad."

"*Looks* bad? It *is* bad, but it's not like you planted him in my house to live in hiding and let me wallow in my ignorance like a fool. Wait, you did. That's exactly what you did."

"I didn't know you'd fall for him," she says weakly. "Jihoon's not your type."

"What does that mean? Super attractive, generous, sweet men can keep walking?"

"No, but you've always dated corporate white guys."

"You know where I work! There's not a lot of choice. It's proximity, not preference." I shake my head. "What would you have done if I recognized him?"

She snorts. "Please. I knew that wouldn't be a problem."

"This is not relevant right now." I get back on track. "What is relevant is the fact you that didn't tell me who he really was."

"Would it matter?"

"That he has a fandom of millions and the international media was searching for him? Yeah, that would have been a good thing to know." Would I have treated him any different if I knew he was rich and famous and wanted? I don't want to think about this and retreat into my justifiable rage.

"See?"

I shake my head. "You're missing the point here. It's not who he is. It's that you lied to me." I want to tell her how hurt I am that she didn't trust me, but I can't come out and say that. The words are too hard, even with Hana. There's been too much tonight for me to expose any vulnerability.

"I couldn't tell you. I'm sorry." She drops back on the bed like an anguished starfish. "It's a huge secret in my family."

"I don't get why you being cousins is such a big deal. He lives in Korea."

She's quiet for a moment. "They had a sasaeng. Do you know what they are?"

I shake my head.

Hana bends over to hug her legs close. "They're fans, but obsessed ones. Stalkers."

"Jihoon had one?"

She nods and tucks her hair behind her ears. "She started by following him around airports. She eventually broke into their dorm and handcuffed herself to his bed."

"Are you kidding?"

"Nope. It was terrifying. StarLune had recently debuted, so they weren't even that big yet. Jihoon's company suggested we keep our relationship secret so fans wouldn't bother us."

"I can't believe your mom went along with it."

"Obviously she would have loved the attention of being Min's aunt. She changed her mind when Jihoon told her what some people had done to an idol's family in New Jersey. They wouldn't leave them alone and followed the kids to school and the parents to work, taking photos. Then one day they broke in to take souvenirs from the guy's childhood bedroom."

"You're kidding."

"It was extreme and unusual, but it happened. Most Starrys are supportive and respectful, but a very rare number of people get obsessed in a bad way."

"That's unbelievable."

Hana pops her head up with a mischievous grin. "Eomma nearly had an aneurysm when StarLune made it big and she couldn't brag to her church group. Especially since Mrs. Park's son kept getting promoted at his firm."

I want to laugh—I can visualize Mrs. Choi's impotent fury—but I don't want Hana to think she's off the hook. "That's all well and good, but this is me. I can keep a secret. I keep secrets for a *living*."

"I know, but it's been ingrained in me that we never talk about Jihoon outside the family." She looks down and picks at her nails. I automatically swat her hand away. "Then he asked me to hold off so he could tell you himself."

"Apparently he was going to tonight."

She sighs. "He said you made him feel free and like himself. He didn't have to pretend or worry about you wanting Min and getting Jihoon. He didn't want to give that up."

That warms me but not enough. "Except he was pretending the whole time. It was all about him and how he felt. What he wanted. Relationships are built on trust and reciprocity, but I was left in the dark."

Hana plucks her lower lip and looks at the ceiling. "The beginning of a relationship is a period of learning," she reasons. "It's when you find out they like raisins in their butter tarts or iron their underwear."

"First, who irons their underwear? Second, this is hardly the same level as finding out they wear dress socks and boxers around the house. Although that's a deal breaker."

"Right, right," she assures me. "I would have told you if he did that."

"Good to know you would have told me something."

She flinches, but I don't take pleasure in twisting the knife. I feel...tired.

"I'm not taking sides," she says softly. "I only want to help you understand why he did it."

I circle back to the main issue, which comes down to two words. "He lied."

"A lie of omission, not commission. He never denied he was in StarLune."

This is stretching it so far it riles me up again. "Why would I ask him that? Do you think I go around assuming everyone is a celebrity in hiding?" Another thought occurs to me. "You don't even like K-pop. You hardly ever play it."

She rolls her eyes. "Right, I'm going against the treaty every proud Korean signs that says we can only listen to trot and idol bands."

"Sorry," I mutter.

Hana nudges me. "Hey, at least now you don't have to worry about dealing with an ex," she says. "Since there wasn't one."

I give her a look. "Huge bonus."

There's a long silence. "How do you feel about him now?" she asks.

"I don't know." I grab some of my hair and start braiding and re-braiding. "Confused. Is the guy I met Min or Jihoon?"

She stands. "Only one way to find out. Get to know all of him."

"Easy for you to say." Do I even want to date a rock star? No, of course not. I should date another lawyer, a steady person who understands me and who isn't leaving the country in days.

"It's icky that you're into my cousin." She grins. "Whatever, half the world is as well."

I flip her off, and she snickers.

"Give him another chance," she says.

"Why?"

She looks at me. "Because you want to."

Maybe I do. Maybe that's enough.

Maybe it isn't.

———————

Alex says he'll send staff to get our belongings, but I hate the thought of someone going through my underwear drawer. "I'm going shopping, and you're paying for it," I tell Alex.

He rubs his eyes until they redden and tear up. "Like that's the biggest problem I've had today. Make sure you keep the receipts. I can't deal with Finance getting on my case on top of all this."

"I can come with you," Hana offers.

I glare at her. "You can sit here and think about what you've done." She hunches down. "Okay."

Once safe inside my room, I splash water on my face and sit on the bed to enjoy the silence. I'm not in there five minutes before a knock sounds at the door.

"Ari?"

It's Jihoon. The mature thing to do would be to open the door, invite him in, and have a civil follow-up discussion.

As if I can do that. I wait until he's gone, then grab my purse and run down the empty hall for the door.

The condo is close to Yorkville, and I head east to the shops. Sitting in a café window is a woman with dyed hair and a brilliant, carefree smile that reminds me of Phoebe. What if people find out my name and go after my family? What if the stress causes Dad's heart to fail again? My entire body goes shivery, and I stop dead on the sidewalk and bite the inside of my cheek. I should tell them on the down low. Or at least Phoebe, to keep an eye on Dad.

Triangle breathing. I take deep, desperate breaths right there as muttering people walk around me with impatient steps. What do I do?

I come back to it later when I'm more in control, that's what. I force one foot in front of the other until I move on autopilot, ducking into my usual stores and getting pajamas, underwear, and some casual clothes. It's Friday, so I don't need a fresh outfit for work tomorrow, but it might be a few days at the condo. I grab three shirts and a suit. Alex's treat.

As I collect my new belongings, my usual logicality seeps back. I'm letting the doomsday attitude of Alex and the others affect me. Nothing is going to happen. No one cares that some singer was in Toronto staying with his cousin, and it'll be a nonstory in a day. Everyone is in crisis overdrive and exaggerating the importance of what's happening because they're stressed.

I head over to the Manulife Centre, where I pick at a damp taco and scroll through my phone. Hana knows better than to text me when I'm mad. She must have told Jihoon, because I have no messages apart from Alex asking me to come by his room when I get back.

Then I put the phone down. The lack of messages from Jihoon could be because he's decided whatever might have happened between us isn't worth the trouble.

That I don't know how to feel about any of this makes me overheated in my skin. I know how I want to feel—furious, betrayed, all those juicy and satisfyingly self-righteous emotions, but at the same time...I can't, not completely. Would I have told me? I want to say yes, but as Jihoon pointed out, knowing you need to say something and getting the words out are two very different beasts.

The same applies to Hana. I poke idly at the disintegrating taco.

We might be best friends, but this is family we're talking about. She couldn't predict the future, and she wasn't wrong when she thought a guy brooding around the house wouldn't be my type. This is Jihoon's fault, I decide. He had to mess it all up by being so likable.

"Ari?"

I know that voice. I whip around.

Twenty-Two

P hoebe stands beside me, her head tilted to the side. "What are you doing here?" she asks.

I gesture to my taco, trying to be normal. I'd thought about texting her a few times since I left her at the record bar, but I didn't know what to say. "Eating."

She eyes the mess on the tray. "That looks unappetizing."

I shove it away. "It is."

"I'm picking up some overpriced snacks as a farewell hostess gift." She shakes a brown shopping bag at me so I can hear the clang of glass jars.

"Leaving already?" I mean to say it like a normal person, but it comes out spiteful.

To her credit, Phoebe doesn't bite. "No, I found a short-term rental. I like to have my own place. Same neighborhood." She waits for a minute, but I'm so drained, I can't think of a good response. Her eyes narrow. "What happened?"

"Nothing."

"Stay here. Watch my bag." She dumps it on the chair beside me and disappears to a café. I sort through her purchases in listless curiosity. Phoebe was always good at choosing gifts—when I was a kid, she got me a stuffed cat I loved so much, I brought it to university with me—and this proves it. She's bought a selection of lovely sauces and pastas to match, as well as a little jar of what looks like marinated cheese. A crispy loaf of ciabatta is wrapped in brown paper and tied with twine. I want to eat it all because my taco hadn't satisfied anything beyond bare physical sustenance.

"Here." She puts a monstrously puffy pastry in front of me, dusted with glittery powdered sugar and filled with greenish cream. I lean down to sniff and sneeze after snorting up the icing sugar.

Phoebe rolls her eyes. "It's food, not cocaine."

"Shut up. What did you get?"

She displays two croissants proudly.

"Almond and cheese?"

Phoebe runs her hand through her shaggy hair before she layers the two pastries together and bites in. I make a face.

"Almond and cheese make a classic combination," she says with a shower of crumbs. "Don't try to derail me. There's something going on. Is it work?"

"Weirdly not."

"That Jihoon guy?"

I run my finger around the edge of the cream puff and lick it off. Pistachio. "What makes you say that?"

"It looked like there was something between the two of you, and you take after Dad."

"What's that mean, I take after Dad?"

She peels her croissant layers apart. "Do you enjoy thinking about, discussing, or in any fundamental way acknowledging feelings?"

"I have feelings."

"I know you do. Want to talk about them?"

"No." At my response, Phoebe raises her eyebrows, and I glare at her. "You sashayed out of my life, and suddenly you have a right to know my innermost thoughts?"

She flushes and looks down. "Sorry."

We sit in a heavy silence, both of us staring at the table. Inside my head is a snarled yarn ball. I want to be mad at Phoebe. I want to be mad at Jihoon and Hana. I can even see that anger, a twisted dark red strand woven through this big mess.

I'm so tired of being angry. I'm tired of my sister not being in my life. Tonight has battered me down enough that I don't have the energy to avoid this conversation anymore. I'm on a roll with awkward talks anyway, right? Might as well keep going.

It takes me a few tries to get the words out. "Why do you never email? Call me?"

Phoebe breathes out hard enough to send her crumbs flying into my lap. "It's hard."

"What's so hard about picking up the phone?"

She rips the corner off one of her croissants. "You tell me."

I clamp my lips shut.

Phoebe continues, "You're always so upset with me when I try. You make a big deal about how busy you are and..." She pauses before giving a little what-the-hell shrug. "It hurts, okay? It hurts that you and Dad insist on thinking I'm some screwup because I don't want what you want."

"You're older than me."

Phoebe eyes me in astonishment. "So?"

"You left when I was thirteen! *Mom* told me you dropped out. You didn't even tell me yourself."

"I was only twenty. I was scared. Dad was so mad, you have no idea. Like, *furious*. He made it clear that I would be a bad influence."

It takes a minute for me to find the words. "Dad told you to stay away from me?"

She frowns. "Not really."

"Then kind of."

"He made it clear you were on a different path in life. Dad's a short-term, narrowly focused workaholic, but he's not cruel like that. It was my choice because I thought it was best."

"I can't believe you didn't talk to me. Me, the person this affected most." I also can't believe we're having this talk in a food court, but now that we've started this discussion, I don't know if I can stop. The red string tightens enough to squeeze the rest of the ball and force out my words.

"I couldn't." Phoebe sounds sad. "By the time I realized how dense I was being, you didn't want to talk. You were always at school or working, and we were at different points in our lives. It got harder and harder. We grew too far apart."

"Yeah." She's right.

"I missed you." Her voice is so quiet, I barely hear it.

I missed you, too. Agitated, I want to get up and go, the same way I did at Longplay, the same way she did when we had coffee. It's easier, and I can focus on what I've told myself matters most. Work, which has always been straightforward, with rules I understand. Work, which is usually controllable and generally predictable.

"I want to have a sister again," she says. "I want to be a sister."

The red yarn snaps under the pressure, and the breath I draw in is so jerky, it hurts. "I don't know what to say."

"Then let's not for a bit, at least about this." Phoebe pulls back but not in a bad way.

"Okay." I take the reprieve gratefully. There's a lot to think through, and I can't right now. My mind hasn't led me to the best places lately, leaving me tentative about everything I thought was a certainty.

"We can talk instead about why you're here when you'd usually be in the office."

I'm too tired to lie and about three minutes away from complete collapse. "It's Jihoon."

She nods. "He's going back to Korea for StarLune?"

My mouth drops open. Phoebe watches me with concern.

"How did you know that's who he was?" I ask.

"After watching that video a few more times, I kind of got into them. Did some research and found out Min's real name is Choi Jihoon, and without the makeup, he looked like the same Jihoon who came to dinner and was spotted in your neighborhood today."

Little shocks zing over me. "You didn't think to text me?"

"I decided you would have told me if you wanted me to know."

"I didn't find out until a couple hours ago."

She laughs but stops when she sees my face. "Oh, you're serious. Then at dinner..."

"I thought he was Hana's cousin and no more."

"Dang." She pinches her lip. "What happened?"

I spill the whole sordid tale, and Phoebe's eyes don't leave my face. A long silence swirls in the wake of my words until she gropes around for my Coke and takes a sip.

"I'm not sure what to say," she admits. "What's your plan?"

"You're looking at it."

"Eating in a food court forever seems unsustainable."

"Not much can happen since he's going back to Korea."

"Video calls exist. Planes exist." She sees my expression. "Can we get some perspective? It's not like he's gone off to some unknown land while you pine away standing on a boulder overlooking the ocean."

All those things might exist, but I don't know if Jihoon wants them. This tentative reconciliation with Phoebe is too new for me to admit this, so instead I say, "He's an idol in Korea, and I'm a lawyer in Toronto."

"Poor Ari," she says, but the tone is kind. "Ari with her whole life mapped out so perfectly. Never having to take a detour. Always knowing where the next stop is. What will you do now that there's another road to take?"

I swing my foot out to poke her leg. "There's no other path."

"Not if you don't see it." She gets up. "I'm due to drop this off. Will you be okay?"

I'm busy frowning at the table, so it takes the words a minute to register, but I nod. "I think so."

"You can call me, Ari. Whenever you want." She grabs her bag. "I'm going to be here a while."

"Thanks. Hey, can you keep this to yourself?" I don't want this story spread to our parents before I'm ready.

"Will do, capitaine." She gives me a rakish salute.

I watch her go and almost see the thread dragging behind her. This time the ball in my chest feels loose. I feel better, and although there's more to be said between us, I only have so much brain space, and this Jihoon thing is time sensitive.

What does it mean to be an idol, anyway? It's an entire world that's unfamiliar to me. I gather my taco and cream puff remains in their wrappings and toss them into the compost bin with a newfound sense of resolution. I need to do some research to know exactly what I'm dealing with. An uninformed decision is a trash decision, for all of Jihoon's heart-over-head preaching.

I text Alex to make sure he's alone because I don't want to talk to Hana and Jihoon until I get myself sorted out. He lets me into his proxy command center when I arrive, his expression tired but satisfied.

"Here's where we are," Alex says, waving me to the cognac-leather Eames lounger as he spins on his executive chair. "It's looking good."

"Is there a horde outside my apartment building?"

"Yes."

"That's good?" We need to synchronize definitions.

"Sure is, because they're singing and not rioting." Alex rolls his neck until his vertebrae pop. "It's supposed to rain, so that will help thin the crowd overnight."

"Then I can go back home."

"About that." His face gets a serious look that means I'm not going to like whatever he's about to say. "Not for two weeks at least. A month is better."

"You've got to be kidding."

Alex rubs his nose. "StarLune has some die-hard fans who will make connections between Mr. Choi and the young, attractive Asian women in the building."

"Alex. You truly thought about those words, decided they were the exact ones you wanted, and let them leave your mouth?"

"Three for three." He's unrepentant. "Again, optics. There are some vicious gossip blogs looking to make a story out of this, true or not. People can be nasty as hell."

I can't believe this won't die down in a few days, so I tell him what he wants to hear. "I'll think about it. What about work?"

I'd already been role-playing how the conversation with Richard could possibly go.

Richard, I'd say. *I want to give you a heads-up that...I've been kind of dating a singer, and if his legions of fans and the media find out, they might start calling the office to get information about me.*

Thank you, Ariadne, he'd reply. *How lovely for you. Who is this singer?*

Then I'll send him a video of Jihoon with his blue hair, dancing while he casts scorching glances at the camera, and oh my God, what am I thinking? Richard's conservative with both big and little Cs. He went to private school. His family has been running things and being conspicuously WASPy since before Canada was a country. He'd consider this a scandal beyond redemption.

"So far, so good. Since your names haven't leaked, your job and family are safe," says Alex. My shoulders sag with relief.

"My sister met Jihoon," I say. "My parents, too."

"As Jihoon, a friend of yours and a cousin of Hana? Nothing else?"

"Since I didn't know there was anything else, yes. Phoebe guessed, though."

"Can she keep quiet?"

"Yes." We may have some issues, but I trust Phoebe not to tell after I asked her not to.

Alex strokes his chin. "Then I'll leave it for now. I don't want to cause more problems by alerting them if they have no idea."

"Won't it be on the news?"

"Will it ever!" He turns on the TV to the twenty-four-hour news channel, which is currently discussing a shortage of hospital beds. "They have it as a developing story. Sadly, it's a slow news day. What I wouldn't give for a political gaffe."

The next segment shows my apartment building, where the news anchor stands with the milling crowd of StarLune fans. "In international celebrity news, it looks like Toronto became a haven for Korean pop star Min of StarLune. The globally popular singer, who was purported missing from his home in Seoul for weeks, was photographed in a local grocery store and had apparently been hiding out in this west-end building."

He turns around. "Are you a fan of StarLune?" he asks a woman holding what looks like a flashlight with a blue heart star at the top. "Are you surprised one of the band members is in Toronto?"

She tosses her fuchsia-streaked hair and looks ecstatic. "No way! The boys have always had a soft spot for the city, and I'm thrilled he was able to come here and relax the way he deserves. We love him. Min, saranghaeyo!" She makes her fingers into a V shape by her face and blows a kiss at the camera.

"Do you have a favorite song?"

The woman starts bobbing her heart star flashlight while belting out a tune I don't recognize. The people in the crowd around her join in, a few dancing with choreographed moves I assume are associated with the song. Others start chanting and the reporter laughs. "There you have it, Kari! A happy group of StarLune fans. The band was last here in the winter, when they sold out two nights at the Rogers Centre as part of their world tour."

"This is messed up," I mutter.

Alex turns it off. "Mr. Choi is the visual, and he's very popular."

I remember that term. "What's a visual?" Right now Alex is my Virgil, guiding me through the nine circles of K-pop culture.

"The best-looking one in the group."

"They're officially ranked by their appearance?" Obviously if there were a hotness list, Jihoon would be first, but what a strange thing.

"It's not a ranking but more a role in the band."

I lower my head, trying to grasp this, as he continues, "Other channels have shown StarLune's airport footage, and they're always masked, or it's concert footage. It's hard to see Mr. Choi's face, so I don't think your parents will make the connection if they see it on the news."

That's a relief, although I'm more worried about people finding out about my parents than them finding out I brought an idol to dinner. "What about Jihoon?"

Alex looks confused. "What about him?"

I swallow hard because, even though I didn't answer the door when he knocked, I'll be unhappy (devastated) if he leaves before we talk. "Has he left for home yet?"

"No." Alex pauses. "We've been trying, but he refuses to go until he sees you."

"What?"

"You heard me, and the others won't go without him." Alex coughs. "Not going to lie here, you'd be doing me a real solid if you talk to him so we can get them all out of Toronto. The Seoul team is much better equipped to deal with this, plus once he's gone, this should die down quickly."

"Tomorrow." I know I need to talk to him again, but I'm drained and also not ready. I want to do more research into who he is first so I can be prepared.

Alex frowns. "It would help me a lot. I can't stress how much it will help if you talk to him as soon as possible. Right now, for instance."

"I said tomorrow. First thing, I promise."

I escape Alex, dragging my shopping bags into my room and noting the heavy security in the main room even though we're in a private penthouse condo. Jihoon won't leave until we talk, which goes far toward mollifying me. It's a bad situation, and ignoring Jihoon and Hana and cutting them both out of my life—I can't forgive one and not the other for the same transgression—isn't a reasonable answer. Well, it might be, but it's not a productive one, even though the juvenile part of me wants to do it to make a point.

The same way I did with Phoebe for years and look how happy that made me. I shove that thought away like I do so many others. It's better that way. Or easier, at least in the moment.

Twenty-Three

*A*lone in my room, I take stock of my surroundings. It's a homier version of an elegant hotel room, minus the branded pens and tip envelope and plus real art on the walls. The floors are deep oak and strewn with patterned area rugs that have a silken slide when I walk over them. After hanging up my new clothes in the closet—which comes with a mirror that illuminates different light settings depending on whether you want to know what you look like in daylight, dim light, or blacklight—I head for the shower.

It's like washing in a showroom. Both sinks are formed from a single block of pale stone with only a slight dip under the faucet. To someone used to a more plebeian white porcelain basin, it's unnerving in its flatness and lightning drainage speed. A full-size set of toiletries from Amorepacific lines up against the tiled wall as if Hyphen keeps this place fully stocked and waiting for VIPs.

I analyze the shower and its multitude of jets before checking the digital pad and tapping the all-over clean, regular heat option. Water flies in from every direction, even angled up from the floor high enough to hit your calves. The steam is magically fanned away before it escapes the stall. I take a shower long and hot enough to boil the day out of my very body and breathe in the smell of money via body washes.

They've even given me the option of rough or fluffy organic cotton towels.

After a thorough slathering with a floral-scented lotion so light it absorbs on contact, I pull on the new pajamas, braid my hair, and clamber into bed with my laptop.

I'm in research mode, and it feels good. I'm in control again.

The first thing I discover is that StarLune has put out an astounding amount of content. I click through pages of interviews, vlogs, music videos, award show and concert footage, dance practices, and relay dances. There are variety show clips, including one where they're all performing in unison while inexplicably dressed in inflatable vegetable costumes. This I watch for sheer entertainment value, but it's not subtitled, and I have no clue what the context, purpose, or public reaction is. This could be a normal thing for K-pop bands to do or wacky beyond belief. Jihoon is a turnip. Kit is a leek, or possibly a napa cabbage. There are thought pieces about their impact and why they're the best or most terrible band in the world.

Then there's the fan content—podcasts and reaction videos and fan cams. There are compilations and profiles and then more videos of band members. There are listicles and lyric translations and GIFs galore and so many inside jokes, I can't even.

I have to. I tap my fingers on my laptop and ponder how to prioritize this information fire hose. The first thing I should do is know all their names. That's an easy search that brings me to a useful starter video.

Two hours later, my eyes are burning and my head is spinning because I have consumed a *lot* of video. This isn't only a world I've been unaware of but an entire universe. I put the laptop aside—the fan has been whirring at a concerning volume for the past ten minutes— and try to calm down.

Alex and the others weren't exaggerating. Now that my eyes are open, I can't believe StarLune existed and I had only the barest inkling. The small sphere of life I've been content with knowing is shameful compared to what I've missed. The degree of fame Jihoon has achieved is more than I can comprehend. According to a *Rolling Stone* article, he's one of the most famous men in the world. Their top videos have over a billion views.

The sleeping video he mentioned is both legit and up to thirty million views. Thirty million people wanted to watch him take a freaking nap. Or ten million people watched it three times or three million ten times each. Any way I slice it, a lot of people were personally invested in watching a guy lie there with his eyes shut.

What bugs me most is that if I had paid more attention to Alex, I wouldn't currently be trying to splash my way out of this pool of ignorance. If I had done the research right away instead of putting it off to the last minute, I'd have recognized Jihoon and his band of merry men. This is what I get for worrying about the clients I wanted instead of the ones I had.

I open the laptop and dive back in to avoid thinking about this. A video of Jihoon singing comes up. Curious, I click it.

Jihoon—Min—is astonishing. There's no other word. The clip is from a concert, and he sings a solo as he dances alone on the stage. When his deep voice goes breathy, it traces along my skin. He moves with smooth effortlessness that must take years of work to achieve.

I can't deal with this. It's time to call in the big guns. I grab my phone. Hana is at my door in less than five minutes.

"I remain very mad at you," I warn as I let her in.

"I know. I completely deserve it."

"I'm willing to table that for now because I need help."

"Understood." She nods. "What help?"

I wave at the laptop. "Jihoon. Min. I have no idea who this guy is. It's like he's two separate people, and I don't know which is the real one."

"They're the same. Min is only his stage persona."

Her phone lights up, and she makes a face. "Hold on."

I glance over and see who it's from. "Oh no." If there's one person who will be more upset than me, it's Mrs. Choi, who is currently blowing up her daughter's phone.

Hana rolls her shoulders. "It's been a real party."

"She's mad?"

In response, Hana shows me about three screens worth of a text block. I catch a few English words, and it's enough to see that, as usual, Mrs. Choi is pulling no punches: lie, shame, embarrass, respect.

What's left of my anger turns to sympathy. Hana's never had an easy time with her mother, and for Mrs. Choi to resort to berating her over text means Hana must have reached the end of her almost limitless patience and started to ignore her calls. She pushes the phone away with a resolute gesture. "Back to Jihoon."

"Do you want to talk about—"

"Jihoon. Yes. Only Jihoon."

"Fine, but—"

"We are not doing this right now."

I catch sight of her red eyes. The kind thing is to let her be. "Okay."

She turns away, and I pretend not to see her dash the back of her hand across her eyes. "His duality confuses you."

"They're too different to be the same guy." I navigate to a video that shows Jihoon wearing a mesh top under a leather harness as he kneels, doing a violent hip thrust. The curves of his thighs in skintight black vinyl pants are honest-to-God catching the stage lights as his fingers trace up his throat to his face...I cough, feeling like the room suddenly became very warm.

"This is weird to watch with you," Hana says.

"Yeah, I get that." I can't look away.

"You need to get to know him when he's Min but not performing, because that's pretty intense." She frowns at the wall before her face clears. "I know!"

She grabs the laptop and pulls up a video of StarLune sitting casually in jeans and hoodies, staring at a video inset on the screen.

"What's this?"

Hana skips an ad. "Reaction videos."

"I saw those. There's lots of screaming."

"No, this is a band reaction. Those were fan videos."

"They sit around watching their own music videos and tape it?" I try for Amused Avenue and end up taking a hard left at Snide Street, where I put myself in cruise.

"It's a thing to not watch the final cut until they're together. Quit being ignorant."

"Hey!"

"Am I wrong?"

I sulk a bit before answering. "No."

She clicks play. There are no English subtitles, but the tones and expressions of a bunch of guys taking the piss are fairly universal.

"I don't see how this helps." My protest is half-hearted because the video they're watching shows Jihoon with a black velvet blazer, no shirt, and a thick chain around his throat. He's so hot, the others whistle and whack him on the back of the head as he covers his face.

"They're telling Jihoon he looks like a snack," Hana translates unnecessarily.

I watch Jihoon laughing with his friends, and I swear, it's the man I know, the thoughtful guy who likes shoes in excessive quantities and talking about cereal brands and leaving notebooks all over the living room. But... "This is filmed," I say. "He's putting on an act. It's his *I'm a regular guy* act."

She blows out her breath in a slow, controlled whistle. "You're impossible. Use your eyes. This is Jihoon. It's the way you're the same Ari goofing around at home as you are the professional Ariadne in the office. Different facets of the same person."

Except Jihoon's transformation is far more extreme, so extreme it's hard to trust. I push the laptop away. "I don't know what to do."

This activates Hana's latent inner counselor, and she sits cross-legged on the bed, the better to examine me with a critical eye. "You need to define what you need to decide. What exactly is it you don't know what to do? Forgive Jihoon? Continue a relationship with him?"

"We don't have a relationship," I point out with some acerbity. "You came home early, and then his global fame got in the way."

"Do you want one? You need to know what you want before you can make a decision on anything."

"What I want?"

Hana nods emphatically, then pulls her hair off from where it's stuck to her ChapStick-covered lips. "Based on your priorities, values, and needs." She looks like she's about to launch into a lecture, so I hold up both hands to pause her.

"I'll think about it."

"What you'll do is get tied in knots trying to convince yourself of a decision that won't mess with your precious career regardless of whether it's the right choice."

"I won't." I definitely will.

Hana leans over and fishes a loonie out of her pocket before handing it to me. "Heads or tails," she says.

"Are you suggesting I let a one-dollar coin dictate my life?"

"Works for deciding between sushi and pizza for dinner, so it'll scale." She taps the coin. "Heads, you never talk to Jihoon or I again. Tails, you accept that we both screwed up for various reasons, mostly because we are human, and you forgive us."

"This is useless."

She makes a tossing motion, so I flip it up in the air before snatching the coin and slapping it down on the back of my hand. We both lean over.

"Heads," she says quietly. "Never talk to us again."

I drop the coin. "Obviously I'm not going to do that."

"Then stop pretending it's an option and move forward."

Tough love Hana is tough. "Even if I forgive him, nothing can happen with Jihoon," I say. "He lives in Korea. He's leaving soon."

"None of that is different from what it was two days ago when you were ready to go over to his place."

"He's a celebrity. I don't like celebrities."

"To repeat, you were doing fine before you knew that, and it's not like he got a new personality in the last six hours. Also you don't know any celebrities."

"I work with them through Luxe."

"You indirectly work with some through Luxe," she corrects. "You also work directly with a bunch of douchebags at Doperly and Twittings, and you seem to manage that well enough. Why are so many of them named after verbs, like Chase or Rob?"

"Don't forget Skip."

"You do not work with a Skip." She sees my face. "You do. I'm so sorry."

"This isn't me." I tug at my hair. "I want to make partner. I want to be the city's top lawyer. I want people coming to me for whatever's the legal equivalent of a TED Talk. I don't chase rock stars."

"Idol," she says. "Not rock star."

"What?"

"Jihoon is a K-pop idol, not some graying old man in leggings screwing barely legal groupies in a tour bus. He's disciplined, works hard, and trained daily for years to get to where he is."

"The same feeling applies."

She puffs out her cheeks. "Look. You're coming at this from the wrong angle. You met him as Jihoon. That's who he is. Min is who he is onstage. It's his performance side."

"He lied to me." Not even a little lie, like *sure, babe, that dress is pretty*. Jihoon's lie blew through the stratosphere.

"Last summer, when that guy at the bar asked for your number, you faked an Irish accent and said you were flying back home to Moose Jaw the next day."

I glare at her. "I hardly think me getting a stranger off my back is on par with Jihoon's story. He played me."

There. It was out. He'd played me—both of them did—and I feel foolish. I mean, how oblivious could I be that I didn't recognize he was lying to my face? I'm a lawyer—a good one—and I couldn't even read that blatant a fib. What does that say about me, about my judgment? My perspicacity?

"Ari." Hana's voice softens. "It's a big world, and you can't be expected to know every part of it. The question is, now that you know, what are you going to do?"

"Nothing. What can I do?"

"For crying out loud." Hana's momentary sympathy evaporates when it butts against the immovable force that is my self-pity. "Will you listen to yourself? You like him. Had fun with him. He likes you." She pauses. "I've never seen you so open with someone, Ari. It's like you've known each other for ages. Yeah, he lived in our place, but you two clicked. Eventually."

I sigh, and this time I know Hana hears it as the defeat it is. "I do like him, but I feel used. And...small. He's surrounded by beautiful, famous women who get him. Who get that lifestyle."

"You are beautiful, inside and out, so shut up. Plus, to Jihoon, you get him."

"Not the pressure of that life. Also they speak Korean."

"Korean is not some alien language where you have to amputate a limb to communicate. Get a goddamn app."

I ignore that. "The distance is a problem. We're both busy at work."

"Those are legitimate concerns," Hana allows.

"I don't know what to do." I always know what to do. I don't act unless I know exactly what the outcome will be. This is so out of the bounds of what I normally experience that I don't even have a blue-print of how to reasonably approach it.

"You don't need to do anything but talk to Jihoon," Hana says.

"Sounds better in theory," I grumble.

Hana leans over and gives me a hug. "I'm sorry I didn't tell you."

"I know." I'm not mad anymore, only worn out.

"Jihoon is as well."

I'm done thinking about this tonight. There's a headache localized entirely in my left temple. "I'll sleep on it."

"You do that." She leaves, and I tuck into bed.

The black-out shades on the window give the room a deep dark-ness that's almost like the inside of a movie theater before your eyes adjust. Scenes play of Jihoon laughing and playing with my hair. How could he not tell me? What else is he hiding? He was so good at show-ing me only the parts of himself he chose, and there I was like a loser, talking to him about real things that mattered to me. Actual feelings about work and my family. I thought it was real, but the time we had was as authentic as a stage set.

A heavy disappointment seeps through me at the loss of what could have been. I wish it could have been different. I wish he lived here and that he was who he said and that we could have tried to build something together. If he'd been a normal guy, we could have gone long-distance. We could have kept connected. But there's that crowd in front of my condo and all the footage of StarLune hurrying toward cars and safety. How can any relationship survive that, even without the dis-tance? I don't compete in contests I can't win, and Jihoon doesn't need me when he has that much public adoration at his fingertips.

I bury my face in the pillow and try to think rationally. This reveal could be for the best. It keeps my time with Jihoon short and mostly sweet, and in a few days, this'll be nothing but a memory. I'll be free again to concentrate on my career.

Exactly what I want.

Twenty-Four

*E*ven though Jihoon has seen me stumble around with tangled hair and eyes puffy with sleep, I take my time getting ready in the morning. It's for me, I assure myself as I fix my hair so it falls loose behind my shoulders in waves from my night braid. Not because I feel intimidated now that I know who he is. Ariadne Hui does not get intimidated by pop culture celebrities, even if Jihoon is on a completely different level than some season three reality TV reject.

However, Ariadne Hui doesn't usually refer to herself in the third person, so it looks like all bets are off.

I did another hour of research when I woke at dawn, unable to sleep and shaken from a nightmare of my office surrounded by television cameras. This time I focused more on StarLune news and concert footage. There are videos of the band arriving and departing various places surrounded by buff black-clad security guards holding back crowds of screaming fans clutching cell phones. Half the time, I can't even tell which one is Jihoon, since they're covered in masks and sunglasses and hats as the flashes strobe over them. The experience looks both physically and mentally unbearable and provides a fresh understanding of his fishbowl life.

It's the concert footage that astounds me, though. I watched stunned as he performed in stadiums for tens of thousands of people.

What kind of person can do that, hold so many people's unwavering attention for hours on end? Hana can talk all she wants about personas and multilayers of self or whatever, but the fact remains that Jihoon is one man, and that one man has people from around the world panting for him and watching videos of him napping. That one man has enough confidence, enough well-earned arrogance, to step on a stage and know he can control the crowd with a single movement.

What does he want with me?

Looks like Ariadne Hui gets a little intimidated by celebrities after all.

This might be the last time we talk, but I want to know everything I should have known in the first place. I feel almost calm. Resolute. Nothing will happen between us because what *can* happen? I was a fool to think otherwise. Despite this conviction, my muscles are so tense my teeth chatter when I finally send the text I've been sitting on for minutes. I'm ready to talk if you're free.

Jihoon's at my door within thirty seconds, but when I open it, he steps back, eyes flickering over my face as if to read the future of the conversation.

"Hi," I say.

This encourages him enough to come in, and I wave him to the table by the window. The curtains are open to show Bloor Street, muted gray from the older buildings stained with pollution and the cloudy morning. Jihoon's white shirt plays up the tan of his skin and reveals the thickness of his neck and little divots of his collarbones. His hair is pushed back from his face, and two small hoops decorate his left ear, and one hangs from his right. I hadn't realized his ears were pierced.

When we're both seated, I look him in the eye. "What else didn't you tell me?" Better to have the great cleanse right now.

"Nothing."

"Do you have a girlfriend?"

His head jerks up. "No, of course not."

"Boyfriend?"

"No boyfriend either."

"Are Kit and Daehyun mad?"

"They are displeased."

This seems like an understatement since they had to come halfway across the world to haul his ass home, but I leave it alone. "Are you going back to Korea?"

"Yes." He tugs on one of the silver hoops. "I have to."

"Why?"

Jihoon wrinkles his nose as he looks out the window. "The company is furious. I have to fulfill my contract." He pauses. "I owe it to my members. StarLune is five people, and no matter what my personal feelings, I need to act in their best interest."

"At the expense of your own?"

He gives me a confused look. "I can't make the decision to break up the band by myself, no matter how I feel. That would be selfish."

"You were going to."

He tucks his hands into the sleeves of his black sweater. "I had a fantasy, and it ended. Like all fantasies."

I keep the questions going. "When are you leaving?"

"Soon. This was terrible timing." Jihoon stares at the ground. "I added to everyone's overwork and the stress we always get when we're releasing new songs. I forced them to lie for me."

"Right." His self-flagellation is making it hard to stay mad at him. We might as well end on a friendly note. I stand from the table and start pacing to get rid of the jumpy energy that's playing over my skin and driving into my bones. "Why did you even start all this with me?"

He lays his head on the table with an audible thump. "I wasn't thinking, Ari. I only wanted you—selfish again. I didn't think of StarLune or the future or even your feelings, only of myself. I felt a connection when I met you that first day. You see me. You treated me like my family does."

"They pull knives on each other?"

"That part, no." He grins, but it quickly slips away. "They don't act like I'm different from anyone else. I'm not an idol, only Jihoon, a man who works as a performer but who also nearly burned down the kitchen making nurungji when he was thirteen. I feel normal with them, and with you. Calm. Safe."

When I woke up, I was sure what I wanted or at least confident as to what would happen. We'd talk, say goodbye, and then I'd be left with memories. When I turn and see Jihoon frowning on the other side of the room, it's clear that I might not have been as certain as I told myself. I like being with him, too, and it hurts to give that up. We've barely known each other a month, but the intimacy of living in the same apartment has made me comfortable with him in a way I don't usually feel. Actually, in a way I never feel, not even with Hana. He lied and the residual of that hurt remains but both Hana and Jihoon have made it clear they had reasons. I might not fully agree, but I understand enough to forgive them.

"People do things for me because they have to or they think it will benefit them." Jihoon runs his hand along the edge of the table. "You never did. At first you seemed so hard and cold, like you are at work, but your actions were kind. Generous."

Pretend it's a legal negotiation. You're working for your client, Ms. A. Hui, and your job is to get all the details and figure out the best plan of action.

"I like things to be organized," I say. "Predictable. This is the opposite of that."

He crosses the room and reaches out to touch my jawline, letting his fingers trace down to my throat. My pulse flutters as he passes over my skin. "Have you thought perhaps you don't crave routine as much as you tell yourself?"

I pull away. "What do you know about people anyway?" He lives the rarified life of a pop star. He never has to interact with the hoi polloi.

Jihoon looks at me in disbelief. "I study people. I watch them.

Do you think I write songs out of the blue? I watch people live and bleed, and I bleed, too. That's what people want, what they need so they don't feel alone."

"I see."

"No, Ari, because you don't bleed—ever. You don't know yourself at all."

"You don't know me well enough to say that," I snap.

"Yet it's true."

I open my mouth to argue...but I can't.

"You saw me, the real me, before all this"—he points around the room—"got in the way. I want you to keep seeing me like that, not as Min. Can you?"

I examine him. He looks tired and worn and painfully genuine. Right now he's Jihoon and not Min. What about when he leaves this room? Who is he then?

"What do you want out of this?" I ask as I walk back to the table and sit. "Us, whatever that is."

"It would be best if I go home and we forget we ever met," he says, looking me in the eyes.

My skin tingles, then goes cold, because these are my own thoughts from last night. "I know."

"Do you want that?" he asks.

"Do you?"

"I asked first."

"You're the one who likes to talk and who caused this mess."

"Then no." Before I can speak, he continues, "I want to be with you, learn you. We're new together, but I see a path. I don't know how it will happen, but that's what I want."

"So do I." I rush the words out without thinking, but they feel right. I let myself believe them even as I wonder what the hell I'm doing. This isn't what I had decided. This isn't a plan based on logic and a cold assessment of the facts.

Living with my heart, I guess. I don't know that I like it.

"Now what?" I ask.

He stands up and leans over, fingers sliding over my fist. "I kiss you," he says seriously. "Then we talk."

I wriggle away. "First we talk."

Now he's the one to start pacing. "I want you to come to Korea with me."

"Whoa, tiger." I blink. "Right now?"

"Soon. For a visit. You can meet the other members, Xin and Sangjun— you would like them. They will like you. We could explore Seoul."

A vacation. I once made travel plans for a friend's trip to Korea, yearning to be there myself as I followed the curves of the Han River on the map with my finger. It's enticing, but...I come to my senses. "Alex says no one knows about me now. If I go to Korea with you, that goes out the window. And you said you'd be busy."

"We would make it work. Newlight would prefer we didn't date because of our image, but I don't have a formal dating ban."

"A what now?"

"We weren't allowed to date as trainees or in the first two years after our debut," he says casually, like this is a normal action for an employer to take. "It's to help us focus on our work and avoid scandals."

"Uh..." I honestly have no response to this.

"Sangjun, one of the other band members, was dating someone for a year. Newlight told him to keep it secret but didn't forbid it. As long as the public doesn't find out, it's not a problem."

"What if they do find out?"

"It compromises that person's safety, and some fans don't like it, but we have ways to keep our privacy." Jihoon leans against the wall. "The distance is an issue because I can't stay here. We have a comeback, and there's much preparation."

"How long will that take?"

He bites his lip. "At least another three months of practice and then promotion, plus the end-of-year award shows. There's also a special fan concert in a month."

"I guess we figure out how to text around a time difference," I say. I've decided this is what I want, so I'm going to go for it.

"Long-distance? You would do that?"

"There don't seem to be other options," I say. "Let's try it, and then we can talk visits."

He already has his phone out and is tapping away. My own buzzes with a calendar invite. "What's this?" I ask.

"The day after our VIP concert. We have free time then, perhaps even a few days." He grins at me. "Seoul is lovely in the fall."

I pretend to consider it. "I do have a few places I wanted to visit."

"I'm sure you will plan the best itinerary." He puts his phone away and comes over to me. "I will, of course, be pleased to accompany you."

"I like to walk," I warn him. Now it's my turn to move closer, almost enough to touch.

A small smile appears on his face, and he pulls my hair over my shoulder to bare my neck. When he leans down to whisper in my ear, his lips brush my skin. "I'm aware," he says, voice almost a purr. "I like to shop."

He doesn't move back when I drift a hand up his chest and tilt my head so my hair brushes his arm. "I can do some shopping if we go to bookstores."

His hand covers mine, clasping it against his heart. "You can't read Korean."

My other hand comes up around the back of his neck, and I press my fingers to his warm skin. He shivers. "Doesn't matter. I like bookstores. And I want to see the pink muhly grass."

"I know the perfect spot for photos. Deal." He drops a tiny kiss on my face, right beside my ear, and pulls back so we face each other. "Now the kissing," he says against my mouth. His hands grip my hips to pull me close.

"Hold on." I wiggle away and accept the calendar invite. "There, it's official."

"Good," he says as he guides me back into his embrace. "I'm glad we've resolved the travel plans."

I don't have time to answer before he acts. It doesn't matter—now is definitely time for the kissing.

I'm not sure if it's because there's a time limit before he leaves, but I don't think I've ever gotten in bed faster with a man in my life. Jihoon murmurs against my neck, his breath warm. I put my hand on his chest and am momentarily distracted.

"Why are you so smooth?" I lean down to check. Totally hairless.

"Laser treatment." He kisses my shoulder, then lets his tongue trace a wandering path. "Easier than shaving all the time."

"How about…" I reach down, and he grabs my hand.

"How about you'll find that out soon enough?" He pins my hand down and tickles me until I'm laughing so hard, I'm breathless, then watches intently as my giggles trail off into little gasps before I pull him down to kiss me. His hand releases mine and drifts down my side as he plants kisses along my throat.

Then he dips much farther down until I'm breathless for a very different reason, and there's nothing else in my mind but him.

Twenty-Five

Two very satisfying hours later, Jihoon's phone buzzes, and he rolls away from where he's curled against me. Because another human in my vicinity is looking at their phone, I have no choice but to look at mine. I lean over, grimacing at the stiffness in my legs, and grab it from the side table. Hidden among the notifications I set last night to keep informed of StarLune and Min posts—and there are many—is a text from Hana. It's a GIF of Jihoon dancing, featuring hip thrusts.

That's where he gets it from. Practice. I approve, feeling his muscles tense and relax as I outline the gorgeously detailed tiger tattoo on his back with my fingers. That there are memes of the man currently in bed with me is as disturbing as you'd expect. He's a public figure who shares his life with a huge and devoted fan base. A terrible and extremely unwelcome feeling rears up, and although it's not one I like to recognize, it's easy enough to identify: inadequacy.

Jihoon leans over and brushes my hair away so he can kiss my shoulder before he buries his face in my neck. When he speaks, the words flutter against my bare skin. "My flight is booked for tonight."

Having fantastic sex with Jihoon right before he leaves indefinitely for Korea is not going in my Best Decisions Hall of Fame, but I regret nothing. I shake off the anxiety about what will happen after today to look at what's happening now, in the moment, or at least in the next few hours.

"Want me to come to the airport with you?" I shiver, and he glances up at the air-conditioning vent before tugging the covers up to my neck.

"I'd love that. No one will see you in the car." He kisses me again, then brushes the tip of his nose against my cheek. He's so affectionate, I can't stand it, and I try not to think about the StarLune fame stuff.

Not happening. The question bursts out before I can stop it. "Do you sleep with your fans?"

"Ari, never." Jihoon turns over to gather me tighter into his arms but pulls away to get off my hair after I squeal. He retakes his spot once he gathers it up and tucks it away.

"Really?"

"None of us would." He kisses my temple, then rests his forehead against my cheek as his hand strokes along my side. "It would be a huge controversy, a scandal. Too risky, and to have a relationship with a Starry would be stressful. You would be worried about disappointing them once they knew the real you, not the idol."

His comments trigger another thought. "Money."

"What about it?" He ghosts little kisses along my arm.

"You're rich."

More unrepentant kisses. "I am."

I yank my arm back and glare at him. "This whole time, you could have been eating in five-star restaurants, but you pretended to be poor."

"I wasn't pretending," he says. "I have money now. For a long time, we didn't. As trainees, we lived in a crowded dorm. Even after our debut, we ate ramyeon and lived in two rooms for the five of us. The ceiling leaked over Xin's bed when it rained."

"Really?"

"He had to sleep with a bucket." Jihoon rolls onto his back, bringing me with him so I lie on his chest. "Idol life doesn't last long either. My money is in boring investments."

I recall one of the videos from my rabbit hole last night. "Don't you collect vintage watches?" One of them had cost over a half a million dollars.

"Those are investments." Jihoon clasps his arms around my lower back and moves the conversation on. "Kit hyeong and Daehyun would like to meet you properly at lunch, with no lies between you."

My stomach growls loud enough to vibrate between us. He laughs. "Hana will come as well."

"I'd like that." I'm curious to talk to Kit and Daehyun now that I know who they are. I can tell how important they are to Jihoon. Plus, they might dish some dirt on his early years. "What about Alex?"

"He says he's busy." He grimaces. "Cleaning up the mess I made."

I'm dressed before Jihoon and go out to the kitchen to fetch some coffee. The fridge incorporates NASA-level technology, and I poke buttons until it disgorges some spherical ice from a slot for Jihoon's cup.

Kit comes in while I'm struggling, and we look at each other. I now know he's StarLune's leader as well as Jihoon's best friend. With everything out in the open, he looks more tired but less tense.

"Coffee?" I say to open conversation.

He passes me a cup that I tuck under the machine. "I heard your flight is booked for tonight," I say.

"It is." Kit's eyes are trained on the slowly filling cup.

I get enough terse answers from my job, where I actually get paid to put up with that shit. I don't need it from him, so I nod and start to leave. Hopefully he'll be in a more talkative mood at lunch, but I can't worry about it now. I've got enough on my plate.

"Ariadne." Kit holds up a hand to stop me. "Can we talk?"

"About what?" I put Jihoon's cup on the counter and take a sip of my own coffee.

An unhappy smile tugs at his mouth. "Jihoon told me you were smart, so you must know."

I automatically go on the offensive. "I assume you want to ask me personal questions about your friend instead of asking him directly."

Under his breath, he mutters, "First Sangjun, now Jihoon." He raises his voice. "We all want to quit sometimes. It can be a hard life, but it's what we chose because the rewards outweigh the sacrifices."

I look at him curiously. He sounds bitter. "Do they?" I ask. "For you as well? All of you?"

The machine beeps but he ignores it. "You have no idea the damage you'll do to him if you don't let this go," he says.

I glare at him, then glance toward the bedrooms and lower my voice. "Don't you mean damage to StarLune?"

"That, too," he says. "Although Jihoon will bear the most pressure. He has no time for a relationship. He's about to start working eighteen-hour days. How do you see yourself fitting in? What will you take from him so he can make space for you?"

Kit has some nerve. I put my coffee on the counter next to Jihoon's because I can feel the tension flowing down my arms, an indicator my hands are about to start shaking. I tamp down my instinctive response, which is to tell Kit to take a long jump off a short pier. He's trying to protect his friend, I tell myself. He's also protecting his precious StarLune and the many millions it makes him, but that perspective is less kind.

"You should ask Jihoon that," I say.

"Jihoon tries to do his best for everyone around him, which means he gets stuck," Kit says slowly.

"Stuck."

"If I want to go left, you wish to go right, and he's in the middle, how can he make everyone happy?"

I decide to be difficult. "I don't want to go right."

"I know you don't want to go right," Kit says through gritted teeth. "I'm using direction as a metaphor for the many priorities competing for his very limited time."

"Yeah, I get that, thanks. I also know he's an adult who came to Toronto by himself, stayed because he wanted to, and is leaving because you're making him. None of it has to do with me, so don't try to paint me as some Yoko Ono stealing your man because that's bullshit, and you know it."

"You've barely known each other a month," Kit says with disgust. "You think it's worth Jihoon risking his career for that? The dream he's worked for since he was a teenager?"

Like I've worked for mine. I don't reply.

"Do you know what the fans will do if they find out about you? You can kiss your privacy goodbye." He eyes me. "Unless that's what you want."

I pick up both coffees and put Hana's advice for dealing with asshole comments into play. "Wow," I say, holding his gaze. For good measure, I shake my head sadly, as if thinking about what a pitiful human he is to say such a disgusting thing. "Wow."

Then I leave.

———

By the time I get back to the room, I see the downside to Hana's advice because I'm brimming with satisfying one-liners I wish I could go back to hurl at Kit. Jihoon hasn't come out of the shower, and I pace the room before deciding not to tell him. I'm sure he's had to deal with Mr. Interference on his own and that the message he received was similar.

The shower turns off as Yuko calls from Luxe. "I know it's Saturday, but are you busy?"

"Yes." This is not the proper professional response, so I try again. "I mean, what's going on?"

"Ines needs you in Niagara. We've been trying to land the Hotel

Xanadu as a client. She set up a last-minute wine tour for some of their important guests, but life sucks, so there might be some issues. She'd like you on hand in case of emergencies."

I glance over my shoulder at the mussed-up bed. "It's not the best time." Also not professional, but this time it's worth it.

"Ari, I'm sorry. This is a big deal for us, and we can't risk a screwup. If you can't go, can you suggest a colleague who can?"

That's not going to happen; I can't let Yesterly and Havings think I can't handle my workload, and there's no one I trust. "I can leave in a few minutes." Thank God Alex had someone drive my car over from my apartment.

"I'll send you the location and tell her you'll be there." Yuko hangs up.

I check around the room for my laptop, which I tuck into my bag. I'm ready to leave by the time Jihoon emerges from his shower.

He looks me over. "What happened?"

"I need to go to work."

"Now?" His face falls.

"I'm afraid so." I try to not feel guilty—this is work, after all, and he's about to leave for the same reason. "It's an emergency."

"Can you go after lunch?"

I shake my head, thankful to have an excuse to miss lunch with Kit. "I'm sorry. I shouldn't be too late."

"Then I'll give this to you now." He hands me a little red box with *Cartier* written in gold script across the top. When I falter, staring, he flips the lid up. "This is to remind you to make time for what matters." He smiles. "Like me. Us."

The loveliest watch I've ever seen is nestled around a tiny black pillow, the little diamonds around the face sparkling under the lights from the bathroom.

"I can't," I say. "I can't take this."

"I disagree." He takes my hand and wraps the leather band

around my wrist. Damn it. Now that it's on, all my protests die. It's gorgeous.

Jihoon looks pleased. "I knew the style would be perfect for you."

I'm freaking out a little, but I manage to say, "Thank you."

He shows me his own wrist. I raise my eyebrows. "We match?"

"I like when couples dress the same back home," he defends himself. He ducks his head, almost shy, making me laugh and tilt my head to catch his eye.

"I don't mind matching you." I line up our arms and take a photo. "Only for me," I assure him. "Not to post online."

"I trust you." He beams, then strokes my wrist with his thumb. "I'll miss being with you every day, Ari."

I go up on my tiptoes to leave a kiss on his jaw, but he twists down to kiss me properly. For those few seconds, I forget about Niagara and the plane that will take him back home in a few hours. Kissing Jihoon is like entering a retreat created for the two of us.

He's the first to pull back this time. "Don't be late," he says, dropping a final kiss on my head.

Now I feel like a true heel for leaving for work. "I'll be back soon."

He doesn't try to stop me, and part of me wonders if I wish he would. I text a quick apology to Hana before heading for Niagara, my mind a mix of Jihoon and work.

Mostly Jihoon.

Better change that to mostly work. Work is here and now, and Jihoon will be gone soon. Work won't.

Twenty-Six

I arrive in Niagara ninety minutes later and hurriedly navigate to a small boutique winery off the picturesque parkway that follows the Niagara River to the waterfalls. Ines waits under a tree, looking as if she doesn't have a care in the world. Her pristine white suit plays up the deep brown of her skin. She's always so put together and often has a perfectly arranged Hermès scarf at her neck. Today's is an eye-catching mix of pale pink and dark green.

"Ari, thank you."

I smile, but a tiny part of me thinks, *I could be having outrageous sex with Jihoon right now*. I tamp that down and focus on the job.

She glances at my wrist, where my new watch catches the sun. "Cartier?"

"It was a gift," I say.

Ines nods in approval.

"What?" I ask.

"Someone values you the way you deserve be valued. It's good to see." She points me to her car. "We'll go together so we can talk."

I check my phone as Ines briefs me. Nothing from Jihoon, and I try not to let it disappoint me. Crowding my phone are more notifications about StarLune. I should turn them off, but I'm also curious about what people are saying. So far, it's still shock and speculation on why he's in Toronto and places where people are sure they saw him. No mention of me or Hana, thank God.

The rest of the afternoon and early evening is a blur as I follow Ines between wineries to smooth out details. Much of what Luxe does is last-minute to accommodate the whims of their clients, who apparently have the future-planning abilities of marmosets. Everything is perfect—the weather is clear and warm, the wine is ready, and I've sacrificed my last day with Jihoon for an overpampered socialite to come enjoy it with her parasitic posse.

The real kicker is that I didn't even need to do much besides look over some contract wording that I probably could have done by phone. Why didn't I push back harder?

During breaks, I check the increasing traffic of StarLune posts. It was a bad idea to set the notifications. I should mute them, but it's like watching a building collapse. I can't look away. Although I've accepted Jihoon—Min—and StarLune are a phenomenon, I don't think I internalized it completely until now. The sheer volume of posts tramples my ignorance into the ground. I put my phone away, promising to only check every hour. Every half hour, I amend, taking one more peek.

When we finish at the final stop, it's almost six, and I want to get back to Toronto. "Are we good?" I ask Ines, trying to keep my voice as patient as possible.

"I'll drive you back to your car." She smiles at me. "It was a relief to have you here although you didn't have much to do. Some of those wineries can be difficult about special clients with no lead time, and I wanted to be prepared."

"Of course," I mutter.

I text Jihoon that I'm on my way back as Ines starts driving. When her phone rings, she puts it on speaker.

"Ines," she says in a smooth voice.

"Hey, Ms. Ines, the guests are gone." It's Gregor, the driver.

"What?" Her hands tighten around the wheel.

"The ladies I was driving around? They're gone."

"Gone where?" she asks. I look at Ines's itinerary as she talks to Gregor and see they should be enjoying mussels while overlooking the Niagara gorge whirlpool right now.

"A waiter at the last place told them about some strip club where the guys only wear steel-toed boots and, uh, tool belts? I guess he called them a cab, and they went over."

I try not to giggle at Ines's face. Tool belts?

Ines, however, handles it like a pro. "Gregor, you stay there in case they come back."

"Will do, boss."

Ines pulls over. "Sorry, I need to take care of this."

"Of course." My leg starts trembling with stress, but it's not like I can walk to my car from here, so the sooner this is dealt with, the faster I'm on my way home. I take a surreptitious look at my phone. StarLune notifications are off the charts, and I clear them all with a swipe. I don't need Jihoon's fame shoved in my face this much.

Ines calls a local contact, who, not surprisingly given the clues, knows exactly which club it is. "It's called the Jackhammer," the woman says with enthusiasm. "Yeah, I can see why they went."

Ines's eyebrows rise as she glances at me. We're both thinking the same thing. "You've been there?" she asks.

"Sure. They have the best nacho poutine around."

Ines hangs up and stares at the phone. "Tool belts," she says thoughtfully.

I try not to laugh. "Where do you think they wear the work socks?"

Her face twitches as she starts the car again.

The bar is about ten minutes away, and Jihoon calls as we enter the little dimly lit foyer. I answer because I want to talk to him in case I'm delayed further.

"Ari? Where are you?"

Although it's not as loud as a dance club, the place is lit up like someone set off fireworks. Ines heads to the right, and I sniff cautiously as I look left. It reeks of fried food, sweat, and Tory Burch perfume, and I raise my voice to talk into the phone so Jihoon can hear me. "I'm at a bar."

"A bar? I thought you were leaving." He sounds more confused than upset. I edge into the main room so I can multitask finding these women and talking to Jihoon, but cheers erupt as a man takes to the stage swinging a sledgehammer. The entire effect is more nerve-racking than arousing as I wait for him to accidentally take out the stripper pole.

"The guests disappeared. We're trying to find...oh my God."

A man dressed in a jockstrap and tool belt has popped up in front of me. "Looking for a good time, baby girl?" he asks, twitching his oiled pecs in my direction. "I like the cute ones. I'll give you a discount, make it good."

There's a choked noise on the phone. "*Ari?*"

Poor Jihoon. "It's for work. I'll call you back." I hang up.

Tool Belt Man drops me a wink. "Boyfriend, huh? Have him come by. I don't mind."

I ignore that. "I'm looking for five women. Mostly blond and they're probably drunk."

He adjusts his belt. "Yeah? Take your pick, baby girl."

I leave my new, almost naked friend and start peering into booths, increasingly desperate to get on my way. The nacho poutine, which is about six inches high, does look good, though. I'm fending off another tool belt handyman and am about to recheck the tables when a text comes from Ines.

Found them, it says. Meet me at the door.

The best message of my life. I race back to the exit and meet with Ines, who's outside taking deep breaths.

"They're good?" I ask.

"Very happy, and I have learned several different applications of the term *flexibility* tonight," she says. "Let me run you to your car. Gregor can pick them up."

I take a photo of the neon sign, including the Pec Popper, who is blowing me a kiss, and send it to Jihoon.

Me: Taking you here next time you're in Canada.

Jihoon: Can't wait baby girl.

Me: Shut up. On my way back.

I delete the next flood of StarLune update notifications, and this time I turn the damn things off. I have plenty of stress already, thanks.

———

I'm going to be late.

Seven thirty comes, and I check my phone. I've kept Jihoon updated on my painfully slow progress, and I see the message I've been dreading. We need to leave for the airport soon.

I can make it, I send back.

Ten minutes later, I've moved about three kilometers. Soon comes another message, read out by my phone.

We have to go. I'll miss you. I glance at the screen to see Jihoon's added a series of hearts and a photo of him blowing a kiss.

There's no way I can get to the condo in time, but I'm going to see Jihoon and that's it. I keep driving as I tabulate my options. I can go to the airport directly, but I won't be able to say goodbye to him in departures like normal people.

I can't make it back, but I have an idea. I text Jihoon. I can meet you. Then I give the GPS coordinates for a gas station off the highway on the way to the airport.

He sends back a series of hearts. Yes.

I hang up and don't bother to check the time as I wait for the traffic to move.

———

The traffic gods bless me with a few breaks, but I'm late to the empty gas station. I check my phone.

> We're here.
> Are you close?

Then, a few minutes later. We have to go for our flight.

God damn the sexy tool belt strippers. I text Jihoon. I'm sorry. Traffic. I'm here. I can't believe I missed you.

I lean back in the seat. Should I call him? I will, the second the tears stop welling up in my eyes.

Now that Jihoon's gone and the chances of seeing him in person for a long time—if ever—are very slim, I admit that I'm perhaps on the brink of something a little more than a crush. Beside me sits my laptop, and I throw it to the back seat with a vicious motion. Work. Was it worth it to disappoint Jihoon so I could be there as a just-in-case for Ines? Staring out the windshield at the bored gas attendant working the cash, I glimpse what Hana's been trying to tell me all these years. Work is work, but it doesn't have to be the entirety of my life. I ignored her because I had nothing else to turn to. Work becomes life when life is empty.

But Jihoon filled it. He slid into the fractures I didn't realize were forming and burst it all open. Now he's gone before I have a chance to smooth the cracks out. The road in front of me is as flat and feature-less as the highway I drove down. Boring. Endless. Dull.

No. Come on, Ari. I'm being dramatic. I survived without Jihoon, and it's not like I'm facing a life of hardship and deprivation because the guy I liked left the country. I have everything that matters—work, health, food, and shelter.

"Get it together," I whisper at my reflection in the window. This isn't like me at all. I don't cry over this stuff because I hardly ever cry. "What's the matter with you?"

The uplifting talk doesn't help, probably because it's not very good.

I pull out my phone and add to my distress by looking at StarLune videos so I can see Jihoon's face. The screen lights up the inside of the car in a garish flicker as I stop on a subtitled interview StarLune did with a Japanese broadcaster. Jihoon tells the interviewer he has no time to date because his career and his fans were the most important loves of his life.

I frown and go to the next video, which features Jihoon and Kit. They're in a practice studio with the video time-stamped two in the morning.

Then Jihoon in an airport, head bowed and almost invisible amid a sea of people.

Jihoon in the center of the stage, tears running down his face as the five members hug and laugh.

Hopes, Hana asked me. What are my hopes? What do I want? I thought I wanted to make my parents proud by being the best lawyer, to succeed at my career. That was my primary focus. It was why I worked so hard, why I felt guilty when I spent time on anything not geared to getting more clients, more money, more accolades.

Even when I loved doing other things. Like making useless itineraries for trips I'd never take. Like reading a book while Jihoon wrote in his notebook or watching a movie with Hana. Those weren't productive, they couldn't be billed, so I never considered them valuable.

The tears start to fall in earnest. There's no one to witness my breakdown, so I let myself go until I'm flat-out crying with belly sobs as I sit alone in my car.

I wanted more time with Jihoon, and now he's back to his old life. He's not going to remember a lawyer he met in Toronto when he's jet-setting around the world. I guess I suspected this would be the end, no matter what he said. We'll text every day, and then one day he'll be too busy and I'll be too proud to call him twice in a row. Then I'll be tired. A day will pass, then two.

Then it will be over, a slow and pitiful disintegration.

I don't want that to happen.

Kit's voice comes back to me. *You've only known each other a month.* He's a dick but he's right. This is nothing but an infatuation.

But I liked being with Jihoon. I liked the person I was when we spent time together. Who is the person I am now, on my own? What do I do now that he's gone?

These are the kinds of questions that normally only come after a lot of wine, and sober me is not prepared to deal with them while sitting in the parking lot of a highway gas station. Nor do I like the fact that they center around a man or another person in general. At least when I'm focused on work, I'm the driver.

I pause and sniffle. No, I'm not. Work is Jihoon in another form—a dependency. I don't like that either, but it's all I know.

I wipe the tears away with the back of my hand. Jihoon will be on the highway by now, and there's no way I'm going to win a high-speed chase down the 401.

There's a knock at my window, and I lurch back in my seat, ready to fight.

Then I see Jihoon's smile, and my heart does a dance as complicated as any StarLune choreography to know that he came back for me.

Twenty-Seven

*Y*ou said you left." I sound faintly accusing when I open the door because I'm having a crisis and having him here in front of me isn't helping.

"I asked the driver to come back when I got your message." He reaches in to undo my seat belt before kissing the corner of my mouth in a peaceful way that makes me think it's his favorite place. "Kit hyeong and Daehyun can wait a few minutes until I get there. Come with me?"

I don't even think but grab my purse and phone before locking the door and following him to a black SUV. Besides the driver, it's only us. Jihoon's dressed in black cargo pants and a tight black shirt, with a mask pulled under his chin. It's the same look he has in other airport news footage, and it strikes me hard that he's about to rejoin a world completely unfamiliar to me.

"Were you crying?" he asks, running his thumb along my cheekbone.

"Of course not." A blatant lie, as I'm not a pretty crier and the evidence is clear on my face.

"Ari. Don't be sad." He puts his hand on my knee and moves us so we're facing each other. "We'll see each other soon."

I lean over and kiss him because I'm not sure what to say. My mind is a chaotic tumble, and I lurch between wishing he would stay to thinking this is all a bad idea to hoping we can make it work. I don't have a plan for this, and I hate it. My phone vibrates and reminds me of the notifications that flowed in over the day. All those people thinking about Jihoon and tracking every moment of his screwy life.

As if aware of my internal turmoil, Jihoon undoes his seat belt, moves over to the center seat, and buckles back in—safety first—before taking my face in his hands. "I'm glad I found you," he says before kissing me so completely, he leaves me panting.

When we come up for air, we're on the highway. Jihoon puts his thumb on my lip, gaze serious. "Now tell me what you're thinking."

Even in the dimness of the car, his features are more dramatic than usual. I think he's...

"Are you wearing makeup?" I ask. I'm a modern progressive woman, but I've never seen a man wearing natural makeup in real life.

"Yes. Do you like it?"

I assess him. "Very much. Is this your usual Min look?" Maybe his makeup is the equivalent of my business skirt suit of armor, the physical indicator that he's about to become more Min than Jihoon. Or I'm overthinking it and he likes wearing eyeliner.

"Our company prefers us to look polished in public." He stretches beside me. "Alex says our fans have been waiting at the airport since morning."

This does not help my anxiety levels. "Did they check the flight times to Seoul or something?"

"We don't usually fly commercial. It's not secure. We have a private plane."

He has a private plane. Jihoon must read the thoughts on my face. "It's Newlight's plane," he hastens to assure me. "I don't own it personally."

"Is that how you got to Toronto without getting tracked? Private plane?"

He shakes his head. "I flew economy class and arrived without my security." He laughs. "I think the person who checked me in isn't a fan. He didn't recognize me."

"How do people know you're leaving today, though?"

He leans over so his forehead touches mine. "Once I was found out, Starrys knew I would have to go back."

My Mafia theory doesn't look so far-fetched after all. "That sounds like you're being kidnapped and also have a monster dose of Stockholm syndrome."

The silence is so long, I wonder if he heard me. "You left me today to work," he says finally. "Did you want to go?"

I falter. I want to say no because it would be rude to tell him yes, but the yes isn't totally accurate either. He understands. "It's the same. I have preferences, but my obligations to the others are more important. Running away because I had a few setbacks was not the best way to deal with my problems." He turns to look at me and makes a face. "Kit hyeong scolded me for being too impulsive, as usual."

"It was dramatic."

"Yes." He seems unbothered that his escape was covered by global media. "Now, tell me about your day."

I'm grateful to have a neutral topic for my mouth to run on about while my brain touches down on every want and every doubt. *What is this, really? What do you think is going to happen after you step on that plane? Not what you want to happen but what will happen each day. What's the plan?*

"Luxe was great, but those women were something else." I glance at his chest. "Can you move your pecs?"

"What?"

"Make your chest muscles jump around."

"I've never tried." He looks down and I can tell by his face he's struggling. Then one side twitches through his shirt, and he looks triumphant.

I give him a slow clap. "Sexy."

"I can also wiggle my ears. Starrys will be impressed I can add this to my list of tricks."

I glance out the window, confirming we've been in the same spot for a while. "I wonder if there's an accident," I say. "The traffic is slower than usual."

He shrugs. "It might be my fault." The connection is lost on me, so he elaborates, "Sometimes so many Starrys come to see us that it causes traffic jams."

How in the world did I think this was a good idea? The man causes freaking traffic snarls. Even more surreal is that he takes it for granted. This is normal to him, a regular occurrence.

"Okay," I whisper.

"It might be an accident," he says. "It doesn't happen all the time."

"You really think that?"

"No," he admits. "It's probably because of me."

His tone is easy enough but with a tension underneath that reflects my own. I'm casting around for a new topic when he speaks.

"Talk to me, Ari. I can tell there's something upsetting you. Is it the traffic? Or that I'm leaving?"

I laugh and then immediately cringe because it sounds so brittle and false. "Of course not. You have work. It's important."

"Why are you speaking like this?" Jihoon shifts away from me to look at my face. "You're important, too. I want us to be together, and you'll visit soon. We can do this."

No, we can't. I wanted to, but real life has clawed its way back in. Ari and Jihoon half a world apart would be hard enough, but layering on a lawyer and a K-pop idol? It's impossible, and I finally acknowledge the truth with a sick finality.

"You'll be busy when you go back," I say slowly, not sure how to say what I need to.

"I'm used to it." His phone buzzes, and he frowns when he checks it.

"What?" I ask.

In answer, he shows me a video of the departure gate swarming with people holding those star sticks and banners. I replay it, almost unable to believe my eyes. "Is that for you?"

"This isn't as bad as it can get." He shuts the video off. "Starrys will be shocked to see Kit hyeong and Daehyun, since that didn't leak," he adds. "It will get the attention away from me."

"Isn't there a VIP terminal or something? Why do you need to go through the crowd?"

He gives me a crooked smile. "For the fans. Newlight wants us seen."

It feels like they want to parade the captured general, but I sense this observation won't be welcome and keep my mouth shut.

It's worse than what I saw outside my apartment, and I can barely take it in. Reading about Jihoon's fame is far removed from seeing it firsthand. I'd been playing with the knife of inadequacy already, and its nasty edge cuts in a little deeper. I text Hana for validation. The airport. That's wild, right?

Her response is the polar opposite to Jihoon's laissez-faire attitude. Totally, she texts. Make sure you're covered when the door opens so they don't see you.

I didn't think of that, but apparently Jihoon has because he starts fussing around with a bag beside him. Out comes a pair of huge sunglasses, a face mask, and a black hoodie. "Here," he says, passing them over. "At the right angle, a telephoto lens can see into the car."

I check the brand. Dolce & Gabbana. I don't even want to know how much they cost, but then again, I'm wearing a watch I could probably sell for a midsize car.

"Aish." He clicks his tongue in dismay. "I forgot the hat." He takes his own and positions it on my head, then brings up my hood.

The disguise smothers me, and Jihoon's expression is not great for my ego. He snaps a photo. "For Hana," he says, showing it to me. I look like a gothic mummy.

"Funny," I say as I pull down the mask and hook it under my chin, glad we're both trying to make the last minutes light. "This is stifling. I can't believe you do this all the time."

He's frowning as he looks out the window, already planning for his life without me.

Slow disintegration or quick chop? I take a deep breath. What's the end goal to keeping this going with him? I always have a goal. Suddenly I wish we had more time to talk about what's going to happen, about us and him and everything, but there's no time left except to say what I know is the smart thing.

Jihoon is thinking with his heart, which means one of us has to think with their head.

"Jihoon." My voice is soft.

"Remember to stay in the corner," he says, glancing out the window.

"*Jihoon.*"

My tone alerts him, and he swings back to give me all his attention. "Ari? What is it?"

My mouth opens and nothing comes out. *It's the right thing to do,* I remind myself furiously. *Get it over with so you can both get on with your lives.*

But all I can do is say his name again.

This time, he understands and his eyes drop. "Ah." He plays with his phone, moving it from one hand to another. "You don't need to say it, Ari. I know."

"This was fun, and I like you, but..."

"But what?" His eyes are wide.

"You know it won't work," I say, staring at my lap to avoid his gaze. "Your life is too different."

"All this is all external," he says. "We are what matters, and we only need to try. Give us a chance, Ari. Take a risk."

I can barely breathe thinking about the crowds waiting for us and the cars, so many cars, on the road. How long did some of those people drive to have a chance to see Jihoon? No, not Jihoon. Min. "I can't," I whisper.

"We talked about this. Don't you believe me that we have a chance?" The hurt bleeds through his voice. I keep rubbing my hands on my thighs to try to get them warm. I hate this conversation, and even worse, I have the horrible feeling I should have kept quiet. It was the right decision, but now that we're here, I want to run away from the consequences of what I've said.

"We didn't talk about it. Not enough."

"Why are you doing this right before I leave?" Jihoon's agitation is contagious. I try to breathe so my voice doesn't shake. He's right. This is an inexcusably bad time, but it's not like it would be better to text him midflight or when he touches down in Seoul. It's better to do this face-to-face.

"When you go back, you'll be busy," I say. "You made that clear."

"Are you trying to tell me you know my schedule better than I do?" he says with a flash of anger. "I know my priorities."

I deserve that, but I know I'm right. "Tell me honestly that you have time for something like this right now." I don't say *me*. That's too hard.

"I want to try."

"Wanting isn't enough when there are only so many hours in a day."

There's a long and deep silence in the car, so intense I can almost see it. I unbuckle the watch from my wrist and hold it out. "I should give this back to you."

"Don't do this, Ari." He looks pleading. "The time I spent with you meant so...please don't do this."

I can't even look at him now, but I thrust the watch out. "I'm sorry."

It feels like forever that my arm is outstretched, but eventually I hear him sigh, a deep sound that could be mistaken for a groan. "This is how it is, then." His voice is soft and musing, almost as if he's speaking to himself. He plucks the watch out of my hand.

My throat is hot and swollen. I want to cry but can't, not in front of him when this is all my own doing.

The car stops, and I peer out the tinted window as layers of security converge on us. My heart stutters with nerves even though I'm not doing a thing except cowering in the back corner of the car. Jihoon takes a deep breath and makes a call, muttering as he scans what's waiting for him outside. He's all business now, and I'm grateful for the change.

"Kit hyeong and Daehyun are out of their car. In thirty seconds, my door will open," he says after he ends the call. "You need to be as far away as possible. Keep your head down."

"I will." Precise instructions are necessary because I'm so far out of my depth, I'm basically in the Mariana Trench.

"May I hug you goodbye?" he asks, hands gripping his knees.

I can only nod. He pulls me close for a moment, his hands tight on my arms and his lips brushing my cheek. "I wish this could be different. I wish you had the courage." His voice is husky. "Bye, Ari."

"Bye, Jihoon." To my shame, my voice hitches because I'm going to cry. Logically I haven't known him long enough to be this attached, but this is beyond anything logical. My heart hammers so hard that I can barely hear the roar of the crowd over the rush in my ears.

Jihoon leans over to tug up my mask and opens his mouth as if to say something. Instead he runs a hand through his hair before the door opens to a flash so dazzling, it's like I've been hit with a spotlight. The pulsating wall of brightness from media cameras and fan phones pushes me farther back as I instinctively cover my face with my arm. Even amid this, Jihoon is careful to only open the door enough for him to climb out, minimizing the crowd's ability to see inside.

He doesn't look back.

"Can anyone see through these windows?" I ask the driver after the door closes.

He's staring at the commotion, mouth slightly open. "No, ma'am, they're completely opaque."

With that assurance, I scoot across to the window to watch Jihoon go. He joins two other men, who must be Kit and Daehyun, and the three of them bow repeatedly as the earsplitting screams become louder, even in the car. A woman tries to fight her way through and is almost tackled by security as the three members of StarLune bow one last time and wave, posing to give the cameras and fans a moment to drink their fill.

"Holy goddamn," says the driver. He glances at me. "Excuse my French. I've never seen a crowd like this, and I drove for Harry Styles."

"Do you think anyone will follow us?" I ask. My wretchedness about Jihoon has been submerged under new and worrying concerns for our personal safety.

"I'll be careful," the driver promises. We watch as Jihoon and his friends are engulfed by even more security and disappear as they enter the airport. The moment the doors shut behind them, the crowds flow into the space they left, chanting and cheering. "Are you ready to go?"

"Yes, please."

"Got it." He puts the car in gear as I check my phone. Unbelievably, Jihoon is trending with video footage from seconds ago. It's weird to see him from multiple angles. He's making a gesture I recognize from my deep dive but don't know the meaning of, so I text Hana, my expert on all things Jihoon.

Me: What's he doing with his hands? It's like he's crossing his thumb and finger.

Hana: Hand heart. Means I like u / love u

Jihoon had turned his body slightly when making the hand heart, almost back toward the car.

Or he's doing it to the adoring fans and I'm reading way too much into it. I must be, because I don't deserve anything from him.

The driver turns around. "Ma'am, do you want to go back to your car or somewhere else?"

"The car." I don't want to leave it overnight at a gas station.

"On our way."

He goes back to driving as I do my best to not think about what happened. I glance over and see my watch sitting on the black leather. Jihoon forgot it. I reach out with shaking fingers and take it back. I can give it to Hana to send to him, perhaps.

I slide the band through my fingers and tilt it back and forth so the diamonds on the watch face reflect the highway lights as I think of the airport crowd. Mob, really. There were so many people screaming and chanting Min's name. *Kay, Min, DeeDee*, over and over, like they were more than men. Their hands had been desperate to touch and their owners to be seen. I can barely put into words how paralyzing it was, and I'd been safe in the car. How did Jihoon feel being exposed like that? What did he think about when the crowds reached for him?

I'll never know.

I straighten in my seat and shove the watch deep in my bag. Then I take my phone and bring up the invite he sent me for after his concert.

It hurts when I decline.

I did the right thing because it's a whole different world that Jihoon lives in. It might be defeatist, but I can see Kit hadn't lied: there's no space in it for me.

Twenty-Eight

The problem with heroic self-denial is that after the feeling of nobility wears off, you're stuck back in your regular life.

But now you're sad.

Jihoon doesn't contact me. I expected that and tell myself it's what I wanted. The problem is that although I thought he would eventually fade into memory, he hasn't. My brain knows I did the smart thing, but my body seems to disagree. I almost physically crave his company, and it takes all my willpower to not watch the several million online clips of him on repeat.

Life isn't doing much to distract me. I have no travel itineraries to plan for friends, and work is somehow both hectic and tedious. Dad calls regularly to bestow advice on how to talk to Richard so I can get ahead. I spend a lot of time making affirmative noises into the phone so I don't snap and tell him his experience helping people navigate adoptions and divorces isn't quite the same as dealing with the suited sharks at Yesterly and Havings. I try to talk to him about his health, but he cuts me off each time. Eventually, I give up because I'm not eager to talk about it either.

Phoebe, surprisingly, has been in touch with me. After I told her what happened with Jihoon, she told me she was around if I wanted to talk.

I didn't want to talk.

Well, I want to talk a little bit, and I can't talk to Hana. Once she got past her initial shock, Hana had refused to talk about Jihoon at all, citing friendship rule number seven.

"Which one is that?" I'd asked. Our friendship rules covered issues such as not leaving each other at a bar, no matter how hot someone was, to total honesty when asked for an opinion on clothing choices. I thought we had six.

"It's like that amendment Americans have about not saying something that will get you in trouble. They're always pleading it in crime shows."

"Friendships don't have a fifth to plead."

"This one does as of now because you'll get upset if I say you're being a total ass about this entire situation and you should grow up and expand your world to give Jihoon and your life outside that awful law firm a chance." She takes a deep breath, having let that all out in a single burst.

"I feel the whole keeping it to yourself thing was more of a hypothetical exercise."

"Sorry." She wraps her arms around her knees. "Sorry. It's that he's a mess, and you're also a mess but also being utterly asinine about this and..."

I hold my hand up to stop her before she runs on again. "You were right, friendship rule seven."

We'd avoided the topic after that, but what she said about Jihoon stung. Despite my better judgment—and honestly, where is that getting me these days?—I tune into one of StarLune's video updates. It's Kit, and beside him is Jihoon. A tight feeling binds my throat when I see him. He looks tired, barefaced, with his hair hidden under a hat and a mask cupping his chin. I watch for a few minutes as the two tease each other about a burned meal.

Jihoon looks like he's been gutted, and the concerned comments in the chat tell me I'm not the only one who noticed that he looks dull and his eyes don't smile. There must be more going on in his life since there's no way I could have done that to him. He told me how busy he was going to be. No doubt it's exhaustion. I can't feel guilty about doing the right thing.

———————

Phoebe meets me in a derelict parking lot that's been transformed into a hidden pop-up patio complete with sand and beach umbrellas. The Beach Boys play softly on the speakers as we drink radlers out of mason jars.

Phoebe kicks off her sandals and digs her toes, blue polish chipped, into the sand. "Almost like being at the beach."

A car beeps its horn as it passes on Dundas Street. "Almost," I say, looking at the chain-link fence that surrounds the lot.

"My new place gets hot at night, so it's nice to be out." She leans her head back, the setting sun lighting up her bleached hair with bright streaks of orange and gold. "Worth it to have my own space, though."

I take a sip of the radler. They've used grapefruit juice, so it's not too sweet. "Don't you wish you could settle down in one place? It must be tiring to keep moving."

She slips on her gigantic sunglasses, which sit on top of her tiny nose and make it look like a button. "Not for me. The same routine is stifling."

"Thanks a lot."

Phoebe's eyes are hidden, but her face moves to look at the couple holding hands to our left. "Why do you think it's a judgment? I don't live my life at you."

"It seems that way."

Off come the sunglasses, but when she looks at me, I wish she'd kept them on. "Why?"

I've already said too much. We may share history, but this

Phoebe—the woman in front of me and not the one I've created in my mind—is a stranger. "Never mind."

"Talk to me, Ari. Please."

I glare at her. "Why do you want the big talk now?"

"Do you want me to apologize for being myself?"

"How about being sorry you left us so you could do it?"

In the silence that follows, the Beach Boys give way to some surf rock band. Phoebe looks at her drink. "I told you before why I did. I don't know how long you want to stay mad or what you gain from it. We nearly lost Dad." She doesn't elaborate after that.

I hate that she makes sense because I have a good seventeen years of sour resentment clinging to me like a sweaty sports bra. What do I gain from this low-level warfare? Nothing except that I can tell myself Phoebe is a flake and her decisions are flaky and thus nothing to make me question my own life. But Phoebe enjoying herself doing my exact opposite makes me wonder if I have the same choices open to me, even now.

She lets that sit for a moment, then leans back in her chair, making it creak alarmingly. "I regret quitting school. I was jealous when you got your degree."

"Jealous of *me*?"

Phoebe rolls her eyes. "You don't even know how proud Mom and Dad are of you. 'Ari's about to graduate. Ari's top in her class. Ari has a fancy-pants job. Ari's life is going so well.'" She says this in a singsong voice that's half-mocking and half-dejected.

"Is that why you never called?"

"Probably. I don't have a good answer." She makes a face. "That sounds bad. I'm not a good person, shit."

We drink our overpriced juice-beer.

"I want to talk about other things," I say.

She looks relieved. "Done."

I cast around for a neutral question. "Where were you before Montreal?"

"Peru, working in a hotel near Machu Picchu for a few months," she says like it's no big deal.

I feel almost shy when I ask her, "Can you tell me about it?"

"You really want to know?"

"I love hearing about people's travels," I say honestly. "I've never been anywhere."

"No?"

"Work."

Phoebe's expression is understanding. "One day we can go somewhere together." She gulps down her radler as this casual offer makes my eyes fly up to her face to see if she's serious. She is. "Okay, tell me when you get bored."

I don't get bored at all. For the next two hours, Phoebe regales me with travel triumphs and mishaps. Missing a flight in LA and meeting a movie star in the bar. Learning how to make espresso from a man who insisted he learned it in Sicily from a Mafia consigliere. She's amusing and wry and makes me laugh so hard my stomach hurts. Then my heart hurts a bit because I could have had this years ago.

She signals the server for the bill. "You know, you could go to Korea. On vacation."

I kick at the sand under my feet. "That ship has sailed."

"I only met Jihoon for a bit, but he seems like a good guy. He'd hear you out, especially if you made an effort to see him."

"The problem is there's nothing to hear out. It was the right decision."

Phoebe drags a finger through the condensation on her glass. "You don't have a single regret?"

"Of course not," I lie.

She looks at me skeptically. "I had a therapist do a thought exercise with me once. Do you want to hear it?"

First I need to get over my sister mentioning a therapist so casually, which is not something she learned to do in the Hui family home. "I don't know."

"Will it hurt to hear?" she asks with exasperation.

"It might," I say.

She smiles. "Yeah, you're right. You should listen, though."

I wave for her to go ahead. Behind her, the server swings the gate open to let in a group of women dressed in tiaras and Hawaiian shirts.

Phoebe takes a drink before she speaks. "I had to make a choice, and the therapist told me to think of the worst thing that could happen. In your example, let's say you reach out to Jihoon. What's the worst that could happen?"

"He rejects me." That bursts out before I can even be embarrassed.

"What happens after that?"

No need to think about this either. "He's out of my life forever." She stares at me, and I stare back before I finally ask, "What's your point?"

"Jesus, this is like pulling teeth." Phoebe runs a hand through her hair. "I'll spell it out. Is that different from your here and now?"

I don't like where this is going, but I shake my head. "No."

"Then you're already living your worst-case scenario." She stands and grabs her bag. "You've nothing left to lose. Think about it."

Phoebe's words pick their way across my mind as I head home. I'm not living my worst-case scenario. A real worst-case scenario is being left in a desert with no water. A squandered romantic opportunity is almost commonplace. It's why there are so many missed connections sections in local newspapers and online. There's no such thing as one true love, and I am 100 percent not living my worst scenario.

I'm *not*.

———

Hana is on the couch when I get home, her head bent so far back she looks like she's auditioning for a part in *The Exorcist: Demon Death Redux*. "Leftovers in the fridge," she mumbles.

I take a good look at her. "How was your mom?"

"Brutal. It's killing me. She won't listen."

Hana had been summoned to the Choi household for another interrogation about her role in the Jihoon incident, which had apparently devolved into her mother's usual nagging about Hana's life.

Tears of frustration leak out from the corners of her eyes. She's been seeing a therapist—secretly, because Mama Choi would dissolve into self-accusations of how she's a terrible mother if she knew—but it's hard to go against your parents. Especially when whatever is done is supposedly done out of love.

"What was it tonight?" I ask.

"Everything. Even this work trip I need to take to Korea in a couple weeks is a chance for her to try to control me. She gave me a nonnegotiable list of what I need to bring back and people I need to see."

I repress the slap of emotion I get when Hana mentions her Korea trip. It's happened a few times, and I don't dwell on it long enough to tell if it's envy or remorse. Although she's going to Busan and not Seoul, I haven't had the courage to ask if she's going to see Jihoon. His watch is tucked in the back of my sock drawer. I haven't looked at it since he left.

Tonight isn't about my heartache, though, but Hana's. I remember what her therapist had told her to do. "Did you set your boundaries?"

"I told her the other day I didn't want her talking about what I eat or how I look."

"That's good," I encourage her.

"Technically, it worked. She didn't say a word about my appearance." She reaches down and fishes around in her bag. "Instead she very generously bought me some new clothes."

I snatch it out of the air when she tosses it over. "Is it a necktie?"

Hana closes her eyes. "Good guess but no. They are pants."

The two of us have similar body types, solidly on the curvier side. These pants might fit up to my knee. I check the tag. They're an extra small. "Wow, this is some Machiavellian-level mind play."

"I'll donate them to a children's charity," she says.

I sit beside Hana and nudge her in the side. "I know you don't like my football coach mottos, but you'll appreciate this one."

She turns to me, one eyebrow raised. "Yeah?"

I nod and lean in. "Fuck it."

This is not witty or classy, but she laughs, and it's enough to get the smile back in her eyes. That's enough for me right now. After she goes to bed, I hide those nasty leggings in my room so Hana won't see them in the morning.

Take that, Mama Choi.

Twenty-Nine

So."

"So," I parrot back. It's a week later, and Alex and I are at a bar after work to prepare for my upcoming initial meeting with Hyphen's in-house legal. Brittany has already told me several times how jealous she is that I'm getting the fun little local clients while she has to spend her time with boring old companies negotiating multimillion-dollar deals. Sometimes she didn't get home for dinner, and Kenny was getting so *mad* about having takeout all the time.

I do my best to be collegial, but it's difficult, especially when I see her coming back with Meredith, both holding coffee from the same place. Brittany is gathering support among the partners, and I need to find a solution. Dad's constant harping on the theme of career advancement doesn't help.

Alex straightens his lapels and puts his hands flat on the table as the visual indicator that he's about to say something important.

"Mr. Choi."

"What about him?" I look at the menu to avoid his gaze.

"Are you dating?"

I can't prevent the slight jerk that shakes the menu and focus on the description for the panko-crusted cauliflower bites. "I don't see how that's any of your business," I say.

"As the man who spent the greater part of a week and most of his sleeping hours trying to hide your existence from the media and a very smart and resourceful fan base, I beg to differ."

Touché. "We're not talking anymore."

His face softens. "Sorry."

"There was no way it would work, and I don't want to discuss it."

"Understood." He puts down his menu. "On the professional side, Hyphen distributes StarLune. I need to know if you can handle it."

I sit back in the chair and glare at him, offended he thinks I can't keep it together. "I can stay professional. We barely knew each other." I can't help choking over the last because it's true but also false.

"Right." He gives me a disbelieving look. "Have you looked through the information I sent?"

I nod, grateful to be on safer ground. "Interesting industry."

"You don't sound convinced."

I turn the menu over. "Most of it is manufactured music."

"You lived with Min of StarLune and can say that." Alex sounds disgusted.

"He wasn't Min when I knew him," I snap, angry to have Jihoon come up again. Work at least used to be my safe zone. "And I said *most*."

"Do you think great actors are artists? Dancers?"

"Yes."

"Then you agree that, say, Dame Judi Dench is an artist."

"Normally I would say yes, but I'm downgrading my answer to *perhaps* because I'm suspicious of the point you're going to make."

"Does Judi Dench write her own parts? Do dancers create their own choreography for *Swan Lake*?"

"You are trying to say I am culturally ignorant and should have some respect."

"I wouldn't phrase it exactly like that, but close." He shakes his head. "You've got some preconceptions that I strongly encourage you to reassess. This is a multibillion dollar industry."

That's something to think about but... "That's the business side. It's the rest that's strange. They audition and get trained and live in group housing like they're in boot camp before some corporate suit sticks them in a band."

"You think the music is more valid if they meet organically."

"Yes."

"Like a symphony does? Or does the first chair violinist also not count as an artist?"

"What about the variety shows where they dress up and whack each other on the ass, like, a lot?"

"Fine," he concedes after a long moment. "Those are bizarre to me, too."

I keep going, pulling on knowledge gathered from my StarLune binge. "Plus, they do the same dance every time for each song."

"The choreography is part of the song, and it's not like a dancer changes their moves for each performance of *The Nutcracker*." He stares off into the distance as if trying to figure out what to say. "It's limiting to think of it that way. These are multimedia experiences that combine music, style, dance, and performance. It's a different concept than you're used to, but that doesn't make it absurd or lesser."

I pause as the drinks get delivered. "You're being surprisingly severe about this."

He wipes a spill off the table. "You've hit one of my sore spots. I spend an inordinate amount of time trying to convince people that bands like StarLune count as legitimate even though they top global charts. It's like people see Asian faces and refuse to believe there's any creativity or artistic merit involved."

"Fine." I try to keep my voice disinterested despite feeling a little attacked. "Now, can we get on to business?"

"This is business."

"Other business," I say. "Tell me what's going on with Hyphen."

"Ari."

"I'll keep an open mind," I promise.

"Good, because I want you to come to Seoul."

"Seoul?" I put my drink down and wonder if I heard him right. *Jihoon lives there,* my brain eagerly reminds me. I could see him. Or I could have, had I not dumped him as he was leaving the country. Work is definitely not a safe zone anymore.

"Yes, and soon. Desiree was supposed to come with me, but she's going on early maternity leave."

I frown. "Isn't this a conflict of interest?"

He shakes his head. "You're not in a relationship with Mr. Choi, and no one but us knows it might have been different."

"Right," I say, trying to ignore the emptiness in my chest I've accepted as permanent when it flares into a precise pain.

"Newlight wants to get to know me while we finalize the North American plans for one of their debut groups. Are you in?"

I twirl a straw around my fingers. I don't usually take vacation time, so Alex's offer provides the chance to travel without feeling as if I'm slacking. In fact, it's a potential career enhancer since I can work closely with Hyphen, and it shows they value me.

These are two good reasons for wanting to go that have absolutely nothing to do with the opportunity of being in the same city as Jihoon.

However, I don't make quick decisions, even though I'm yearning to go, and I need to check with the partner in charge. "Let me get back to you."

"You don't need to see Mr. Choi while we're there. We won't be working directly with StarLune."

I shift uncomfortably on the vinyl seat. "I wasn't thinking about that."

"If you say so." He gives me a long look, but I steer the conversation back to Hyphen, and that's what we talk about the rest of the night.

———

The next day at the office is colored by fantasies of what I can do if I go to Seoul, combined with worry about being out of the office for a week, even if it's on business. I have a feeling, almost like dread, that if I leave, something will go wrong.

I look up from my screen and notice my water glass is empty. Better get something to drink before I start to shrivel.

The kitchen at Yesterly and Havings is all chrome and glass, a high-design contrast to the country club elegance that fills the rest of the office. A small hall leads from the open seating to a recessed snack area custom-made to catch the loud and unwary.

Or the uncaring like Brittany, whose voice drifts out as I step unseen into the space.

"I don't understand," she says. "I've tried to make it clear so she knows it's okay to be Chinese, that it's the same as being like us. I don't see color, anyway."

"You're trying, and that's what's important." This is Meredith speaking.

"I'm doing my best, but it's so hard to tell what she's thinking." Brittany sounds miserable. "I know she's jealous because Richard asked me to join the Beaconsmith meetings."

"You were asked because you deserve it," says Meredith with righteous indignation. "You work hard. Like I told you the other day at lunch, if she worked as hard, she'd get those accounts as well."

"She got upset with me when we met because she thinks I said her name wrong, but people get my name wrong all the time. It doesn't bother me."

"Brittany." Meredith's voice is as warm as a talk show therapist about to lay down some life lessons. "You can't let people make you feel bad for being a strong, competent woman and a fantastic lawyer. Don't drop to their level."

"You're right," says Brittany. "When they go low, we go high."

"Exactly," approves Meredith.

At this moment, vision narrowed to a tunnel, I weigh several options.

Option: Make myself known and use this as a teachable moment to create a more tolerant world.

Analysis: I am not capable of this.

Option: Walk in there, look them both right in the eye to watch them squirm, then leave.

Analysis: I might seem like this kind of person, but it's aspirational.

Option: Leave and forget I heard anything to save Brittany and Meredith embarrassment.

Analysis: Most likely course of action.

"I mean, I don't want her to feel bad," says Brittany. "It must be hard when you're obviously the diversity hire and the rest of us got here because we put in the work."

"We're impressed with how fast you're learning, and it's because you try," soothes Meredith. "Your mother is very proud of you, Brittany. You're a good fit with us."

I turn around so fast, I nearly stumble on my own feet. I'm taking option three, but it's not to save them embarrassment. It's to prevent my own.

In my office, I lower myself in the leather chair. The room smells expensively good from the subtle air freshener they pump through the office to negate any indication of human occupation. I don't realize I'm shaking until a sharp pang shoots through my jaw from how hard I'm clenching my teeth.

I reach for my phone and then pull back because I can't talk about this, not to anyone.

There are two kinds of shameful experiences. The first category is normal but mortifying, like falling down the stairs when you're trying to make an entrance or saying something inane. They fade with each retelling and eventually get reworked until they become cringey but hilarious anecdotes that happened to a fictional past you. They lose the ability to cause any more indignity.

The second category causes damage. They're hailstorms where the ice takes up space so deep in your very bones that it's impossible to melt. These are the unwelcome eye-openers, when you're forced to face something you could damn well do without. If the first is falling down the stairs, the second is getting shoved from behind by the person you trust most in the world. Those never stop bleeding, and telling those stories, if you can, only rips them raw again. Usually you don't.

You end up eventually owning the first kind. The second owns you.

If anyone should be uncomfortable here, it's those two women and not me. Yet I'm the one who's been cut down and made smaller because at some point my ancestors came from Asia and not England. I don't even speak the language: Phoebe always called us dim sum Chinese. Despite the fact that I know jack about the motherland, I'm not allowed to be Canadian, only Chinese Canadian. My doubled descriptor seems like it halves my belonging, making me a permanent outsider. I don't even know how to fight the Brittanys and Merediths without somehow feeling that I'm selling out a heritage I've never even related to.

Even though the Brittanys have a head start, I'd believed Dad when he insisted hard work would get me where I wanted to be. For the first time, I see he was too optimistic. Or Brittany really is the better lawyer, a better fit. How would I ever know if the problem is my talent or me? Although I've been paddling like mad in the Yesterly and Havings lake, all these conversations have been happening underneath that I'm not involved in. Hana had once warned me to watch out for this, but I'd ignored her. I was different. It didn't apply to me.

I rub around my eyes, careful to not make my upset visible by smearing my mascara. At least it clarifies one of my decisions. I text Alex because I can't be sure my voice won't shake. **Send me the flight information.**

I was going to be the best damn lawyer at Yesterly and Havings. Now I'm not sure that's even what I want, so I might as well get a trip out of it.

There's no way I'm bringing a souvenir back for Brytaghnghie, though.

Thirty

usiness class," I say to Alex as we board, trying to hide my excitement. Stressed though I am about Jihoon, this is my first time on a plane. "Extravagant."

"Company pays for the upgrade if a flight's over eight hours," he says complacently as he wipes down the armrests with enough sanitizer to make my eyes water.

I sit stiffly in the seat before slowly relaxing enough to take in my surroundings. The air smells oppressively neutral, and everyone is unpacking books and devices as they get comfortable for the trip. They all look bored.

I have a week's work with Newlight before I meet with Hana, which I'm thrilled about. Our trips to Korea overlap, and I've taken some vacation days (screw you, Yesterly and Havings) so we can explore Seoul before she goes south to Busan. Hana didn't mention meeting with Jihoon or the strangeness of me taking vacation days in a very obvious way that makes it clear she's waiting for me to bring it up.

I poke the bag stuffed under the seat in front of me with my toe. It's filled with work files I should go through, but I was up late last night paging through documents, and I want a break. The problem is, if I don't work, I brood about whether I should have told Jihoon that I'll be in Seoul.

Because I didn't. I have no idea what I even want. To meet? To talk? And say what?

Alex was kind enough to give me the window seat, and I make the best of it, craning my head to look at the runway and the surrounding dry brown grass. I'm about to pull out the in-flight magazine to see what restaurants they recommend in Phnom Penh when the screen in front of me flickers to life with the safety video. It's in Korean and subtitled in English.

I blink, and Alex makes a strangled noise beside me. "No way," he manages to get out. "That's not..."

"It is." It's StarLune, dressed in dapper suits and singing about where the exits are on this airplane.

He elbows me. "Breathe," he says as Daehyun goes into a rap to inform me that in times of emergency, my seat cushion can be used as a flotation device.

Alex and I watch the rest of the video, which includes a huge dancing life vest and a trippy segment of them going down the inflatable slides to land on what looks like Jupiter. I pray the plane doesn't crash for real because I haven't absorbed any of this life-saving instruction. Jihoon looks...good. He looks incredible.

At my most crass level, I can't believe I tapped that. More importantly, I'm kicking myself for being such a coward and letting him go without a fight. He was right. I made excuses because I didn't have the courage to take a risk.

Worse, I didn't let him go. I *made* it happen. It was 100 percent all my fault.

My seat rumbles under me, and I have a moment of fear. Soon I'll be in the air, dependent on technology and the human understanding of aerodynamics to keep me alive. All Jihoon-related thoughts disappear as the plane taxis forever before it accelerates. Everyone still looks bored.

I turn to Alex, who laughs when he sees me. "Liftoff never gets old for me either," he says. Then he passes me some gum. "For your ears."

I know the exact moment the plane tilts up to the sky as it lifts off and briefly wonder if the tail will hit the ground. Then we're travelling up, and I nearly dislocate my neck to watch as the city below transforms into a map. We circle around over the long lines of the highways, ovals of running tracks, and even little dots of aquamarine from people's pools. When we go higher, I realize for the first time that fog is actually a low cloud. I've been walking through clouds. We keep climbing until even the clouds are under us, strangely solid in appearance.

Only then do I sit back with a smile. Alex says something, but between my ears and the roar inside the plane—I didn't know it would be this loud—I can't hear him. He gives me a thumbs-up, and I nod.

By the time there's a glass of white wine and a package of rice crackers in front of me, I've calmed down enough to not look out the window every minute, since it's all the same cloud cover. I click through the movies, but there's nothing I want to watch, even if I could hear the dialogue. Alex is already asleep beside me.

With my airplane amusement options exhausted, I decide now is the perfect time to do something I've been avoiding. Alex had told me to check out some StarLune fan accounts for research, even though we'd be working with Newlight's other groups. It's a work thing, I assure myself. Not a weird stalker thing.

I go to StarLune's social media. It's mostly staged photos and selfies, so I scroll down to the comments. Although the vast majority are emojis and GIFs, there are a few thoughtful ones that I investigate.

Thanks to the in-flight Wi-Fi, the next hour is eye-opening as I follow messages and replies and comments. Plenty celebrate StarLune's outlandish good looks, but countless others talk about the music and its impact. The best thread I find says, *moots, what's been the best thing about having @_starlune_ in your life?*

The first post is a GIF of a sweaty Jihoon dancing, and I linger on this before moving on. The tweet has over five thousand replies, and they range from *a playlist that got my lazy ass to the gym* to *I was in a really bad place and their lyrics saved my life.*

Lifting my eyes to the screen on the chair in front of me, which shows a little airplane zooming its way westward toward the Pacific, I'm forced to the difficult conclusion that I am a child. Not even a child. I am the insecure emo teenager glaring out under overgrown bangs who hates everything on principle so I can feel superior. I can't do that anymore because Jihoon is, factually, a cultural icon for a reason. Despite my averred dislike for celebrity culture, when I scroll through the comments, I have to admit that my legal career, which for the most part involves helping the rich get richer, is not having this level of positive impact on the world.

Although slightly proud of myself for reaching this breakthrough of self-discovery, I don't like it. I'm a lawyer. I look at the facts. I didn't do that with Jihoon because I let my preconceptions get in the way of learning. I'm ashamed of myself for not giving Jihoon's work the respect it deserves. Worse, not even the consideration that it needed respect. I didn't think about his work past the fame, and I wonder if our conversation at the airport would have been different if I had.

Alex wakes up and grabs a squished-looking bottle of water that pops back into its regular shape once he cracks it open. He glances at my phone after he takes a few sips. "Turning into a Starry?"

"No!" I flip the phone over. "Research, like you told me."

He smiles smugly. "You tell yourself that."

Before I can clap back, a yawn so huge it's close to dislocating my jaw splits my face. Alex tucks my phone into my bag. "Get some rest," he says. "We've got a few hours to go, and you're going to be working hard this week. Newlight doesn't waste time."

His voice comes through a fog because I'm already drifting off, thinking about Jihoon and what might have been had I not been so wrongly sure of what was possible.

———

Our arrival at Incheon Airport is undramatic and the exact opposite of the mayhem I know greets StarLune. I'm an exhausted swirl of weary body and keyed-up brain from finally being in another country after dreaming of it for so long. Even the endless immigration line does nothing to dampen my enthusiasm. I went on a plane. I'm out of Canada. I'm in a different country with unfamiliar stores and food and rules, and I don't understand a word being said around me. Beside me, Alex thumbs through his phone mumbling at the messages from Newlight, but I want to drink in everything about this sterile airport environment. The border guard asks me why I'm here and for how long, and I do my best to not grin at him like an absolute fool.

Luggage collected, we get out of the airport and into our car, where I lean my head against the window to take in the scenery. Although it looks like the kind of highway you'd see connecting any industrialized city, there are a slew of minor differences. Korean signs, obviously, and people drive faster than in Toronto in cars that all seem to have tinted windows. As we cross a huge bridge, I think of how big the world is and how I've spent my time longing for a fancier office to look down on it instead of exploring it in person. I don't want to miss a moment and have reached the point of trying to lift my eyelids with my fingers to keep my eyes open before I give in and end up dozing. Alex pokes me awake when we arrive at the ornate door of a luxury hotel. The valets bow when we arrive and rush to help us with our bags, which are lit up by the marquee that covers the main door.

Our rooms are adjacent but don't have an adjoining door, so Alex drops off his bag and comes to see me. Given the sumptuous atmosphere of the rest of the hotel, I was expecting a Versailles look, or at least a Las Vegas winner's suite, but the room is a standard size and painted a calming gray. Even the photos on the walls are tasteful black-and-white landscapes.

Alex checks his phone. "It's now eight in the evening Seoul time on Monday. It was Sunday when we left Toronto."

"Right." I'm barely listening. I've never been this far from home, and the sight outside my window draws me in. From here, Seoul looks like most other cities, and I'm itching to go out to feel like I've left Canada.

"Ari." Alex sounds exasperated, but he's smiling at me.

"Sorry." I shut the curtains and take a deep breath. I'm here to work. "Have they changed the schedule?"

"Let's walk and talk," he suggests. "Did you do a travel plan?"

I scoff. Do I have a plan? Of course I have a plan. For the first time, I was able to do an itinerary for myself, which is written in purple ink in my travel notebook. "There's a café I want to try. It's close." All the walls are made of plants, with furniture from repurposed tree stumps. There's even grass on the floor, according to the pictures.

"I'm in."

Five minutes later, we're on the street, which has a wide side-walk and looks like a financial district, with lots of gray buildings. I'm almost immediately sidetracked by a brightly lit convenience store, and Alex and I share a single look before we enter. There's a big seating area with microwaves and a hot water urn. Alex looks around.

"How wedded were you to the café?" he asks. "I love convenience stores. They're like cultural microcosms."

I look at the shelves upon shelves of snacks I've never tried or known existed. "Travel is about flexibility."

We each grab a purple plastic basket and start browsing. I select some strawberry milk and a box of Choco Pies, which look like the cookie-marshmallow-chocolate wagon wheels from home. Alex grabs Spam on a stick, eyes wide with joy. "Do you know how hard it is to get food with Spam at home?" he asks as he pops it into the microwave after we pay.

I only nod because I'm biting into a sandwich with tangy egg salad and spaghetti on white bread. It's kind of nasty and also amazing, and I realize I haven't thought about Jihoon all night.

Then I look over at a display of canned coffee and see him emblazoned on the side.

Right. He's a huge celebrity with endorsements, and I'm in his territory. My mood plummets, but I hide it from Alex, who is chatting about what to expect tomorrow. Newlight has it packed tight, including social events. "There's a company party," Alex says. "They've had a good quarter and want to celebrate."

"Do I have to go?" I don't like corporate parties.

"Yes, because I have to, and I'm not enduring it alone."

We look out at the street at the people passing. "Are you going to contact Mr. Choi?" he asks.

"No."

Alex looks pained. "Up to you, but if you want something, don't waste time not going after it."

"Right now, all I want is for tomorrow's meeting to go well," I say, bringing the conversation back to work. He takes the hint, and we're soon yawning over the table of food wrappers.

"Time for bed," he says, rubbing his eyes. "This was a good idea. We'll check out that café tomorrow."

Back in the hotel, I roll up in the crisp white sheets and try not to think about why Alex's comment about wasting time bothers me so much. Then the thought comes to me that this is nothing new. Wasting time is what I've been doing for years. I just didn't realize it.

That night, I dream about canned coffee and photo shoots.

Thirty-One

We're ready bright and early for Newlight. Although there's almost zero chance of seeing Jihoon in the corporate office, I have a shaky feeling in my chest, like my heart is vibrating.

"Why isn't the GPS working?" says Alex, squinting at his phone map as he turns it upside down and to the side, trying to line it up with what he thinks is north. "Newlight is in Gangnam, same as the hotel."

Because we're losers, we begin humming "Gangnam Style" and doing the horse dance with our hands. The driver keeps his eyes professionally on the road, no doubt used to clueless foreigners.

We pass through what looks like a typical urban center but with more designer stores and pull up at the Newlight building, a midsize skyscraper with the corporate logo, a stylized torch, emblazoned on the top. After passing through the revolving door, we arrive in the next century.

"Stop staring," Alex mutters, trying to look blasé. "You look like you've never set foot outside the village."

In my defense, there's a lot to see. The entire lobby is sheathed in white plastic tiles so bright the reflection of the sun through the huge round windows hurts my eyes. Holograms of StarLune and Newlight's other groups dance along the edge of the walls. I avert my gaze from a twelve-foot-tall Jihoon with chocolate-toned hair wearing a suit that's been shredded to reveal the sapphire-encrusted satin lining. Non-holographic yet fashionable people stride past us with purpose and impeccable grooming and style, making me feel duller than usual.

Alex's cool demeanor doesn't crack until a little green robot with a smiling faceplate rolls up to greet us in perfect English. "Mr. Williams and Ms. Hui of Hyphen Records. Welcome to Newlight Entertainment, where innovation is content. Please follow me."

"Innovation is content," I murmur to Alex. "I know the winner of the buzzword bingo game."

"It's better than *shut up and give us your money*," he says. "I guess we go with the robot." I hum a few notes of "Thus Spoke Zarathustra," the theme song for killer AIs, and Alex tugs on his lapels. "I'll follow anything as long there's coffee at the end of it," he says.

The robot, which plays a soft acoustic version of "Candor" as it moves, takes us to a glass elevator where we stand in silence because I'm unsure of whether I should make conversation with it or if it's recording us. When we arrive at our floor, the door opens to a hall-way that is also doused in light.

"I should have brought sunglasses," I say, retreating into jokes to mask my anxiety.

Alex is staring at the rows of trophies and framed metallic records. "I've never seen so many awards in one place outside a museum," he says with awe. "There's an entire section for StarLune." I'm not sure what sort of a sound I make, but Alex peers over. "Are you okay?"

"I'm fine." My voice squeaks, and I cough and try again, pitching it as low and confident as when I speak in a meeting. "I'm fine."

I'm something, that's for sure, surrounded by airbrushed images of Jihoon. From the vinyl images that cover the wall, his face beams down on me with the same soft smile he has in the morning, sleepy-eyed as he dozes over his coffee. I look down at the polished floor because thinking of Jihoon as a person is not convenient at the moment. This 2D image is Min, and Min is not mine.

Nor is Jihoon.

I want him to be. A rush of possessiveness flashes over me, immediately followed by a disappointment so sharp, I taste it like blood in my mouth.

Yeah, I'm living my worst-case scenario.

"Remind me to hit the gift store," Alex says as he continues down the hallway after the robot.

I catch up when he pauses at another display case, this one with a row of trophies showing what looks like a mermaid. "The what?"

"Newlight merch is a huge moneymaker. StarLune has their own snack-food line."

Once we get into the boardroom, it's like any business meeting but with more bowing. I can match the people from the dossier Alex gave me, so I know the woman in the black dress is Hyesu, Newlight's head of publicity, the man in the navy suit is her assistant, and the man in gray is their legal, my equivalent. There's a translator, but Hyesu is fluent in English, as is Wonho, the lawyer. Both went to school in the United States.

The morning passes quickly, with the usual formal introductions and small talk. After we watch a corporate video that has better production value than a Marvel movie, Hyesu pulls out her laptop.

"Let's get to it." In seconds, spreadsheets and timelines display on the wall in front of us. We hunker down to work, and it's satisfying to be able to focus entirely on a single client. It might not be Beaconsmith, but it's a fascinating look at the industry. I feel naive for my argument with Alex at the bar now that I have a better sense of what's involved.

"This group, Kay-Ent-Kay." I stop when Alex kicks me under the table.

"Kinetic," he interjects smoothly.

"Of course, my apologies." Because naturally KntK would be pronounced *Kinetic*.

The day passes without further incident, and Alex and I go back to the hotel, change, and stagger out to the cute café. We drink raspberry-champagne lattes, the most bonkers item on the menu, while digging our toes into the floor grass and barely talking. I didn't know jet lag drained you so bad. I don't even have energy to worry about contacting Jihoon. Hana, bless her, has limited her messages to suggestions on the street vendor foods I have to eat, and Phoebe concentrates on giving me updates on Dad and photos of dogs she sees in the park, all captioned, **Hail Lord Pugglesworth**, regardless of breed. In a way, both of them being so careful to avoid talking about Jihoon makes me think about him more.

Back at the hotel, I send Hana a text with photos of the convenience store food I picked up on the way (a cup of ice with a mango drink pack to add in) and debate replying to Phoebe. If she's trying, I will, too, so I send her photos of the hotel room and tell her about my day.

Phoebe: **There's a gift store?**

Me: **I'll get you something.**

Late that night, I start a text to Jihoon.

Then I delete it, because what can I say?

I could say I made a mistake, but then we're back to where we started, him in Korea being a big-ass idol and me living in Toronto. There's no point.

So I lie in bed, staring at the ceiling and listening to my heart argue with my obtuse head.

Thirty-Two

I hate parties.

No, I'm looking forward to this event. Then I repeat it, out loud and with zest. "I am looking *forward* to this corporate *party*. I *am* looking forward to this *corporate* party."

The affirmation doesn't help. I am *not* looking forward to this corporate party.

After the workday, I force myself under a cold shower, filling the bathroom with pained yelps but knowing it will be worth it to feel slightly more alert. In twenty minutes, my hair is up in a high bun because I can't stand it on my neck in this unseasonable heat, my black dress is on, and I have a good red lip and even a cat eye. Alex, who looks like a movie star in charcoal pants and one of those suit vests with the satiny-looking back panel, nods in approval when I meet him in the hallway.

We slide into the cab, and he gives an address on the other side of the Han River. Seoul is enthralling, and I want to investigate every street and alley we drive past. So far I've only seen around the hotel and the commute to Newlight, which is sad. More pathetic is that putting off pleasure for work is standard for me. At least I feel bad about it now, so that's growth of some kind. The next but distant stage is doing something about it.

The neighborhood we arrive in is surprisingly multicultural compared to the office in Gangnam. "Itaewon," says Alex as we get out of the cab and walk to a small alley lined with a green carpet. "Gay town, party town, and where a lot of foreigners hang out."

We halt in front of a chrome door etched with tulips that swings open on silent hinges when we cross a dark square cut into the carpet. I wait for another robot to come up, but instead beautiful women smile and bow as we enter. I can't help but suck in my stomach because they have waists so cinched they resemble wasps, an impression heightened by the black-and-yellow dresses they wear and hair that rises above their very pale faces in sculpted bouffant styles. Fresh sympathy grows for Hana if this is the obviously not impossible but very difficult body standard she's being compared to by her mother.

Hyesu and her team are there to greet us, lit by the spotlights that gleam down on the bars lining the room. Smeared glasses litter the tables, and the sickly sweet smell of alcohol floats in the air.

"Ariadne!" Wonho comes up, already at the level of drunk where his eyes are hazy and a slight slur makes him hard to understand over the loud music. Yet his tie remains a work of art, and he hasn't even downgraded to a French tuck. "You need a drink."

"Thanks, but I'm fine."

It doesn't take. He plucks one from a pretty tray that's flashing LED lights into the glasses so they glow and hands it over, then he waits until I sip it. Only when the glass is empty does he smile contentedly.

The first hour of the night passes. Wonho introduces me to his colleagues, and Alex chats to Hyesu at one of the bar counters nearby. The atmosphere is overwhelming, and my skin feels too humid from everyone's breath. Not helping are the idol holograms that cluster in tableaux near the bar, similar to the ones at Newlight headquarters. More of the groups are recognizable from my meetings, and I'm pleased to identify KntK as well as StarLune.

When Wonho is distracted, I escape to a quiet corner. Tilting my head against the wall, I survey the crowd, noticing how many people StarLune keeps employed. There's the staff at Newlight, the stylists, dancers, and videographers. It's a mini economy, and most of it comes directly from StarLune. Jihoon wasn't lying when he said his decision impacted more than only him.

Programmers, too. Newlight has propelled their technology game to boss level with a set of holograms that make their way around the room, so realistic I could have sworn it was StarLune in the flesh. They've dressed the images in blazers and black jeans, and when I peer closer, the faces are extraordinarily expressive. I knew Korea was light-years ahead of Canada, but the expertise here is more than I can imagine. A slight aura seems to follow the band and people melt out of their way because it would be weird to have Kit walk through you like a ghost.

I catch sight of the Jihoon hologram, and my breath simply stops. He has lilac hair trimmed in a sleek undercut that emphasizes his bone structure. As I stare, Alex appears at my side from the opposite direction. "We've put in enough of an appearance," he says. "Want to head back to the hotel or look around Itaewon?"

"Itaewon so we can see the oldest jazz bar in Korea, but in a minute." Bemused, I move across the room to get a better look at Jihoon. Longing for the real man itches along my fingers.

Ariadne Hui, you are an absolute and utter jackass to have done what you did.

"This technology is phenomenal," I say. The black boxes lining the ceiling must be projecting the holograms.

Alex follows me. "What are you talking...oh no. Oh *no*."

As I step close to the hologram, I reach out to see what happens to my finger in the light. A murmur goes up around me.

"Ari!" Alex grabs my arm before I make contact.

I freeze as I recognize the light citrus cologne. Computer generations don't wear cologne.

The not-hologram Jihoon looks right at me.

"Oh my God," I say. "You're real." Then I cringe.

"Jesus, Ari," mutters Alex as he tugs at me. "How much did you drink?"

Jihoon at least keeps his cool, although his eyes look a bit wild. "Min of StarLune." He's so close that when he bows, a breeze flows over my sweaty skin.

Two issues occur to me simultaneously: I'm not supposed to know Jihoon, and I've basically accosted the guest of honor at my client's event. Behind Jihoon, Kit stares at me. Correction, everyone stares at me. I must have broken a thousand etiquette rules in the past twenty seconds.

Kit nudges Daehyun, and the two of them cast me cold looks that I only see out of my peripheral because I can't take my eyes off Jihoon. Then Kit steps forward to pull Jihoon subtly away. It's like the spell is broken as the rush of blood in my ears gives way to the driving techno beat of the music and the buzz of Newlight's entire staff complement gawking at me. Hyesu bustles forward, bowing and speaking quickly. It must be along the lines of *she's a blundering Canadian, please cut her some slack because she has no idea how to behave like a functioning adult.*

Jihoon smiles at her, then leans over to speak in English. "Would you like an autograph? We love to meet our fans. Starrys are so important to us."

I feel my face go purple, but his expression is completely earnest, like we've truly never met and I'm nothing but a starstruck fan. I should let him have this brief triumph, because God knows I deserve it. I might not have a choice but to let him have it because I can barely breathe, let alone think of a retort.

So I only stare at him. He stares back, smile fading until his gaze darkens and his eyes flick across my bare neck to my lips.

Alex clears his throat. "Well, this is fun, wow, so great," he says. "A pleasure to meet you."

He leads me away, hissing, "Don't even think about looking back. Not one fucking glance, am I understood?"

He must be mad if he's swearing, but I can't help peeking over my shoulder. Jihoon's watching, his teeth biting so hard into his lip that I can see the indent. I wish I could smooth it out, but I've humiliated myself enough for one evening.

"You up for that jazz bar?" Alex asks once we're outside.

"I only want to die." My voice is muffled behind my hands.

"Hotel it is."

In the cab, Alex throws himself back with a groan. "How did we not know they'd be there?"

"You know, it was fine." I've recovered a bit. "I looked like an awestruck fangirl, nothing too bad."

"Says you. I thought you were going to rip off that Bottega jacket and climb the poor guy like a tree." He gives me a penetrating look. "You didn't tell him you were here."

"I tried, but I couldn't do it." My mind is all over the place. "You can recognize who designed a blazer?"

"Yes, and it's not difficult to tell someone you're in Seoul. It's three words. *I'm*, there's one. *In*. Two. *Seoul*. Three, there you go."

"They were hard words," I say.

My phone buzzes. Jihoon.

You're here.

Alex looks down at my phone, which lights up the back of the cab. "I don't know why you're playing this game with yourself."

"It's not a game." He's right. Everyone is right. I want this, so why can't I admit I was wrong and ask him to give me another chance?

Alex looks at me with raised eyebrows.

It might be the drinks, but I give him the truth. "I don't know what I want, okay?" The words rush out faster than the traffic we're speeding through. "I thought I did, and now I don't know. What if I'm wrong about this, too? I want it all to be simple again."

"It never was simple," Alex says. "It was small. Now you're opening up."

"Thanks, I hate it."

"Think of it like a new city to explore," he suggests.

"Except if I make the wrong choice in a city, I can grab a cab or check a map. This is my life, and if I screw up, that's it. It's a one-way ticket."

We go silent as we cross the bridge. Most bodies of water at night are a little freaky, because how can you look at a black ocean and not get worried about being dragged out to sea by a giant squid? But there's something about a dark river that's eternally romantic. I wish I could appreciate it better, but Alex's words rise in me with the same power as a sea monster.

"Do a pros and cons list." Alex's voice breaks in on my thoughts.

"Those don't work."

"I know. I did one before asking Ben to marry me. The con side was much longer than the pros, starting with his parents."

"You got married, though." I glance at his wedding band. I'd seen photos of the ceremony in Costa Rica, both the grooms in custom-made linen suits with Bermuda shorts and gigantic smiles.

"Because there was one pro that negated every con. Every last one. That's when I realized it's not a pros and cons list, it's a weighting. If I weighed all my concerns against all the benefits, what would win out?"

Now I'm interested. "What was the pro?"

He grins. "I'd written *Ben*, in all capital letters. He was all that mattered."

I glance back at my phone. There are so many cons: the distance, work, the fame. Then that one weighted pro: it's Jihoon.

I really liked him. Like him. I can't stop thinking about him, but more than that, what my existence could be with him. More intense and richer. Deeper and broader. I wish I hadn't been such a quitter. I wish I'd given my life half the attention I give to work, that I'd valued myself as much as I had a law firm that couldn't care less about me. I wish I'd given us a chance to be something.

Alex reaches over to give my hand a squeeze. It's warm and comforting as we drive through the busy Seoul streets. Then he releases me and looks out the window to give me space to think.

When I take out my phone, l let my heart lead the decision.

It takes three tries for me to type out a reply that doesn't have any typos from my trembling thumbs. Then I read it over again. I'm about to read it one more time before my finger unilaterally decides to commit to this course of action, dragging my brain along with it.

I'd like to talk to you, my reply reads. To apologize.

The reply comes blessedly fast: I'm free tomorrow night.

This time I don't wait or bother with checking my message, so what I send back says, yse.

He understands. I'll send you the address of a café.

When I look up, Alex takes one glance at my beaming face and bursts out laughing. I don't even care.

I get to see Jihoon again.

Then there's a pause and another message comes in. You looked lovely in that dress. Good night, Ari.

I don't hate parties that much after all.

Thirty-Three

The next day drags, and before I leave, Jihoon texts me where we can meet.

Jihoon: It's safe but wear a mask and hat.

Safe. I'm meeting a man who needs to consider safety when going for coffee. Despite his money and fame, Jihoon lives in a bubble.

By the time I get to the café, I've discarded seven different starters as to how I'm going to apologize. None of them seem adequate yet all seem beyond my ability to manage.

The café is in a side alley and, absorbed in my interior role-play, I walk past the entrance and have to double back. The moment I tap the button to open the door and walk in, a smiling woman wearing an ivory apron bows and waves for me to follow her. The café is empty but gorgeously decorated like an old library, with green lamps and dark wood and books piled on side tables surrounding plush club chairs. She points me up the back staircase.

The decor on the second floor is similar but features pretty tea sets instead of books. I notice all these details with a sense of desperation as I try to avoid thinking about what's going to happen. I don't want to have this conversation. I would sell my soul to skip the next twenty minutes so I can deal with the fallout of what Jihoon has to say without having to live through the actual words.

There's a table near a window, and at the table sits Jihoon, eyes trained on me. A black slide loafer dangles from the toes of his crossed leg.

He stands to greet me, and I peer at him. "What happened to your eyes?"

That wasn't one of my planned openers, but it's too late. Well, it's no worse than some of them, so I commit and give a weak wave toward his face. "Your eyes. They're blue." More of a grayish blue, the color of a battleship, but now is not the time to get pedantic.

"Contacts," he says. "For a photo shoot."

"Oh." Right now, I'm Smaug lying on that bed of loot, the jewels encrusting me, but the second I start talking, my words will reveal that one soft spot on my underbelly for him to stab or stroke.

I don't even wait for him to sit down, because the stress is too much for me. Gone is the cool and collected Ari who can handle a client meeting without batting an eye.

"I'm sorry. I'm sorry I said we shouldn't see each other. I'm sorry I didn't try. The contacts look good. I know you have every right to be mad. I'm sorry."

"Ari, breathe." He doesn't touch me, but his voice is gentle.

I take a huge gasping breath and avoid looking at him because I don't know what to do next. I hate this. I hate talking about anything emotional. I hate being vulnerable and hoping, praying the other person doesn't make a joke to lighten the mood when I'm not ready to be laughed at or make me feel silly or cut me down for having those feelings. I hate having to give that amount of trust, even to Jihoon.

"We'll talk," he adds. I look up quickly and he nods me to the table. His face is drawn and pale under his tan skin, and his arms are crossed.

We sit down in chairs low enough that I land with an inelegant *oomph*. The silence thickens as I look anywhere but at him and he looks at me. Finally I understand he's going to wait me out, so I steel myself and raise my eyes to his.

"I panicked," I say softly. Eye contact makes all this harder, especially with those contacts, but I power through. "I saw the crowds, and it was all so strange, and I choked."

"What worried you?" His hands are tucked under the table so I can't see them.

"I'm not sure." I frown. "A bit of everything? The fame, for sure. The distance. We've only known each other a month. We're busy."

He nods. "Those are all reasonable concerns that we discussed before I left. You're using the panic as an excuse when you simply weren't convinced even after we talked."

I wince. "We might not have discussed them enough."

"Then why didn't you say so? Why didn't you ask me what I thought or if I had the same fears?"

This makes me frown. "Because we'd talked about it already?"

"Yes, and you continued to have those thoughts. Instead of telling me, instead of communicating, you acted. You acted alone."

That's true, but... "I did it because you were happy with trying."

"I was," he says simply. "I was happy to try. I wanted to try because I don't know the future. You were scared to even do that, and you should have told me."

"I wasn't scared."

"You're lying." His voice is sharp.

"It was a shock to see the airport," I say, plucking at a loose thread on the chair. "You told me, but I didn't understand how famous you were until I saw it myself."

Jihoon pushes away the cup he's been playing with. "I was the same person."

"Let's be real. Say we date. We can't go see a movie in the spur of the moment. Apparently we can't even go to a coffee shop without a disguise. Even if we wanted coffee, it's a thirteen-hour flight."

"Others have made it work." His jaw is set. "We could have, too. You didn't want to make the effort."

"That's unfair." I yank the thread out completely and fiddle with it. "I didn't want what we had to fade away."

"You wanted to keep control."

That sounds both very bad and like me. I nod. "I guess I did, although I didn't say that to myself at the time."

"Yet here you are. None of those things have changed. What do you want from me, Ari?"

I take a deep breath and go for it. "I miss you. I miss talking to you and knowing you were there." I take another deep breath, wondering if I'm going to start hyperventilating from sucking in all this oxygen, and force the words out. "I screwed up, and I know it. I want to try again."

It's out. I put all the cards on the table. He can get up and leave, but at least I won't have the regret of never letting him know. I won't live my worst-case scenario. Well, that might happen, but at least I gave it the same effort I would a work project. More, because feelings are much harder to deal with than a memo.

"When you told me it was over, at first I thought it was a joke," he says mildly. Now he's looking away from me, over my shoulder. "A very unfunny and cruel joke."

Shame is the worst feeling. I try not to hide in my chair and instead accept the repercussions of my actions. "I'm sorry."

"I didn't know what changed. I thought you were using me, and when I was leaving, you didn't need me anymore."

This snaps my head up. "Never!"

"No?" His smile is twisted. "I'm surrounded by people who only want me for what they can get."

"Jihoon, I didn't even know you were in StarLune or rich until I'd already fallen for you." My face heats. That was too much information.

He assesses me carefully across the table. "Would you have contacted me if I hadn't seen you last night?"

"I don't know." I look down at the red thread twisted around my fingers. "I was psyching myself up to it. Started a few texts. Deleted them."

He gives me a small seedling of a smile. "What do you see happening, Ari?"

Be honest, my inner lawyer tells her client, Ms. A. Hui. "You to forgive me, first. I know I need to earn your trust back. I want to try, really try. If you want."

"We need to talk about all those things you kept bottled up." I frown, and this makes him groan. "Emotional openness is the only way I'm willing to forgive you."

"How much openness?" I ask cautiously.

"Ari. As much as is needed."

"Okay," I say. "We have different standards, though, if past history is an example."

"I want the Ari I knew in Toronto before she got scared," he says. "The one who talked to me about her life and listened to me talk about mine."

That I can do. I think I can do it. I will definitely do my best to try to do it. "All right," I say with more confidence than I feel. He looks at me, and I speak more firmly because I have to fix this with Jihoon. "Yes. I will, if I can get the Jihoon I knew before Min."

"That man is always here." Jihoon pinches his lip thoughtfully. "Kit hyeong will call me a fool and say you'll break my heart again."

I glance up. "You can break mine this time."

"I'd prefer we didn't break anyone's anything." He slides the decorative teacup back and forth across the table. "You hurt me, Ari. I need you to know that, although I probably deserved it after lying to you in Toronto."

"I know." I keep his gaze this time and let myself feel the crush of regret around my heart. "I handled it badly."

He stands up and comes around the table to my side, where he drops on the arm of my seat to run his hand along my hair. "It's a deal. Again."

I blink at him uncertainly. "It is? You? Ah...with me." How articulate. I can't even think of the words because he's so close and his hand has moved from my hair to clasp the back of my neck. I freeze for a moment because I didn't think he'd say yes, even after all that negotiation.

He bends down, those unnaturally light eyes fixed on mine. "Yes. Shall we seal it with a kiss?"

I groan. "That's so corny, oh my..."

Jihoon shuts me up with his mouth. My hands come up to brush the hard muscles of his chest and his heart races under my fingers through the thin shirt. It's a sweet kiss, no more than a flutter against my lips. It's also not enough because after that torture, I want more. I sit up and lean into him as his arms wrap around me.

"Jihoon-ah!" A woman's sharp voice comes from the other side of the room, and Jihoon leaps away. Her face has a hugely infectious smile, and she waves two menus as she winks.

He bows, but she only laughs. They speak together for a moment before she turns to me.

"It is nice to meet you," she says. "I am Eunyoo."

Her English is halting but miles better than my Korean. "Annyeonghaseyo," I say, remembering that Jihoon once said this was the more formal greeting. "Hello. I'm Ari."

She looks affectionately at Jihoon, and whatever she says causes him to duck his head and go red. Then she lays the menus down and leaves.

"What did she say?" I demand.

"She says I need to eat well." He picks up the menu and goes to his seat to peruse it with his full attention.

"What else?" His color hasn't gone down.

"Nothing."

"Jihoon."

"Because I need the energy," he mutters.

"For what?"

"You know. Performing." I say nothing and he huffs. "She said I need to stay strong to keep you happy."

I watch in astonishment as the flush travels to the tips of his ears, turning them fuchsia. He won't look me in the face, and this shyness from a man who can eye fuck an arena of fans into a screaming mass is hilarious. I take pity on him and change the topic. "How long is the break you're getting today?"

He almost pouts. "Until ten tonight."

"Oh." That's not long.

"I'm due back for practice because of the concert," he says as if in apology.

I look at him carefully. "Have you been eating?" He's skin, muscle, and bone, and his jawline is much sharper. I had noticed last night but had put it down to the lighting.

"Comeback," he says. "We all lose weight. It's expected."

"That's not healthy." He's as streamlined as a greyhound.

"Not at all healthy. It's the industry."

"How long can you keep this up? Performing, I mean?" I already hold my back when I have to bend over.

"A good question." He glances down at himself. "I don't know. StarLune debuted ten years ago. We're veterans but not superhuman."

"What comes after being an idol?"

"I could host a variety show," he says. "Act in a drama or shift into full-time producing. Songwriting."

"That seems like a better match than variety shows." I hesitate. "Your songs are incredible."

His eyebrows lift. "You listened to manufactured K-pop?"

I wrinkle my nose at being deservedly called out. "I was wrong."

He laughs. "An unexpected but appreciated vote of confidence."

He comes over and tucks himself into the chair beside me. I lean into him, taking physical satisfaction in his closeness.

"Now, tell me why you are in Seoul stalking idols at parties," he says.

"I really did think you were a hologram," I excuse myself as he slides his arm around my back.

"I don't know how to take that, to be honest."

"As a compliment. I'm here with Alex to work on some of the North American promotions for bands under Newlight. Not StarLune, though."

"For how long?"

"A few more days."

He picks up his phone and brings up the calendar. "The concert is soon, and I'll have some time off after. Can you stay longer?"

"Ah, I am actually staying longer."

"You are?" He glances over with those unnervingly pale eyes.

"I'm taking some vacation time. Hana is stopping over in Seoul for a couple days before she does a training course in Busan. We were going to explore."

"She didn't tell me that." He tucks my hair behind my ear. "You will both stay with me."

"We have a hotel."

Jihoon waves his hand. "My place is safer, and we can see each other. You can come to our VIP concert."

I want this and know Hana would love it, so I don't need any convincing. "We'd love to."

"When Hana leaves, we will tour the city, you and I together."

"That we can do." I rest my head on his shoulder then lift it to smile at him. "I have an itinerary."

"I have no doubt you would have the best one. Perhaps I can add some secret spots to it."

It feels like we're back in Toronto, normal people instead of celebrity and noncelebrity. Jihoon's always been touchier than me, soothed with physical contact, but I didn't realize how much he depends on it until he drapes himself over me, hands stroking my arms as if reminding himself of how I feel. Even though the conversation is going smoothly, I have this nagging feeling that it shouldn't be going as well as it is.

"Why are you so quick to forgive me?" I ask suddenly. "I would have made me work for it way more."

He plays with my hair. "What's the point of that? We both acted poorly and have learned from it."

"I guess."

"You forgave me before, and I did the same. You're here and we talked. People make mistakes, and it's not productive to hold grudges forever or keep score. I'd prefer to be happy."

He moves back to his seat when Eunyoo brings us hotteok, pancakes filled with syrup so sweet, it hurts my teeth.

"I should have made these for you when I was in Toronto," he says.

"The pancakes you did were good. More chocolate chips than batter."

He nods, satisfied. "Good. I miss the cereals, though."

It's an oddly domestic conversation. A relationship is built on tiny everyday interactions, casual comments, and brief touches. I didn't know how much I missed it and, as Jihoon licks the syrup off the side of his hotteok, how I would like to have this all the time.

This is not like me. Previous relationships were in a very specific compartment in my mind. I had work, home, friends, family, and the occasional boyfriend with very little overlap. That's not how it is with Jihoon. I like him in my home life and that he and Hana are friends apart from me. I like the way he intersected and intertwined with me in Toronto like no one else has.

Jihoon reaches over and tugs my hand across the table so he can trace the lines on my palm, his touch rippling through my whole body. He's not even looking as he does it, but his absentminded desire for us to touch makes me weak.

Eunyoo comes up and whispers to Jihoon. Both of them look serious. "Gamsahamnida," he says quietly. She leaves, feet tapping lightly on the stairs as Jihoon rubs his knuckles into his hand.

"What?" I ask.

"There's someone from a fan site outside. They must have followed me."

Thirty-Four

S omeone followed him. Right, that's a common occurrence. "Run that by me again. A fan site?"

"Websites run by fans that post photos of us."

I take a deep breath and become lawyer Ariadne, based on data and not emotion. "If they followed you, do they already have photos of me?"

We pull out our phones. After a minute of scrolling, he looks up. "Nothing. You?"

"Nope."

Since I've remained in problem-solving mode, I bypass the many unrelated questions I have and stand to look out the window. "Would the fan site person have a professional-looking camera?" I ask.

"Yes." He stands, but I wave him back, looking intently out the window like I'm a spy. Out front of the café is a woman with black hair pulled into a low ponytail, two cameras slung around her neck and her phone in her hand.

"Why doesn't she come in?" I ask.

He looks out the other side, angled to stay hidden. "Good fan sites respect our personal space and privacy. She would think it incredibly rude to intrude."

I turn to him. "Jihoon, she's followed you here and is waiting right outside the door to get a photo of you. That's not respecting your space."

"She's not touching me or approaching me. She's not threatening. She usually only covers appearances on our schedule, so her even being here is unusual." He bites his lip. "My own fault. It's been happening more since I came back."

This is so out of my realm of comprehension that it takes a few moments to try to wrap my head around his reality. "There is a woman outside waiting to take photos of you, and you're scared to leave because of it. That's not normal."

This causes him to burst out laughing. "Of course not, but it's what my life is. Usually I wouldn't care, but I want to protect you, Ari."

I move to next steps. "Do we stay here all night?"

"Eunyoo has a plan. I'll distract her by going out the front while you leave out the back door for the car. You and Yeong, the driver, can pick me up out front." He's confident, and since this is his world and not mine, I have to trust him.

He catches me around the waist before we head downstairs and lifts my chin with one finger. "Did I say how pretty you look today?" he says.

"I'm more than looks." I sniff theatrically even as I feel my face go red. I forgot how much I love Jihoon's spontaneous compliments.

He grins. "I haven't been able to tell you how smart and creative you are for a long time, but I'll do that soon as well." He bends to kiss me, his lips slotting in perfectly to mine. For a moment, that's all I know—his hands on my waist and his kiss. Then Eunyoo calls from the bottom of the stairs, and Jihoon hands me a mask.

To my surprise, his plan works. While I wait downstairs, Jihoon leaves and lingers in the door so anyone waiting in the back alley will leave to follow him. I give Eunyoo a wave and dash out when the car appears, falling into the back seat so dramatically that Yeong stifles a laugh before he guns it and heads around the corner.

The car slows, and I duck down as the door opens. Jihoon jumps in beside me with a cup in his hand.

"Eunyoo thought it was more realistic to come out with a drink," he says, seeing me look at it. "I think we're safe. Did you see anyone?"

"No but better ask Yeong."

Jihoon leans over and has a long discussion that concludes when he turns to me and says, "He didn't."

It's like those subtitled movies where six minutes of dialogue gets translated to *good idea.*

"Now what?" I peer out the car window to look for other photographers.

"If you don't mind, Yeong will drop me at practice first. Anyone following us will wait there until I come out later tonight, so he'll be free to take you to your hotel."

Anyone following us. I only nod. "Right, but I meant us. What happens now, to us?"

"Ah." He kisses my hand. "We take it day by day. No plan."

I do my best to smile, but the thought of no plan makes me nervous. He's worth the effort of living with my heart, but I don't know how. I'm years out of practice. Decades, maybe.

"We need to talk," I say. "About how this is going to work. Logistics."

"That will be the first thing we do once our special concert is over," he promises. "I look forward to a deep and sincere discussion."

"Ah, yeah." I hope my eyes don't resemble those of an emotionally stunted deer in the headlights of an overly empathic truck, but Jihoon takes my hand.

"It will be easy," he soothes. "If you're honest with me and with yourself."

"Not helping."

Jihoon's phone is almost vibrating off the seat with the number of messages coming through. He simply picks it up and turns it off, the most thoughtful thing a modern man can do, before briefly pressing his forehead against mine. "I'm sorry, Ari." He sounds regretful. "This life is stifling. At least when I'm busy, I don't think about it. Work is an excuse."

Work is an excuse. Jihoon has a disconcerting habit of expressing thoughts I didn't know had been circulating in my own mind. When I'm doing due diligence or checking over documents, I don't have to think about what a fucking useless way I'm spending the time I have on this planet.

Here lies Ariadne Hui.

She wrote memos no one read.

Now she's dead.

Lost in thought, I watch the night city pass by the car windows, Jihoon at my side with his hand on mine. He's humming low to himself, little snippets of songs that start familiar but soon twist and alter into new melodies that curve around my mind. I think about cool water washing over my skin and the way the sun feels when it beats down through the thick, wet heat of a summer day. He changes the tune, and it turns bluer, filling me with longing for a place I've never been. Kaukokaipuu, the Finns call it. I write it on the first page of each new travel notebook.

I don't realize I've let out a lingering sigh until Jihoon calls my name. "Ari?"

"Yes?" My eyes almost hurt from the intensity of looking out the window while not seeing what's in front of me.

"Tell me what's bothering you." He shifts on the seat. "Is it me?"

"Not you." I lift his hand to more comfortably fit my fingers with his and nestle my head back into the car seat to look through the sunroof. "You said work is an excuse."

"I did."

"Work has been my life for as long as I remember," I say to the distant sky. "First school, then the office. My parents expected the best from me. You know Phoebe dropped out and is basically a nomad. It drives my father nuts to see her waste her life."

"Yet you seem envious of her."

"I don't know if law was my goal or Dad's. Phoebe got to do what she wanted, and I'm stuck with what he wanted for me." I say it louder than I planned and then stop, shocked when I hear the words and how angry they are.

"Then, Ari, make a different choice. Like your sister did."

I glare at him. Easy enough to say when it's not you who has to deal with the backlash. "A choice that will worry and disappoint them the way she did? I was always the good one."

"They survived your sister leaving school."

"Sure, but they weren't happy." I make a face. "I don't want to talk about it anymore."

He smiles and looks down at me. "I'll be here when you do." My hair is over my shoulder, and he slides a lock through his fingers before deftly tying it into a loose knot and undoing it. "This is the first time I haven't adored a comeback," he says thoughtfully. "Before, I was worried and tired but excited for fans to hear our work."

"Why?"

"When I was with you in Toronto, I had no expectations on me. I could do whatever I wanted, without people fussing about where I was or what I was wearing. No one watched me. I had space to think and dream."

Although I've slowly come to grips with the idea that being an international celebrity isn't all skittles and beer, part of me wants to point out that being a millionaire with staff to take care of the boring parts of life is hardly a tragedy. That would be grossly unfair because neither is being a lawyer with loving family and friends and kick-ass benefits and a pension plan. I have all that I should need to be happy; so does Jihoon. Yet both of us greedily want more, to selfishly carve out the extra that makes life worth living instead of going through the motions every day.

"What did you dream about?" I ask.

"Impossible things. You know I write some of our songs." He rubs his arms. "People think mine are fun ones, light and happy. I want to grow and move in different directions."

"Then you should."

His smile is sardonic. "The company likes things how they are."

"Not messing with a good thing," I say, remembering the conversation we had on my balcony. "You said you tried to do things on the side. Was it your songwriting?"

He freezes up, and this tension is so unusual, I turn to face him. "Jihoon?"

He only shakes his head, and soon we pull up to the Newlight building. "Turn to me for a second," he says. He snaps a photo, then gives me a lingering kiss. "I'll see you soon. I'll find the time."

This time when he leaves, he takes what remained of my regret and sadness with him. It's going to be hard, but I'm in it to win it, even if it takes the open communication Jihoon threatened. I can do that for him.

Back at the hotel, I'm alone with my thoughts until an email from Yesterly and Havings comes through. It's to all staff, congratulating Brittany on her nomination for a prestigious excellence award, the one I hoped they would select me for.

I wait for the fury to come. It doesn't. It stings but it doesn't burn.

Another email comes in, this time from Luxe. Ines has found someone to take on the role she offered me, so no need to worry.

I get into bed and pull the duvet over my head. My entire body feels empty, and for the first time, work isn't there to soothe me. A loudspeaker squawks outside my window, and when a peppy song starts to play, I peer out of my blanket cave, wondering what it is. Alex would know. I should have had him take me on a musical tour of the city to experience K-pop myself instead of learning it from a computer screen.

A musical tour of the city. Ideas start to flow as I consider how this could look.

Excited, I sit up and start to make some notes. Slowly, without me noticing, anything to do with Yesterly and Havings drifts quietly to the back of my mind.

————

"Water," rasps Alex, hanging in my doorway with an ashen face. "I beg you. Coffee."

I give a weak wave toward the coffeemaker on the desk, and he stumbles in.

"That was..." I pause as I try to force my lethargic brain into thinking while controlling my nausea. "Intense."

The last day working with Newlight had passed without incident. Then they took us out to say goodbye.

I was unprepared.

The night had started well, at a BBQ place familiar to me from the ones Hana and I go to in Koreatown, with a little vented brazier on the table to cook the meat. I nibbled on some fried tofu and drank the first of what would be many drinks.

So many drinks. I texted Jihoon before we left, and he warned me it would be a long night. I didn't realize how long.

"They must have iron livers," says Alex now with deep respect.

After dinner, we went to the noraebang for karaoke and more drinking. Thank God I'd had the foresight to turn off my phone, which saved me the dread of one of the Newlight staff seeing a text from Jihoon and the more dominant fear of sending him an incredibly bad booty call message.

Makeup sex rocks, but I'm trying to be classy here.

Clutching our coffees, we go to Alex's room so he can finish packing. He struggles as he lifts his bag to check the weight. "Who would have guessed souvenirs were so heavy?" he says.

"You bought StarLune snow globes for your team and the convenience store's entire stock of spicy dried squid snacks for Ben."

"Worth it." Alex's face brightens as it always does when someone says his husband's name. "He loves those snacks and they're impossible to find at home. Did you see where I put the honey butter chips?"

"We ate them last night when we got back to the hotel."

Alex glances into the trash, which contains the empty, crackly evidence of our drunken cravings. "Shoot. We ate the crab chips, too."

Alex finishes packing, and we go out for lunch. Hyesu had recommended haejangguk, which is apparently a hangover-curing soup, so we get that for Alex and sundubu jjigae for me.

"Are you happy with the week?" I ask, picking up the wide metal spoon when the food comes. The rich smell of the soft tofu stew makes me feel better already.

"I didn't get together with an idol like some people, but it was productive." He ignores the look I give him and eats some banchan. "I got tons of content for my podcast, too."

Alex runs a music history podcast on the side. This seems like a good segue to my musical tour idea.

"I was thinking about your podcast," I say, all faux casual, no big deal. "What do you think about running music history tours?"

"What, in Toronto?" He sounds doubtful, and I try to not take it negatively.

"No, like you take a bunch of like-minded nerds on a music history tour in London or LA or whatever. Luxe does the planning. You host."

There's a long pause. "Do you have my phone tapped?"

"Why? You like it?"

"I've been playing with the same idea." Alex sounds excited and he's never overtly excited—he's too much the smooth PR guy. "I was going to ask you for advice. The trip you planned when Ben and I went to Greece was incredible."

This makes me laugh, partly with relief and partly with excitement.

"I already have something," I say. I'd taken the notes from the other night and turned them into a proposal.

"Send it to me. I'll read it now."

Alex spends the rest of lunch shifting between his food and making suggestions on my proposal. Once we're happy, we pause.

"Will Yesterly and Havings be okay with you doing this?" he asks, nibbling on some bean sprouts.

I shrug. "Gotta live while you can."

He shoots me an astounded look. "Who are you? Ari would never say such a thing."

I ignore that. "I'll send it to Ines later. I think she'll like it."

We finish eating, and after Alex heads to the airport, I sit on my bed. It's with unfamiliar delight and no small degree of stress that I switch on my out-of-office email notifications.

I'm officially on vacation, so I pull my proposal up on my laptop to read it over one more time. Alex's suggestions were solid, and I can visualize how the tour would work. I know it would do well.

Then I send it. Like that, one click and it's gone. Looking at my cursor on the screen, I wonder why there are no undercurrents of *should* or *what about*. Instead my mind ticks over more ideas in a satisfied, steady rhythm.

That Yesterly and Havings is not front and center is disconcerting because it's been one of my only concerns for my entire professional life. What I can do to impress Richard. How to get more work. How to win. It was all I thought I wanted, but work was a thing I did, not a thing I was deeply connected to. It was transactional.

Now something's shifted, and I don't know who I am anymore. We'd done a Who Is Jihoon Day in Toronto. Now I wish I'd done that Who Is Ari Day as well.

It would have been useful.

Thirty-Five

*H*ana arrives later in the afternoon. Jihoon asked Yeong to collect her from the airport, and after they pick me up from the
hotel, we head to Jihoon's apartment. It's near Itaewon in a neighborhood called Hannam-dong, close to most of the places we want to see
over the next couple days. We're both dozing when my phone dings
with some photos from Jihoon. The first is the whole band dressed
as princes in lush velvet and brocade and tight pants laced at the
front with high boots, standing in what looks like a baroque fairy-tale
throne room in outer space.

The second is of him and Kit, back-to-back and looking at the
sky. The last is of him, alone, standing near a rock with a light saber,
King Arthur style. He's looking straight at the camera with his tongue
touching his lip, dangling a crown from his hand. I make an ungodly
noise, and Hana is instantly awake.

"Is that Kit?" Her eyes bug out as she looks at the second photo.
Then she blinks. "Hoonie sent you their concept photos? Unedited?"

"I guess. He said they had a shoot today."

"Do you have any idea how secret these are? StarLune's concepts
might as well be stored in Fort Knox. If these get leaked, there will be
chaos in the fandom."

"I'm not going to leak them," I protest. I can't stop looking at the photos. He's not even a person right now, and it's clear why they're called idols. This is Min, not Jihoon. The uncertainty stirs in my chest again but is immediately quelled by knowing he trusted me enough to send the shots.

Hana scrolls through the photos. "Starrys are going to go nuts with how hot these are. It makes sense with the hints Newlight's been dropping about the new album."

I make a face and content myself with sending a series of fire emojis to Jihoon.

"You don't know anything about what they're planning, do you?"

"We don't talk about that a lot." We texted frequently but haven't been able to meet again thanks to his punishing schedule.

She glares at me. "Pretending he isn't who he is isn't helpful."

It takes me a minute to parse this out, but when I do, I decide to ignore it. "I was busy. This was a work trip."

"You were busy ignoring the fact that you are dating Jihoon and Jihoon is a vocalist for StarLune."

"We're not *dating*." Not if dating includes actual dates.

She waves this away. "If you're not seeing anyone else, then it's close enough."

"Hana, I am doing my best, but it's an adjustment." Another photo comes in. Jihoon has his jacket open, and he's wearing a sorry excuse for a shirt, thin lace that covers nothing. I brandish the phone at her to prove my point. "This is not what regular guys do. We're going to talk about it after the VIP concert."

"Good." Satisfied to know there is a talk scheduled, Hana relaxes and leans over me. "Tell him to send one of Kit. Sangjun, too."

I grab my phone protectively. "Tell him yourself."

"I'm not supposed to see these, remember? Because they're under lock and key, but apparently you've recalibrated your boyfriend's give-a-fuck-ometer to zero."

"He's not my boyfriend." Not officially.

She does a *yap-yap* motion with her hand. "Whatever."

A final photo comes in, a selfie. It's Jihoon again, same outfit, same incredibly toned lace-covered chest, but he's blowing a kiss.

In this territory, Jihoon is a visual king, and as a mortal, I can't compete. I poke Hana, and we make monster faces to send back.

We drive up to what looks like a regular apartment complex, although the Pentagon-tight security checkpoints we need to negotiate indicate it's not for average people at all. There are three-sixty-degree cameras tucked into trees and mounted on walls, small robots buzzing along the paths, and guards patrolling the grounds. The driver drops us off at a painting-filled lobby decorated with a chandelier ornate enough to grace czarist Russia at its most opulent.

Like a hotel, there's a concierge who greets us with a friendly smile but whom I suspect is a combat master ready to take down intruders. I wouldn't be surprised if tucked under the desk is an AK-47 and panic buttons that would cause gates to slam down on all the entrances. Hana deals with the details and soon hands me a fob. "Here. Your key."

She taps hers against the numberless pad in the elevator, and when we arrive at the floor, it opens right into the apartment. It's one of those design elements that looks good in movies but feels strange. I need a hallway.

We walk into a foyer with vertical lights hanging from the ceiling, which must be fifteen feet high.

We're here, I text Jihoon.

His response comes immediately. Home within an hour. Make yourself comfortable.

"They've renovated since I was last here," Hana says as she explores. To call this place an apartment is an understatement. It's so cavernous it echoes, and it includes a music room with a piano and guitars as well as the multiple bedrooms. The floors are polished stone and covered by pretty rugs. It's a lot to take in.

"This one is yours," Hana says, peeking into one of the rooms.

"Why?" I'm in the main bathroom, which has a separate shower and jacuzzi tub, but I go over. "Wow."

A gorgeous bouquet of primroses and tiger flowers stands on the desk, and orchids decorate the side tables. I check the other room. "This has flowers, too," I point out.

"Gerberas," she says. "Pretty."

"Why did he give me a guest room instead of asking me to stay with him?"

She sits on the bed and stretches her arms back. "I assume this is about Jihoon, and I further assume it was because he wanted you to have your own space."

"Doesn't he want, you know." I make a wiggle motion with my hand. "To be together?"

Hana makes a moue of distaste. "I'm two doors down."

"You know what I mean."

She sits up. "Let me check my Jihoon translator." She rubs her temples and closes her eyes like a fairground psychic. "I'm getting vibes that...let me see...okay, it's coming through, and the spirits say you should use your words and ask him yourself."

"Hana, come on."

"Communication is central to a healthy relationship. I keep telling you this."

We bring in our suitcases, and I continue to investigate while Hana showers. She joins me while I'm staring into a small fridge I found in the kitchen. After a peek over my shoulder, she pushes me aside to rifle through because it's stuffed full of skin-care items instead of food. "He's got the full Beauté Diable line," she says, pulling out a package with reverent hands. "This is a fifty-dollar sheet mask."

"Let's see if they have anything to eat besides retinol serums." I'm nauseous, but it could be from either anticipation or hunger.

She opens the larger, non-cosmetics fridge and some drawers

before admitting defeat and handing me a banana. "Not much apart from microwave rice and ramen."

"Aren't they millionaires?"

She points at the cosmetics fridge. "Millionaires with priorities."

We eat the bananas standing in front of the floor-to-ceiling windows in the living room as we debate stealing Jihoon's sheet masks to alleviate the physical effects of Hana's jet lag and my residual hangover. The Han River looks gray and sad under a cloudy late-afternoon sky, and my tension rachets up with each minute that passes.

When the door finally opens, it's a surprise even though I've been waiting for it. Jihoon comes in first and drops his bag on the floor before kicking off his shoes and crossing the room in long strides to wrap me in a hug that feels like home. He keeps his arm around me as Kit comes over to greet Hana with a smile and a tight embrace while watching me with distrust over her shoulder. It gives his face an interesting expression, and I make sure to give him a big toothy grin to be a jerk, even though his contempt is well-earned after what I did to Jihoon at the airport in Toronto. He shuts his eyes.

Any worries I had about Jihoon's welcome and what it would be like to see him after the café talk melt away as he keeps me tucked in tight. Both men are coiffed and made up and look more like models than flesh and blood, but they pepper Hana with enthusiastic questions about the flight, the drive from the airport, and if we're hungry.

"You only have dehydrated pucks," says Hana. "That's not food."

"Easily rectified." Kit pulls out his phone and puts in a sushi order before heading off to take a shower.

Jihoon runs his hand down my arm. "Let me change."

Alone again, Hana and I fall into a weary silence. "After I eat, I need to sleep," she says.

"Jihoon says they need to leave again anyway." He showed me their schedule, and it was packed from morning to night with interviews, show appearances, practices, and rehearsals. The new album and the concert are keeping them busy.

She doesn't answer, but her head nods down onto her chest. With Jihoon here, some of my stress has transformed into exhaustion, and I relax on the couch beside her, barely registering the dip of the cushions when Jihoon comes back to burrow into my side. It's restful to have him here, not doing anything but breathing.

Conversation over dinner is a mess of Hana and I trying to keep our eyes open and both men's phones flashing with notifications every few seconds. The two of them do their best to keep to English but occasionally drop back into Korean when a message comes through.

"You should rest," Jihoon says as they get ready to go. He's barefaced and dressed in gigantic maroon sweats that hang off his lean frame. Kit is already at the door pulling on his shoes. "We'll be late, but I'll text."

He doesn't kiss me goodbye, which I do my best to not read anything into. Hana barely waits for the door to close before she stumbles down the hall, muttering about jet lag. I turn out the lights and linger in the living room, comfy in an oversize chair. The city is on display, and too lazy to go to bed, I watch the lights flicker on and off as people go about their business. Finally I drift off, head resting on the side of the chair and hands tucked in my lap.

"Ari?" A gentle touch on my shoulder wakes me up. Coming out of a deep sleep means I'm not sure exactly where I am, but Jihoon is sitting on the floor beside me.

"Hi."

Now he smiles, but he looks weary. "I'm sorry I'm late."

I sit up straight and rub my eyes. "What time is it?"

"Past two." He leans against my knee, and I run my hand through his hair. "Why are you not in bed?"

"You gave me my own room." In my half-awake state, it's easier to say what's bothering me. "Is it because you want your space?"

Jihoon looks up at me and blinks. "I was being respectful. I know you don't like to be woken up, and I have to leave early."

That's thoughtful and he's right, I do hate waking up. I can make some sacrifices, though. "We don't have much time."

Perceptive as he is, he reads between the lines to what I want to say. "I want to see you when I can, too." He urges me up and leads me to his room.

It's bigger than the one he gave me but has the impersonal air of a hotel. I climb on the bed and look around. "You didn't decorate much."

"I'm not here enough to bother." He says it indifferently as he sorts through some bottles on the desk.

This time, instead of letting it go, I take a page from the Book of Jihoon and simply ask what I want to know. "Why is it not worth the bother to make it homey?"

Jihoon stops, and I watch his face in the mirror as his eyes move over the room. "Your place in Toronto," he finally says. "You had some photos up and little figurines on the desk that you liked."

"They're ceramic birds," I say. "Two in a cage, one in flight. Hana gave them to me."

He sits down on the bed beside me. "When we were younger, Newlight did a lot of filming in our rooms. Fans would dissect everything they saw, so there were no secrets. We learned to hide anything truly personal."

"Do they film in this apartment?"

He shakes his head. "Kit hyeong and I refused. We needed some space to be ourselves." We both look around the bare room, and he gives a small laugh. "I suppose the old habits stuck with me."

"You must have some art or something you enjoy."

Jihoon jumps from the bed and goes to his closet, where he pulls out a small wooden bowl. It's carved from a knot and polished to a dull glow. "I bought this last year from a street vendor," he says, curving his hands around it. "The person didn't know who I was, and we haggled for ten minutes. Usually people try to give me things for free because it's good for promotion."

He puts it down on the desk, frowns, and shifts it to the left. Then he's in the closet again. This time he brings out a statue of a tiger, a strange dark work that mixes Tigger's goofiness with the menace of a wild animal. "From an artisan in Thailand," he says. "She begged me not to display it because she didn't want to be overwhelmed by Starry requests."

"Why not?"

"She wanted her work to go to people who appreciated her skill, not those who wanted one because I did."

"They can be one and the same," I point out.

He nods in agreement. "I agree, but she said time would tell. Not everyone knows our fans the way we do."

Jihoon studies the newly decorated desk before giving it a nod of satisfaction and me a quick kiss. I'm already dozing when he comes back from the shower. Once he's in bed, I pull him up so his head tucks under my chin, his long body half covering mine. "Tell me you want to be here," he says in a low voice.

"I do."

I can feel him smile. "It was like coming home to see you in the chair. I haven't felt like that in a long time."

"How are the rehearsals?"

He makes a humming sound, the muscles in his chest and stomach shifting against me. "Difficult but manageable."

I'm not sure if it's worse to ask or not to ask, but I decide to keep going. "Are you worried about what happened last time, when you were at Olympic Stadium?"

Jihoon's arms tighten around me, and he buries his face in my hair. "Every time we rehearse."

"Hold on a sec." I wriggle away from him and grab my wallet from my room.

He looks at the little silver hand I press into his palm when I return. "What's this?"

I sit cross-legged next to him on the bed. "I was tense studying for my bar exam." That's putting it lightly—I'd never been so stressed in my life. "I was having an awful day and nothing was going right when I found this on the ground. It was like the universe was giving me a sign." I rub my nose. "I know it sounds silly, but I brought it into my exams."

"A good-luck charm."

"More of a reminder. When I touched it, I told myself I'd worked hard and I could do it. You can't do anything about the luck, but you can control the effort."

"Now you're giving it to me." He sits up as well, duvet bunching around his waist.

I look over. "You work hard, Jihoon. I know you can do it."

His eyes flash between me and the hand, which has the fingers outstretched as if waving a cheery hello. "Thank you." He gets up and puts it in his wallet, then gives it a small pat after he zips the pocket shut.

When he gets back to bed, I draw him in until we're lying with our legs tangled together.

"How tired are you?"

He stirs with interest beside me, rolling up on one elbow and looking down. "I feel slightly more alert now."

"Then thank me better," I tell him.

He grins. "That I can do."

And he does.

Thirty-Six

*H*ana and I spend a happy day wandering around Seoul and eating until we feel like we're going to explode. Bindaetteok follows mandu follows bibimbap. Hana helps me find vegetarian options since a large portion of the food seems to revolve around pork belly.

It's not until she's with me that I understand what had been lingering in my mind since I arrived. It's a shift to be in a city where most people resemble me because they're Asian. I glance over as we sit on a bench in Hongdae, watching the buskers. "This feels strange. Everyone looks like us."

"I know." She sips her lilac-colored boba tea. "You get used to looking different back home."

"Asian as descriptor."

She laughs. "Yeah, your defining quality in a crowd. Here, it's irrelevant. I get looked at for my nose shape or my shoes, not for being Korean. I like it, at least to visit. It feels restful."

We finish our drinks and head for our next destination.

———

The next day is the special VIP show, and I wake to a selfie of Jihoon holding the hand talisman and making a heart with his fingers. Despite the dark night of the soul that brought him to Toronto, Jihoon is fully engaged in what he's doing. A buzz of energy sparks off him.

I want that feeling, too. I got a glimpse of it when working on Alex's music proposal. At Yesterly and Havings, I only have the satisfaction of completing the job and that's it. I want more.

"Are you getting ready?" Hana's voice is at the door.

I put the phone away, deciding to redirect my misgivings about work into a markedly more trivial concern, which is that there's nothing I want to wear tonight. I have not a single garment that will kick-start the confidence I need to stand out among the multiple-step-skin-care gorgeous people who will be screaming for StarLune.

Hana comes in as I'm poking disconsolately through my boring clothes. She looks cute, I observe with resentment. Loving resentment. Envious loving resentment, even though I never saw the point in dressing with style since most of my day was spent at work and lawyers aren't generally lauded for their fashion-forward approach.

"I hate my clothes," I say. "I need to go shopping."

She closes her eyes and bends her head. "I have waited years to hear you say that," she breathes. "You've made me the happiest woman in the world."

"Please stop. I want a bit of change, that's all."

"You never want change," she says. "You want certainty. You eat the same thing. When a pair of shoes wears out, you buy the exact same ones as replacements and get upset if you can't."

"You're exaggerating."

She ignores that. "You haven't even cut your hair in a decade."

"I get trims."

"You get trims." Her eye twitches.

"Wanting a new pair of pants is hardly earth-shattering."

"The pants are not the point." Her eyes and mouth open wide as if she's had an epiphany. "Hold on."

"What?"

"This isn't about the pants at all." She points at me. "You're in psychological terra incognita, and it's driving you bats."

"That's ridiculous." I dig through my clothes and toss a shirt—plain, black—into the suitcase.

"Nope." Hana nods vigorously. "Here you are away from your Tuesday laundry and your meal prep and your predictable Steves and Garys or whoever you deal with at work. You, my friend, are in a situation you can't regulate and you're spinning."

I go to the window and yank the curtains open to reveal the bucolic forest view even though we're basically in the middle of Seoul. Being rich is nice. "You make it sound like I'm some sort of control freak who can't function unless I'm standing on top with a whip."

"I don't kink shame."

"Hana."

She stands and lifts one of my—plain, black—shirts to her chest. "You've always had your life planned. Law school. Law firm. Live close to your parents. You never had to make a choice, Ari. Now you can and it's scary."

"I don't know what this has to do with buying pants."

She lifts her eyebrows at me. "You should think about it, then."

"Sometimes pants are only pants." I check the time. We're getting behind on the schedule I have planned. I can make do with the clothes I have. "Anyway, yesterday we went all historical with Gyeongbokgung Palace and the museums, so today I thought a walk along Cheonggyecheon Stream. Then lunch at Gwangjang Market and a surprise for the afternoon."

"Nope. We're going shopping."

"But..." I think of the itinerary I've set out.

"For an hour," she wheedles. "The stream and all those cute places will be there after we shop. Think of it as an experience."

"We can shop in Toronto."

"Trust me, not like this."

I catch sight of another one of my plain black shirts. "Okay. Only for a bit, though."

Hana leaps out of my room, voice echoing down the hall. "Let's do one of Jihoon's ridiculously expensive masks before we go."

With our skin fully hydrated, we go downstairs, where Hana enters an animated discussion with Yeong, who generously agreed to drive us around. The two of them check their phones like they're planning a heist before Hana nods and we head off.

"We're going shopping in Myeongdong." She gives me an appraising look. "There's a lot, so it might be a little overwhelming for a baby consumer."

I let that pass. "I don't even know what I want."

She's almost bouncing. "You want to look good for Jihoon tonight."

"It sounds bad when you phrase it like that."

"Jihoon's seen you in sweats, and he likes you, but you want to blow his socks off."

I do want to, but I don't want to admit that out loud.

"You want to kiss boring black goodbye," she continues.

"I like wearing black," I protest.

"I said *boring* black. We can get you some interesting black."

Interesting black seems like a contradiction, but I'm warming up to the whole idea. "I need new things for work. I don't want to look like a lawyer when I go into Luxe. Or Hyphen."

Hana glances over my hair, tied back in a smooth bun, and my nude lipstick. "Got it."

During the rest of the ride, she pulls up various social media accounts to get a sense of what I like. It's a frustrating exercise for both of us, since what I like and what I feel comfortable in are not the same thing. By the time we arrive at a bustling district filled with people and vertical shop signs, I'm certain this is a bad idea. Hana taps me on the shoulder. "It's only pants," she says.

Pants can be only pants. Me in new pants is still me. I cheer up.

Hana and Yeong map out a more fulsome plan of attack, alternately pointing or frowning at various stores. They turn to me and purse their lips, then Hana shakes her head. Yeong says something that makes Hana's eyes widen, and they start nodding.

"This is so cool," she whispers as Yeong gets on his phone.

"What is?" I'm suspicious because we have conflicting ideas on what counts as cool.

"There are salons that cater to idols, where they get their hair and makeup done."

"No, Hana."

"I don't want to beg," says Hana.

"Good. It's demeaning for both of us."

"But I will," she continues, undaunted. "Please, please pretty please with a cherry on top, let's go to Jeebie's."

"Hana."

"I won't let them do anything drastic, I swear."

"Why do you want to go so badly?"

She blinks. "Because this is a once-in-a-lifetime experience with some of the top stylists in a country famous for its style? They'll make us so hot."

"We're hot now," I remind her.

"Yeah, but exceptionally hot. We'll be hottified."

"That's not a word." Despite my quibbles, I admit that sounds kind of appealing. Also, it will make Hana happy. "All right. We can go."

She claps her hands. "Shopping first."

Thirty-
Seven

*H*ana sips her coffee as I stretch my shoulders, in pain from carrying about twenty shopping bags. I'm sitting with my back to the window because across the street is a huge billboard featuring StarLune dressed in jeans and white T-shirts. Jihoon has followed me around this entire morning, a ghostly presence that pops up on drink bottles, skin care, portable face fans, and digital advertising screens. Name any item at random and somewhere in the city, there's a StarLune branded version or a StarLune ad for it. After the first seven or eight sightings, I'd become somewhat inured, but I draw the line at having his billboard in my face while I chug an iced matcha latte.

"I need to buy some luggage," I say, nudging a bag with my foot.

She stirs her caramel drink. "Leave your old clothes here."

"I can't..." I trail off because I could. After dressing for the Yesterly and Havings ecosystem for years, it was pleasant to be able to contemplate buying a hot-pink shirt. I didn't because it was ugly, but for so long, I'd simply not thought it was an option.

I like having options. Why had I let myself get so constricted? Phoebe might not have a lot in her bank account, but at least she's had experiences. All I have is the memory of my billable hours.

"We'd better get going," Hana says, waving to a black car on the street. We haul the bags over, and Yeong leaps out to help us load them into the trunk. They almost fill the back of the SUV.

"He says it looks like we had a successful trip," Hana translates.

I already have my eyes closed. Shopping was exhausting. "Online from now on." Or I think that's what comes out, because I'm already falling asleep.

Hana shakes me awake when we arrive at Jeebie's, its glass storefront lit with a pinkish glow. Walking into the salon is like entering an alternate world where very different standards of beauty apply and the norm is so far to the right of the bell curve, it's off the graph. Dazzling people mill around. Perfectly applied eye makeup abounds. Hair is every color of the rainbow. Even Hana stops dead in the doorway to take it in.

Once we recover, we get our bearings, and Hana approaches the front desk, which is at least ten feet long but only a foot wide and made of some resinous polymer that shifts under the light like mercury. I expect the receptionist to be aloof and judgmental, but she gives us a wide smile and a bow as she greets us.

"They have an English-speaking stylist for you," Hana says as a woman in a white robe leads us upstairs.

"This place looks very expensive," I say, watching a guy with bone structure made of razors sleeping in a chair as a man bleaches his hair.

"Jihoon's paying. He has an account here."

Of course he does. A woman comes out with cotton-candy-pink hair tied into a high twisted braid that reminds me of a style I'd see on the Whos of Whoville. She's dressed in matching pink, with pink lips and eye makeup, and looks confidently incredible. I have a momentary daydream of walking into Yesterly and Havings with that bubblegum look. Would Richard pretend not to notice, too well-bred to comment on my appearance, or would I be sent home to change like a rebellious high schooler?

"I'm Nayeon," the stylist says before leading me to a chair in a small room. She sits me down and leans on the counter, head to the side like an intelligent bird. "What can I do for you today?"

"I'm not sure," I say honestly.

She purses her lips. "We can work with that," she reassures me. "Is this for an event, or do you want a change?"

"I have an event tonight, but I also want a change." I wrinkle my nose. "Sorry. I'm not helping."

Nayeon laughs. "It's hair and makeup. It can seem like a huge deal, but it's not. It's transient, a way to play. You can wash your face later. You can grow out your hair or wear a hat."

I never thought of that before. Slowly, I nod. "I want to look like me," I say. "But...different. A bit different."

"Sure." She walks around me, her face assessing as she runs her hands through my hair. "To confirm, no blue hair?"

"No."

"Green?"

"I would prefer not."

"Got it." She winks at me. "You want to watch me work, or you want to do the classic makeover surprise reveal?"

"Surprise." My answer astonishes me.

She swings the chair around. "You got it."

Nayeon talks to me as she works, chatting about living in New York, where she went to college at Parsons before working as a stylist for some K-pop bands. "The schedule was too much," she says. "I had no life. It was even harder for the idols."

"How so?"

Nayeon lifts my hair with both hands. "Too much scrutiny, and they have to be cautious of every single thing. One step out of line and it could be the end of your career or even your band. The pressure is enormous." She starts snipping again. "What's the event tonight? Do you want to be super glam?"

"It's the StarLune concert." There's no harm telling her. I

bet all the stylists here are sworn to secrecy, and I'm on Jihoon's tab anyway.

Her eyebrows raise. "Lucky. You'll need staying power because those shows are intense. Who's your bias?"

I know what this is now—my favorite in the band. Might as well be honest. "Min."

"I like X, so it's good we don't have to fight," she says. "We want Min to see you from the stage so he can fall in love and run away with you, and that's not going to happen if you've got mascara running down your face."

Nayeon is careful about asking me for input—do I want curls, light lipstick or dark, how much hair trimming will I allow?—and ends with a shoulder massage that almost has me purring.

She does a final dusting on my face and steps back with a big smile. "Tell me what you think."

She swings me around at the same time as a beat drops on the speakers as if to herald the new and improved Ariadne Hui.

Nayeon is a magician. My hair is down but has more presence, if you can say that about hair. I stayed clear of bangs ever since the school photographer kept calling me China Doll on my grade eight picture day, but I now sport a thick line of bangs that frame my face and make my eyes pop. I love it. She takes a mirror and shows me how she's cut layers to form the back into a pointy shape.

Then there's the face. I look nothing like my usual professional made-up self, which is designed to make me less memorable, not more. My cheeks are faintly flushed, and my lips look like ripe summer cherries. My skin is creamy, if slightly freckled, glass. Nayeon explains how to recreate the look, and I barely listen as I turn my head from side to side to watch my hair settle. Despite the high gloss on my lips, not a strand sticks to them. Nayeon grins and grabs a tube out of a drawer that she holds up. "Lip varnish," she says before tucking it into my bag with a wink.

"Very nice." Hana comes in with a big grin, and my painted mouth falls open. Her hair is shorter, a bob that comes under her ears, and her look is sultry. She looks like she can go croon some jazz hits while lying on a piano in a red satin dress. "Worth spending Hoonie's money."

"I'll pay him back."

She snorts. "As if he'll let us."

We thank Nayeon, who is beaming with pride at her work, and head down to the reception area. I strut with a little more swing than usual and am self-aware enough to be embarrassed even as I toss my hair. After all, lawyers aren't sex kittens. Strong, confident women aren't sex kittens. Then I pass a guy so ethereal he glows, and when he does a double take, eyes wide in appreciation, I preen a bit.

I decide I can be all those things if I want.

Yeong is waiting, and he gives us a bow.

"He says we looks lovely," Hana translates after he speaks.

We get in, me shaking my hair because it feels so light and smooth, and I reach into my bag, already red in the face at what I'm about to do. "Can you ask if Yeong is free to drop something off?"

She eyes the box. "A present?" She speaks to Yeong and nods. "No problem, he says."

I pass over a little box, tied with a ribbon. "It's for Jihoon. Can Yeong bring it to him? I'm not even sure where he is right now."

Yeong hides a smile, and he takes it as Hana dies with curiosity beside me. I don't know why I bought him a pair of earrings—I know the stylists usually pick out a selection for them to wear—and they're only simple hoops but with a design of little watch faces etched on the thick metal. I thought of him when I saw them.

Hana doesn't say anything about it.

———

Tired but looking phenomenal, we stumble back to the condo and dump our bags on the floor before grabbing some fancy water from the fridge and collapsing on the couch. I look at my haul with satisfaction. It'll take me time to sort through my new clothes, which have green and red and blue among my beloved but now strikingly cut black, and even longer to get used to wearing them.

I can't deny it was a very illuminating day, even without the museums.

Hana wriggles her toes in the thick rug and checks the time. "Two hours until we need to go. You know what you're going to wear tonight?"

Not at all, so that's the cue to drag everything to my room, where I stop dead at the sight of a box on the bed. "Hana?" I call.

She comes in as I pick up the long box, which is swathed and knotted in an emerald velvet that catches the light in a complex pattern. Hana dances with impatience as I pick it open with my nails to reveal a plain black box. Inside, tissue paper dotted with silver teacups is carefully folded over. I push it aside to reveal something black.

Hana's eyes bug out as I pull out a blazer. "That's a Harhawk."

I don't recognize the brand. I shake it out, and Hana gasps. It's exactly the kind I would wear to work except this sucker is turbocharged. The wool, which gleams with a subtle woven black-on-black pattern, is soft under my fingertips, and the lining is a lovely pale blue silk patterned with more teacups.

"Try it on," Hana insists. She's got the green velvet wrapped around her throat like a scarf.

I pull it on over the shirt I'm wearing, and it fits as if it's been custom-made. Hana fusses over me, exclaiming over the hidden details. There are soft cuffs inside the sleeves so I can push them up, and pockets line the inside of the jacket in a row. Inside one is a small box I toss on the bed. An inside button at the back means I can cinch it for a tighter fit, and when Hana tests it, the blazer doesn't wrinkle at all around the waist. Then we find out it has a detachable bottom panel to turn it into a long jacket with a belt and another to make it flare at the hips in what Hana calls a peplum. She stands back with her hands on her waist.

"That thing is a work of art," she says. "You know that Harhawk's waiting list is as long as one for a Birkin bag? They have to decide to sell to you."

"A brand for the rich and famous." Celebrities.

She flicks me on the arm. "Plus people they think deserve them. The brand is a social cooperative. Profits go to help girls get educations and fund microloans for women entrepreneurs."

She sees my confusion. "Jihoon is one of their global ambassadors. The members support gender and sexual diversity acceptance, too. Daehyun gave a song to an LGBTQ charity under a different name because Newlight wouldn't let him do it officially, but everyone knew. StarLune keeps all their lyrics gender-neutral. Didn't you notice?"

"The lyrics are mostly in Korean."

"They wear *dresses*."

"I thought that was a stylist thing."

She closes her eyes. "I cannot believe you."

I can't believe me either, to be honest. My internet research was appallingly selective, and I don't want to dwell on why I was more interested in the footage of them getting mobbed by screaming fans than the stories about their charitable work.

Hana grabs the box I found in the pocket. "Open it, open it."

I obey and nearly drop the box on the floor. It's a pair of earrings. Thin chains with diamonds that might be a lot of carats dangle from thin gold hoops. They're so pretty, Hana sucks in her breath beside me, and we both reach in to touch the gems with tentative fingers.

"I can't accept these," I say automatically.

"The hell you can't. Give them to me if you don't want them."

I clutch the box to my chest. "It's too much."

Hana grabs my hands to lift one of the hoops and holds it up to her ear, checking out her reflection. "You know Jihoon bought my parents' mortgage out for them, right?"

I blink. "Seriously?"

"Mom was so pissed." Hana grins. "Said he was showing off. Then she burst into tears and said he was the best nephew ever."

"They're family, though."

"Buying gifts is his love language," she says. "He wants you to know he cares. When I visited him in Seoul last time, he wouldn't let me pay for a thing. I had to sneak out to get him a bottle of whiskey as a host gift."

"I don't know if I like that."

"Because you can't reciprocate?"

"In part." The silver earrings I got him now look so cheap, I feel embarrassed.

She perches on the edge of the bed like a wise owl. "Because you've been raised to be an independent and modern woman who doesn't need a man to get by, who can't be bought by material goods, like a *bribe*, and who can make her own way in the world, thank you very much."

I frown, fingers petting the soft green fabric I took from Hana. "You say that like it's a bad thing."

"Would you feel bad accepting flowers from someone?"

"No."

She taps my earrings. "Look at it as scale. For Jihoon, these are the equivalent of flowers."

"I don't think that's entirely true."

"Relationships are not an exercise in absolute equality," she says in exasperation. "From each according to their ability and to each according to their need."

"That was Marx's description of communism."

"It's perfectly applicable. Also you *need* those earrings."

I vacillate because Jihoon's gifts are wildly overgenerous but also really fucking awesome.

"How did he know the jacket would fit?" I wonder, looking in the mirror.

"I told him," Hana says unrepentantly. "We're the same size, so I can borrow that dream of a blazer. Win-win."

"You're unreal."

She laughs and tugs it off me. "Now let me try."

If I tuck it in the closet with the rest of my new clothes, well. It *is* a nice jacket.

Thirty-Eight

*D*on't worry, you look good." Hana checks me over for the tenth time. "I can't believe you had the option to look like this all the time and deliberately chose not to. What's the matter with you?"

In the end, I went for all white, a pair of high-waisted, wide-legged pants cinched with a silver belt and a satin halter tank. The shoes are red flats, and my hair is in a high pony that shows off my new bangs and my new earrings. My heart hammered when I looked in the mirror, and Hana's quiet, "Damn, you look expensive," when I came out didn't help. My Cartier watch, which I brought with me, is clasped around my wrist.

Yeong drops us at a private side entrance, and we make our way to our seats. They're incredible, front row and in a bend of the stage. It's a smaller space—only seating twenty thousand—and Hana tells me that's deliberate, to give an intimate feel. StarLune videos are already playing on the screens that line the stage.

People scan me over when I walk by, and it's hard to stay calm. I'm not used to being looked at like this, but part of me likes it.

Full disclosure: all of me likes it. I spend so much time at work trying to blend in that I get a subversive pleasure out of being noticed for looking good as myself, not for looking different.

My phone buzzes. **Are you here?**

I send him a selfie of Hana and I, and my phone rings almost immediately.

"Look to the left," Jihoon says. "Your left."

There's a set onstage with a small black curtain I wouldn't have noticed unless I was looking. It twitches, and then I see him. It's only a moment but enough to notice his smile when he sees me.

"You look..." He doesn't continue as a burst of conversation comes from behind him. "Stay there, and I'll have someone bring you backstage after."

"Like a groupie."

"Yah, Ari, you know better."

"Thank you for the gifts. I love them."

"You deserve to have things as special as you, and I thought the jacket would be more welcome than the shoes I promised you back in Toronto." He pauses. "Enjoy yourself."

Smiling from the compliment, I pass on the message to Hana, who is ecstatic at the idea of seeing the band after the show. "They'll be sweaty." She swoons. "Panting from exertion. Chests heaving."

"Gross."

"Shut up." She laughs. "It's fun to look."

Hana hands me a pair of earplugs. There's no opening band for StarLune concerts, and the lights cut out at exactly seven, leaving us in a warm shared darkness lit only with the light sticks that fans wave around. A screen lights up in center stage with a video of StarLune set to a hypnotic driving beat.

Beside me, Hana's already screaming. I'm too stunned to even think. This entire experience is physical and visual overload. The noise batters at me, and I want to cover my ears with my hands. I've never been to a real concert in my life, and this is so much different than I expected that it's hard to take in. It's not a show but an extravaganza. There are screens hanging everywhere. There's *infrastructure*.

Jihoon's growl blasts out from the speakers. Hana jerks me forward, screaming even louder.

When the white lights pierce the darkness of the venue like knives, we're both hugging and yelling. It's so cathartic that when Jihoon's voice stops and the pounding beat starts up again, my knees weaken. The screens explode with red lights, and now Daehyun's voice roars out, attacking me right down to my bones. On the other side of me, a girl shrieks as if she's been stabbed, and the light sticks held by the fans pulse with the music in a kaleidoscope of coordinated color all around the arena. People are chanting, and it takes me a minute to realize it's the band members' names.

By the time the center screen lifts, I can barely breathe. StarLune rises from the stage backlit with spotlights, and all they do is stand there as they're revealed to the howling audience. The lights flash on, and they pose for a single perfect moment. They're dressed in white, gold, and black, complementary but not identical. Jihoon's face, the flawless mask of an idol, fills the screens. His lips are perfectly pouted, his jawline sharp enough to cut diamond. He doesn't look real.

Jihoon breaks the pose to glance at Kit, who's next to him, and the crowd roars. He turns back and tilts his head as if judging us. He doesn't smile.

The crowd loves it. I love it.

Jihoon's the first to move down the flight of steps, one hand in his pocket and his swagger so utterly breathtaking that Hana pounds me on the arm. "Holy *shit*, that's my boy," she hollers.

I can't answer because I have my hands up to my mouth like I've seen a ghost. The five of them walk to the center of the stage and stop. For a blessed moment, the crowd's din lowers to only thunderous.

Then Jihoon lifts his mic, and the five move as one.

I don't take my eyes off him for almost three hours, and by the time they're done, both Hana and I collapse back into our seats, spent. Except for a few breaks to change outfits—when they would play videos on the screens that showed StarLune as spies—and to talk to the audience, the band had been in action the entire time.

"That was…" I can't even finish and flutter my shirt to try to dry some of the sweat.

"It was." Hana's voice is so hoarse from screaming, she can barely speak over a whisper.

I thought I'd feel silly for cheering Jihoon on, like I was some sort of rah-rah fangirl, but the hell with that. He was astounding, but he wasn't Jihoon on that stage. He was Min, StarLune vocalist and idol, and he was utterly in his element. He deserved to be admired for the work he put in and how he pulled it off. Around us, people are buzzing and taking photos. I'm too wrung out to move.

When the venue is about half-empty, a man comes to the barricade, security cards dangling from his neck, and makes eye contact with us. He nods to an exit around the side of the stage.

Beside me, Hana is chanting, "*Ohmygodohmygodohmygod*," and I know exactly what she means, because although I'm trying to be cool, the whole backstage thing is nerve-racking. Part of me wants to tell Hana I'll meet her at home because I feel suddenly shy about seeing Jihoon. He was alive on that stage. No matter what he said, he was made for this.

We follow the security guy through a maze of cinder-block corridors, and when we arrive, the space is nothing like I expect. For one, it's small and crowded, with women in artistically ripped crew sweatshirts chattering as they sort through portable hanging closets, people eating from a buffet, and people handing each other drinks as they lounge on black leather couches.

I hear Jihoon laugh in the corner, and my eyes seek him out. Here in this busy little room, he's nothing like the megastar I saw onstage. He's only Jihoon. His gaze catches mine, and for a moment, there's no one in the room but the two of us.

Of course, like all perfect moments, it slips away almost before I notice it happening.

A silence settles as people see us. Jihoon bounces over to make an introduction to the room at large. When Hana bows and I wave, the eyes on us become less distrustful. I'm about to ask how he introduced me, but Jihoon leans over.

"What did you think?" He drips with sweat, shirt open halfway down his chest and an ice pack draped around the back of his neck.

"I loved it." That's all I can say, but Jihoon smiles at me as he pushes his hair off his face. "You were unreal."

"We worked hard," he says.

Kit comes up, and we look at each other.

"I could tell," I say honestly. "You were fantastic."

Kit's smile is reluctant but real as he gives me a small bow. "Thank you." He pulls Hana away to chat with him and Daehyun. Apart from a slight tap on my arm, I barely notice her go because I'm filled with conflicting emotions as I try to separate the man in front of me from the performer I witnessed dominating the stage and twenty thousand people.

"You look beautiful," Jihoon says. He leans down, but then his eyes flick around the room and he straightens. "Do you want to see what it's like on the stage?"

"Yes." The weight of the stares around us makes me nervous.

"We need to wait for the arena to clear out." He brings me to an empty side room and collapses on the couch.

I sit beside him. "What's it like, being onstage?"

He smiles, and his nose wrinkles adorably. "When it's good, it's a mix of nervousness and excitement and anticipation. Knowing a performance is coming fills me with a buzz, and being onstage is the only way I can release it. It took me a long time to get here, though."

"It did?"

"I had such bad stage fright in the beginning they almost cut me from the band. Compare that to Kit hyeong. For him, performing is like an addiction. He craves the stage for itself, but I want only the connection the stage brings."

He sees me frowning.

"When I started, I wasn't sure I wanted to be an idol, but I knew music was for me. Our producer asked me, 'Do you want to write songs or make music?'"

"That sounds like the same thing."

"It's not. I could be in a tiny room in Busan writing songs, but I need to share them with others and get their ideas. I need them out in the world. It's a constant tension between fame, which I endure, and creating, which I need. Before you say anything, I accept I love the attention I get onstage." He gives me a wry look. "Contradictions."

"Is it worth it?"

He rubs his face against the side of my neck. His skin is cool from the ice pack. "I don't know."

"Then what are you going to do?"

"Think about it later." He runs his lips along my neck, making me shudder, before settling back with a low growl. "I need to stop. Anyone can come in."

Good call. There's a snack table, and Jihoon takes another bottle of water and a plate for the two of us to pick at. It's a combination of Korean and Western food, a mix of junk and healthy. Jihoon eats chips and carrots, sushi and pizza, while I work through the dough-nuts, twisty and covered with sugar. Finally, he glances at the clock.

"That's enough time," he says, standing and then extending his hands to haul me up.

I follow him back through the corridors to what looks like a lift. One hand catches me around the waist as the other pulls my ponytail off my shoulder.

"Wait a moment," he says into my neck. Then he calls out to a hidden someone, and a grunt comes from somewhere in the back.

"The crew is safe. Everyone works for Newlight and signs NDAs with their contracts." Jihoon steps with me onto a platform. "Hold on."

That's all the warning he gives. The platform rises, and when I crane my neck up, I see what I thought was the bottom of the stage is actually a hole and the darkness is the distant arena ceiling.

I try to imagine what it feels like to be Jihoon, standing here as people scream for him, but I can't. It's completely foreign to me.

"How do you feel?" I ask. "When the platform rises?"

"For this show, we started off with mics instead of headsets. I think of how it feels, pressing into my palm." He traces a line down my hand. "I listen to the crowd." He nods to the left. "Sangjun stood there, and he always waves at me before we start a show. That's when it feels real."

The platform surfaces, and I take a cautious step onto the stage. It's bigger than it looked from my seat, and there are crosses and lines taped on the floor. Quietly I watch Jihoon as he stares out at the empty seats, his face blank.

"What if something goes wrong when you're onstage?"

"Things go wrong all the time. Daehyun once fell and took me down with him. We nearly rolled off the stage. I've dropped hand mics. One ended up in a fan's lap, and she fainted. I forgot the lines to a song, and Xin covered for me. Tonight the lights were wrong for the second song, and Kit hyeong's voice broke. A few years ago, he would have cried all night."

To think I get stressed stumbling on a curb if there are people around.

Jihoon's now talking softly as if to himself. "We've played hundreds of live shows, and there are two things we can depend on. Something will always go wrong."

He pauses until I prod him. "The second?"

"That we'll get through it together."

There it is, that utter faith in his friendships that brings a lump to my throat. It's not only the rush of the adulation I don't want to compete with—it's this, his loyalty to his friends. That's why he came back to Seoul in the first place, because he couldn't let them down.

I hug him close. "You didn't look nervous at all."

He leans against me. "We show it in different ways," he says. "Daehyun paces and whispers his lines. Xin does a dance move over and over." He demonstrates a pivot-twist-arm thing. It's simple but so smooth that if you put a gun to my head and told me to replicate it or die, I'd have to tell my mother I loved her as I waited for the inevitable.

"How about you?"

"I had your talisman in my pocket," he says. "It steadied me."

Jihoon flops down to lie on the stage, and I break away to walk around, noting the dusty marks of their feet all over. How does he manage to do that much dancing and singing without passing out? I couldn't walk downstairs for two days after Hana made me go to a booty blaster class. I drift back to sit beside him, only giving a quick thought to the integrity of my white pants.

"You were actually singing?" I ask. "No lip-synching?"

He sits up and gives me a sour look. "Ari, really. I'm a professional."

"You were dancing. Like, hard. With jumps." My voice bounces like a ball if I walk too fast.

"It's a performance. Our fans wouldn't be happy if we stood in one spot like statues for three hours."

"It must be hard to keep it up."

"I have excellent stamina." His delivery is so straight that at first I don't see the smirk on his face. Then I burst out laughing.

"Don't be nasty."

"Fine, but it's true."

He pulls out a tube of lip gloss and runs it over his mouth in a far sexier way than I thought even possible.

"What are you doing?" I croak.

"My lips are dry. You want some? It's pomegranate." He holds it out to me.

"No, I mean you're a pop star. You put on lip gloss." It's weirding me out to see Jihoon do regular Jihoon things when an hour ago he was on this very stage making his fans scream their brains out.

Jihoon laughs so hard, he drops the tube, and since I've already sacrificed my white pants to the stage dust, I roll over after it. When I hand it back, he grabs my hand. "It's only me," he says. "I sing. I get dry lips. You do law. You get dry lips. Same thing."

This is so wrong, I don't even know where to start. Instead I say, "My lips are perfectly hydrated."

Jihoon's eyes drop down, and he licks his freshly pomegranated mouth. "Really? I should check."

He leans in, but I'm distracted again. This time it's the silver hoops in his ears. "Are those?"

Jihoon touches one with gentle fingers. "The ones you bought me. I wanted you with me onstage."

Worry floats away as Jihoon's hand snakes around my waist to pull me in tight against him, and he bites softly on my lower lip. I can almost taste my pulse as it surges.

Then he pulls back, finger tracing my eyebrow. "Do you want to go home?"

"Toronto home or your apartment home?" I ask.

"Toronto eventually. Apartment first."

I nod and his face breaks open in a huge smile. "Let's go."

Thirty-Nine

The next day I go with Hana to the train station. Even though Jihoon offered to fly her, Hana wants to take the KTX train because "it goes over three hundred kilometers an hour!" I hadn't known she had a thing for trains.

"Try to sit with the baseball team," I tell her as Yeong hauls out her luggage and she thanks him.

She looks at me. "A *Train to Busan* joke? Predictable."

I wave her off and get back in the car. A few minutes after I arrive at the condo, Jihoon comes in, Kit trailing behind him. Both men look utterly beat, but Jihoon smiles and envelops me in a hug before resting his cheek on my head. "This was worth surviving the early morning photo shoot," he says.

"We can stay in if you're tired." I pull back to look him over.

Jihoon makes a face. "I'll fall asleep, and I have plans for us."

"Have fun." Kit lolls over the couch in a melodramatic reenactment of *The Death of Marat* and then collapses to the floor. He sounds uncharacteristically friendly, which I attribute to his fatigue.

Jihoon prods Kit's prone body with a toe. "We'll be back tonight. Don't wait for dinner."

"Be smart, Jihoon-ah," Kit says, rolling over on his back. "Can you drag me to my room before you go?"

"No." Jihoon steps over him lightly.

We head off. "What did Kit mean by being smart?" I ask.

"Don't be seen."

I stiffen at Kit being Kit after all. Jihoon grabs my hand and holds it. "It's not you," he says hurriedly. "I mean, it is you because I'm trying to protect your privacy, but it's not you personally, if that makes sense."

"I get it." I do but I feel uneasy. It's like he's ashamed of me. "Where are we going?"

"What shoes are you wearing?"

"That's your concern. My shoes."

He sighs. "For walking, Ari, not style. I want to know if you can go for a hike."

"I'm good." I don't need to glance down to check that I'm wearing comfortable flats.

"Perfect. Seoul has many mountains."

"We're climbing a mountain?" I'm intrigued, but also, mountains are high.

"We'll do an easy path," he says. "Not up to the summit."

We chat idly about nothing in particular as we drive north out of the city, and now that I'm looking, I can't believe I haven't noticed how mountainous it is here. Seoul is so modern that the green that rises all around almost seems to fade into the background.

"Here we are," Jihoon announces. "Bukhansan Mountain."

He hands me a face mask that I dutifully don as I weave my hair into a tight braid. Jihoon pulls on a bucket hat and a mask, and there's no way anyone can recognize him because all you can see is his—admittedly very pretty—eyes. Then he dons sunglasses and those are hidden, too.

The mountain trail is moderately busy, and I soon learn to dodge older women wielding technical hiking sticks like weapons. It reminds me of home, with the autumn leaves glowing red and gold in the sun and a cool bite to the air.

Jihoon takes my hand, and we walk for about ten minutes, each of us wrapped in our own thoughts but enjoying the other's presence. Occasionally he takes out his phone to jot down a note, and I lean on a rail and let my mind wander. This is the first time in years I haven't been thinking about work, and it's a little worrisome. I should be scheming and plotting about how to raise my profile, especially given Brittany's rising star.

I don't want to. I feel at rest, my mind calm. Jihoon taps away as he hums, absorbed in the fragments of lyrics and melodies that he wants to capture before they fade. Law was never that. It was a duty, and I'm competitive and egotistical enough to want to be the best, but I never loved it. I was never inspired the way Jihoon is right now.

My hand goes white on the rail. I'm never going to be the best lawyer in the city, at Yesterly and Havings or anywhere else. I don't want it enough, not anymore. I don't know if I ever did or if I simply repeated that story to myself until I believed it.

Beside me, Jihoon rolls his neck in a circle. I reach up to stroke his nape, rubbing the tight muscles under his warm skin. He smiles. "Thank you."

"You're deep in thought."

He looks at me out of the corner of his eye. "What's your favorite song of ours?" he asks me.

"Only Us."

"Why?"

I pull up the English translation of the lyrics on my phone. "I like this verse," I say, pointing at the screen.

He hooks his head over my shoulder to see.

When we stand together
Our knees are scratched rough
Filled with sand and pebbles
The lost cousins of boulders

The hidden children of the mountains
That used to encircle us

Brushing our palms down
The dust flies up like dice on a throw
Your hand on mine
Our feet lost in the dunes
My hand slips in your sleeve
Your arm warm against my side
Where I'll keep it close forever

I found "Only Us" when I was on the plane, and something about the image caught my attention. There are pages of debate about the meaning, but when I read it through, I agreed with the consensus, that it's about two people who leave everything to be together.

Unlike the other StarLune videos, which are slickly produced dance numbers with high-concept wardrobes, the video for "Only Us" is grainy and looks low-budget. The band wears ripped jeans and T-shirts, with mussed hair and ambitious eyeliner. There's a sixth person, grayed out so you can't tell their gender or age, and they all try to leave in turn before a door opens and light streams out. Only the faceless sixth person gets through, and they don't look back when the door closes. The video ends with the image of the door, now weathered and faded, cracking open again.

I read over the lyrics. "It's not as poppy and light as some of StarLune's other songs."

He gives me a wry smile. "The ones I write."

"They're good!" I don't want to insult him, but it's not like he doesn't know that. Anyway, they're chart-toppers.

"The ones Daehyun writes are more to your liking? Like this one?"

"Well…"

"I wrote 'Only Us.'"

I frown. "Are you sure?"

"I know my own song, Ari."

I look back at the lyrics to find the songwriting credits. "It has both your names."

Jihoon props his foot up on a rock and leans out to survey the trees. "It does. His name is first. 'Dance Royalty,' on the other hand, has my name first."

I pull him back on the path so we can keep walking. "You need to explain this."

"You saw Daehyun. Met him."

"Yes."

"How would you describe him?"

"Brooding, sort of quiet and dark. Tough."

Jihoon laughs. "He's a clown in private. Plays tricks on everyone, always having fun. He doesn't like the cameras, so he shuts down when we have to do interviews or we're filming. They used that as his image when we debuted and built on it. How about me?"

"Ah." How to answer this with tact. "Bright and playful?"

"Of the two of us, who do you think loves bubbly pop, designed to get people laughing and dancing? Who would like the kind of music to listen to in the rain when you yearn to be happy but you've forgotten how?"

"Oh my God." I stop dead, causing a woman behind me to tap me with her walking stick. I jump out of the way with an apology, and she barely adjusts her visor before striding on. "You're kidding. You wrote the songs people think are Daehyun's."

He nods. "While he wrote the ones people associate with me."

"Holy shit. Isn't that, like, fraud?"

"Technically no. We're both on the songwriting credits, and we collaborate, but the company wants to maintain the images they created for us. They don't lie, but they promote the idea that I write the light songs and Daehyun writes the dark ones because they think that's what appeals to our fans."

I walk for a bit, mulling this over. "I don't want to say the fun songs aren't as good as the other ones," I say carefully. "The fans love them, and they cheer people up."

"We want to make people happy."

"Your songs are the ones people keep talking about and theorize about, the ones they turn to when they need to feel seen. Doesn't it bother you that people think Daehyun writes them?"

He looks down and nods. "It should be enough to have StarLune do my songs," he says. "Yet I'm selfish."

We walk along. "Do you not like the songs people think are yours? Daehyun's?"

"I do. I love them. To write a song that sticks like that is a gift, and Daehyun is a genius."

"I hear a *but*."

"I want to do more. I feel like a liar to the fans. I want to talk to them freely about my music but the company won't let us." He toes at a fallen leaf.

There's something dark in his voice. "What else?"

"I want to write more songs like the ones I love and to explore where that can take me, but they don't chart as well. The company wants us to focus on Daehyun's style for the next album. His songs, even though people will think it's me. It's success some would kill for, but it makes me feel sick."

There's a long silence, and I can tell he's struggling. I take his hand and wait until he speaks again. "Perhaps my songs don't chart as high because they're not good enough," he says in a low voice. To hear Jihoon unsure about his talent is shocking. Of all the things I thought he would be 100 percent sure of, his ability tops the list.

"You know fans love them."

"Because they're StarLune. Would they love them the same if they didn't know it was me?"

"That's an impossible question."

He frowns at the trees, and I take his other hand, rubbing the cool skin to get some warmth in them. "Hey," I say. "I've done nothing but complain about my work to you. It's your turn." It bothers me that I can't see his full face under his mask. I want to reassure him, but I'm not sure how, here in public. I rub harder, hoping he can tell I want him to keep talking.

"It's not an impossible question. I sent some songs out. My own songs, under a false name. They were rejected." He looks down at me. "The rejection came right before I went on stage for our final tour show. I'd never doubted myself like that before."

"Jihoon, no." I lean in to give him some comfort. "You should talk to the rest of the band about this. Does Newlight accept every song you and Daehyun write for StarLune?"

"No." His answer is reluctant.

"Not every song is going to work. Sure, fans might be more willing to listen, but they wouldn't remain if you started producing garbage."

"Starrys are very loyal," he says doubtfully.

"Because you deliver."

He brightens a bit, then fades. "If Newlight wants only Daehyun's sound, and no one will take my songs when they don't know it's me, what do I do? Who am I if I'm not Min and a songwriter for StarLune?"

I tuck his arm in mine. "You're also Jihoon, and you'll keep trying until you make it happen."

He smiles then, a real smile, and pulls me close. "Thank you, Ari."

Forty

We keep walking up the increasingly steep trail, and tension continues to build between us like a wall. There's a flat rock up ahead that's a bit off the main path. I lead him over and sit.

"Are you tired?" he asks.

"Sit beside me." He does, and I take his hand and put it between my hands and then my knees to keep it warm. "Tell me what else you're thinking."

"There's nothing else." He tries to tug his hand away, but I'm an expert at recognizing signs of avoiding feelings. That Jihoon is balking means it's big, and I wonder how to get him to open up. I depend on him to take the lead on these things.

"We never talked about how this will look when I go back to Toronto," I say, taking a shot. "We haven't had the talk about the future."

He pulls away slightly, and I know I've hit it. "Have you changed your mind?" I ask carefully.

The few seconds it takes for him to respond nearly kill me. "No." When he finally answers, the confidence in his voice lets me relax a bit, and the wall dissolves. He looks up. "I was worried you had."

The relief I feel is all-encompassing. "No way."

He laughs and leans his head against mine. "I still have our walking trip to Spain booked in the calendar for next year," he says.

"That's amazing, but I'd also like some shorter-term plans."

"How long until I see you again?" he asks as he looks out at the trees.

I look at my watch as if that will help. It doesn't. He smiles and holds his own wrist out to show his matching Cartier. "It's the first time I've worn it since Toronto," he says.

This time, it's me who gets a thrill at us matching. I give him a quick kiss on the cheek through the masks. "Plans," I remind him.

"I won't be able to come back to Canada for a while," he says.

"I understand. Will you be happy?"

"Away from you?"

I give him a shove soft enough for him to know it's only affection. "Being so busy and adding to your collection of little hotel soaps."

He makes a face. "I bring my own. Those are too harsh for my delicate celebrity idol skin."

"My question was not really about soaps."

"I don't know." He frowns and fixes his hat. "I don't know anything anymore."

"I thought you went with heart over head," I say.

Jihoon's laugh is so biting, I blink in surprise. "I suppose that only works when your heart isn't split exactly in half." Then he shakes his head. "I'll be happy knowing you're comfortable, and to be comfortable, you need a plan. Let's do one."

We sit and talk like two admin assistants booking their C-suite bosses. We talk about his schedule. We talk about calls and short visits. We look at calendars and his touring plans, with no dates in North America for the foreseeable future, and I tell him what kind of workload I have as I try to make partner. Like children, we even come up with a secret sign for him to use in his video chats.

All that is easy. What comes next is harder. "Have you thought about the future after StarLune?" I ask. His contract with Newlight is another four years.

Jihoon shifts over, and I close the rest of the distance. "I'm not going to sign again."

"What?"

"I'm getting old," he says simply. "I don't want to be learning choreo when I'm thirty-two, and I don't want to disappoint the fans if I need to slow down. I don't want to be on these schedules. I want to make my own. I want to dress myself for events in clothes that don't have to match four other men."

"Your music?"

"That's the only thing I want besides you. I would get out now if I could do it without letting the others down."

A few months ago, I would have told Jihoon that you need to watch out for yourself first, but now I don't know if I believe that. The strength he gets from his relationships with the band and the support they share is astonishing. "Have you talked to the others?"

He shakes his head. "I will, but I only decided a while ago. You were a catalyst for thoughts I was too scared to let surface. I can't be the one to split up StarLune, but the days are becoming a struggle. I need to grow. It's like an itch I can't get, but it's all I can think about."

We sit quietly as I scroll through my calendar. "This is going to be hard," I admit. "Really hard. Your life is next-level."

"You're scared, even now."

That makes me pull back. "There's a lot to be worried about."

"Yes, but I'm less worried when I know we're doing it together. We need to depend on each other."

"That's not what I do." I rub at my face under the mask. "That's the hard part. You have Kit and the rest to help you. I don't do that. I'm not used to it."

Jihoon turns me around to see my face. "What are you really frightened of here, Ari? Is it my career? The distance? The fame?"

"I'm afraid you'll leave." I can't even look at him. "That you'll wake up one day and look around and realize that it's too hard and that will be it."

He pulls his mask down to look at me. "Do you work hard at being a lawyer?"

"Yes."

"I work hard, too. All the time, every day. I'm not afraid of work. I know it's hard for you. We'll be apart, but you won't be alone. I promise."

He tugs my mask down, shushing my protest with a finger on my lips before he lowers his hands. "No one is around, and I need to see you when I say this. You are worth the work. We are worth the effort. I can't speak for your feelings, so I'll speak about my own. No one makes me feel alive like you do. Millions of people see me, but no one makes me feel as seen as you."

I risk looking in his eyes, and it's intense. He said no one saw him, but I feel the same way. He's not glancing over my shoulder or fidgeting with his phone. All his focus is on this moment, him and me and what we can be together.

I believe him. This is worth it. "Okay," I say.

His face relaxes into a smile. "Okay."

We sit on the rock for another minute, wrung out by the discussion, but Jihoon's words warm me from the inside. Then I get antsy. I want to walk. I want to talk. I want to... His phone buzzes.

Jihoon checks it and raises an eyebrow. "The apartment is empty."

"It is?" I pull my mask back up and so does he.

"Mmm, yes. We could head back."

I give a mock gasp. "And miss hiking to the top of a mountain?"

"The mountain will always be there, but hyeong will eventually come home."

"That settles it. Home." After all, I deserve a reward. This emotional honesty stuff is hard.

"I love a woman who knows what she wants." He leads me down the path.

———

We have a slow and lazy afternoon in bed, filled with silly jokes and irrelevant observations. A few times, I look over and marvel at the strangeness of the entire situation. Min from StarLune coils like a cat next to me, blinking lazily as he talks about why it's good to add mayo to cup ramen, although honestly that sounds repulsive.

It's nice. Nicer than nice, and not because it's Min. Because it's Jihoon and I'm falling in love. No surprise, he's easy to love. His words from earlier keep coming up in my mind. *You are worth the work. We are worth the effort.* He didn't mention what I can offer, how many hours I bill. It's only about me, Ari, as a person, and us as people.

Food arrives—not mayo noodles—and we dive in as if we're starving, which Jihoon, given the amount of energy he expends practicing and how he needs to fit into the world's tightest pants, might actually be. I look around the room as we eat. "I keep thinking of tours Luxe could do. Like one here in Seoul."

Jihoon raises his eyebrows. "If it's not based around StarLune, I'll be hurt."

"It's like you read my mind. First, we'll have a guided tour of your apartment, including your state-of-the-art cosmetics fridge."

"The products are better cold," he protests.

"Make sure you keep some dirty clothes on the floor for authenticity and preferably a note to Kit about how you're out of milk or something horribly domestic. Sign it with a lipstick kiss."

He snorts. "That sounds like a fanfic."

"No doubt." I pause with my chopsticks halfway to my mouth. "Do you read those?"

He goes red. "No."

"Liar."

"We might have looked when we were younger."

"Jihoon."

"What?" He fishes around to put a tofu tidbit on my plate. "How could we not?"

"I mean...because it's kind of narcissistic?"

He burrows into his food. "We wanted to know what our fans were thinking."

I wave my hand for him to continue.

"They were thinking some extremely imaginative things that I don't think are physically possible unless one is a gymnast. Sangjun and I couldn't look at each other for a week."

I roll my eyes. "Anyways, a K-pop tour would work. Or food, those are popular. They don't have to be personally guided. Your location could trigger stories on your phone when you arrive in specific areas. Like it's serendipity." Another thought comes to me. "We can partner with vendors, and you can pick up food samples as you go."

"I would do that. They sound like the one you took me on in Graffiti Alley."

I deflate. "Yeah, there's a ton of things like this."

Jihoon grabs my hand and kisses the palm. "That doesn't matter. There are thousands of lawyers as well but only one Ari."

"I suppose."

He gives me a sharp look. "An Ari who is more animated talking about this new opportunity than she ever spoke about law."

"That's true." It feels strange to say it out loud, like I'm betraying something.

Kit comes in before Jihoon can reply, dressed in comfortable sweats. We wave him toward the food, and he washes his hands before sinking into a chair and helping himself. "Hana is gone?" he asks.

"Took the train this morning," I remind him.

"Ah, I didn't get a chance to say goodbye. I should text her." He pulls out his phone and sends a text before starting to check his messages.

Then his head shoots up, and he mutters to Jihoon.

When Jihoon's face goes white, I know there's a problem.

Forty-One

I go numb. "Hana, is it Hana?"

Jihoon shakes his head rapidly. "No, no. Nuna is fine."

My relief is short-lived, because if this entire thing with Jihoon has taught me anything, it's that phones are the medium through which global-scale problems arrive.

"Something was leaked," I surmise, putting the deductive powers of my highly trained legal brain to use. "Photos from today."

Both men nod.

"Of the two of us."

Again with the nods. My phone is in my room, so I hold out my hand, and Kit passes his over without comment.

We're in the background of a casual selfie, and the person's face is blurred for privacy. They caught the exact moment when our masks were both off as we sat on the rock. My face is up and his is down. It looks exactly like two people about to kiss, and there might as well be a tagline written in cute font across our chests.

"What's the caption say?" I ask, doing my best to speak around the lump in my throat. Oddly, it's not the photo itself that bothers me but that it captured such a private moment. I'd never felt possessive about an experience before.

Kit takes back his phone. "It identifies Jihoon and a woman. No name for you yet." He scrolls down. "Apparently you met on a trip to Korea when Jihoon was a trainee and have been in touch since. That's from an unidentified source. Wait. They're saying Newlight has been keeping you apart for years."

"Who says this?" I demand.

Kit doesn't look up. "They. The internet."

In the middle of this, Jihoon's phone rings, and he starts pacing the living room as he talks.

"You're taking this well," I say to Kit. He's not bursting with an *I told you so.*

"No," he corrects me. "I'm not, but I can deal with that later. Now we solve the problem."

That sounds ominous, but before I can reply, Jihoon hangs up. He looks furious as he snaps at Kit, who walks away with his hands in the air.

"I need to go to the company," Jihoon says, taking my wrists. "Ari, I am so sorry."

I nod, but in a way, it's a relief. I don't have to wait for the worst to happen because it's here.

"I can fix this." Jihoon sounds urgent. "Let me handle this. I know I can fix it."

"How?" I'm genuinely curious.

"I have a few ideas. Do you trust me?"

"I'd be more confident if I knew what you have planned," I say. "Let me come to the office with you."

"That would be a bad idea. I need to focus, and there will be media out front. Too many fans, both at the gates here and at Newlight. We can't expose you to that."

Fair enough. I take a deep breath and try to stop it from coming out shaky. "I understand," I say. Although it's terrifying to relinquish any semblance of control, I'm trusting him not to hurt me the same way he trusted me back at the café.

Relief breaks over his face, and he kisses me. "Good."

Then he and Kit are gone. I'm left in the empty apartment for exactly three minutes before I get a call.

"Hey, Hana," I say.

"Jihoon texted me. Oh my God. I can get my local partner to cover me for a day and come up from Busan if you need me."

"I'm okay. Jihoon said he's going to fix it." I sit down. "I'm going to trust him."

There's a long silence. "You don't trust anyone to do anything," she says.

"He says he has this."

"What's the plan, then?"

"Not sure."

"How are you doing?"

"You know those fish that live at the bottom of the ocean and when they drift up, the lack of pressure makes them explode?"

"Yes."

"Like that. In minutes, I will be exploded fish guts all over this fancy apartment."

"Hell of an analogy, but I get it." She coughs. "Are you looking at social media?"

"No."

"You want me to tell you what's going on?"

"Definite hard no."

"Okay." Her fingernails tap against the phone. "At least you weren't identified. Call if you need me."

I manage one hour and seven minutes.

One hour and seven minutes with nothing from Jihoon.

One hour and seven minutes of pacing.

One hour and seven minutes of staring at my phone, torn between wanting to check it and knowing I shouldn't for my own mental health. Fuck it. I'm about to grab the phone when Hana calls me at one hour and eight minutes.

"Ari." Hana's voice is low and serious.

"I don't want to know."

"You do." Her voice breaks. "They know who you are. Your name is out."

Before this, I considered it pure hyperbole when someone said they needed to sit down because their knees went weak. I can now say this is not an exaggeration at all because my legs turn to jelly so fast, I stumble.

If they know who I am, they'll learn too much about me. My work, my family. Yesterly and Havings, *Richard*, will never put up with this kind of publicity. I have an image of my dad getting harassed at his law office and their house surrounded by StarLune fans. The internet can dig up dirt on anyone. I'm boring as hell, but I don't know what Phoebe's done while she's been out of my life.

No, get the facts. First get the facts.

Even as I stare at the floor, wordless, messages roll in from Alex.

Hey, text me when you can.

We have an issue. Text me.

"I need to go," I croak. I disconnect and start fear scrolling, desperately searching for information. I keep my eyes half-closed as if that will somehow mitigate the experience the way it does for horror movies. It doesn't.

Where are you text me

Call me

Do not answer your phone to anyone except me I'm calling now

The phone rings—Alex—but I decline it. I don't want to talk to him until I find out what's going on for myself.

StarLune's Min dating Canadian lawyer

K-pop dating scandal

Min Gfriend identified: Who is Ariadne Hui?

Fans demand apology from StarLune's Min

There are comments about me, and while there a large subset who are vocal in their support of Jihoon, many are less positive. There's disbelief Min would date anyone, let alone someone like me. I'm too big. Not pretty. Old. Canadian and Chinese, so a double whammy of foreign. A nothing and a nobody. A few defend Jihoon's right to pursue a relationship but in a conceptual way, not one with me specifically.

I decline another call from Alex.

WHERE ARE YOU CALL ME NOW

Multiple threads are combing through the band's lyrics to decide which ones are about me, which is romantic but untrue. The stories get wilder by the minute with zero evidence and have shifted to a narrative about me as a temptress rather than Jihoon and I as star-crossed lovers.

answer your phone its me alex

If it weren't me they were talking about, this experience would be a fascinating psychological study into how people make connections out of nothing. Since it is me, it hovers right at terrifying.

Another call from Alex. I decline again, needing a moment to absorb what's happening. To process it.

UREGENT

Had I run a marathon, I don't think my heart rate could be higher or my body more exhausted, so I put the phone down and walk over to the window on shaky legs. Seoul lies out in front of me, and it hits me that in this city and others, legions of fans are currently talking about me. I feel cold. Jihoon does online chats with over a million people watching. How can you even train to deal with that level of scrutiny?

Unable to resist the lure of the phone—it's not FOMO but POMO, petrified of mob outrage—I check again before the reality of this hits me. My name is trending. My name is a goddamn hashtag.

I reach the bathroom right before I throw up.

————

I've barely rinsed out my mouth when I grab my phone. Jihoon said he was on this, so I shoot him a text that links to one of the stories about me. Me, specifically by name.

His reply comes up instantly. **I'm sorry. I know. Trust me, Ari. Be strong.**

I've seen how people get eviscerated on social media. I've been part of the conversations as my clients decide whether it's safer to cut an outspoken or offensive employee loose rather than feel the weight of the internet's judgment.

I look at his message. **I trust you,** I write back. **I know you're busy dealing with this, and I trust you.** Then I think about what he said on the mountain, and I type three words.

I love you.

The message—the declaration—sits on the screen as I tap my fingers on my knee. Telling Jihoon how I feel fills me with exhilaration instead of fear about his reaction. I can do this. I need to do this.

I send it.

Then I wait for a response that doesn't come.

Forty-Two

The next hour or so is a blur. I spend a good deal of time in the bathroom staring at my reflection and wondering what to do in between checking to see if there's a reply from Jihoon.

There's nothing. That's fine. He's busy with a crisis.

But my stomach feels tight.

A familiar number comes up when my phone rings—Richard's assistant. He must have heard about what's going on, although I have no idea how since he's not one to follow gossip sites. I debate answering, but the need to make sure things are good at work is too strong to resist. I need to mitigate whatever Richard's heard.

"Please hold for Mr. Havings," she says. She doesn't wait for me to agree before she puts me on hold. It's about seven in the morning back in Toronto. She's never liked me, so I'm spitefully glad Richard hauled her out of bed to make the call because doing his own is beneath him. A minute later, Richard's smooth, cultured voice comes through.

"Ariadne, hello."

"Richard, good morning." My voice shakes, so I leave it at that.

"I had a call from Karina," he says.

It takes me a second to compute this. "The communications manager?"

"Yes. She received a message about you from a television channel, ZedTV or some such thing."

He waits for me to pick up the story.

"ZZTV." No. Oh no.

"That's it. Is there something we should know?"

It's the oldest trick in the book, to let someone hang themself with their own rope, but I'm a lawyer, too. "Something you should know?" I repeat. He can say it himself.

"Karina tells me you are involved with a celebrity, a member of some Asian singing group. South Korean, I believe."

Something about how he says it makes my hackles rise, as if where Jihoon is from makes this whole thing somewhat ludicrous.

"Exactly so." A desire to be contrary rears up. "He's a Korean performer. A K-pop idol."

The long pause says exactly what Richard thinks of this. "Idol." He rolls the word around in his mouth. "Yes, Karina mentioned that."

Sounds like good old Karina gave him a thorough briefing. "What did ZZTV want?" I ask.

"To confirm you were one of our lawyers. Karina says you're listed on our website, which is no doubt how they discovered your connection to us. She's updated the site so you no longer appear."

He downgraded me to being merely a connection and then erased me, as if working at Yesterly and Havings around the clock for years meant nothing. Before I can answer, he continues, "Karina assures me she's equipped to deal with the issue."

"She is?" The last I checked, her biggest task was doing the staff newsletter. In which, I also remember, she insisted on featuring me in Yesterly and Havings's first and only Face of Diversity! column. Hana had it on the fridge for a month, laughing every time she looked at it.

"Karina is very well qualified. Her mother is on the hospital board with me. I've decided it will be best for you to take some time away until this gossip dies down."

I nearly drop the phone and have a moment of inelegant clutching to get it back up to my ear. "I beg your pardon?"

"Karina has pointed out that your relationship with this man does not match the image we'd like to maintain with our clients."

I drum my fingers on my chest, feeling the soothing thumping against my sternum. I should tell Richard that we're only friends and the whole thing was blown out of proportion. That might change his mind. Then I see the tiger statue on Jihoon's desk.

No. I'm not going to do that. Jihoon is important, and I'm not going to hide him away. "My relationships are private, as are anyone else's in the firm."

"We are a serious group, Ariadne. This absurd pop culture media talk isn't the type of thing we'd like to be associated with."

"Are you firing me?"

"Of course not. You're an excellent lawyer," he chides. "I'd like you to take a month off until this calms down. We'll redistribute your clients. You'll agree with me there's a risk to their privacy."

"I don't agree," I say, fist clenching at my side. "I'm unsure how anyone would find out which are my clients unless someone at Yesterly and Havings tells them." If the leak comes from the client side, they can't complain about the publicity.

"I understand you think that." Richard's voice doesn't change because he's been at this for decades longer than I have. "However, I look at the bigger picture, and we need to prioritize the firm."

I give it one last attempt. "Richard, clients like Hyphen and Luxe won't care—"

He doesn't let me finish. "My decision is made, Ariadne." I can tell he's pissed I spoke up. "We can assess your role when you return. It would be unfortunate to lose you permanently, but this is best for now."

After giving me instructions on how to pass over my clients, he hangs up, and I do my best to not hurl the phone against Jihoon's lovely stone floors. The only thing calming me down is my faith that Jihoon will get this under control soon. He has to, because I'm about to lose it.

I go back to social media, unable to stay away, and refresh to see a statement from Newlight posted thirty seconds ago. My heart thumps hard enough to bruise my rib cage as I inch past the Korean to the English translation posted underneath.

Hello. This is Newlight Entertainment.
We would like to address an issue concerning one of our artists, Min of StarLune. Recently, a photo was published of Min with a woman. There is no personal connection between the two. The woman is a fan who approached Min when he was visiting family in Toronto and at a private party after she pursued him to Seoul. She interfered with Min during a walk on Bukhansan mountain where he went to reflect after last night's successful VIP concert.

Min would like to assure all his fans that he is safe and apologizes for any concerns Starrys may have. Starrys and StarLune are his only priorities. The safety of our artists is paramount and actions by individuals that intrude on their privacy will not be tolerated.

Thank you.

At the bottom is a shot of me staring at Jihoon at the Newlight party. I know my expression reflects my shock at seeing him, but I can also see how it can be read as wide-eyed adoration.

I read it twice, then once more.

I have a few issues, to put it mildly. The first is a general WTF bafflement that a company would put out a statement like this at all. That's going up there with the variety shows in the cultural relativism category.

LILY CHU

The second is a much stronger and more specific WTF. This was how he fixed it? He disassociated us so my name is out of it, which is good, but he might as well have punched me in the gut. He basically told the entire world I was a delusional fan he had nothing to do with. I won't be viewed as Jihoon's seducer in the collective Starry fandom mythology but this is so much worse. I bring up the party photo again. What was he thinking to let this happen?

I dial Alex's number almost on autopilot. He must have known, and I need to get the background before I confront Jihoon.

Alex picks up. "Good God, finally. Do you deliberately plan your day around ruining mine?"

"No."

"Sorry." He sounds exhausted. "It's been a hell of a year, and it's not even nine in the morning. How are you coping?"

I ignore his question. "Did you know about the statement from Newlight?"

"I haven't seen a statement." He sounds puzzled. "Give me a second."

Muttering comes through the phone as he reads through. "Photos...interfered...what the...Ari, I had no idea. That photo is from the party. That's not what happened. They didn't tell me. Newlight only asked us to monitor North American media."

"Jihoon said he'd fix it." I do my best to not break down. If Yesterly and Havings taught me anything besides how to write a concise memo, it's that crying during a business call is akin to having a neon sign around your neck that says WEAK, GO FOR THE JUGULAR. I like Alex, but this is hard training to fight against.

Alex's laugh is cynical. "Yeah, he fixed it alright. It's the only thing Newlight could have done, I suppose."

"You're joking. Branding me as a sasaeng fan was their best solution?"

"No, that's total bull and I'm sorry. I meant from their perspective.

They must have panicked and overreacted to stop the scandal for StarLune."

"I'm not a scandal!" The volume of my voice shocks me as much as it does Alex, who pauses for a moment.

"I apologize," he says. "I didn't mean it that way."

I don't even care about his apology. "They could have said I was a friend. They could have said almost anything else. Now this is what I am to people, and I can't control any of it. I'm not even a *who* anymore. I'm a *what*. I'm not Ari but a desperate StarLune fan with no sense of reality. This is so..." I can't even find the words but sink into a chair, head in my hand as I work to get my breath normal.

"I'm sorry, Ari."

"Whatever," I mutter. This mess isn't Alex's fault, but I have the ignoble desire to take it out on someone, and Jihoon, the real cause of the problem, isn't here. "Forget Newlight and StarLune. I need a plan for me."

"Ari, we should talk about how you feel—"

"Can you help me or not?"

"I'll call your family. If you come home, you can stay at the same condo as before, both you and Hana." He hesitates. "There may be some fans around your apartment again."

"May be?"

"Will definitely be."

I shut my eyes. "Thank you. Can you call my family in twenty minutes? I want to talk to them first."

"Done. Tell me if you need help with flights."

"I will."

I can be upset later. Now I need to talk to Dad before Alex does. I don't dither before I call because this can't be over fast enough. "Hi, Dad."

"Ariadne. Back from Korea? I hope you got some good work done so you can get back to your real clients."

"Soon." I sit down because I feel shaky. "Alex Williams from Hyphen Records will be calling you in a few minutes."

He chuckles. "Have you quit law to get a record deal?"

I manage a weak noise that impersonates a laugh. "Ha, yeah. Very funny, Dad. Do you remember Jihoon?"

"He came for dinner. Nice kid."

"He's a performer, here in Korea. He's pretty big."

"Like that Justin Bibber?"

"Bieber and kind of." I cough. "The media found out we're friends, and Alex is worried reporters might come talk to you." No need to go into the details of what Newlight did.

"Us?" He sounds confused. "Why?"

"To find out more about me."

"I see." He clicks his tongue in his habitual thinking sound. "Make sure you keep Richard Havings in the loop."

"I already spoke to him."

"Good."

"He put me on a month's leave to protect the firm's reputation."

"He did?" There's a long pause. "It makes sense from his perspective. You know this will affect your chances of being made partner. This is serious."

Being made partner. He isn't even concerned my name has been announced for the world, or enough of it, to drag through the mud. Partner is all he cares about. "I guess it might."

"You were doing so well. We were so proud of you."

Were, not *are*. "I know," I say.

"What's going on with you? I'd expect this from—" He stops suddenly to prevent the next words, which I know are *Phoebe, not you.*

"I didn't plan this." My answer is sharp, and Dad receives it with a disapproving silence that soars across a continent and an ocean. I know from the articles he sends that he expects me to be cool under pressure, but this is far beyond handling an unruly meeting.

"We'll wait for the call," he says. "I appreciate the update."

When he hangs up before I can reply, I know he's more upset than I thought. Part of me, that little girl who will never grow up, wants to call back and beg forgiveness and tell him that I'll fix it with Richard.

A text comes in from Phoebe: Do you know you're a hashtag?

Me: Yes

Phoebe: You ok?

Me: No

Phoebe: I promise I won't tell them how you cried when mom washed your teddy bear.

Me: Thanks.

Phoebe: 🖤

I see a few missed calls from Hana, but I don't want to talk to anyone.

Instead, I go to my room and pack.

Forty-Three

I'm not so immature that I'm going to run off without talking to Jihoon. I *am* sufficiently immature that I'm ready to leave right after I talk with him since there's no way it's going to be a rewarding conversation. That final and still unanswered text I sent to him stands as the most regretted action of my entire life, even worse than when I got a perm.

There are reasons I never open myself up. The disappointment. The hurt. The humiliation at reading it all wrong.

I slick my hair back in its usual bun and pull on the clothes I arrived in. Then I wait.

When Jihoon arrives back at the apartment, it's night, and the Seoul buildings glow through the window. He's alone and pauses at the door to take off his shoes, head bent low and hand lingering on the wall to support himself.

I stay silent as he comes into the living room because I'm not sure what to say. He joins me at the window, eyes lingering on my bun. "This is not how I wanted it to go," he says.

"You told them I was a sasaeng." It's not even a question.

"That's not what I agreed Newlight would put out," he says as he reaches for me. I step neatly to the side to keep some distance between us, and his hand falls to his side.

"No?"

"I approved a statement that said the photo was misleading. I didn't want to say anything at all, but the company insisted."

Misleading. I bite my cheek. "What exactly did you want the statement to say?"

"That you are a friend of my cousin."

I wait but that seems to be it. "Not that we're involved."

He pulls on his earring, the one I gave him. "No. The statement I wanted would be clear that we are not in a relationship. Now is not the right time to announce it."

"What's so bad about admitting we're together?" I demand. "Am I that terrible a choice?"

"I'm sorry, Ari. There's nothing wrong with us dating, but it needs to be planned carefully. It's not safe for you, and we also need to focus on our comeback. I can't let the others down, and I'd be too distracted with this if our relationship came out."

At the purely intellectual level, it's quite the experience to be denied so publicly, especially since we never had the official What Are We relationship talk. It's like a koan: What is the sound of dumping a girlfriend who wasn't a girlfriend?

"What distraction? You tell them the truth. People will understand you're entitled to your life."

In the reflection on the window, he looks tired and so do I, my tight bun causing unflattering shadows to fall on my face.

"The company originally wanted to remove me from the band," he says. "To apologize and go on hiatus."

I step back. "For seeing someone?"

"You know some fans don't like it," he says, rubbing the back of his neck. "They were circulating a petition to have me removed because I wasn't fully dedicated to StarLune."

"That's what you did, then. You let them throw me under the bus for your career because a few people made a fuss about a part of your life they have no right to interfere with." I desperately want a time machine so I can take back that fucking text.

"No. I told them to issue a correction. Kit hyeong is at the office fighting with them now, but I needed to see you to explain." He takes my hand. "We can figure this out."

I shake him off. "You made your choice clearly, unequivocally, and on a global platform," I say. "You let Newlight smear me in front of millions of people, and you stood aside."

"I can't openly go against our company like that," he says, running a rough hand through his lavender hair. "You don't understand. I'm fighting back, but it has to be done right."

"It's not enough to have them say I'm not a sasaeng. The right thing is to tell the truth." This is embarrassing now, like I'm forcing him into a relationship he doesn't want.

"I had no choice. Ari, you need to understand what's at stake. I've been with StarLune for over a decade. The members are my family. It's not only about me but also their lives and the careers they've dedicated everything to."

"I get that."

"Then you'll understand that we make our decisions together and always have. It's our greatest strength. It's not like I can threaten to leave. I can't toss StarLune away for—"

He halts, and I fill in the blanks. "For me," I say.

"I didn't mean it like that. It's not you, Ari. It's the timing, that's it. I want you in my life, but for now we can't be public. Soon, I swear."

"You said we were worth fighting for." White lights line the bridge in the distance.

"We are."

This actually makes me laugh. "I told my work that it was all true, and they put me on leave. They would have anyway, but at least I stood up for us. You wanted to make sure the world knew I was nothing to you."

"That's not true." He takes my hands between his. "It's that this involves more than us. Stay with me. Please. Give me a chance."

"Will you put out the truth? Right now? That I'm not a sasaeng and we are dating because I'm more than your cousin's friend?"

His silence is answer enough. Later is the time to decide how to work through the mix of shame and fury that fills me. Now is the time to get out of here with what's left of my pride intact.

"I lost my *job*," I tell him. "I lost my reputation. What did you lose?"

"You don't even like your job."

"It's what I chose, and it's as valid. Your money and fame don't make you more important. They don't make your name more precious." I glare him. "You aren't even happy with what you do. Or was all that anguish about finding your true artistic self another lie?"

The flash of pain on his face is instantly replaced with anger, and he pins me with a look. "You're ready to leave no matter what I say."

"That's not true."

"No? I see your bags, Ari, so don't tell me about giving up when you hit an obstacle." He doesn't wait for me to reply. "It's awful, but no one else is affected if you lose your job. With me, the entire team is impacted."

"Then it's a numbers game to you. This way, only I get hurt, and it's worth it if everyone else is happy."

"I didn't say that."

"You didn't have to say the exact words. The sentiment is clear enough. You chose StarLune."

"You're the one making me choose, Ari. Give me some time."

It takes me a moment to find my breath because I'm livid. "Every time I apply for a job, people who search me online will see this, as if being your stalker is all I have to offer."

"I told you I didn't want that to go out." His usually low voice is rising to match mine.

"Yeah, that's what you *say*, but let's look at what you *did*. You didn't retract it."

"We're working on it."

"If you'd wanted it done, it would be done. You'd have found a way. I'm going to have to rebuild my life, while your biggest problem will be having Daehyun's name first on the credits for the song you're going to write about this."

Jihoon reaches out, but I step back with my hand up. "No way are you coming near me." I shake my head. "You know what I said in my last text?" Things can't get worse, so I might as well address this elephant in my mind.

"Yes."

"Forget it. Forget this all happened."

"Ari, please." His voice is so soft. "I want to talk to you about that. I was waiting. Let's talk."

I turn to the window and answer his reflection. "No."

He bows his head. "If that's what you want."

Then he's the one to leave.

Forty-Four

I don't cry in the car but look rough enough that Yeong casts worried glances through the rearview mirror. Finally I give him a brief smile. He's a nice guy, and I didn't even get a chance to buy him a thank-you gift.

"Gwaenchanayo? Okay?" he asks slowly enough for me to understand.

"Gwaenchanayo." I'm not, I'm a mess, but there's no way Yeong is paid enough to deal with my drama.

He's unconvinced, and the language barrier is enough that we have to leave it at that. His silent sympathy flows to the back seat, where I huddle against the door.

I didn't see Jihoon again, but that could be because I left as soon as I was sure I wouldn't see him in the hall. Yeong was already in the lobby, so I didn't need to call a cab, which was convenient since a common taxi probably couldn't penetrate Jihoon's famous-person security. I wondered if Yeong had been asked to wait, if Jihoon knew I would leave. Or if he wanted me to.

Yeong drops me off under the awning of a luxury hotel that glows gold and unloads my bags. We both bow, him with considerably more grace than me.

"Gamsahamnida," I say, proud I remember how to say thank you.

A low bar, and I should aim higher than toddler-level Korean when in Seoul. Richard once told me a client had to improve his English if he wanted to be taken seriously. He didn't say anything when I pointed out it was the man's sixth language and most people at Yesterly and Havings spoke only one despite learning French in school.

Confirmed: Richard truly is a dick.

The moment Yeong drives away, I search my phone for another hotel. I don't want Jihoon finding me, even though I suspect it won't be a problem. He made his choice, and it wasn't me. Despite the pretty words, it was never going to be me because I can't win against his relationships with his bandmates and his fans. Enjoying my company isn't enough when he stacks it up against his entire life and lifestyle, the routines and habits of his world.

While I have my phone out, I block Jihoon's number and his email. We've said what we needed. My hand hardly shakes as I pick up my bags and head to the new hotel, a comfortable middle-range place that's a good two stars below the one Yeong left me at. I collapse on the bed after checking in. I need to book a flight out. I need to call Hana. Alex. I need…to do nothing.

An hour later, I stop staring at the ceiling and look at my phone, which has accumulated messages like plaque. I don't have the energy to check through them but send a text to Hana to say I'm heading home. A second goes to Alex, asking for help with a plane ticket to Toronto as soon as possible.

Alex: Done. Flight leaves tomorrow. Check your email. I'll meet you at Pearson.

I swing my feet to the floor and stretch, thoughts zigging through my zagging mind, when Phoebe calls. "We talked to that Alex guy," she says without preamble.

"How mad was Dad?"

"Worry about yourself first," she says. "This won't send him into a heart attack."

"What if—"

"Ari, enough. He's an adult and capable of taking care of himself. The question is how are you?"

"I don't know," I say. "It's a lot."

"Did you talk to Jihoon?"

I snort. "Did I ever."

"It didn't go well?"

"You saw the statement."

"Yeah, Alex showed us."

Great, now my whole family knows my shame. "After he told the world I was a stalker, he said he didn't want anyone to know about our relationship. As a finale, he picked his band over me. I'm leaving for Toronto tomorrow."

Phoebe groans. "I can't believe you didn't even talk it over with him."

I goggle at the phone. "I did talk to him. How do you think this happened? Telepathy?"

"Did you keep an open mind? He was probably in a tough place."

"The best way to get out of that place was not to brand me a sasaeng."

Phoebe makes a nasal noise that sounds like disagreement. "That was a bad choice for sure, but his company did that, not him."

"If he had his way, the statement would have said I was nobody. That's a real step up."

"It's not fantastic, but you know it's not safe to be named as Min's girlfriend."

"First, I'm more than Min's anything. Second, you're taking his side." I pace the room. "I can't believe you."

"Of course I'm not, but it doesn't sound like you were ready to hear him out."

"That's rich coming from you of all people. You're so scared of people knowing the real you that you move around the world to avoid it. You can't even hold a job down."

She sucks in her breath. "Doesn't look like you can either, does it?" she says venomously.

I don't even answer. I hang up and turn the phone off.

Stomping indignantly around the room muttering to myself isn't enough. I need to get the hell out. I leave my phone by the bed but make sure to write down the hotel's name before hitting the street, because if there's one thing this moment requires, it's comfort carbs. I lose myself in the fast-flowing crowd, seeking out some of Hana's recommended Seoul street foods. No one looks at me because everyone is thinking about themselves: their own heartbreaks and joys and boredoms and dreams. Eventually I come across a vendor stirring a deliciously fragrant bubbling pan filled with red sauce and thick noodle things that I recognize as tteokbokki and exactly what I need.

With double the cheese, the container has a satisfying heft when I give a test lift in my hand. I sit on a bench and briefly wonder if it's rude to eat on the streets before shrugging and digging in with the little wooden stick. The rice cakes are pillowy, and the sauce has the perfect amount of sweet spice.

After eating, I drift like a sated jellyfish through the crowds, stomach full and mind vacant. In the near future, within hours in fact, I'll have to make some decisions, but right now I allow myself the indulgence of not thinking.

Or I try to. I try very hard, but all I can picture is my phone, abandoned upstairs in my hotel room. It's Schrödinger's phone, keeping any and all options possible, from Jihoon's public reversal and declaration of love to some other mass humiliation. It, and by extension me, exists in a zone of possibility. Despite what happened—and it was objectively lousy—I'm not ready to admit it's completely over with Jihoon. As long as I don't look at that phone, there's hope.

What a sad, desperate person I am.

"That's pathetic," I whisper to the colored contact lenses lined up against the wall of the store I've ended up in without noticing. "You are being pitiful."

Back at the hotel, I avoid looking at my phone to keep that tiny flame of hope alive and instead set the alarm on the high-tech clock that's part of the wall. One night of avoiding my problems is acceptable. One night and tomorrow I'll start fresh.

Fresh, jobless, and alone.

———

Happy digital chirps wake me up. I silence the alarm and lie back, tingles trailing up and down my legs as I try to pinpoint what's wrong, because things aren't right. I'm not even sure where the hell I am.

The nerve-racking ignorance only lasts a few more seconds before my eyes fly open and I sit upright, already queasy at the thought of having to endure this day. I can avoid it for a bit longer by not looking at my messages until after I shower.

Nope. My hands might as well be controlled by a puppeteer because they reach for my phone before I know I'm doing it.

First the texts. Hana's compassion lifts off the screen, a foil to my sister's question marks and note telling me to grow up. Yuko with a virtual hug via emoji. My dad, wanting to know how I plan to convince Richard to give me my job back.

The emails. One from Karina the communications manager that gets instantly deleted. Ines casually mentions that Yesterly and Havings assigned a new lawyer and she's looking forward to my return. Spam messages reminding me it's time to take advantage of sales. There are also a stream of messages from Starrys who must have figured out my address from other Yesterly and Havings emails. These I delete en masse without doing more than glancing at the all-capped and unflattering subject lines. Then I remove my Yesterly and Havings account from my phone for good measure.

I refuse to look at social media and drag my ass out of bed to make coffee, each step taking all my focus. Rinse the mug. Rifle through the pods to find a dark roast. Insert pod. Swear at forgotten water. Add water, reinsert pod. Watch the little dial show me how long it will take until the water heats.

Don't think of anything else. Only each drip of coffee.

The mug comes into the shower with me, where hot water beats down on my head as I sip the gradually diluting and increasingly soapy espresso.

Everything happens as it should. I check out and pay. Get in a cab and go to Incheon. Check in. Wander around the beautiful airport staring mindlessly at gate numbers and duty-free stores and dodging fellow travelers. The day is bright and sunny, and the clear blue sky through the windows makes me feel small and leaden.

In the business-class lounge, the first thing I do is look for Jihoon, because that's what should happen, right? He comes rushing in to reveal his love and atone for the error of his ways by filling the lounge with surprise flowers and balloons. There might be a band. There should absolutely be one, since he's *in a goddamn band* that he values over everything. At least an acoustic guitar.

There's no band. No flowers except for some decorative willow branches in vases. The only people are bored business travelers pecking at devices and adjusting their dark suits. That's when it hits me that we are done.

I go into the bathroom and cry.

Not for long, though, because I have things to do. Once I take my red and puffy eyes back to the lounge, I delete Jihoon's information, feeling nothing as my fingers tap him out of my life. I tell Hana I'm good but need some space. Then I run out of steam.

Luckily, the lounge is fancy and filled with distractions like elegant little matcha cakes and mochi and a bar. I very carefully hide my phone in my bag and down three vodka sodas before I board the plane and fall asleep.

Forty-Five

"H ey, Ari." Alex's voice comes in a distressingly mild way over my
phone as I wait for my luggage in Toronto, headachy, miserable, and with a tongue so dry I can tap Morse code on it. "There's a
bit of an issue."

"Of course there is. I can get a cab. Is the invitation to the secret
condo open?"

"Sorry, that was ambiguous. I'm here. The problem is I'm
not alone."

I get a five-dollar bottle of water from the vending machine and
take a sip that gets absorbed into my mouth before I can even swallow.
Those vodkas I had in the lounge in Incheon were not the only ones
over the course of the flight, and I regret the decisions that brought
me to this point because it's hard to cope when simultaneously drunk
and hungover. "Not alone."

"Looks like someone got your photo at Incheon airport and
people here figured out flights. I'm looking at"—I hear some muttered
calculations—"yeah, I'd say three camera crews and a good fifty fans."

"Why?" The luggage conveyor belt starts up, and the first
bag drops.

"Do you want me to go into an exposition on the cult of celebrity and parasocial relationships in modern society and how it's

a substitute for the sense of community we lost in the postindustrial era?"

"No. Do they look mad? Like they want to tear me apart?"

He hums. "I'd say curious."

"Great."

"Are you okay?" he asks. "You sound bad."

"Vodka."

"Shit, Ari."

"Give me a break, Alex."

"Did you change, or are you in the black joggers and white shirt you were wearing when you left?"

"How did you know what I was wearing?"

"Social media."

I don't even have the energy to be horrified. "Of course I didn't change." I sat on my ass ten kilometers up in the sky for a trillion hours being unhappy, watching terrible movies I could barely hear over the thrum of the plane and falling asleep/passing out. Was it a healthy way to cope? Whatever.

"That's good, I can recognize you. Put your hair in a braid. Have a hat?"

"No."

"Mask?"

I fish a crumpled one out of my pocket. "Yes, and sunglasses."

"Good. You've seen media footage of what it can be like," he says. "There will be cameras and noise, people shouting your name. Uh, or other things, so I need you to ignore that and keep walking."

"What kind of things?"

"I don't know, ridiculous stuff about leaving Jihoon alone." He sighs. "Tune it out. If they're here at the airport to see you, they probably have an unbalanced perspective on their relationship with the band as well."

"I'll try."

"Good. Go down the right ramp, and I'll be about three meters away from the convenience store wearing a red hat."

My first bag slides down to the carousel. "An unusual fashion statement."

"I'd like to never speak of it again, but there's a good chance ZZTV will have it plastered on their home page in about eight minutes."

We hang up. I tug my bags to the floor and make my way to arrivals. Alex wasn't lying. As soon as the door opens to reveal me, a man calls my name, and a barrage of lights goes off. I don't know how Alex expects me to keep moving without falling over my feet, but I do my best, even though my eyes are bugging out behind my shades and my back bends with more than the weight of the new clothes in my bags. A woman screams, "Jihoon loves Starrys, not you, loser." I automatically turn to answer, but a voice sounds beside me.

"C'mon, girl." I nearly thrust my arm out for protection before I recognize Alex in his red hat. "Let's go, you're doing so good. Get your head high, that's right."

He takes my bags, continuing to murmur like I'm a skittish horse, and leads me out to a car, where he hands the luggage to a woman and ushers me in. The camera crews have followed us out, and I try not to duck.

He runs his fingers over his head, hideous hat discarded on the seat beside him. "Are you okay?"

"No. That was weird."

"I know." His quiet words are sympathetic. We don't have the kind of relationship where we hug, but that goes out the window with everything else I've come to expect from my life when Alex pulls me in close. I bury my face in his expensively clad shoulder and let him pat my back until the hot feeling fades from my eyes. I won't cry. I *won't*.

"Jihoon contacted me," he says.

I pull away. "When did he turn from Mr. Choi to Jihoon?"

Alex adjusts his lapel. "About the twelfth time I had to field a call from him since yesterday. Hana won't talk to him, and he was terrified you were in danger. He wants to talk to you."

This time, I look him right in the eyes. "Mr. Superstar doesn't always get what he wants."

"That's unfair."

"I appreciate your help in getting me home and through that clusterfuck at arrivals, but screw you, Alex."

There's a pause. "I deserved that. What are your plans?"

"To take some time to think." I've never had that. I went from high school to university to law school and straight to work. At graduation, my friends' parents got them copies of *Oh, the Places You'll Go!* with teary handwritten variations of *the world is yours, explore and be happy.* I got the gratification of meeting expectations.

"You can have Hyphen's condo for as long as you want. We have some places for you and Hana to look at if you take my very strong suggestion that you move. She said she's back next week."

"You spoke to Hana?"

"She wanted to talk about the statement. The yelling made my ears ring."

We pass the silver silos of the Molson's brewery, the gigantic Canadian flag hanging limp and dejected. "It was an asshole move for them to do."

"For us, yes. For them, self-preservation and protecting their investment." He ponders. "Also, they are kind of assholes."

I must have fallen asleep, because the next thing I know, Alex is shaking me awake. "We're here."

He comes with me upstairs and points out he had the fridge filled with groceries. Then he tells me to keep a low profile and "for the love of God and your own mental health, don't go on social media. At least your accounts are private."

When I'm alone, I put down my bags and lie down on the couch. Then I cry again, but it's the last time. I swear.

Forty-Six

*T*here are recurring proverbs in cultures around the world that indicate a certain universal nature to specific parts of the human experience.

It never rains but it pours.

Bad things never walk alone.

Poor luck comes in threes.

All roundabout ways of saying when life sucks, it sucks hard.

A few months ago, if you had asked me to write a personal profile, it would have said I'm a lawyer with a strong work ethic and not much else. It wouldn't have touched on the fact that I am also apparently appalling at self-reflection—although looking back, the terseness of that mock profile makes it abundantly clear—and ghastly when it comes to handling a breakup with finesse.

Apparently I'm also a masochist. Instead of trying to climb out of this funk, I lie on the couch with my greasy bangs hanging limp on my forehead and watch all StarLune's videos, eyes glued to Jihoon. Then, for fun, I torture myself with their latest online chats. Kit and Daehyun eat some gimbap, and Xin shows about half a million people a loophole in some video game. It's all very normal guy stuff played out in front of a huge audience with long pauses to stare at the screen and respond to fan comments.

I sit through all of them in the hopes of seeing Jihoon. Or hearing his name.

Tragic, but at least there are no witnesses to my shame.

A new video was posted last night, and it's subtitled, so I debate between heating up a box of frozen simulated chick'n nuggets, which is all the cooking I can handle, or watching it. My laptop takes the decision out of my hands through the miracle of auto-play. Looks like the nuggets will have to wait twenty-eight minutes and seven seconds.

It's Sangjun, whom I never met properly but is now as familiar to me as my own family from the amount I've seen him through various media. He looks drained, dark eyes peeking over a white face mask he eventually tugs under his chin. I sip from the can of warm, flat Diet Coke balanced on my chest beside my laptop and listen to a man I don't know speak in a language I don't understand.

When the door opens behind him, he seems honestly shocked to see Jihoon. I am, too, so much so that I jolt upright and topple the can on my lap. Ignoring the pop soaking my sweatpants, I bring the screen closer as my heart beats hard enough to drown out what they're saying. Like Sangjun, Jihoon's eyes are a bit puffy and ringed with purple. He's bundled in an oversize blue jacket with the hood pulled up so far, it almost comes down to his eyebrows, and his hands are tucked in the front pockets.

The chat to the left goes even faster than before with little star and moon emojis and *miss you oppa!* My eyes toggle between the subtitles, the chat, and watching Jihoon before I give up and admit I'm going to watch the damn thing at least three times to focus on each one.

At least there's not a lot to parse out because it's banal. Jihoon says he was in the Newlight building doing some work and wanted to say hi to Starrys. The two men stare at the screen, frowning occasionally at the comments and briefly triggering my regret that Jihoon's band members have been pulled into our mess. Then Jihoon's mouth gives a sad twist, quick enough to miss had I not been staring unblinkingly. He gives a little wave and says he's off to the studio. Having mastered the subtitles and feasted my eyes on what little of Jihoon I can see, I replay for the comments.

I should not have done this. Most of them are about how much they love StarLune in a variety of languages, but occasionally someone will write in English.

Is that woman still bothering you, oppa? You deserve better.

She should be in jail.

Love us first, Jihoon.

I'm glad you're okay, Min. She was a bad person.

Then I see the comment that made Jihoon react. *Min oppa, you look sad. Don't be sad. You deserve happiness.*

I go back to the video and notice something I missed because I was looking at his face. Jihoon makes the tiniest gesture with his hand before he goes, touching his thumb and his pinkie together. It's the same one we decided on, the silent *I'm thinking about you.*

I slam down the cover of my laptop. That's enough for today.

———

After two more days, trial and error shows me the exact formula for responding with the least amount of effort to keep the people in my life off my case. This gives me plenty of time to lie on the couch and think big thoughts, which include but are not limited to:

My career, which is in tatters and I should attend to posthaste.

My reputation, now trashed by Newlight. At least the gossip is dying down, helped by the firm Alex hired that specializes in restoring online reputations.

New apartments I should be viewing and don't want to.

Jihoon, who hung me out to dry.

Climate change, an enormous problem I contribute to by existing.

My online shopping, which I should chill on because no one needs seven pairs of sweatpants and consumerism leads directly to the point above. Also I don't have a job to pay for it.

Dad, who is after me daily about Yesterly and Havings and has offered to intercede with Richard.

Phoebe, because I don't want to fight with her.

All this means I don't do a damn thing, even when Ines emails how much she loved the music proposal I sent before my entire life went down the drain. I toss my phone down, unable to summon the motivation to reply, let alone reply enthusiastically.

I'm busy not thinking about any of these issues when there's a knock at the door. Since it might be the delivery of another outfit designed for the sloth life, I force myself off the couch, where my body has stretched an indent in the leather cushions, and check the peephole.

Phoebe stares right back. "Open the door, Ari. I know you're in there. I can smell the pizza boxes."

When I do, she shoulders past before I even say hello, leaving me to close and lock the door behind her. Phoebe puts her bag of groceries on the counter and surveys the surroundings, gaze picking out the half-empty takeout containers, balled-up socks, and open laptop, then lingering on the empty bottles of wine. I have no defense. It looks bad, the portrait of a woman who has 100 percent lost the plot.

Because it is in fact the apartment of a woman who has at least 96 percent lost the plot.

"How did you get through security?" I finally ask.

"I have my ways," she says. "It smells like a raccoon's ass in here."

"How would you know? Been hanging with a lot of raccoons?"

She doesn't dignify my feeble retort with a reply, instead marching to the kitchen, where she pulls out a bowl and a fork and then opens the container of precut fruit she brought. The sweet smell of pineapple spills out, and the corner of her mouth turns up when she hears my stomach grumble.

"Here." She shoves the bowl over, and I take a bite, my salivary glands aching with the first taste of freshness I've had in days. While I eat, she rummages under the sink for a garbage bag, fills it with trash before she even leaves the kitchen, and then grabs another to tackle the living room.

I want to talk to her but can't find a way over the wall of our fight. *You don't bleed, ever. You don't know yourself at all.* A rich tide of unwarranted bitterness rises in me toward Jihoon. It's his fault I'm here, unsteady and confused, instead of powering my way to a corner office. Lousy Jihoon came into my life with his lousy heart-over-head ideas and damn it.

I watch Phoebe work and try to excavate the words stuck in my throat, that I'm sorry. Are they the hardest words to say? Better or worse than saying *you're important to me*?

Better or worse than saying *I love you*?

"Spit it out. You're giving me a headache." Phoebe cracks a pizza box in half to fit it in the bag.

"Spit what out?" I can't help falling into my old defensive pattern.

"Ari." Phoebe doesn't look up as she moves around the living room, as if I'm a wary animal she doesn't want to antagonize with eye contact. "Say it."

At Yesterly and Havings, I had to hold my bow carefully and calculate the impact and the meaning of each word before releasing it. Now the words tumble out inelegantly, like a child emptying a box of blocks onto the floor.

"I'm sorry for what I said, Phoebe. I'm sorry I wanted to hold on to my anger more than I wanted to be a good sister. I should have reached out instead of blaming you for doing the same thing as me."

Her eyes have widened with every word. "That wasn't what I expected."

I'm panting from the effort of getting all that out. "What'd you think I was going to say?"

"That I'm a failure who doesn't know what she's talking about." When she looks at me, her eyes glimmer. "I know you and Dad think there's something wrong with me because I have no savings. No home. No ambition to be the best."

I want to protest that I don't think that at all, but she'd know it was a lie. Instead, I say, "It's different from how I live."

"That doesn't make it bad. You were partly right the other day. I might be scared to settle down, but what you don't get is that I wouldn't change my life at all. I love moving around and meeting new people. It's how I am, and it might not be what Dad wants or what you respect, but it's my life. Not yours and not his."

I feel worse. I let my envy—because now it's clear what it was—block me from the joy she has in living how she wants. I could have been part of that, too. I could have visited her. I could have widened my horizons, but I wasted all that time. All those experiences. All that *life*.

Phoebe doesn't move from the living room, where she works the edge of the garbage bag between her fingers, the plastic stretching thin and almost splitting.

She doesn't look up. "You like being the good girl, with all the praise and the head pats." Her smile twists as she drops the garbage bag to the ground. We both ignore the boxes that spill out. "You needed me as a foil. Can't have a good girl unless there's a bad one."

I'm a horrible person, because she's right again. She's kicking me when I'm down, but I deserve it, and this needs to be said. I let myself think she was a mess to make myself feel better. I'm so arrogant.

You don't bleed, ever. You don't know yourself at all.

This is why. Because it hurts when you have to dig deep.

"I don't know what to do," I say. "I don't how to break this habit."

"Ari admitting she doesn't know how to do something?"

That's it. The tears come hot and hard, spilling from the dam I stuff all my feelings behind. "I'm sorry." It's all I can say because every emotion has come to those two words, over and over.

"You know," she says conversationally, "I'm the one in therapy, but you should be there beside me. You've got some issues."

"I want to fix this."

She holds up her hand. "Let's unpack this 'fixing' idea. You're

important and part of my life, but I am about me. You are about you."
She kicks the garbage bag aside to walk across the room before grabbing my arms so I have no choice but to look up at her. "It's not about fixing because it's not broken. We're two people with some baggage that we'll work through because we love each other."

She must see my confusion because she smiles, and this time, it's gentle. "We'll be there for each other. Don't judge me. It's all I ever wanted from you, and you've never given it to me. I don't think I gave it to you either."

I take a deep breath. My skin is raw. My throat is dry. "That's it?"

"I mean, it'll probably be a bit bumpy at first, but yeah. We move forward from here. We be here for each other."

"I'm sorry I was a hostile jerk."

"I'm sorry I snitched on you to Mom and Dad to take the pressure off me for failing gym when you tried to change the B to an A on your report card in grade four."

"I knew it. I knew that was you!" My forgery had been perfect. I'd been grounded for a month, three weeks for getting the B in the first place and then a week for the lying.

She puts her arm around me. "You know I love you."

"Ditto."

"Ari, jeez, c'mon."

I touch my head to hers and take a deep breath. "I love you, too."

"Good." She claps her hands together. "Now it's time to talk about you."

"I'd rather not."

"I know, but Hana got my number from that Alex guy and texted me," she says. "Says you're a mess."

"Thanks."

"Not like I couldn't see that for myself," she continues. "Dude sure did a number on you."

"Aren't you on Jihoon's side?" There's the bitter me coming out again, and I wince. "I didn't mean it like that."

"I think you did, but you're clearly out of practice, so I'll let it pass. For the record, I didn't say he was a blameless angel, only that you could have stayed to talk it out instead of taking off." She settles into the high stool beside me. "Now it looks like you're not even mad."

I fork up more pineapple. "How can I be mad he put the needs of the collective over me?"

"Because this is not *Star Trek II: The Wrath of Khan* and he is not Spock?"

"I don't know what you're talking about."

"*Wrath of Khan*? When Spock..." She sighs. "Never mind. The point is he didn't have to make that choice."

"He felt he did. Isn't it the same thing?" I shake my head. "I know he was under a lot of pressure."

"You can be angry about it."

"It's just..." I push the pineapple away. "Even if he didn't know they were going to say I was some sort of deluded fan, he also didn't want to tell the truth."

"You're sad because he broke your trust."

I drop my head. "I guess. Not to mention Dad's furious with me. Worse, he's disappointed."

"Oh no. Hold up. Let's tackle that one. It's okay if people are disappointed. It's more about them than you."

"I guess," I say uncertainly.

"I know you've internalized some shit about needing to be stable or responsible, but Mom and Dad aren't made of glass. You don't need to structure your life around them."

"Dad's invested in me being a lawyer. It means a lot to him."

"Who's more invested in your life? You or him?"

I know the correct answer is me, but I don't know if it's the honest one.

Phoebe puts her elbows on the counter. "Look, your life is not Dad's life. You can't keep trying to fulfill what he couldn't."

I frown. "What do you mean?"

"All this big law stuff."

"Dad didn't want to be in a law firm. He wanted his own business." That's what he always told us, that he wanted the freedom of doing his own thing.

"He didn't have a choice. You think it's bad now? How many Bay Street firms do you think were hiring Chinese lawyers back then?"

"That doesn't mean he got rejected."

She looks uncomfortable. "I may have overheard him talking to Mom when we were younger. He didn't come out and say it, but it was clear what happened."

"You might have misinterpreted."

"Possibly, but can you look at your firm and tell me I'm wrong?"

She's not but... "I'm not sure what you're trying to say. If anything, this makes me feel worse."

"No, no." She shakes her head so hard, her hair flies out. "That's the exact opposite of the point I'm making. Again, it's got nothing to do with you. This is a Dad thing."

"What do I do, then? About this whole mess?"

She lets me change the subject. "I can't tell you that," she says. "I do know nothing will happen if you sit here in this dirty apartment feeling sorry for yourself. That's not the Ari I know. Now get off your duff. I'm not doing all this cleaning by myself."

———

The fresh apartment sparks a need for change, which means it's time to make some plans. The day after Phoebe's visit, I go to High Park and climb a small fence to reach my favorite picnic bench beside Grenadier Pond. It's warm, so I can sit in the wan autumn sunlight to assess my choices.

I spread my notebook to a fresh page and jot down a list of options for my future life.

Yesterly and Havings
Ines
Travel
Back to school
Live off the land as a hermit
Other (please specify)

I leave the notebook to walk a few steps in a personal cleansing ritual, then come back and look at my list again.

Time for inspiration. I go to my StarLune playlist and click on "Two of Swords." I have a complicated set of thoughts about Jihoon, but this song reflects exactly what I'm going through. How does he manage to distill my tangled mess of thoughts into a melody? I suppose it comes with the territory of being an award-winning songwriter.

When I open my eyes, I let myself feel before I think. A big black line goes through Yesterly and Havings. Another goes through school and then hermit life. I shove the book away and pace to the pond's edge. Making those lines filled me with so much energy, I need to burn some off. I don't need to go back to Yesterly and Havings. Richard and Brittany can be out of my life completely.

I don't owe them anything, and I don't owe Dad my career.

This begs the question of who I am if I'm not a lawyer, but this isn't a dystopian future where citizens need to tattoo their profession on their foreheads. It can be an ongoing question for future Ari. Back at the table, I pick up my notebook, idly doodling a series of dashes as I consider my options. They look like little negatives, all the things I'm excising from my life. Removing. Deleting. I very deliberately add a thin vertical line to the center of each dash. I don't have to only remove. I can add and grow.

I can make those negatives positives.

I want to start my life for real, and it's fine if I figure it out as I go.

Forty-Seven

This is a new look for you." Ines waves an approving hand. My hair is loose, and I'm in a Kelly-green dress with a short skirt that would have raised every eyebrow at Yesterly and Havings.

"I quit my job." The conversation with Richard had been brief and exhilarating. He hadn't even tried to get me to stay. I screamed with relief the second the call ended, possibly even while disconnecting, before dancing a little jig around the kitchen, middle fingers raised to the phone in a final salute.

"Good, you were wasted there," she says. "What will you do?"

I smooth the front of my dress. "I have an idea."

She waits, and it's now or never. "I can't ask this officially because I don't want be seen stealing a client, but I want to join Luxe as your part-time in-house counsel." I'd realized by the pond was that it wasn't necessarily law I hated. In fact, I enjoyed a lot of the actual work. The culture was the problem.

Ines temples her hands as Yuko stops typing to eavesdrop. "Part-time. The rest of the time?"

"I want to create tours for you, like I did for Alex. I know they can be successful."

There's a long silence. "You've thought this through, Ari?"

"Yes. I have five proposals ready, plus an overview of the industry and what gaps they fill." The plan came to me in the middle of the night, and I initially pushed it aside as completely unworkable. I also couldn't stop writing down ideas. Hana, who had kept watch on me since she'd come home from Korea, was the one to point out I lost nothing by trying.

So here I am, trying.

Ines smiles, lips a crimson slash against her dark skin. "Then it's a good thing I called Richard Havings yesterday to tell him the new lawyer he'd given me was the most vacuous human I'd ever met and Yesterly and Havings was fired unless I had you back."

"What did he say?"

She adjusts her skirt. "He didn't give me what I wanted, which is you. I told him I was leaving."

Elation fills me. "He wouldn't like that."

Ines raises an eyebrow. "I don't care."

"There was some controversy when I left." I want no secrets. "I assure you it wasn't about my work."

Yuko leans over. "Are you referring to Newlight's statement that you stalked Min of StarLune on two continents?"

"Ah, yes." I glare at her. "Thanks for describing it so concisely to Ines."

She gives me a wicked grin. "Revenge for not letting me get a peek while he was in Toronto. I don't think you're a stalker, by the way. Newlight is full of assholes, everyone knows that, and then there were the watches."

"The what?"

"You were wearing matching Cartiers, and I know for a fact, because Ines told me, that you got yours as a gift and not as a sasaeng move."

I blink. "That's observant."

"It was all over my social media. The matching watches, not the gift part. Only I knew that. Plus, that photo of the two of you was...

wow." Here she holds her hands to her chest. "No one's ever looked at me like that. Like you were his world."

Yeah, he did, at that moment. I don't want to think about it.

"I won't ask if you're secretly together, but I'm not opposed to you telling me," Yuko adds.

"Your personal life is personal," Ines says firmly. Then she holds out her hand. "Welcome, sweeting. We want you here."

I take a deep breath because I need to confirm I can get what I really want. "How about the tours?" I ask.

She leans back. "The one you did for Alex sold out in hours. You have an eye for what people want. It's a deal." She smiles. "You got the jump on me, Ari. I was going to ask you to do more anyway."

Yuko whoops and pulls out the champagne. "Time to celebrate!"

As I sip the cool champagne and talk shop with Ines and Yuko, I think about how funny heartbreak is. It sounds so dramatic. My heart is broken. My heart is split in two. Cleaved.

The unfunny thing about heartbreak is that it's not dramatic at all. It's simply there as a background ache that ebbs and flows. Like now. As Yuko digs out a package of sriracha cashews, the pain that comes when I think of telling Jihoon about my new job comes sharp and fast, a stab to the heart.

I bleed.

———

The hurt waves in over the weeks. Like when Hana and I move into our new place with a view of the CN Tower. Not sending Jihoon a photo leaves me empty.

Like when I see a man walking down the street with his pet lizard zipped into his jacket to keep warm, the animal's head tucked under its human's chin. There's a soft twinge when I think of how Jihoon would laugh.

Like seeing the online hype for StarLune's mini tour, which sold out venues in record-breaking time. Or when I hear the full album and read the glowing reviews. When there's a billboard in Yonge-Dundas Square featuring Jihoon in that prince outfit and lilac hair.

"Why can't I get over him?" I ask Hana one lazy Saturday morning, the early winter snow falling lightly outside.

"He's a Choi," she says, microwaving milk for hot chocolate. "We're pretty great."

"Hana."

There's a beep, and she pulls out her cup. "He made a mistake, a big one, but you're punishing yourself. Did you want to leave him in Seoul or think you should?"

"Both. It was a big deal when he didn't stand up for me." I can't overlook that, although I've come around to understanding the impact on the group.

"Remember, at the beginning of this whole *thing*"—here she gestures as if to encompass the past, present, and future—"I asked what you hope for?"

"Vaguely."

"Shut up, I know you do. It's time to put it in action again."

"Yeah, since it worked so well last time."

"It does when you're honest with yourself." She reaches for her phone and taps for a moment. "If you need some help."

I check my messages. "An email account with a password?"

"I'll go out for a bit." Her look is so kind, it kicks my confusion right past nervous into extreme trepidation. "Call me when you're ready."

I don't answer because I'm already logging in. The account name provides no clues, and as usual, it takes extra-long to load up because the gods of the internet are attuned to knowing exactly when you need urgent access to something and enjoy thwarting you at every turn.

Then I'm in, and my whole body freezes. It's a regular email account with forty-six unread messages from Jihoon. The last one's dated from earlier in the week. I sit up straighter. Obviously I'm going to read the messages, but I debate over the order before deciding to check the earliest one first.

It's an email Jihoon sent in August, when he was in Toronto. I scan it without absorbing any of the words. Then I slow down and read it again before clicking through to the next.

Ari—You mentioned the email account your friend had for memories and I thought I would do it for you. Last week you took me on a tour of the city and I watched you laugh. It was lovely to see. You're often so serious and I like that about you too. I like everything about you.

Ari—Tonight I kissed you and there was a song there, I felt it. I didn't care because you were with me. The song could wait. For the first time, the song could wait.

Ari—Kit hyeong and Daehyun are here and I'm scared they'll tell you my secret. My time with you has been precious. I felt like me again, Jihoon, and not StarLune's Min. I'd forgotten what that was like and I can't bear to lose myself like that again. No wonder I couldn't believe in my songs if I couldn't even believe in me.

Ari—Hana said I should have told you who I was before but I had no words. A lyricist with no words, what a joke.

Ari—Why? You broke my heart at the airport but Kit hyeong told me this was impossible. We hadn't known each other long enough for it to hurt this much but it does. He doesn't understand that the time doesn't matter, only how I was with you and you were with me. I tried to hide it from him but I couldn't. The plane ride was endless.

Ari—I don't know why I keep thinking of you. People usually want gifts or favors from me but not you. What was it, then?

Ari—We are in Seoul together, and I can pretend we are a normal couple. I like it. I like you. I took this photo in the car because the lights played on your face like a galaxy and I was lost among the stars.

Ari—You're gone and I don't blame you but I already miss you. I went to the hotel Yeong brought you to but you weren't there.

Ari—I made a mistake. You were right. I should have retracted the company's statement when they refused to change it and gone public with the truth. I told myself it would make things worse for everyone but I was wrong. The members are shocked. We always said StarLune was more than ourselves but Kit hyeong told me our strength comes from supporting each other as individuals. They're furious at the company, who won't listen to any of us. They're disappointed in me but not as much as I am in myself.

Ari—Alex won't tell me a word but he says you're safe.

Ari—I'm so sorry. I know I did wrong. You were right. I gave up when I should have protected you. I should have tried harder. I should have done more.

Ari—You're back in Toronto. You had to endure that terrible crowd because of me but my heart lifted to see you.

Ari—I woke up early to go for a walk. It's getting colder so I hope you wrap up well and stay healthy. Please make sure to eat.

Ari—I had Alex hire a company to restore your reputation. I hope this helps you.

Ari—I know you won't be watching but I made our sign today on Sangjun's livestream. It made me feel better.

Ari—I've been thinking about the music I want to make. I spoke to Daehyun and he feels the same but had been scared to tell me. It was good to speak with him about this, and I wish I had that courage long ago. We told the others as well.

Ari—It's three in the morning but I can't sleep. We were in the dance studio today for hours and I thought it would tire me enough to rest but I lie awake thinking of you.

The messages are a mix of what he's doing that day and how he feels, like journal entries. Some are only a line, and some are longer, almost a full screen. I don't realize I'm crying until a tear drops on the keyboard.

The last message is from last week.

Ari—We're about to go onstage. How can I love and hate

something so equally? StarLune is everything to me but it took you away. I thought it was bad before I left for Canada but that was an acute pain that I could dig out like a sliver. This new pain is all through me. I continue to fool myself that that you remain in my life through these messages but it's getting harder.

I shut the laptop and lie back on the couch, letting the tears stream down my face and puddle in my ears. It's disgusting and I don't care.

Hopes, Ari.

I want to be with Jihoon.

Shit, despite everything, I want to be with Jihoon.

How can I be with a man who twice broke my trust, when he didn't tell me who he was and then when he let Newlight put out that statement and wanted to deny our relationship? I call Hana.

"What's with these messages?" I demand. "What's he trying to pull?"

"I imagine he is a man trying to do the best he can."

"He had a chance to make a difference, but when push came to shove, he never did."

"No." She sounds sad.

"How did you get that email?" I ask.

"He sent it to me the other day, but I wasn't sure if you were ready." A car honks in the background. "I'm on my way home. I was going to get Thai for dinner."

"Yeah." I'm too drained to cook.

Or think.

God, I hate Jihoon.

No, I don't. That's the problem.

Forty-Eight

O n a cold day in late November, I arrive home to Hana napping on the couch. I move quietly to let her sleep as I make some tea and check the secret email. I do it every day and can't tell if it's a punishment or reward.

Ari—the tour is complete and it was breathtaking and exhausting. Now I have time to think about what might have been and what I could have done different. I have too much time.

I wonder if I should write back. He must see that the messages are being read, but he never mentions it.

A knock at the door disturbs my thoughts. Hana must have ordered takeout. I check the peephole.

Dear God. Hana's mom stands peering at the door, holding a covered dish. I muffle a groan. Talking to Mrs. Choi can be difficult even on a good day, and today was mediocre at best.

I slide on my socks across the wood floor. "Hana."

She throws an arm over her face. "Sleeping."

"Your mother is here."

This gets her eyes open. "What?"

"Your mom is outside the door." There's another knock, and we share a look.

Hana's lips go thin. "I was over there yesterday."

"We can pretend we're not home."

To my surprise, Hana sits up. "You know what? No." She throws the blanket on the floor, strides over to the door, and flings it open.

"Why did you take so long?" Mrs. Choi marches to the kitchen, where she uncovers her dish. The rich smell of kimchi fried rice spills out.

Hana remains at the door. "Eomma, I told you when I left your house that we have food."

"You have bad food," she corrects. "Good food equals good thoughts."

Hana looks like she's going to explode, so I step in to give her a moment. "Hi, Mrs. Choi. I was about to cook, but we can keep this for later."

"The Chinese don't know good food," she says as if this is canon.

Hana comes into the kitchen. "I said to please call before you come over. I might be busy."

Mrs. Choi scoffs. "Too busy for your eomma?" She looks through our cabinet and flicks her finger at the hot chocolate. "You shouldn't drink that. No wonder Mrs. Lee's boy didn't like you. You need to try harder."

For the first time in my life, I witness Hana Choi rendered speechless. She stares at her mother as if ticking off the ladder of lines the woman has crossed. She can't say it because that's her mom standing there, interfering but still family. Hana glances over at me, and I nod at her. I'm here for her, however she handles this.

That must be what she needs, because when she turns back to her mother, her head is high.

"Eomma," she says. "You weren't invited over."

Mrs. Choi doesn't even look up from where she's hunting in a drawer for chopsticks. "I don't need an invitation. We're family."

"You do." She takes a breath. "Please leave and call to ask if you can come next time."

This is a night of firsts, because now it's Mrs. Choi's turn to be without words. She looks to me as if for confirmation, but I keep my face a rock. Then her mouth opens and closes like a fish.

"You don't want your terrible mother here? You're ashamed of me? Keeping secrets?"

Hana doesn't move. "I love you, but I need you to listen to me. I've asked you a dozen times to not talk about my love life or how I look or what I eat. I don't want you to come over uninvited. From now on, when those things happen, I'm going to leave or ask you to leave."

Mrs. Choi's hand is on her throat. "How can you say this to your own mother?"

"I'm saying it because I love you and I want to keep seeing you. If you don't respect me, we can't do that."

"Respect." Mrs. Choi glares at her, voice getting high. "What do you know of respect? I raised you! We came here so you would have a better life. *You* should respect *me*."

"I do. I also need some space."

I'm in awe of Hana right now. I thought it was hard to talk to Phoebe, but Hana's gone right into the bear's den. I can tell how scared she is by the way she picks at her leggings with one hand, but she's standing up for herself.

"Your father will be ashamed of you, speaking to me like that."

Hana doesn't reply, but she doesn't lower her eyes. The staring contest between the two Choi women lasts for another few seconds, and then to my shock, it's Mrs. Choi who breaks.

She slams the cutlery drawer shut and spins around to grab her rice. "Only dutiful daughters deserve my cooking," she says.

Then she leaves, slamming the door behind her. I rush to lock it and then turn to check on Hana. She looks almost dazed. "What the hell did I do?" she whispers. "I've never seen her so mad."

"Hey, you did good. It was hard but you did it."

She bursts into tears as I hug her. "Am I a bad daughter? She's right. I do owe her respect. She's done so much for me."

"Hana, you can love your mom and want to live your life."

She doesn't reply, but after a few minutes, she moves from sobs to sniffles. "I thought she was going to cry."

"I know you feel bad."

"I feel terrible." She rubs her eyes. "I had to."

"You did."

"Thanks for staying here. It helped."

"Anytime. Kind of wish she left the food, though. Your mom is a great cook."

Hana hiccups and starts laughing. Soon we're both laughing, and it feels like a cure.

———

Ari—Daehyun and I met with the agency about our songwriting. They insist it's better for StarLune to keep things the way they are. I gave in and hated myself again. Daehyun is unhappy and so is Kit hyeong, since they rejected his solo project. I hope you are keeping warm. I check the weather in Toronto every day. Watch for the snow.

I pull my coat tighter around me as a barrier against the cold wind while I stand in front of Dad's office building.

It's been years since I've been here. I don't want to be here now, but some things are better said in person, and the formality of the office might be helpful. The other night, Phoebe and I had been at dinner when she finally exploded on him for pressuring me to beg Richard to end the leave he put me on. I hadn't had the guts to tell him I'd already quit and was working at Luxe. I'd told myself it was for his own good because of his heart, but it was because I was a coward.

After seeing Hana confront her mom, I made up my mind. I always thought I had control in my life and of the decisions I made, but now I see that as long as I'd let him determine my path, however indirectly, none of those choices had been mine in the first place.

I push open the lobby door. The elevator is waiting, but instead I climb the stairs to the second floor.

"Oh my, Ari." Gloria, Dad's assistant, gives me a big smile when I lean around the door. "Look at you. It's been so long. How are you?"

"Good, thanks. You?"

"Can't complain." She checks her monitor. "Is your dad expecting you?"

"No. I was in the neighborhood. Thought I'd come say hi."

Her eyebrows rise slightly because she knows the chances of me coincidentally being in the neighborhood are slim. All she says is, "He's free if you want to go in."

Nope, I do not want to go in to have this conversation, but I force myself through the door. Dad looks up from behind the desk. "Ari? Is everything okay?" He half stands, hands flat on his desk and eyes wide.

I shut the door behind me. "I wanted to talk to you."

He sighs. "This couldn't have waited until I was done with work? You should be trying to get your job back. You made a mistake, and you'll have to earn back their trust. It's getting too late."

My nervousness transforms into anger at how one-track he is. He hasn't even asked how I am. I'm more than my job, but not to him. "I don't want to."

He frowns. "Don't be childish. You're a bit upset, but you know better. Swallow your pride and apologize. Show Richard you can handle it."

"No, Dad, I'm done with them."

"Don't say that. I should have called him for you."

"I quit my job, and I'm never going back to Yesterly and Havings. I hated it there. I'm not even sure how much I want to be a lawyer."

That was graceless, but the relief I feel once the words are out is immense. No more lies. We'll have to learn a new way to relate to each other that's not work based. I wonder if we can.

Dad lowers himself and stares at me. "You foolish girl. What were you thinking? You'll never get a chance like that again. If you quit, you've wasted your life."

"I was wasting my life when I was there."

He's talking over me before I finish. "You need to think this through. This is your future at stake. What's going on with you? You used to be so steady. I never had to worry about you, not like Phoebe."

"This isn't about Phoebe. It's about me."

He blows out his breath and turns to his screen. "If that's what you came to say, I need to get back to work."

I start to leave, but there's an itch in my mouth. I've started this, so I might as well get it all out.

"I haven't said everything."

He raises his eyebrows and puts his hands on the desk in a move of exaggerated patience.

"I only went into law to make you happy. You wanted Hui and Hui or Bay Street Hui, and Phoebe was never going to do that."

Dad picks up a pen and looks over my shoulder. "Is this because of—" He frowns. "Jihoon?"

"It's not."

He looks up. "No?"

This rankles. "I am perfectly capable of making a decision without a man."

He puts the pen down. "You know I didn't mean it like that. I only want what's best for you."

"How about you let me decide what's best for me?"

Dad stiffens. "I don't appreciate that, Ari. There's no need to speak to me with that tone."

This is the hardest thing I've ever had to do, but I take my courage in hand. I walk over behind the desk, wrap both my arms around his thin shoulders, and say, "I love you, Dad. I love you, but I'm done being what you want me to be."

For a long moment, I don't know what he's going to do, but then he gives a little shake, so I release him, and he pulls away without looking up. "I want you to reconsider Yesterly and Havings when you're calmer."

"I'm very calm. I know you wanted me to be a lawyer," I say. "I didn't know what I wanted. Now I know what I don't want."

"I'm not happy about this, Ari. You're showing a huge lack of judgment." He purses his lips. "It's a mistake."

"If it is, it's my mistake to make. Not yours."

He gestures as if to indicate washing his hands of my decision and keeps his eyes trained on the monitor.

I'm almost out the door when he calls me back.

"Ari?"

"Yeah, Dad?"

He glances down. "Drive safe."

I can hear the *I love you* under his words, but I don't press him. I said my piece, and this will have to do. "I will."

Then I go back out to the cold.

Forty-Nine

February is the shortest and longest month on the calendar. It's been over four months since I left Seoul, and my life has been turned around. Alex's second music tour sold out in a day. I'm now creating the K-pop tour because he's on board to do a whole music series in conjunction with local artists in different cities. Ines asked me to do on-the-ground negotiations for her luxury travel again when the other guy quit, and this time I jumped at it. I can finally experience everything I've put off. Phoebe and I made tentative plans to travel together and meet someone she knows in Malta who might be a good connection.

In summary, I have a lot to do, but instead of doing any of it, I'm rereading the emails Jihoon sent me. For the hundredth time, I wonder if I should write back. What would I say?

I'm not sure. Phoebe and Hana were correct—Jihoon was a man struggling to do the right thing. I even have new sympathy for him. He spent his career working with StarLune and putting them first. Protecting his members was his default. I even get why he wanted to lie about who I was. Safety and timing were good reasons, but I was too hurt to see it then, and I'm too stuck to do anything about it now.

I tuck my legs under me and huddle under a fuzzy blanket. I wish all this soul-searching had resulted in me being able to leave those feelings behind, but the twistiness in my heart is enough to tell me what I wish weren't true: the pain hasn't gone away because I am very much in love with Jihoon.

Ugh. *Come on, brain, do your job. Reason this feeling out of existence and let me live my life, I beg of you.*

I give my brain a count of five to take some action. Nothing.

I twist the coin in my pocket before I pull it out to toss lightly in my hand. I need to make a decision, but I'm not even sure what the question is. What would be heads, and what choice would be tails?

I throw the coin in the air and grab it in my fist, staring at my knuckles.

Then I tuck the coin in my pocket without looking. It doesn't really matter, after all. The moment the coin flipped in the air, I knew what I wanted because it hasn't changed.

After all this, I want Jihoon back. I want us.

I check the email, and there's a new message.

Ari—I wrote a song. It was the first song I wrote where I could write the music I wanted. Daehyun is tired of hiding as well, and this time we stood up to the company. The others came with us for support but I never would have had the nerve had it not been for you. Thank you for this gift.

There was a mural in the alley you took me to with a tiger flower. I think of it often because that was the true image of my life, the desire to be loved, but intimately and not on the world stage. I wish you could hear this song but I don't think I'll see you. You never reply to these messages and they only drag out the pain.

I won't be checking this email again. Goodbye, Ari.

Panic. Sheer panic. I don't know why I thought Jihoon's one-sided emails would continue forever, but I did. I read it again, and knowing he'll never see my answer gives me a sense of liberation.

This time, I click reply.

Jihoon, I hope this email finds you well.

I make a face.

Hi Jihoon!

No, oh my God.

Dear Jihoon: With regards to your last email.

I bang my head against the back of the couch.

Then I take a deep breath and start typing.

Jihoon—I read your messages. All of them, many times. I didn't reply because I didn't know what to say. I'm going to try now because knowing you'll never see this makes it easier to say what I've been thinking about since I came home.

I know you're sorry for what happened. I don't like it but I understand. You felt you didn't have a choice.

It hurt, though. It really, really sucks to be told you're first and then to find out that you're not. That I was more like eighth, after the members and band and fans and music. When you wanted to say I was nothing but an acquaintance, I felt dismissed. I was insignificant, and I'd never felt like that with you.

But you're part of StarLune. I expected you to make decisions based on us as individuals but you considered the impact on everyone else as well. I thought in islands and you saw the ocean. It wasn't wrong but I couldn't see that.

I made some big changes in the past few months. My life is going okay now, actually. I quit law. I'm going to be traveling. I'm doing what I wanted but it seems empty without you. It's not going as well as it could because I miss you. I think of the Jihoon I met here in Toronto and I miss us. I'm glad you found your music again. I know you'll write the songs people need to hear.

I wish we could find our way back to what we had but I don't know how and it's too late.

Ari

———

"Pass the char siu bao." Dad doesn't look at Mom, who mutters about sodium intake.

We're at our usual dim sum restaurant, since Mom wanted a family lunch and Phoebe and I privately agreed that a neutral and public place would be preferable. It's the first time we've been together since I told Dad I'd quit at Yesterly and Havings. My other news, given over the phone, that I was now what he called a glorified tour guide, had gone over equally well.

Phoebe passes him the BBQ pork buns as I pour another cup of jasmine tea, dark leaves swirling in the bottom of my cup. So far, the conversation has lurched from the weather to my work to Phoebe's work. Mom must have put the fear of God into Dad, because I swear his lips began to form the Y in Yesterly and her gaze snapped to him like a laser. He shut up.

Mom's excited to tell us about her new exercise class that's "like Zumba but better, with poles."

Phoebe looks at her curiously. "Ski poles?"

"No, stuck in the ground. I'm learning to swing on them."

I choke. "You're taking pole dancing?" Phoebe pinches me under the table.

Mom nods happily. "It's very good for muscle toning. I'll need it for the beach."

Phoebe's eyes narrow. "What beach?"

"We're going to Mexico for a week. Your father can explore Mayan temples while I snorkel in the ocean. They have barracudas and sea turtles."

My sister and I stop eating. "Vacation," I say. "You, Dad?"

He shrugs and doesn't look up from his rice. "It makes your mother happy."

Phoebe's mouth hangs open. "Whoa," she whispers. I agree. It's like witnessing a unicorn prance along the dim sum carts. I do my best to keep the conversation going so he doesn't clam up.

"What temples are you thinking of visiting?" I ask.

Dad's chopsticks waver over the deep-fried shrimp dumplings before he turns to the steamed ones with a heavy sigh. "I'm not sure yet."

"I can help you out," I offer, trying to keep my voice casual even though my heart jitters. "I've done a few itineraries for friends going to Riviera Maya."

He nods, attention on the food. "Okay."

"Okay?" I was ready for a rejection, so it takes me a minute to absorb this.

"Might as well put your knowledge to use."

Phoebe winks and sends me a discreet thumbs-up, but I barely pay attention.

I'm going to plan Dad the best freaking excursions ever.

And find a pole dance studio for Mom while I'm at it. As long as she never makes me watch.

———

The notification on my phone announces that Jihoon's about to start a new livestream. I can recognize his name, Min, in Hangul now. A glutton for punishment, I pull out my laptop to see his face better. It's been three days since I sent that email, and I haven't checked it again. Part of me is glad to have gotten it off my chest, but most of me is psychically wallowing in an overflowing pool of loss that will hopefully drain over time.

I turn on the livestream as Hana comes in. "I was about to ask if you wanted to watch this," she says.

I pat the couch beside me, and she squeezes my shoulder as she tucks in. Jihoon appears on the screen, but unlike the usual room they film from, he's outside. Hana sucks in her breath, and I squint at the screen as the comments explode with theories on where he is. He wears a black beanie and black puffer jacket, and there's snow on the ground. Behind him is a concrete wall, but I can make out what looks like a painting to his right. It looks more like Toronto than Seoul, but I guess all cities have pockets of similarity. I don't look too long at the scenery because my attention is on him. This is the last time I watch, I promise myself. The very last time. I can't keep punching myself in my own face.

He looks to the side of the screen, I assume reading the comments.

"Phone must be on a tripod," Hana mutters. I don't answer, because first, that's truly irrelevant to me, and second, I'm taking in every aspect of his appearance. His hair has grown out a bit, and under the beanie, I can see it's back to black. He's barefaced, and this makes him more like Jihoon than Min. I can almost picture him lying with his legs up on the couch, telling me about his day as he always did, hair flopping in his face until he shoved a bandana on to keep it back. All those little details I didn't know I kept as memories.

A few seconds later, he nods as if he's ready.

"Hello." He bows quickly, eyes crinkling as he looks up and smiles. "I'm going to speak in English for this." He speaks briefly in Korean, breath puffing in the cold, and the chat lights up.

"This isn't usually where I talk to you, but I have something special I want to share." He smiles at the chat. "Yes, it's a song, one I wrote recently. It's never been performed before, but now that our mini tour is done, I'd like you to hear it."

"What?" squeals Hana. "A new song?" That, along with the comments, tells me this is not the usual order of things.

"Did he tell you this was happening?" I ask.

She shakes her head. "Only to make sure you tune in."

Before I can quiz her on this, Jihoon is speaking.

"This a bit different from what you've come to think of as my sound. I hope you like it because it's the kind of music I'm going to create from now on."

"What's he doing?" mumbles Hana. I told her about Jihoon and

Daehyun and their songwriting credits. "Is he going to come out and tell people what's been happening?"

I shake my head. "He wouldn't," I say. "There might be rumors, but he won't confirm them unless they do it together as a group."

She glances over. "That sounds exactly like him."

Jihoon has been reading the comments, and when he looks up, his expression is discouraged. I wonder what he expected to see. "I'll play it now. Please forgive any mistakes. It's called 'Turns.' When it's done, you can tell me what you think on my new social media account."

"His what?" bleats Hana. "They're not allowed individual accounts. Newlight controls a single one for the whole band."

Jihoon's face fades, and up comes the image of a field and a winding path. Along it grow vibrant orange flowers. Tiger flowers.

"Did he shoot a music video for his surprise livestream song?" asks Hana in disbelief. "What is he doing? Is this a solo?"

Jihoon's velvet voice comes on. The flowers fade as the image becomes Jihoon in a sound booth. Hana starts to translate, but I touch her hand. Right now, I want to concentrate on his voice.

Then come words I recognize because the chorus is in English.

Tiger flower
Every turn I take
I see only your reflection
A silhouette in the setting sun traced with red
Tiger flower
Through the maze I walk, tracing your fading path
My watch measuring steps instead of hours
I drop to my knees to see you, touch you
Tiger flower
I need you

I wanted that. I want that. Goddamn Jihoon. I can't stop staring at the screen where Jihoon is singing, eyes closed in the booth. His right hand is held up, and his finger makes a circle with his pinkie. Our sign.

Molasses slow, it occurs to me this is our song, the song we talked about in Toronto. I recognize the melody and some of the lines. He took our messing around and made it art.

Kit joins in the next chorus, and their voices rise in a duet before the rest of the band comes in. It's a haunting tune, and I tear my eyes away to check the chat. It's moving too fast for me to even read, but I catch the occasional English word as people try to describe what they hear: beautiful, yearning, passion, genius.

Then it fades, and the screen is blank. Jihoon is gone, the livestream over.

I jump to my feet, shaking my laptop. "What happened? Make it come back." Frantic, I close the window and bring the browser back up. Nothing. "Hana, check your phone. Where did he go?"

Hana sits like a statue on the couch, mouth open. She looks over to where I'm now on social media, trying to find out what the hell is going on. The internet is in full meltdown, and #MinSong and #Turns are already trending. "Ari."

"What?"

"That song's for you."

To hear her say what I was thinking causes me to stop what I'm doing. "How do you know?" I ask, wanting to know what she heard.

"The maze. The thread. Ariadne. He's talking about you. It's for you."

I need to find those lyrics ASAP. "There was nothing about a thread."

"Right, that was the Korean part. The lyrics are about following a thread out to the light. Ariadne gave Theseus the thread to find his way out of the maze."

I collapse on the couch, staring between Hana and my phone. "Did he tell you he was doing this?"

She shakes her head and glances at her phone. "Wait. He mentioned his new social media." She taps in the search and brings up a new account headed with a casual selfie of Jihoon. The follower count clicks up and up as I watch. It has a single post. A tiger flower.

Hana taps again. "Holy shit. Kit. Sangjun. Xin. Daehyun. All of them have launched their own accounts and under their own names, not their stage names."

She shows me, and every member of the band has posted the same image as Jihoon in solidarity, and each already has likes in the hundreds of thousands. "Newlight is screwed," she crows. "This is unbelievable. StarLune is finally taking control."

I nod, barely listening. That this is unprecedented is clear from the comments, and I'm scrolling so fast, I'm accidentally liking posts when my fingers tap hurriedly on the screen.

"Check that email," Hana says. "Check it right now."

I do. There's another message.

Ari—I miss you.

"Tiger flowers," I murmur, thinking about the video. "He talked to me about them."

"They're Jihoon's birth flower," Hana supplies.

"He mentioned it."

"Did he tell you the meaning?"

I shake my head and swipe at my eyes. "He'd only told me the meaning for primrose." Loveliness.

"*Please love me.*" She grabs my hand, hard. "That's what tiger flowers mean. He's told two million people he's in love with you."

Fifty

The alley. The background to the livestream was familiar for a reason. I know the place because I took Jihoon there myself. He's not in a Canadian-looking neighborhood of Seoul. He's here, in Toronto.

"I need to go," I blurt. Then I don't move, looking between the door and the screen. Do I want to do this again? I said in my email that I didn't know how to get back to what we were, and Jihoon's given me a path. I want to take it but am unsure if I have the guts.

"Hey." Hana's voice is quiet. "You know there's no limit to happiness, right? Like no happiness police that will take everything away if things are going too well."

I make a face at her. "Of course I do."

"I don't think so." She pauses as if collecting her thoughts. "You don't act like it. When things go your way, you never celebrate. You always look for what can go wrong as if the light's too bright when you're happy and you need a cloud to make you comfortable."

"I'm not..." I can't finish the sentence.

"It's okay to want to be happy with another person," she says. "It's scary to not know what will happen and how someone will react. You're a good person, Ari. You won't be able to fuck it up too bad if you're honest."

"Thanks?" Hana's not always the best at pep talks.

"Now get your man."

"Right." This is what I want, and I'm going to grab that thread he's offering. I marshal my courage and throw on some unstained pants. There's a cab right outside, and I hop in. "Queen and Portland."

When I arrive at the empty alley, I start searching. I don't remember the tiger flower painting at all, and the murals change, so I don't even know if it will still be there. I walk slowly, looking at the images of gates and faces and cats until I find it by an open garage, so vibrant and gorgeous, I don't know how I missed it when I was with Jihoon.

It takes up a full door, and I step closer to see each of the petals is a stylized tiger outlined in red.

"Ari?"

My head snaps up because Jihoon is standing behind me. He didn't leave. He stayed until I could come after him. I now know I would have gone to Seoul to find him again but this is way more convenient.

I rub my cold hands together because I forgot my gloves. "Hi." As openers go, it's not great, but cut me some slack.

He doesn't move. This is terrible. Shouldn't he be throwing his arms around me or kissing me passionately? The movies told me that's what happens after the grand gesture.

The grand gesture, which oh my God, he did. The ball's in my court. I talked feelings with Phoebe. I hugged my Dad. I can do this. I'm going to Jihoon this and lay it all out. Writing that email was easy compared to this. I'm nauseous, and my legs are trembling. I'm scared, but I have to stop the bleeding.

"I get why you made your choice," I say. "It hurt me because I thought I mattered to you but you let Newlight just…do that to me. Then you wanted to erase who I was to you."

That is without a doubt the hardest thing I have had to say. I can't have hope without vulnerability, so I push on. "I really liked you. I fell in love with you."

Nope, that was the hardest. *Almost done, Ari. Keep going.*

"You told me to trust you, and I did. You said you'd fix it, but you stepped on my heart and crushed it. It was probably karmic payback for what I did to you at the airport, but it was awful. Really awful."

There, it's out.

"You said you wanted us to find our way back to what we were," he says.

"You read the email."

He nodded. "I couldn't help but hope you'd written, so I kept checking despite promising myself not to. Were you being truthful?"

I nod and look up to try to prevent the tears from falling. "I was."

"I'm not sure we can go back to that," he says. "The past is over, and those people are a little wiser now."

I take a breath. "Then we don't go back. We move forward."

"You would do that without knowing what's to come?"

"Yes." No hesitation.

Jihoon stuffs his hands in the pockets of his puffer jacket. "I'm leaving StarLune. We're disbanding."

"What?" This isn't what I thought he'd say.

"After you left, I had to face what I'd done. StarLune has been my life for a decade, and I love it, but the band is my past, and you can be my future."

"You can't leave the band," I say. "It's too important to you."

"We made the decision together. StarLune is made of people, and those four people will always be with me. That's why we posted the same photo on our social media. We have others planned to show we support and love each other."

"All of you?" I eye him hesitantly.

"Yes. We all need this. You are not wrecking StarLune."

"The internet will say I am."

"We'll tell our fans the truth, that we've talked and the cracks have been there a long time but none of us wanted to be the first to say it. We need to grow in our own ways." He looks at me. "I want you to be part of that journey. If you'll have me."

I take a half step forward, and it's enough for him to cover the distance between us and wrap me in his arms. His mouth is on mine before I can answer, but the kiss tells him what he needs to know.

I'll have him.

He encloses me in his puffer jacket, wrapping it around me until we're in a bubble. "I love you, Ari. When you sent that text in Seoul, I was almost bursting to tell you how I felt, but I wanted to tell you in person."

"Really?" Since I still sometimes woke at night regretting that message, this is a relief.

"Yeah." He breathes into my hair. "It turned out to not be an opportune time."

I grin despite myself. "This is definitely a more suitable occasion, but you should say it again to make sure."

"I can do that." He kisses the corner of my mouth. "I love you."

"Good." I make him wait until he's fidgeting, then rub my nose on his warm neck. "I love you, Jihoon. And Min. I love all of you."

His heart pounds, matching mine. "Thank you," he whispers.

"What's next?" I murmur against his mouth.

"I don't know." He pulls me closer to shelter me from the cold. "What do you think's next?"

"I don't know, either." I don't have a goal. I don't have a plan.

That's fine, because Jihoon's arms are warm, and he's smiling only at me.

Epilogue

Hello, this is Newlight Entertainment.
We have some news about StarLune. Although we have negotiated, as of April, StarLune—Kay, Min, DeeDee, Sangjun, and X—will no longer be artists under Newlight Entertainment. Newlight strongly denies any bad faith actions or wrongdoings in the song credits of its artists.

———

To all the Starrys,
This is StarLune. You might have seen the announcement from Newlight Entertainment and we wish to give you more details about why we ended our contract ahead of time. Although we are disbanding, all the members of StarLune remain close friends and are eager to support each other in our future careers as we grow as artists and individuals. This was a choice we made as a team, as we have always made our decisions.

We stand by our comments regarding the deceptive songwriting credits and cannot stay with a company that doesn't respect our artistic contributions. Jihoon and Daehyun are proud of their work and each other. We apologize with all our hearts for misleading Starrys and hope you will forgive us.

Jihoon will take a hiatus from performing to continue in his songwriting career and music production. He will be making a new home outside Seoul, creating the music he loves.

Daehyun will focus on music production and will also make music to bring joy and light to fans.

Sangjun and Xin are proud to announce the launch of StarRise Entertainment, where artists are treated with freedom and respect. Global auditions for artists of all genders will begin soon.

As the first signed artist with StarRise Entertainment, Kitae will be launching a solo career with a new album due in several months. Please give him your love!

For all your love and support over the years, we thank you from the bottom of our hearts. You were always the stars lighting the path through our night sky.

Kitae, Jihoon, Daehyun, Sangjun, and Xin

————

"Are you coming?" Phoebe pokes her head in my hotel room. "We have time for a coffee by the water before the meeting."

My role at Luxe has transformed since I started almost a year ago. My tours have been such a success that I've been put fully in charge of their development. We're getting another lawyer—not Brittany—to do the luxury group travel contracts. This is my last one to negotiate, and Phoebe is here to introduce me to her Maltese contact. She moved back to Montreal in June, so I don't see her as often as I'd like, although we text most days.

"Almost ready." I pull on my usual disguise, a hat and sunglasses. The chances of being recognized here in Malta are slim, but I've had enough run-ins with the media and StarLune fans to be cautious.

Life has been, as Hana calls it, an absolute gong show but in a wonderful way. "Turns" charted in multiple countries, which gave a euphoric Jihoon the confidence he needed to commit to his songwriting path. Min of StarLune's romantic gesture to his alleged and now disproven stalker caused a media frenzy that I don't think I could have survived on my own. Jihoon brought me to Seoul, which offered much better security, and held my hand through the entire situation. Newlight was zero, possibly even negative, help, but the rest of StarLune supported us publicly and privately, as did idols from other groups. The furor grew when Jihoon explained the story on a livestream, right from the moment we met to the false statement, to an audience of over six million viewers.

"I should have said something to clear her name sooner, and that's on me. I'm grateful to have Ari in my life and that her heart was big enough to forgive me," he said, looking at the camera. "My hope is that you are all able to find the same joy we bring each other."

There are people who don't like it, but that stream reassured most of the fans who truly did want Jihoon to be happy and caused a backlash against Newlight. When Xin announced he was seeing someone, it was accepted almost immediately. They're a cute couple.

In any case, gossip about StarLune's relationships was instantly overshadowed by the announcement of StarLune disbanding. Some Starrys held vigils outside Newlight and accused me and Xin's partner of breaking them up. The band fought back hard. My time in Seoul means that I know all Jihoon's friends well now. It bothers him a bit to know that Kit and I will never be buddies, but he's satisfied we respect each other.

In fact, it was Kit who turned the tide about StarLune's disbandment when he laid it out in a message to their fans. He was honest and emotional as he described how proud they all felt to love and encourage each other as they sought new paths.

"Being part of StarLune was beautiful, but it's time for a new era," he said, staring into the camera earnestly. "No one can be the same as they were a decade ago. You aren't and we aren't either."

Then, he took a long silent look at the comments, which made me laugh with how weird it was to watch Kit read the screen to himself as millions viewed him breathlessly. Jihoon, who was watching it with me, nudged me in the side. "Quit it," he said.

"Sorry."

Kit spoke again. "StarLune is over, and it's no one's fault. We've always known it would never last forever, and we're grateful we could close the band on our own terms. We love you, and we love each other. Please let us grow to be the men you helped us become."

Jihoon beamed with pride and posted the clip on his social media with a line of hearts, stars, and moons. Now that they were out of their contract, Jihoon and the others took great pleasure in checking in with former Starrys and encouraging those who were having bad days, a personal interest that helped fans adjust. Newlight's CEO getting involved in a financial scandal didn't hurt either, and their continued denials about forcing Jihoon and Daehyun into pretending about the songwriting credits—which included leaked emails threatening to cancel the group's debut if the two members didn't play along—was one of the final nails in the company's coffin.

Now, months later, most of the controversy has died down, allowing the former members of StarLune to make waves in their new chosen paths and me to travel to Malta with my sister.

"Let's go," Phoebe says, and we step out into the Valletta streets. The bright sun reflects off the light stone of the city, and I pull my hat farther down, already sweating in the fall heat.

"You hear from Jihoon?" she asks as we go down a flight of steps.

"He called earlier," I say. "They're done with Kit's new EP, and he took two of Jihoon's songs."

Jihoon had been in Seoul for the past week working with Sangjun and Xin's new company. As well as signing Kit, StarRise has two rookie groups debuting in a few months, and Jihoon loves spending time with them. I went by the studio with him once and was struck at how gently he treated these kids who idolized him. StarRise is determined to give the trainees a supportive environment, and Jihoon is happy to drop in with advice when he can.

He's also making a name for himself with his own songs and continues to collaborate with Daehyun, both thrilled to have the freedom to talk about their work with their fans. Daehyun's last song was for a girl group who hit the U.S. charts for the first time. He called us at three in the morning when he found out, and we popped champagne right there for an impromptu transpacific celebration.

Phoebe points to a small alley. "We can take a shortcut here. You leave tomorrow, right?"

I nod. Jihoon is leaving Seoul to fly into Paris, where we'll do some shopping (him), visit some museums (me), and climb the Eiffel Tower (both). We've also sent our hiking gear ahead to Saint-Jean-Pied-de-Port, where we'll start walking the Camino de Santiago. We only have a few days, but we can always come back to where we left off.

My phone buzzes with an alert: *Jihoon and Ari Super Awesome Getaway*. It's the calendar invite Jihoon sent from my living room last year, but now it's been updated to say: *Jihoon and Ari Super Awesome Getaway. The first of many. I love you.*

Jihoon has added a new selfie in the notes section. It reads, *Always thinking of you, Ari.*

I blow the selfie a kiss and step out of the alley to a view of the ocean, the city ringing the harbor like a partial corona. Phoebe grins at me. "Not bad, huh?"

I smile back at her. "It's perfect."

And right now, it is.

Acknowledgments

It was another year of very interesting times. Which means, for many of us, it wasn't great.

You might have found solace in knitting or baking or playing board games. I found it in K-pop, and *The Comeback* is the result of consuming hours and hours (and hours) of content that made me truly happy. I *loved* writing this book, and I hope you enjoyed reading about Ari, Jihoon, and Hana. And if you're intrigued and looking for starter playlists, check my website: lilychuauthor.com.

As always, many people contributed to this book. Mistakes are always my own, though!

My agent, Carrie Pestritto, who is a hugely supportive human.

The fantastic editor team of Allison Carroll from Audible and Mary Altman from Sourcebooks. I'd also like to thank the Audible and Sourcebooks teams for all their work.

My first readers helped shape the book: Candice Rogers Louazel, Allison Temple, Farah Heron, Jackie Lau, Rosanna Leo, and Yen Conrod Tran.

Graci Kim, who not only provided excellent comments but also generously provided sensitivity feedback and was kind enough to answer questions about Korean food to etiquette to everything.

Thank you also to the lawyer who answered my questions about their firm under the strict understanding they would remain absolutely anonymous.

My biggest thanks and all my love go to Elliott and Nyla, who are my favorite people.

PS: You might wonder if Jihoon and StarLune are based on any specific idol or band. They are not. I swear!

About the
Author

Lily Chu lives in Toronto, Canada, and loves ordering the second-cheapest wine, wearing perfume all the time, and staying up far too late reading a good book. She writes romantic comedies with strong Asian characters.

You can learn more at lilychuauthor.com and @lilychuauthor.